P9-CAM-507

Sophie Kinsella

The Undomestic
Goddess

A Dell Book

THE UNDOMESTIC GODDESS
A Dell Book

PUBLISHING HISTORY
Dial Press hardcover edition published July 2005
Dell international mass market edition / January 2006

Published by Bantam Dell
A Division of Random House, Inc.
New York, New York

This is a work of fiction. Names, characters, places, and incidents
either are the product of the author's imagination or are used
fictitiously. Any resemblance to actual persons, living or dead, events,
or locales is entirely coincidental.

Library of Congress Catalog Card Number: 2005048488

Dell is a registered trademark of Random House, Inc.,
and the colophon is a trademark of Random House, Inc.

ISBN-10: 0-440-29652-8
ISBN-13: 978-0-440-29652-2

Printed in the United States of America

www.bantamdell.com

OPM   10 9 8 7 6

To Linda Evans

PRAISE FOR SOPHIE KINSELLA'S NOVELS
THE UNDOMESTIC GODDESS

"Kinsella is at the top of the chick-lit game. . . . [She] skewers high-powered city life, while delivering a romantic comedy anyone who subsists on takeout will appreciate. . . . Light yet filling."   —*New York Post*

"*The Undomestic Goddess* is a fast, fun read that delves a little deeper."   —*Cleveland Plain Dealer*

"A delightful, fluffy novel of great charm and wit. Take it along on your next trip for several diverting hours."
                                                        —*Contra Costa Times*

"Another charming winner from the delightful Kinsella."
                                                        —*Booklist*

"Kinsella has given her heroine enough charm to make you care enough to stick with her through her trials, intrigues and romances."   —*New York Daily News*

CAN YOU KEEP A SECRET?

"Venturing beyond Saks and Barney's, the bestselling author of *Confessions of a Shopaholic* and *Shopaholic Ties the Knot* entertains readers with backstabbing office shenanigans, competition, scandal, love and sex. . . . Kinsella's down-to-earth protagonist is sure to have readers sympathizing and doubled over in laughter."
                                                        —*Publishers Weekly*

"Chick lit at its lightest and breeziest . . . filled with fabulous clothes, stalwart friends and snotty enemies waiting to be taken down a peg."   —*Orlando Sentinel*

The Undomestic
Goddess

One

Would you consider yourself stressed?

No. I'm not stressed.

I'm . . . busy. Plenty of people are busy. I have a high-powered job, my career is important to me, and I enjoy it.

OK. So sometimes I do feel a bit tense. But I'm a lawyer in the City, for God's sake. What do you expect?

My handwriting is pressing so hard into the page, I've torn the paper. Dammit. Never mind. Let's move on to the next question.

On average, how many hours do you spend in the office every day?

~~14~~

~~12~~

~~8~~

It depends.

Do you exercise regularly?

~~I regularly go swimming~~

~~I occasionally go swim~~

I am intending to begin a regular regime of swimming. When I have time. Work's been busy lately, it's a blip.

Do you drink 8 glasses of water a day?

~~Yes~~

~~Someti~~

No.

I put down my pen and clear my throat. Across the room, Maya looks up from where she's rearranging all her little pots of wax and nail varnish. Maya is my spa beauty therapist for the day and is in her forties, I'd say. Her long dark hair is in a plait with one white streak woven through it, and she has a tiny silver stud in her nose.

"Everything all right with the questionnaire?" she murmurs.

"I did mention that I'm in a bit of a hurry," I say politely. "Are all these questions absolutely necessary?"

"At the Green Tree Center we like to have as much information as possible to assess your beauty and health needs," she replies in soothing yet implacable tones.

I glance at my watch. Nine forty-five.

I don't have time for this. I really do not have the time. But it's my birthday treat and I promised my best friend, Freya.

To be more accurate, it's *last* year's birthday treat. Freya gave me the gift voucher for an "Ultimate De-stress Experience" just over a year ago. She's my oldest school friend and is always on at me for working too hard. In the card that came with the voucher she wrote *Make Some Time For Yourself, Samantha!!!*

Which I did fully intend to do. But we had the Zincon Petrochemical Group restructuring and the Zeus Minerals merger...and somehow a year went by without my finding a spare moment. I'm a lawyer with Carter Spink. I work in the corporate department on the finance side, and just at the moment, things are pretty hectic with some big deals on. It's a blip. It'll get better. I just have to get through the next couple of weeks.

Anyway, then Freya sent me *this* year's birthday card—and I suddenly realized the voucher was about to expire. So here I am, on my twenty-ninth birthday. Sitting on a couch in a white toweling robe and surreal paper knickers. With a half-day window. Max.

Do you smoke?

No.

Do you drink alcohol?

Yes. The odd glass of wine.

Do you eat regular home-cooked meals?

What does that have to do with anything? What makes "home-cooked" meals superior?

I eat a nutritious, varied diet, I write at last.

Which is absolutely true.

Anyway, everyone knows the Chinese live longer than we do—so what could be more healthy than to eat their food? And pizza is Mediterranean. It's probably *more* healthy than a home-cooked meal.

Do you feel your life is balanced?

~~Yes.~~

~~N~~

Yes.

"I'm done," I announce, and hand the pages back to Maya, who starts reading through my answers. Her finger is traveling down the paper at a snail's pace. Like we've got all the time in the world.

Which she may well have. But I seriously have to be back in the office by one.

Maya looks up, a thoughtful expression on her face. "You're obviously quite a stressed-out woman."

What? Where does she get that from? I specifically put on the form, I am *not* stressed-out.

"No, I'm not." I hope Maya's taking in my relaxed, see-how-unstressed-I-am smile. She looks unconvinced.

"Your job is obviously very pressured."

"I thrive under pressure," I explain. Which is true. I've known that about myself ever since . . .

Well. Ever since my mother told me, when I was about eight. *You thrive under pressure, Samantha.* Our whole family thrives under pressure. It's like our family motto or something.

Apart from my brother Peter, of course. He had a nervous breakdown. But the rest of us.

I love my job. I love spotting the loophole in a contract. I love the thrill of negotiation, and arguing my case, and making the sharpest point in the room. I love the adrenaline rush of closing a deal.

I suppose just occasionally I do feel as though some-one's piling heavy weights on me. Like big concrete blocks, one on top of the other, and I have to keep holding them up, no matter how exhausted I am . . .

But then everyone probably feels like that. It's normal.

"Your skin's very dehydrated." Maya is shaking her head. She runs an expert hand across my cheek and rests her fingers underneath my jaw, looking concerned. "Your heart rate's very high. That's not healthy. Are you feeling particularly tense?"

"Work's pretty busy at the moment." I shrug. "It's just a blip. I'm fine." *Can we get on with it?*

"Well." Maya gets up. She presses a button set in the wall and gentle pan-pipe music fills the air. "All I can say is, you've come to the right place, Samantha. Our aim here is to de-stress, revitalize, and detoxify."

"Lovely," I say, only half listening. I've just remembered that I never got back to David Elldridge about the Ukrainian oil contract. I meant to call him yesterday. Shit.

"Our aim is to provide a haven of tranquility, away from all your day-to-day worries." Maya presses another button in the wall, and the light dims to a muted glow. "Before we start," she says softly, "do you have any questions?"

"Actually, I do." I lean forward.

"Good!" She beams. "Are you curious about today's treatments, or is it something more general?"

"Could I possibly send a quick e-mail?"

Maya's smile freezes on her face.

"Just quickly," I add. "It won't take two secs—"

"Samantha, Samantha..." Maya shakes her head. "You're here to relax. To take a moment for yourself. Not to send e-mails. E-mail's an obsession! An addiction! As evil as alcohol. Or caffeine."

For goodness sake, I'm not *obsessed*. I mean, that's ridiculous. I check my e-mails about once every... thirty seconds, maybe.

The thing is, a lot can change in thirty seconds.

"And besides, Samantha," Maya goes on. "Do you see a computer in this room?"

"No," I reply, obediently looking around the dim little room, at posters of yoga positions and a wind chime and a row of crystals arranged on the windowsill.

"This is why we ask that you leave all electronic equipment in the safe. No mobile phones are permitted. No little computers." Maya spreads her arms. "This is a retreat. An escape from the world."

"Right." I nod meekly.

Now is probably not the time to reveal that I have a BlackBerry hidden in my paper knickers.

"So, let's begin." Maya smiles. "Lie down, please, under a towel. And remove your watch."

"I need my watch!"

"Another addiction." She tsks reprovingly. "You don't need to know the time while you're here."

She turns away, and with reluctance I take off my watch. Then, a little awkwardly, I arrange myself on the massage table, trying to avoid squashing my precious BlackBerry.

I did see the rule about no electronic equipment. And I did surrender my Dictaphone. But three hours without a BlackBerry? I mean, what if something came up at the office? What if there was an emergency?

If they really wanted people to relax, they would let them *keep* their BlackBerrys and mobile phones, not confiscate them.

Anyway, she'll never see it under my towel.

"I'm going to begin with a relaxing foot rub," says Maya, and I feel her smoothing some kind of lotion over my feet. "Try to clear your mind."

I stare dutifully up at the ceiling. Clear mind. My mind is as clear as a transparent . . . glass . . .

What am I going to do about Elldridge? He'll be waiting for a response. What if he tells the other partners I was lax? What if it affects my chances of partnership?

I feel a clench of alarm. Now is not the time to leave anything to chance.

"Try to let go of all your thoughts. . . ." Maya is chanting. "Feel the release of tension. . . ."

Maybe I could send him a very quick e-mail.

Surreptitiously I reach down and feel the hard corner of my BlackBerry. Gradually I inch it out of my paper knickers. Maya is still massaging my feet, totally oblivious.

"Your body is growing heavy . . . your mind should be emptying . . ."

I edge the BlackBerry up onto my chest until I can just see the screen underneath the towel. Thank goodness this room is so dim. Trying to keep my movements to a minimum, I furtively start typing an e-mail with one hand.

"Relaax . . ." Maya is saying in soothing tones. "Imagine you're walking along a beach . . ."

"Uh-huh . . ." I murmur.

David, I'm typing. *Re ZFN Oil contract. I read through amendments. Feel our response should be*

"What are you doing?" says Maya, suddenly alert.

"Nothing!" I say, hastily shoving the BlackBerry back under the towel. "Just . . . er . . . relaxing."

Maya comes round the couch and looks at the bump in the towel where I'm clutching the BlackBerry.

"Are you hiding something?" she says in disbelief.

"No!"

From under the towel the BlackBerry emits a little bleep. Damn.

"I think that was a car," I say, trying to sound casual. "Outside in the street."

Maya's eyes narrow.

"Samantha," she says ominously. "Do you have a piece of electronic equipment under there?"

I have the feeling that if I don't confess she'll rip my towel off anyway.

"I was just sending an e-mail," I say at last, and sheepishly produce the BlackBerry.

"You workaholics!" She grabs it out of my hand in exasperation. "E-mails can *wait*. It can all *wait*. You just don't know how to relax!"

"I'm not a workaholic!" I retort indignantly. "I'm a lawyer! It's different!"

"You're in denial." She shakes her head.

"I'm *not*! Look, we've got some big deals on at the firm. I can't just switch off! Especially not right now. I'm... well, I'm up for partnership at the moment."

As I say the words aloud I feel the familiar stabbing of nerves. Partner of one of the biggest law firms in the country. The only thing I've ever wanted, ever.

"I'm up for partnership," I repeat, more calmly. "They make the decision tomorrow. If it happens, I'll be the youngest partner in the history of the firm. Do you know how big a deal that is? Do you have any idea—"

"Anyone can take a couple of hours out," interrupts Maya. She puts her hands on my shoulders. "Samantha, you're incredibly nervy. Your shoulders are rigid, your heart's racing... it seems to me you're right on the edge."

"I'm fine."

"You're a bundle of jitters!"

"I'm not!"

"You have to *decide* to slow down, Samantha." She looks at me earnestly. "Only you can decide to change your life. Are you going to do that?"

"Er... well..."

I stop with a squeak of surprise, as from inside my paper knickers there comes a judder.

My mobile phone. I shoved it in there along with the BlackBerry and turned it onto VIBRATE so it wouldn't make a noise.

"What's that?" Maya is gaping at my twitching towel. "What on earth is that... quivering?"

I *can't* admit it's a phone. Not after the BlackBerry.

"Erm..." I clear my throat. "It's my special... er... love toy."

"Your what?" Maya looks taken aback.

The phone judders inside my pants again. I have to answer. It might be the office.

"Um . . . you know, I'm reaching a bit of an intimate moment right now." I give Maya a significant look. "Maybe you could . . . uh . . . leave the room?"

Suspicion snaps into Maya's eyes.

"Wait a moment!" She peers again. "Is that a phone under there? You smuggled in a *mobile phone as well*?"

Oh, God. She looks furious.

"Look," I say, trying to sound apologetic. "I know you've got your rules and everything, which I do respect, but the thing is, I *need* my mobile." I reach under the towel for the phone.

"*Leave it!*" Maya's cry takes me by surprise. "Samantha," she says, making an obvious effort to keep calm. "If you've listened to a single word I've said . . . you'll switch the phone off right now."

The phone vibrates again in my hand. I look at the caller ID and feel a twist in my stomach. "It's the office."

"They can leave a message. They can wait."

"But—"

"This is your own time." She leans forward and clasps my hands earnestly. "*Your own time.*"

She really doesn't get it, does she? I almost want to laugh.

"I'm an associate at Carter Spink," I explain. "I don't *have* my own time." I flip the phone open and an angry male voice bites down the line.

"Samantha, where the hell are you?"

It's Ketterman. The head of our corporate department. He's in his late forties and his first name is John, but no one ever calls him anything except Ketterman. He has black hair and steel glasses and gray gimlet eyes, and when I first arrived at Carter Spink I actually used to have nightmares about him.

"The Fallons deal is back on. Get back here now. Meeting at ten-thirty."

Back *on*?

"I'll be there as soon as I can." I snap the phone shut and look ruefully at Maya. "Sorry."

I'm not *addicted* to my watch.

But obviously I rely on it. You would too, if your time was measured in six-minute segments. For every six minutes of my working life, I'm supposed to bill a client. It all goes on a computerized time sheet, in itemized chunks.

11:00–11:06 drafted contract for Project A
11:06–11:12 amended documentation for Client B
11:12–11:18 consulted on point for Agreement C

When I first started at Carter Spink it freaked me out slightly, the idea that I had to write down what I was working on, every minute of the day. I used to think: *What if I do nothing for six minutes? What am I supposed to write down then?*

11:00–11:06 stared aimlessly out of window
11:06–11:12 daydreamed about bumping into
           George Clooney in street
11:12–11:18 attempted to touch nose with tongue

But if you're a lawyer at Carter Spink, you don't sit around. Not when every six minutes of your time is worth money. If I let six minutes of time tick away, I've lost the firm £50. Twelve minutes, £100. Eighteen minutes, £150. And the truth is, you get used to measuring your life in little chunks. And you get used to working. All the time.

Two

As I arrive at the office, Ketterman is standing by my desk, looking with an expression of distaste at the mess of papers and files strewn everywhere.

Truthfully, I don't have the most pristine desk in the world. In fact . . . it's a bit of a shambles. But I am intending to tidy it up and sort out all the piles of old contracts on the floor. As soon as I have a moment.

"Meeting in ten minutes," he says. "I want the draft financing documentation ready."

"Absolutely," I reply. Ketterman is unnerving at the best of times. He just emanates scary, brainy power. But today is a million times worse, because Ketterman is on the decision panel. Tomorrow morning at nine a.m., he and thirteen other partners are holding a big meeting to decide on which associates will become partners this year. All the candidates gave presentations last week to the panel, outlining what qualities and ideas we would bring to the firm. As I finished mine, I had no idea whether I'd impressed or not. Tomorrow, I'll find out.

"The draft documentation is right here...." I reach into a pile of folders and pull out what feels like a box file with an efficient flourish.

It's the wrong one.

Hastily I put it down. "It's definitely here some-where...." I scrabble frantically and locate the correct file. Thank God. "Here!"

"I don't know how you can work in this shambles, Samantha." Ketterman's voice is thin and sarcastic.

"At least everything's to hand!" I attempt a little joke, but Ketterman remains stony-faced. Flustered, I pull out my chair, and a pile of articles and old drafts falls in a shower to the floor.

"You know, the old rule was that desks were com-pletely cleared every night by six." Ketterman's voice is steely. "Perhaps we should reintroduce it."

"Maybe!"

"Samantha!" A genial voice interrupts us and I look round in relief to see Arnold Saville approaching along the corridor.

Arnold is my favorite of the senior partners. He's got woolly gray hair that always seems a bit wild for a law-yer, and flamboyant taste in ties. Today he's wearing a bright red paisley affair, with a matching handkerchief in his top pocket. He greets me with a broad smile, and at once I feel myself relax.

I'm sure Arnold's the one who's rooting for me to be made partner. Just as I'm equally sure Ketterman will be opposing it. I've already overheard Ketterman saying I'm very young to be made a partner, that there's no rush. He'd probably have me pegging away as an associ-ate for five more years. But Arnold's always been on my side. He's the maverick of the firm, the one who breaks the rules. For years he had a labrador, Stan, who lived under his desk, despite the complaints of the health and safety department. If anyone can lighten the atmosphere in a tricky meeting, it's Arnold.

"Letter of appreciation about you, Samantha." Arnold beams and holds out a sheet of paper. "From the chairman of Gleiman Brothers, no less."

I take the cream vellum sheet in surprise and glance down at the handwritten note: . . . *great esteem . . . her services always professional . . .*

"I gather you saved him a few million pounds he wasn't expecting." Arnold twinkles. "He's delighted."

"Oh, yes." I color slightly. "Well, it was nothing. I just noticed an anomaly in the way they were structuring their finances."

"You obviously made a great impression on him." Arnold raises his bushy eyebrows. "He wants you to work on all his deals from now. Excellent, Samantha! Very well done."

"Er . . . thanks." I glance at Ketterman, just to see if by any remote chance he might look impressed. But he's still frowning impatiently.

"I also want you to deal with this." Ketterman puts a file on my desk. "Marlowe and Co. are acquiring a retail park. I need a due diligence review in forty-eight hours."

Oh, bloody hell. My heart sinks as I look at the heavy folder. It'll take me hours to do this.

Ketterman's always giving me extra bits of mundane work he can't be bothered to do himself. In fact, all the partners do it. Even Arnold. Half the time they don't even tell me, just dump the file on my desk with some illegible memo and expect me to get on with it.

And of course I do. In fact I always try to get it done just a bit faster than they were expecting.

"Any problems?"

"Of course not," I say in a brisk, can-do, potential-partner voice. "See you at the meeting."

As he stalks off I check my watch. Ten twenty-two. I have precisely eight minutes to make sure the draft documentation for the Fallons deal is all in order. Fallons is our client, a big multinational tourism company, and is acquiring the Smithleaf Hotel Group. I open the file and scan the pages swiftly, checking for errors, searching for gaps. I've learned to read a lot faster since I've been at Carter Spink.

In fact, I do everything faster. I walk faster, talk faster, eat faster . . . have sex faster . . .

Not that I've had much of that lately. But two years ago I dated a senior partner from Berry Forbes. His name was Jacob and he worked on huge international mergers, and he had even less time than I did. By the end, we'd honed our routine to about six minutes, which would have been quite handy if we were billing each other. (Obviously we weren't.) He would make me come—and I would make him come. And then we'd check our e-mails.

Which is practically simultaneous orgasms. So no one can say that's not good sex. I've read *Cosmo*; I know these things.

Anyway, then Jacob was made a huge offer and moved to Boston, so that was the end of it. I didn't mind very much.

To be totally honest, I didn't really fancy him.

"Samantha?" It's my secretary, Maggie. She only started three weeks ago and I don't know her very well yet. "You had a message while you were out. From Joanne?"

"Joanne from Clifford Chance?" I look up, my attention grabbed. "OK. Tell her I got the e-mail about clause four, and I'll call her about it after lunch—"

"Not that Joanne," Maggie interrupts. "Joanne your

new cleaner. She wants to know where you keep your vacuum-cleaner bags."

I look at her blankly. "My what?"

"Vacuum-cleaner bags," repeats Maggie patiently. "She can't find them."

"Why does the vacuum cleaner need to go in a bag?" I say, puzzled. "Is she taking it somewhere?"

Maggie peers at me as though she thinks I must be joking. "The bags that go *inside* your vacuum cleaner," she says carefully. "To collect the dust? Do you have any of those?"

"Oh!" I say quickly. "Oh, *those* bags. Er . . ."

I frown thoughtfully, as though the solution is on the tip of my tongue. The truth is, I can't even visualize my vacuum cleaner. Where did I put it? I know it was delivered, because the porter signed for it.

"Maybe it's a Dyson," suggests Maggie. "They don't take bags. Is it a cylinder or an upright?" She looks at me expectantly.

"I'll sort it," I say in a businesslike manner, and start gathering my papers together. "Thanks, Maggie."

"She had another question." Maggie consults her pad. "How do you switch on your oven?"

For a moment I continue gathering my papers. "Well. You turn the . . . er . . . knob," I say at last, trying to sound nonchalant. "It's pretty clear, really. . . ."

"She said it has some weird timer lock." Maggie frowns. "Is it gas or electric?"

OK, I think I should terminate this conversation right now.

"Maggie, I really need to prepare for this meeting," I say. "It's in three minutes."

"So what shall I tell your cleaner?" Maggie persists. "She's waiting for me to call back."

"Tell her to . . . leave it for today. I'll sort it out."

As Maggie leaves my office I reach for a pen and memo pad.

1. How switch on oven?
2. Vacuum-cleaner bags—buy

I put the pen down and massage my forehead. I really don't have time for this. I mean, vacuum bags. I don't even know what they look like, for God's sake, let alone where to buy them—

A sudden brain wave hits me. I'll order a new vacuum cleaner. That'll come with a bag already installed, surely.

"Samantha."

"What? What is it?" I give a startled jump and open my eyes. Guy Ashby is standing at my door.

Guy is my best friend in the firm. He's six foot three with olive skin and dark eyes, and normally he looks every inch the smooth, polished lawyer. But this morning his dark hair is rumpled and there are shadows under his eyes.

"Relax." Guy smiles. "Only me. Coming to the meeting?"

He has the most devastating smile. It's not just me; everyone noticed it the minute he arrived at the firm.

"Oh. Er . . . yes, I am." I pick up my papers, then add carelessly, "Are you OK, Guy? You look a bit rough."

He broke up with his girlfriend. They had bitter rows all night and she's walked off for good. . . .

No, she's emigrated to New Zealand. . . .

"All-nighter," he says, wincing. "Fucking Ketterman. He's inhuman." He yawns widely, showing the perfect white teeth he had fixed when he was at Harvard Law School.

He says it wasn't his choice. Apparently they don't let

you graduate until you've been OK'd by the cosmetic surgeon.

"Bummer." I grin in sympathy, then push back my chair. "Let's go."

I've known Guy for a year, ever since he joined the corporate department as a partner. He's intelligent and funny, and works the same way I do, and we just some-how . . . click.

And yes. It's possible that some kind of romance would have happened between us if things had been different. But there was a stupid misunderstanding, and . . .

Anyway. It didn't. The details aren't important. It's not something I dwell on. We're friends—and that's fine by me.

OK, this is exactly what happened.

Apparently Guy noticed me his first day at the firm, just like I noticed him. And he was interested. He asked Nigel MacDermot, who had the next-door office to him, if I was single. Which I was.

This is the crucial part: I was single. I'd just split up with Jacob. But Nigel MacDermot—who is a stupid, stupid, *thoughtless* behind-the-times moron—told Guy I was attached to a senior partner at Berry Forbes.

Even though I was single.

If you ask me, the system is majorly flawed. It should be clearer. People should have engaged signs, like toi-lets. Taken. Not-Taken. There should be no ambiguity about these things.

Anyway, I didn't have a sign. Or if I did, it was the wrong one. There were a slightly embarrassing few weeks where I smiled a lot at Guy—and he looked awkward and started avoiding me, because he didn't want to

a) break up a relationship or b) have a threesome with me and Jacob.

I didn't understand what was going on, so I backed off. Then I heard through the grapevine he'd started going out with a girl called Charlotte who he'd met at some weekend party. They live together now. A month or two later we worked together on a deal, and got to know each other as friends—and that's pretty much the whole story.

I mean, it's fine. Really. That's the way it goes. Some things happen—and some things don't. This one obviously just wasn't meant to be.

Except deep down . . . I still believe it was.

"So," says Guy as we walk along the corridor to the meeting room. "What was Ketterman in your room for earlier?"

"Oh, the usual. A due diligence report. Have it back by yesterday, that kind of thing. Like I'm not snowed under already."

"Everyone wants you to do their work for them, that's why," says Guy. He shoots me a concerned look. "You want to delegate anything? I could speak to Ketterman—"

"No, thanks," I reply at once. "I can do it."

"You don't want anyone to help." He sounds amused. "You'd rather die, smothered by a heap of due diligence files."

"Like you're not the same!" I retort.

Guy hates admitting defeat or asking for help as much as I do. Last year he sprained his leg in a skiing accident and point-blank refused to use the crutch that the firm's doctor gave him. His secretary kept running after him with it down corridors, but he'd just tell her to take it away and use it as a coat stand.

"Well, you'll be calling the shots soon. When you're a partner." He cocks an eyebrow.

"Don't say that!" I hiss in horror. He'll jinx it.

"Come on. You know you've made it."

"I don't know anything."

"Samantha, you're the brightest lawyer in your year. And you work the hardest. What's your IQ again, six hundred?"

"Shut up."

Guy laughs. "What's one twenty-four times seventy-five?"

"Nine thousand, three hundred," I say grudgingly.

Since I was about ten years old, I've been able to do big sums in my head. God knows why, I just can. And everyone else just goes, "Oh cool," and then forgets about it.

But Guy keeps on about it, pitching sums at me like I'm a circus performer. This is the *one* thing that irritates me about him. He thinks it's funny, but it actually gets a bit annoying. I still haven't quite worked out how to get him to stop.

Once I told him the wrong number on purpose—but that time it turned out he actually needed the answer, and he put it in a contract and the deal nearly got wrecked as a result. So I haven't done that again.

"You haven't practiced in the mirror for the firm's Web site?" Guy adopts a pose with his finger poised thoughtfully at his chin. "Ms. Samantha Sweeting, Partner."

"I haven't even thought about it," I say, feigning indifference.

This is a slight lie. I've already planned how to do my hair for the photo. And which of my black suits to wear.

"I heard your presentation blew their socks off," says Guy more seriously.

My indifference vanishes in a second. "Really?" I say,

trying not to sound too eager for praise. "You heard that?"

"And you put William Griffiths right on a point of law in front of everybody." Guy folds his arms and regards me humorously. "Do you ever make a mistake, Samantha Sweeting?"

"Oh, I make plenty of mistakes," I say lightly. "Believe me."

Like not grabbing you and telling you I was single, the very first day we met.

"A mistake isn't a mistake." Guy pauses. "Unless it can't be put right." As he says the words, his eyes seem to hold an extra significance.

Or else they're just squiffy after his night of no sleep. I was never any good at reading the signs.

I should have done a degree in mutual attraction, instead of law. It would have been a lot more useful. Bachelor of Arts (Hons) in Knowing When Men Fancy You And When They're Just Being Friendly.

"Ready?" Ketterman's whiplash voice behind us makes us both jump, and we turn to see a whole phalanx of soberly suited men, together with a pair of even more soberly suited women.

"Absolutely." Guy nods at Ketterman, then turns back and winks at me.

Three

Nine hours later we're all still in the meeting.

The huge mahogany table is strewn with photo-copied draft contracts, financial reports, notepads covered in scribbles, polystyrene coffee cups, and Post-its. Take-out boxes from lunch are littering the floor. A secretary is distributing fresh copies of the draft agreement. Two of the lawyers from the opposition have got up from the table and are murmuring intently in the break-out room. Every meeting room has one of these: a little side area where you go for private conversations, or when you feel like breaking something.

The intensity of the afternoon has passed. It's like an ebb in the tide. Faces are flushed, tempers are still high, but no one's shouting anymore. The Fallons and Smithleaf people have gone. They reached agreement on various points at about four o'clock, shook hands, and sailed off in their shiny limos.

Now it's up to us, the lawyers, to work out what they said and what they actually meant (and if you think it's the same thing, you might as well give up law now) and put it all into a draft contract in time for more negotiations.

When they'll probably begin shouting some more.

I rub my dry face and take a gulp of cappuccino before realizing I've picked up the wrong cup—the stone-cold cup from four hours ago. Yuck. *Yuck*. And I can't exactly spit it out all over the table.

I swallow the revolting mouthful with an inward shudder. The fluorescent lights are flickering in my eyes and I feel drained. My role in all of these megadeals is on the finance side—so it was me who negotiated the loan agreement between Fallons and PGNI Bank. It was me who rescued the situation when a £10-million black hole of debt turned up in a subsidiary company. And it was me who spent about three hours this afternoon arguing one single, stupid term in the contract.

The term was *best endeavors*. The other side wanted to use *reasonable efforts*. In the end we won the point—but I can't feel my usual triumph. All I know is, it's seven-nineteen, and in eleven minutes I'm supposed to be halfway across town, sitting down to dinner at Maxim's with my mother and brother Daniel.

I'll have to cancel. My own birthday dinner.

Even as I think the thought, I can hear the outraged voice of Freya ringing in my mind.

They can't make you stay at work on your birthday!

I canceled on her too, last week, when we were supposed to be going to a comedy club. A company sell-off was due to complete the next morning and I didn't have any choice.

What she doesn't understand is, the deadline comes first, end of story. Prior engagements don't count; birthdays don't count. Vacations are canceled every week. Across the table from me is Clive Sutherland from the corporate department. His wife had twins this morning and he was back at the table by lunchtime.

"All right, people." Ketterman's voice commands immediate attention.

Ketterman is the only one here who isn't red-faced or weary-looking or even jaded. He looks as machinelike as ever, as polished as he did this morning. When he gets angry, he just exudes a silent, steely fury.

"We have to adjourn."

What? My head pops up.

Other heads have popped up too; I can detect the hope around the table. We're like schoolkids sensing a disturbance during the math test, not daring to move in case we land a double detention.

"Until we have the due diligence documentation from Fallons, we can't proceed. I'll see you all tomorrow, here at nine a.m." He sweeps out, and as the door closes, I exhale. I was holding my breath, I realize.

Clive has already bolted for the door. People are on their mobile phones all over the room, discussing dinner, films, uncanceling previous arrangements. There's a joyful lift to the proceedings. I have a sudden urge to yell "Yay!"

But that wouldn't be partnerlike.

I gather up my papers, stuff them into my briefcase, and push back my chair.

"Samantha. I forgot." Guy is making his way across the room. "I have something for you."

As he hands me a simple white package, I feel a ridiculous rush of joy. A birthday present. He's the only one in the whole company who remembered my birthday. I can't help glowing as I undo the cardboard envelope.

"Guy, you really shouldn't have!"

"It was no trouble," he says, clearly satisfied with himself.

"Still!" I laugh. "I thought you'd—"

I break off abruptly as I uncover a corporate DVD in a laminated case. It's a summary of the European Partners presentation we had the other day. I mentioned that I'd like a copy.

I turn it over in my hands, making sure my smile is completely intact before I look up. Of course he didn't remember my birthday. Why would he? He probably never even knew it.

"That's . . . great," I say at last. "Thanks!"

"No problem." He's picking up his briefcase. "Have a good evening. Anything planned?"

I can't tell him it's my birthday. He'll think—he'll realize—

"Just . . . a family thing." I smile. "See you tomorrow."

The main thing is, I'm going to make dinner after all. And I won't even be late! Last time I had dinner with Mum, about three months ago now, I was an hour late after my plane from Amsterdam was delayed. Then she had to take a conference call halfway through the main course. It wasn't exactly a success.

As my taxi edges through the traffic on Cheapside, I quickly rifle in my bag for my new makeup case. I nipped into Selfridges in my lunch hour the other day when I realized I was still using the old gray eyeliner and mascara I bought for a Law Society dinner a year ago. I didn't have time for a demonstration, but I asked the girl at the counter if she could just quickly sell me everything she thought I should have.

I didn't really listen as she explained each item, because I was on the phone to Elldridge about the Ukrainian contract. But the one thing I do remember is her insistence I should use something called "bronzer powder." She said it might give me a glow and stop me looking so dreadfully—

Then she stopped herself. "Pale," she said at last. "You're just a bit . . . pale."

I take out the compact and huge blusher brush and start sweeping the powder onto my cheeks and forehead. Then, as I peer at my reflection in the mirror, I stifle a laugh. My face stares back at me, freakishly golden and shiny. I look ridiculous.

I mean, who am I kidding? A City lawyer who hasn't been on holiday for two years doesn't have a tan. I might as well walk in with beads in my hair and pretend I've just flown in from Barbados.

I look at myself for a few more seconds, then take out a cleansing wipe and scrub the bronzer off until my face is white again, with shades of gray. Back to normal. The makeup girl kept mentioning the dark shadows under my eyes too, and there they are.

Thing is, if I *didn't* have shadows under my eyes, I'd probably get fired.

I'm wearing a black suit, as I always do. My mother gave me five almost identical black suits for my twenty-first birthday, and I've never really broken the habit. The only item of color about me is my bag, which is red. Mum gave that to me as well, two years ago. At least . . . she gave me a black one originally. But on the way home I saw it in a shop window in red, had a total brainstorm, and exchanged it. I'm not convinced she's ever forgiven me.

I free my hair from its elastic band, quickly comb it out, then twist it back into place. My hair has never exactly been my pride and joy. It's mouse-color, medium length, with a medium wave. At least, it was last time I looked. Most of the time it lives screwed up into a knot.

"Nice evening planned?" says the taxi driver, who's been watching me in his mirror.

"It's my birthday, actually."

"Happy birthday!" He eyes me in the mirror. "You'll be partying, then. Making a night of it."

"Er . . . kind of."

My family and wild parties don't exactly go together. But even so, it'll be nice for us to see one another and catch up. It doesn't happen very often.

It's not that we don't want to see one another. We just all have very busy careers. There's my mother, who's a barrister. She's quite well-known, in fact. She started her own chambers ten years ago and last year she won an award for Women in Law. And then there's my brother Daniel, who is thirty-six and head of investment at Whittons. He was named by *Money Management Weekly* last year as one of the top deal-makers in the city.

There's also my other brother, Peter, but like I said, he had a bit of a breakdown. He lives in France now and teaches English at a local school and doesn't even have an answering machine. And my dad, of course, who lives in South Africa with his third wife. I haven't seen much of him since I was three. But I've made my peace about this. My mother's got enough energy for two parents.

I glance at my watch as we speed along the Strand. Seven forty-two. I'm starting to feel quite excited. The street outside is still bright and warm and tourists are walking along in T-shirts and shorts, pointing at the High Court. It must have been a gorgeous summer's day. Inside the air-conditioned Carter Spink building you have no idea what the weather in the real world is doing.

We come to a halt outside Maxim's and I pay the taxi driver, adding a large tip.

"Have a great evening, love!" he says. "And happy birthday!"

"Thanks!"

As I hurry into the restaurant, I'm looking all around for Mum or Daniel, but I can't spot either of them.

"Hi!" I say to the maître d'. "I'm meeting Ms. Tennyson."

That's Mum. She disapproves of women taking the name of their husband. She also disapproves of women staying at home, cooking, cleaning, or learning to type, and thinks all women should earn more than their husbands because they're naturally brighter.

The maître d'—a dapper man who is a good six inches shorter than me—leads me to an empty table in the corner and I slide into the suede banquette.

"Hi!" I smile at the waiter who approaches. "I'd like a Buck's Fizz, a gimlet, and a martini, please. But don't bring them over until the other guests arrive."

Mum always drinks gimlets. And I've no idea what Daniel's on these days, but he won't say no to a martini.

The waiter nods and disappears, and I shake out my napkin, looking all around at the other diners. Maxim's is a pretty cool restaurant, all wenge floors and steel tables and mood lighting. It's very popular with lawyers; in fact, Mum has an account here. Two partners from Linklaters are at a distant table, and I can see one of the biggest libel lawyers in London at the bar. The noise of chatter, corks popping, and forks against oversize plates is like the huge roar of the sea, with occasional tidal waves of laughter making heads turn.

As I scan the menu I suddenly feel ravenous. I haven't had a proper meal for a week, and it all looks so good. Glazed foie gras. Lamb on minted hummus. And on the specials board is chocolate-orange soufflé with two home-made sorbets. I just hope Mum can stay long enough for pudding. I've heard her say plenty of times that half a dinner party is enough for anybody. The trouble is, she's not really interested in food. She's also not that interested in most people, as they're generally less intelligent than her. Which rules out most potential dinner guests.

But Daniel will stay. Once my brother starts on a bottle of wine, he feels obliged to see it through to the end.

"Miss Sweeting?" I look up to see the maître d'. He's holding a mobile phone. "I have a message. Your mother has been held up at her chambers."

"Oh." I try to hide my disappointment. But I can hardly complain. I've done the same thing to her enough times. "So . . . what time will she be here?"

I think I see a flash of pity in his eyes.

"I have her here on the telephone. Her secretary will put her through. . . . Hello?" he says into the phone. "I have Ms. Tennyson's daughter."

"Samantha?" comes a crisp, precise voice in my ear. "Darling, I can't come tonight, I'm afraid."

"You can't come at *all*?" My smile falters. "Not even . . . for a drink?"

Her chambers are only five minutes away in a cab, in Lincoln's Inn Fields.

"Far too much on. I have a very big case on and I'm in court tomorrow—No, get me the other file," she adds to someone in her office. "These things happen," she resumes. "But have a nice evening with Daniel. Oh, and happy birthday. I've wired three hundred pounds to your bank account."

"Oh, right," I say. "Thanks."

"I assume you haven't heard about the partnership yet."

"Not yet."

"I heard your presentation went well. . . ." I can hear her tapping her pen on the phone. "How many hours have you put in this month?"

"Um . . . probably about two hundred . . ."

"Is that enough? Samantha, you don't want to be passed over. You've been working toward this for a long time."

Like I don't know that.

Still, I suppose I should be glad she's not badgering me about whether I've got a boyfriend. Mum never asks me about my personal life. She expects me to be as focused and driven as she is, if not more so. And even though we don't talk very often anymore, even though she's less controlling than she was when I was younger, I still feel apprehensive whenever she rings.

"There will be younger lawyers coming up behind," she continues. "Someone in your position could easily go stale."

"Two hundred hours is quite a lot . . ." I try to explain. "Compared to the others—"

"You have to be *better* than the others!" Her voice cuts across mine as though she's in a courtroom. "You can't afford for your performance to slip below excellent. This is a *crucial time*—Not *that* file!" she adds impatiently to whoever it is. "Hold the line, Samantha—"

"Samantha?"

I look up in confusion from the phone to see a girl with long swishy blond hair, wearing a powder-blue suit, approaching the table. She's holding a gift basket adorned with a bow, and has a wide smile.

"I'm Lorraine, Daniel's PA," she says in a singsong voice I suddenly recognize from calling Daniel's office. "He couldn't make it tonight, I'm afraid. But I've got a little something for you—plus he's here on the phone to say hello. . . ."

She holds out a lit-up mobile phone. In total confusion, I take it and press it to my other ear.

"Hi, Samantha," comes Daniel's businesslike drawl. "Look, babe, I'm snowed under. I can't be there."

Neither of them is coming?

"I'm really sorry," Daniel's saying. "One of those things. But have a great time with Mum, won't you?"

I take a deep breath. I can't admit she blew me off too. I can't admit that I'm sitting here all on my own.

"OK!" Somehow I muster a breezy tone. "We will!"

"I've transferred some money to your account. Buy something nice. And I've sent some chocolates along with Lorraine," he adds proudly. "Picked them out myself."

I look at the gift basket Lorraine is proffering. It isn't chocolates, it's soap.

"That's really lovely, Daniel," I manage. "Thanks very much."

"Happy birthday to you . . ."

There's sudden chorusing behind me. I swivel round to see a waiter carrying over a cocktail glass with a sparkler. *Happy Birthday Samantha* is written in caramel on the steel tray, next to a miniature souvenir menu signed by the chef. Three waiters are following behind, all singing in harmony.

After a moment, Lorraine awkwardly joins in. *"Happy birthday to you . . ."*

The waiter puts the tray down in front of me, but my hands are full with phones.

"I'll take that for you," says Lorraine, relieving me of Daniel's phone. She lifts it to her ear, then beams at me. "He's singing!" she says, pointing to the receiver encouragingly.

"Samantha?" Mum is saying in my ear. "Are you still there?"

"I'm just . . . they're singing 'Happy Birthday' . . ."

I put the phone on the table. After a moment's thought, Lorraine puts the other phone carefully down on the other side of me.

This is my family birthday party.

Two cell phones.

I can see people looking over at the singing, their smiles falling a little as they see I'm sitting on my own. I can see the sympathy in the faces of the waiters. I'm trying to keep my chin up, but my cheeks are burning with embarrassment.

Suddenly the waiter I ordered from earlier appears at the table. He's carrying three cocktails on a tray and looks at the empty table in slight confusion.

"Who is the martini for?"

"It was . . . supposed to be for my brother . . ."

"That would be the Nokia," says Lorraine helpfully, pointing at the mobile phone.

There's a pause—then, with a blank, professional face, the waiter sets the drink down in front of the phone, together with a cocktail napkin.

I want to laugh—except there's a stinging at the back of my eyes. He places the other cocktails on the table, nods at me, then retreats. There's an awkward pause.

"So anyway . . ." Lorraine retrieves Daniel's mobile phone and pops it into her bag. "Happy birthday—and have a lovely evening!"

As she tip-taps her way out of the restaurant, I pick up the other phone to say good-bye—but Mum's already rung off. The singing waiters have melted away. It's just me and a basket of soap.

"Did you wish to order?" The maître d' has reappeared at my chair. "I can recommend the risotto," he says in kind tones. "Some nice salad, perhaps? And a glass of wine?"

"Actually..." I force myself to smile. "I'll just get the bill, thanks."

It doesn't matter.

We were never all going to make a dinner. We shouldn't even have tried to set the date. We're all busy, we all have careers, that's just the way my family is.

As I stand outside the restaurant, a taxi pulls up right in front of me and I quickly stick my hand out. The rear door opens and a tatty beaded flip-flop emerges, followed by a pair of cutoff jeans, an embroidered kaftan, familiar tousled blond hair...

"Stay here," she's instructing the taxi driver. "I can only be five minutes—"

"*Freya?*" I say in disbelief. She wheels round and her eyes widen.

"Samantha! What are you doing on the pavement?"

"What are *you* doing here?" I counter. "I thought you were going to India."

"I'm on my way! I'm meeting Lord at the airport in about..." She looks at her watch. "Ten minutes."

She pulls a guilty face, and I can't help laughing. I've known Freya since we were both seven years old and in boarding school together. On the first night she told me her family were circus performers and she knew how to ride an elephant and walk the tightrope. For a whole term I believed her stories about the exotic circus life. Until her parents arrived that first Christmas to pick her up and turned out to be a pair of accountants from Staines. Even then she was unabashed and said she'd lied to cover up the *real* truth—which was that they were spies.

She's taller than me, with bright blue eyes and freckled skin, permanently tanned from her travels. Right now her skin is peeling slightly on her nose, and she has a new silver earring, right at the top of her ear. She has the whitest, most crooked teeth I've ever seen, and when she laughs, one corner of her top lip rises.

"I'm here to gate-crash your birthday dinner." Freya focuses on the restaurant in suspicion. "But I thought I was late. What happened?"

"Well . . ." I hesitate. "The thing was . . . Mum and Daniel . . ."

"Left early?" As she peers at me, Freya's expression changes to one of horror. "Didn't turn *up*? Jesus Christ, the *bastards*. Couldn't they just for *once* put you first instead of their frigging—" She stops her tirade; she knows I've heard it all before. "Sorry. I know. They're your family. Whatever."

Freya and my mum don't exactly get on.

"It doesn't matter," I say, shrugging ruefully. "Really. I've got a pile of work to get through anyway."

"*Work?*" Freya looks appalled. "Now? Are you serious? Doesn't it ever *stop*?"

"We're busy at the moment. It's just a blip—"

"There's always a blip! There's always a crisis! Every year you put off doing anything fun—"

"That's not true—"

"Every year you tell me work will get better soon. But it never does!" Her eyes are filled with concern. "Samantha . . . what happened to your life?"

I'm silent for a moment, cars roaring along behind me on the street. To be honest, I can't remember what my life used to be like. As I cast my mind back over the years, I recall the holiday I had with Freya in Italy, the summer after A Levels, when we were both eighteen.

My last window of real freedom. Since then work has gradually, almost imperceptibly, taken over.

"I want to be a partner of Carter Spink," I say at last. "That's what I want. You have to make . . . sacrifices."

"And what happens when you make partner?" she persists. "Does it get easier?"

The truth is, I haven't thought beyond making partner. It's like a dream. Like a shiny ball in the sky.

"You're twenty-nine years old, for Christ's sake!" Freya gestures with a bony, silver-ringed hand. "You should be able to do something spontaneous once in a while. You should be seeing the world!" She grabs my arm. "Samantha, come to India. Now!"

"Do what?" I give a startled laugh. "I can't come to India!"

"Take a month off. Why not? They're not going to fire you. Come to the airport, we'll get you a ticket. . . ."

"Freya, you're crazy. Seriously." I squeeze her arm. "I love you—but you're crazy."

Slowly, Freya's grip on my arm loosens.

"Same," she says. "You're crazy, but I love you."

Her mobile starts ringing, but she ignores it. Instead, she rummages in her embroidered bag. At last she produces a tiny, intricately worked silver perfume bottle haphazardly wrapped in a piece of purple shot silk, which is already falling off.

"Here." She thrusts it at me.

"Freya." I turn it over in my fingers. "It's amazing."

"I thought you'd like it." She pulls her mobile out of her pocket. "Hi!" she says impatiently into it. "Look, Lord, I'll be there, OK?"

Freya's husband's full name is Lord Andrew Edgerly. Freya's nickname for him started as a joke and stuck. They met five years ago on a kibbutz and got married in Las Vegas. He's tall and phlegmatic and keeps Freya on track during her wilder moments. He's also amazingly witty once you get past the deadpan exterior. Technically, their marriage makes her Lady Edgerly—but her family can't quite get their heads round this idea. Nor can the Edgerlys.

"Thanks for coming. Thanks for this." I hug her. "Have a fabulous time in India."

"We will." Freya is climbing back into her taxi. "And if you want to come out, just let me know. Invent a family emergency . . . anything. Give them my number. I'll cover for you. Whatever your story is."

"Go," I say, laughing, and give her a little push. "Go to India."

The door slams, and she sticks her head out the window.

"Sam . . . good luck for tomorrow." She seizes my hand, suddenly serious. "If it's really what you want—then I hope you get it."

"It's what I want more than anything else." As I look at my oldest friend, all my calculated nonchalance disappears. "Freya . . . I can't tell you how much I want it."

"You'll get it. I know you will." She kisses my hand, then waves good-bye. "And don't go back to the office! Promise!" she shouts over the roar of her taxi.

"OK! I promise!" I yell back. I wait until her cab has disappeared, then stick my hand out for another.

"Carter Spink, please," I say as it pulls up.

I was crossing my fingers. Of course I'm going back to the office.

I arrive home at eleven o'clock, exhausted and brain-dead, having got through only about half of Ketterman's file. Bloody Ketterman, I'm thinking, as I push open the main front door of the 1930s-mansion block where I live. Bloody Ketterman. Bloody . . . bloody . . .

"Good evening, Samantha."

I nearly jump a mile. It's Ketterman. Right there, standing in front of the lifts, holding a bulging briefcase. For an instant I'm transfixed in horror. What's he doing here?

"Someone told me you lived here." His eyes glint through his spectacles. "I've bought number thirty-two as a pied-à-terre. We'll be neighbors during the week."

Please tell me this is not happening. He *lives* here?

"Er . . . welcome to the building!" I say, trying as hard as I can to sound like I mean it. The lift doors open and we both get in.

Number 32. That means he's only two floors above me. I feel like my headmaster has moved in. Why did he have to choose *this* building?

The elevator rises in silence. I feel more and more uncomfortable. Should I attempt small talk? Some light, neighborly chitchat?

"I made some headway on that file you gave me," I say at last.

"Good," he says curtly, and nods.

So much for the small talk. I should just cut to the big stuff.

Am I going to become a partner tomorrow?

"Well . . . good night," I say awkwardly as I leave the lift.

"Good night, Samantha."

The lift doors close and I emit a silent scream. I cannot live in the same building as Ketterman. I'm going to have to move.

I'm about to put my key in the lock when the door to the opposite flat opens a crack.

"Samantha?"

As if I haven't had enough this evening. It's Mrs. Farley, my neighbor. She has silver hair and gold-rimmed spectacles and an insatiable interest in my life. But she is very kind and takes in parcels for me, so I try to tolerate her intrusiveness.

"Another delivery arrived for you, dear," she says. "Dry cleaning this time. I'll just fetch it for you."

"Thanks," I say gratefully, swinging my door open. A small pile of junk leaflets is sitting on the doormat and I sweep them aside, onto the bigger pile building up at the side of my hallway. I'm planning to recycle them when I get a moment. It's on my list.

"You're late home again." Mrs. Farley is at my side, holding a pile of polythene-covered shirts. "You girls are so busy!" She clicks her tongue. "You haven't been home before eleven this week!"

This is what I mean by an insatiable interest. She probably has all my details logged somewhere in a little book.

"Thanks very much." I reach for my dry cleaning, but to my horror Mrs. Farley pushes past me into the flat, exclaiming, "I'll carry it in for you!"

"Er . . . excuse the . . . er . . . mess," I say as she squeezes past a pile of pictures propped against the wall. "I keep meaning to put those up. . . ."

I steer her hastily into the kitchen, away from the pile of take-away menus on the hall table. Then I wish I hadn't. On the kitchen counter is a stack of old tins and packets, together with a note from my new cleaner, all in capitals:

DEAR SAMANTHA
1. ALL YOUR FOOD IS PAST ITS SELL-BY DATES. SHOULD I THROW AWAY?

2. DO YOU HAVE ANY CLEANING MATERIALS, E.G. BLEACH? COULD NOT FIND ANY.

3. ARE YOU COLLECTING CHINESE FOOD CARTONS FOR ANY REASON? DID NOT THROW THEM AWAY, JUST IN CASE.

YOUR CLEANER JOANNE

I can see Mrs. Farley reading the note. I can practically *hear* the clucking going on in her head. Last month she gave me a little lecture on did I have a slow cooker, because all you needed to do was put in your chicken and vegetables in the morning and it didn't take five minutes to slice a carrot, did it?

I really wouldn't know.

"So . . . thanks." I hastily take the dry cleaning from Mrs. Farley and dump it on the hob, then usher her out to the door, aware of her swiveling, inquisitive eyes. "It's really kind of you."

"It's no trouble! Not wishing to interfere, dear, but you know, you could wash your cotton blouses *very* well at home and save on all that money."

I look at her blankly. If I did that I'd have to dry them. And iron them.

"And I *did* just happen to notice that one of them came back missing a button," she adds. "The pink and white stripe."

"Oh, right," I say. "Well . . . that's OK. I'll send it back. They won't charge."

"You can pop a button on yourself, dear!" Mrs. Farley is shocked. "It won't take you two minutes. You must have a spare button in your workbox?"

My what?

"I don't have a workbox," I explain as politely as I can. "I don't really *do* sewing."

"You can sew a simple button on, surely!" she exclaims.

"No," I say, a bit rankled at her expression. "But it's no problem. I'll send it back to the dry cleaners."

Mrs. Farley is appalled. "You can't sew a button on? Your mother never taught you?"

I stifle a laugh at the thought of my mother sewing on a button. "Er . . . no. She didn't."

"In my day," says Mrs. Farley, shaking her head, "all well-educated girls were taught how to sew on a button, darn a sock, and turn a collar."

None of this means anything to me. *Turn a collar.* It's gibberish.

"Well, in my day . . . we weren't," I reply politely. "We were taught to study for our exams and get a career worth having. We were taught to have opinions. We were taught to use our *brains*," I can't resist adding.

Mrs. Farley doesn't seem impressed. "It's a shame," she says at last, and pats me sympathetically.

I'm trying to keep my temper, but I've worked for hours, I've had a nonexistent birthday, I feel bone-tired and hungry, Ketterman is living two floors above me—and now this old woman's telling me to sew on a *button?*

"It's not a shame," I say tightly.

"All right, dear," says Mrs. Farley in pacifying tones, and heads across the hallway to her flat.

Somehow this goads me even more.

"How is it a shame?" I demand, stepping out of my doorway. "How? OK, maybe I can't sew on a button. But I can restructure a corporate finance agreement and save my client thirty million pounds. That's what I can do."

Mrs. Farley regards me from her doorway. "It's a shame," she repeats, as though she didn't even hear me. "Good night, dear." She closes the door and I emit a squeal of exasperation.

"Did you never *hear* of feminism?" I cry at her door. But there's no answer.

Crossly, I retreat into my own flat, close the door, and pick up the phone. I speed-dial the local wood-fired pizza company and order my usual: a capricciosa and a bag of Kettle Chips. I pour myself a glass of wine out of the fridge, then head back into the sitting room and flick on the telly.

A *workbox*. What else does she think I should have? A pair of knitting needles? A loom?

I sink down onto the sofa with the remote and flick through the TV channels, peering vaguely at the images. News . . . a French film . . . some animal documentary . . .

Hang on. I stop flicking, drop the remote onto the sofa, and settle back on the cushions.

The Waltons. On some obscure syndicated channel. I have not seen *The Waltons* for *years*.

Ultimate comfort viewing. Just what I need.

On the screen the whole family's gathered round the table; Grandma's saying grace.

I take a swig of wine and feel myself start to unwind. I've always secretly loved *The Waltons*, ever since I was a kid. I used to sit in the darkness when everyone else was out and pretend I lived on Walton's Mountain too.

And now it's the last scene of all, the one I always waited for: the Walton house in darkness. Lights twinkling; crickets chirping. John Boy talking in voice-over. A whole huge houseful of people who love one another. I hug my knees and look wistfully at the screen as the familiar music tinkles to its close.

"Good night, Elizabeth!"

"Good night, Grandma," I reply aloud. It's not like there's anyone to hear.

"Night, Mary Ellen!"

"Good night, John Boy," I say in unison with Mary Ellen.

"Good night."

"Night."

"Night."

Four

I wake at six a.m. with my heart pounding, half on my feet, scrabbling for a pen, and saying out loud, "What? What?"

Which is pretty much how I always wake up. I think nervy sleep runs in the family or something. Last Christmas at Mum's house I crept into the kitchen at about three a.m. for a drink of water—to find Mum in her dressing gown reading a court report, and Daniel swigging a Xanax as he checked the Hang Seng Index on TV.

I totter into the bathroom and stare at my pale reflection. This is it. All the work, all the studying, all the late nights . . . it's all been for this day.

Partner. Or not Partner.

Oh, God. Stop it. Don't think about it. I head into the kitchen and open the fridge. Dammit. I'm out of milk.

And coffee.

I *must* find myself a food-delivery company. And a milkman. I reach for a Biro and scrawl 47. *Food delivery/ milkman?* at the bottom of my TO DO list.

My TO DO list is written on a piece of paper pinned up on the wall and is a useful reminder of things I'm intending to do. It's yellowing a bit now, actually—and the ink at the top of the list has become so faint I can barely read it. But it's a good way to keep myself organized.

I should really cross off some of the early entries, it occurs to me. I mean, the original list dates from when I first moved into my flat, three years ago. I must have done some of this stuff by now. I pick up a pen and squint at the first few faded entries.

1. Find milkman
2. Food delivery—organize?
3. How switch on oven?

Oh. Right.

Well, I really *am* going to get all this delivery stuff organized. At the weekend. And I'll get to grips with the oven. I'll read the manual and everything.

I scan quickly down to newer entries, around two years old.

16. Sort out milkman
17. Have friends over?
18. Take up hobby??

The thing is, I *am* meaning to have some friends over. And take up a hobby. When work is less busy.

I look down to even later entries—maybe a year old—where the ink is still blue.

41. Go on holiday?
42. Give dinner party?
43. MILKMAN??

I stare at the list in slight frustration. How can I have done *nothing* on my list? Crossly, I throw my pen down and turn on the kettle, resisting the temptation to rip the list into bits.

The kettle has come to a boil and I make myself a cup of weird herbal tea I was once given by a client. I reach for an apple from the fruit bowl—only to discover it's gone all moldy. With a shudder, I throw the whole lot into the bin and nibble a few Shreddies out of the packet.

The truth is, I don't care about the list. There's only one thing I care about.

I arrive at the office determined not to acknowledge this is any kind of special day. I'll just keep my head down and get on with my work. But as I travel up in the lift, three people murmur "Good luck," and walking along the corridor a guy from Tax grasps me meaningfully on the shoulder.

"Best of luck, Samantha."

How does he know my name?

I head hurriedly into my office and close the door, trying to ignore the fact that through the glass partition I can see people talking in the corridor and glancing in my direction.

I really shouldn't have come in today. I should have feigned a life-threatening illness.

Anyway. It's fine. I'll just start on some work, like any other day. I open Ketterman's file, find my place, and start reading through a document that codifies a five-year-old share transfer.

"Samantha?"

I look up. Guy is at my door, holding two coffees. He puts one down on my desk.

"Hi," he says. "How are you doing?"

"Fine," I say, turning a page in a businesslike manner. "I'm fine. Just . . . normal. In fact, I don't know what all the fuss is."

Guy's amused expression is flustering me slightly. I flip over another page to prove my point—and somehow knock the entire file to the floor.

Thank God for paper clips.

Red-faced, I shove all the papers back inside the file and take a sip of coffee.

"Uh-huh." Guy nods gravely. "Well, it's a good thing you're not nervous or jumpy or anything."

"Yes," I say, refusing to take the bait. "Isn't it?"

"See you later." He lifts his coffee cup as though toasting me, then walks off. I look at my watch.

Only eight fifty-three. The partners' decision meeting starts in seven minutes. I'm not sure I can bear this.

Somehow I get through the morning. I finish up Ketterman's file and make a start at my report. I'm halfway through the third paragraph when Guy appears at my office door again.

"Hi," I say without looking up. "I'm fine, OK? And I haven't heard anything."

Guy doesn't reply.

At last I lift my head. He's right in front of my desk, looking down at me with the strangest expression, as if affection and pride and excitement are all mixed together under his poker-straight face.

"I should not be doing this," he murmurs, then leans in closer. "You did it, Samantha. You're a partner. You'll hear officially in an hour."

For an instant I can't breathe.

"You didn't hear it from me, OK?" Guy's face creases briefly in a smile. "Well done."

I made it. I *made* it.

"Thanks..." I manage.

"I'll see you later. Congratulate you properly." He turns and strides away, and I'm left staring unseeingly at my computer.

I made partner.

Oh, my God. *Oh, my God.* Oh, my GOD!

I'm feeling a terrible urge to leap to my feet and cry out "YES!" How do I survive an hour? How can I just sit here calmly? I can't possibly concentrate on Ketterman's report. It isn't due until tomorrow, anyway.

I shove the file away from me—and a landslide of papers falls on the floor on the other side. As I gather them up I find myself looking anew at the disorderly heap of papers and files, at the teetering pile of books on my computer terminal.

Ketterman's right. It is a bit of a disgrace. It doesn't look like a partner's desk.

I'll tidy it up. This is the perfect way to spend an hour. 12:06–1:06: office administration. We even have a code for it on the computer time sheet.

I had forgotten how much I detest tidying.

All sorts of things are turning up as I sift through the mess on my desk. Company letters...contracts that should have gone to Maggie for filing...old invitations...memos...a Pilates pamphlet...a CD that I bought three months ago and thought I'd lost...last year's Christmas card from Arnold, which depicts him in a woolly reindeer costume...I smile at the sight, and put it into the *things to find a place for* pile.

There are tombstones too—the engraved, mounted pieces of Lucite we get at the end of a big deal. And... oh, God, half a Snickers bar I obviously didn't finish eating at one time or another. I dump it in the bin and turn with a sigh to another pile of papers.

They shouldn't give us such big desks. I can't believe how much stuff is on here.

Partner! shoots through my mind, like a glittering firework. *PARTNER!*

Stop it, I instruct myself sternly. Concentrate on the task at hand. As I pull out an old copy of *The Lawyer* and wonder why on earth I'm keeping it, some paper-clipped documents fall to the floor. I reach for them and run my gaze down the front page, already reaching for the next thing. It's a memo from Arnold.

Re Third Union Bank.
Please find attached debenture for Glazerbrooks Ltd. Please attend to registration at Companies House.

I peer at it without great interest. Third Union Bank is Arnold's client, and I've only dealt with them once. The bank has agreed to loan £50 million to Glazerbrooks, a big building-materials company, and all I have to do is register the security document within twenty-one days at Companies House. It's just another of the mundane jobs that partners are always dumping on my desk. Well, not anymore, I think with a surge of determination. In fact, I think I'll delegate this to someone else, right now. I glance automatically at the date.

Then I look again. The security document is dated May 26th.

Five weeks ago? That can't be right.

Puzzled, I flip quickly through the papers, looking to see if there's been a typo. There *must* be a typo—but the date is consistent throughout. May 26th.

May 26th?

I sit, frozen, staring at the document. Has this thing been on my desk for *five weeks*?

But...it can't. I mean...it couldn't. That would mean—

It would mean I've missed the deadline.

I can't have made such a basic mistake. I cannot possibly have failed to register a charge before the deadline. I *always* register charges before the deadline.

I close my eyes and try to remain calm. It's the excitement of being partner. It's addled my brain. OK. Let's look at this again, carefully.

But the memo says exactly the same thing as before. Attend to registration. Dated May 26th. Which would mean I've exposed Third Union Bank to an unsecured loan. Which would mean I've made about the most elementary mistake a lawyer can make.

There's a kind of iciness about my spine. I'm trying desperately to remember if Arnold said anything about the deal to me. I can't even remember him mentioning it. But then—why would he mention a simple loan agreement? We do loan agreements in our sleep. He would have assumed I'd carried out his instructions. He would have trusted me.

Oh, Jesus.

I leaf through the pages again, searching desperately for some loophole. Some miracle clause that will have me exclaiming "Oh, of *course*!" in relief. But of course it's not there.

How could this have happened? Did I even notice this? Did I sweep it aside, meaning to do it later?

What am I going to do? A wall of panic hits me as I take in the consequences. Third Union Bank has lent Glazerbrooks £50 million. Without the charge being registered, this loan—this multimillion-pound loan—is unsecured. If Glazerbrooks went bust tomorrow, Third

Union Bank would go to the back of the queue of creditors. And probably end up with nothing.

"Samantha!" says Maggie at the door. Instinctively I plant my hand over the memo even though she wouldn't realize the significance, anyway.

"I just heard!" she says in a stage whisper. "Guy let it slip! Congratulations!"

"Um . . . thanks!" Somehow I force my mouth into a smile.

"I'm just getting a cup of tea. D'you want one?"

"That'd be . . . great. Thanks."

Maggie disappears and I bury my head in my hands. I'm trying to keep calm, but inside is a great well of terror. I have to face it. I've made a mistake.

I have made a mistake.

What am I going to do? I can't think straight—

Then suddenly Guy's words from yesterday ring in my ears, and I feel an almost painful flood of relief. *A mistake isn't a mistake unless it can't be put right.*

Yes. The point is, I can put this right. I can still register a charge.

The process will be excruciating. I'll have to tell the bank what I've done—and Glazerbrooks—and Arnold—and Ketterman. I'll have to have new documentation drawn up. And, worst of all, live with everyone knowing I've made the kind of stupid, thoughtless error a trainee would make.

It might mean an end to my partnership. I feel sick—but there's no other option. I have to put the situation right.

Quickly I log on to the Companies House Web site and enter a search for Glazerbrooks. As long as no other charges have been registered against Glazerbrooks in the meantime, it will all come to the same thing. . . .

I stare at the page in disbelief.

No.

It can't be.

There's a new debenture in Glazerbrooks' charge register, securing £50 million owed to some company called BLLC Holdings. It was registered last week. Third Union Bank has been bumped down the creditors' queue.

My mind is helter-skeltering. This isn't good. It's not good. I have to talk to someone quickly. I have to do something about this now, before any more charges are made. I have to ... to tell Arnold.

Just the thought paralyzes me with horror.

I can't do it. I just can't go out and announce I've made the most basic, elementary error and put £50 million of our client's money at risk. What I'll do is ... is start sorting out the mess first, before I tell anyone here. Have the damage limitation under way. Yes. I'll call the bank first. The sooner they know, the better—

"Samantha?"

"What?" I practically leap out of my chair.

"You're nervy today!" Maggie laughs and comes toward the desk with a cup of tea. "Feeling on top of the world?"

For an instant I honestly have no idea what she's talking about. My world has been reduced to me and my mistake and what I'm going to do about it.

"Oh! Right. Yes!" I try to grin back and surreptitiously wipe my damp hands on a tissue.

"I bet you haven't come down off your high yet!" She leans against the filing cabinet. "I've got some champagne in the fridge, all ready...."

"Er...great! Actually, Maggie, I've really got to get on...."

"Oh." She looks hurt. "Well, OK. I'll leave you."

As she walks out I can see indignation in the set of her shoulders. She probably thinks I'm a total cow. But every minute is another minute of risk. I have to call the bank. Immediately.

I search through the attached contact sheet and find the name and number of our contact at Third Union. Charles Conway.

This is the man I have to call. This is the man whose day I have to disturb and admit that I've totally messed up. With trembling hands I pick up the phone. I feel as though I'm psyching myself up to dive into a noxious swamp.

For a few moments I just sit there, staring at the keypad, willing myself to punch in the number. At last, I reach out and dial. As it rings, my heart begins to pound.

"Charles Conway."

"Hi!" I say, trying to keep my voice steady. "It's Samantha Sweeting from Carter Spink. I don't think we've met."

"Hi, Samantha." He sounds friendly enough. "How can I help?"

"I was phoning on a . . . a technical matter. It's about . . ." I can hardly bear to say it. "Glazerbrooks."

"Oh, you've heard about that," says Charles Conway. "News travels fast."

The room seems to shrink.

"Heard . . . what?" My voice is higher than I'd like. "I haven't heard anything."

"Oh! I assumed that's why you were calling. Yes, they called in the receivers today. That last-ditch attempt to save themselves obviously didn't work. . . ."

I feel light-headed. Black spots are dancing in front of my eyes. Glazerbrooks is going bust. They'll never draw up the new documentation now. Not in a million years.

I won't be able to register the charge. I can't put it right. I've lost Third Union Bank £50 million.

I feel like I'm hallucinating. I want to gibber in panic. I want to thrust down the phone and run.

"It's a good thing you phoned, as it happens," Charles Conway is saying. I can hear him tapping at a keyboard in the background, totally unconcerned. "You might want to double-check that loan security."

For a few moments I can't speak.

"Yes," I say at last, my voice hoarse. "Thank you." I put down the receiver, shaking all over.

I've fucked up.

I have fucked up so big, I can't even . . .

Barely knowing what I'm doing, I push back my chair. I have to get out.

Five

I walk through reception on autopilot. Out onto the sunny lunchtime street, one foot in front of the other, just another office worker among the midday crowds.

Except I'm different. I've just lost my client £50 million.

Fifty million. The amount is like a drumbeat in my head.

I don't understand how it happened. I don't understand. My mind keeps turning it over. Over and over, obsessively. How could I have not seen . . . how could I have overlooked . . . It must have been put on my desk, then covered up with something else. A file, a pile of contracts, a cup of coffee.

One mistake. The only mistake I've ever made. I want to wake up and this will all be a bad dream, it happened to someone else, it's a story I'm listening to in the pub, agog, thanking my lucky stars it wasn't me. . . . But it is me.

My career is over. The last person at Carter Spink who made a mistake like this was Ted Stephens, who lost a client £10 million in 1983. He was fired on the spot. And I've lost five times that.

My chest feels tight; I feel like I'm being smothered. I think I could be having a panic attack. I sit down on a bench set against some railings and wait to feel better.

OK, I'm not feeling better. I'm feeling worse.

Suddenly I jump in terror as my mobile phone vibrates in my pocket. I pull it out and look at the caller ID. It's Guy.

I can't talk to him. I can't talk to anybody. Not right now.

A moment later, the phone tells me a message has been left. I lift the phone to my ear and press 1 to listen.

"Samantha!" Guy sounds cheery. "Where are you? We're all waiting with the champagne to make the big partnership announcement!"

Partnership. I want to burst into tears. But . . . I can't. This mistake is too big for tears. I thrust my phone in my pocket and get to my feet again. I begin to walk faster and faster, weaving through the pedestrians. My head is pounding and I have no idea where I'm going.

I walk for what seems like hours, my head in a daze, my feet moving blindly. The sun is beating down, and the pavements are dusty, and after a while my head starts to throb. At some point my mobile starts to vibrate again, but I ignore it.

At last, when my legs are starting to ache, I slow down and come to a halt. My mouth is dry; I'm totally dehydrated. I need some water. I look up, trying to get my bearings. Somehow I seem to have reached Paddington Station, of all places.

Numbly, I turn my steps toward the entrance and

walk inside. The place is noisy and crowded with travelers. The fluorescent lights and air-conditioning and the blaring announcements make me flinch. As I'm making my way to a kiosk selling bottled water, my mobile vibrates again. I pull it out and look at the display. I have fifteen missed calls and another message from Guy. He left it about twenty minutes ago.

I hesitate, my heart beating with nerves, then press 1 to listen to it.

"Jesus Christ, Samantha, what *happened*?"

He doesn't sound cheery anymore, he sounds totally stressed. I feel prickles of dread all over my body.

"We know," he's saying. "OK? We know about Third Union Bank. Charles Conway called up. Then Ketterman found the paperwork on your desk. You have to come back to the office. Now. Call me back."

He rings off but I don't move. I'm paralyzed with fright.

They know. They all know.

The black spots are dancing in front of my eyes again. Nausea is rising up inside me. The entire staff of Carter Spink knows I messed up. People will be calling each other. E-mailing the news in horrified glee. *Did you hear . . .*

As I'm standing there, something catches the corner of my eye. A familiar face is just visible through the crowd. I turn my head and squint at the man, trying to place him—then feel a fresh jolt of horror.

It's Greg Parker, one of the senior partners. He's been in the States, I remember. He'll have just got in on the Heathrow Express. Now he's striding along the concourse in his expensive suit, holding his mobile phone. His brows are knitted together and he looks concerned.

"So where *is* she?" His voice travels across the concourse.

Panic hits me like a lightning bolt. I have to get out of his line of vision. I have to hide. Now. I edge behind a vast woman in a beige mac and try to cower down so I'm hidden. But she keeps wandering about, and I keep having to shuffle along with her.

"Did you want something?" She suddenly turns.

"No!" I say, flustered. "I'm . . . er . . ."

"Well, leave me alone!" She scowls and stalks off toward Costa Coffee. I'm totally exposed in the middle of the concourse. Greg Parker is about fifty yards away, still talking on his mobile phone.

If I move, he'll see me. If I stay still . . . he'll see me.

Suddenly the electronic Departures display board renews itself with fresh train information. A crowd of waiting travelers grab their bags and newspapers and head toward platform 9.

Without thinking twice, I join the throng, hidden in their midst as we sweep through the open barriers and onto the train. It pulls out of the station and I sink into a seat, opposite a family all wearing London Zoo T-shirts. They smile at me—and somehow I manage to smile back.

"Refreshments?" A wizened man pushing a trolley appears in the carriage and beams at me. "Hot and cold sandwiches, teas and coffees, soft drinks, alcoholic beverages?"

"The last, please." I try not to sound too desperate. "A double. Of . . . anything."

No one comes to check my ticket. No one bothers me. The train seems to be some sort of express. Suburbs turn into fields, and the train is still rattling along. I've drunk three small bottles of gin, mixed with orange juice, tomato juice, and a chocolate yogurt drink. The chunk of icy fright in my stomach has thawed and I feel weirdly distanced from everything around me.

I have made the biggest mistake of my career. I will have lost my job. I will never be a partner.

One stupid mistake.

The London Zoo family have opened packets of crisps and offered me one and invited me to join in their game of Travel Scrabble. The mother even asked me if I was traveling for business or fun?

I couldn't bring myself to answer.

My heart rate has gradually subsided, but I have a bad, throbbing headache. I'm sitting with a hand over one eye, trying to block out the light.

"Ladies and gentlemen." The conductor is crackling over the loudspeaker. "Unfortunately . . . rail works . . . alternative transport . . ."

I can't follow what he's saying. I don't even know where I'm headed. I'll just wait for the next stop, get out of the train, and take it from there.

"That's not how you spell *raisin*," London Zoo mother is saying to one of the children, when the train suddenly starts to slow down. I look up to see that we're pulling into a station. Lower Ebury. People are gathering up their bags and getting off.

Like an automaton I get up too. I follow the London Zoo family off the train and out of a tiny, twee country station. There's a pub called The Bell across the road, which bends round in both directions, and I can glimpse fields in the distance. There's a coach waiting, and all the passengers from the train are boarding.

London Zoo mother has turned round and is gesturing at me. "You need to come this way," she says helpfully. "If you want the bus to Gloucester?"

The thought of getting on a coach makes me want to heave. I don't want the bus to anywhere. I just want an aspirin. My head feels like it's about to split open.

"Er . . . no, thanks. I'm fine here." Before she can say anything else, I start walking down the road.

I have no idea where I am. None.

Inside my pocket, my phone suddenly vibrates. It's Guy. Again. This must be the thirtieth time he's rung. And every time he's left a message telling me to call him back, asking if I've got his e-mails.

I haven't got any of his e-mails. I was so freaked out, I left my BlackBerry on my desk. My phone is all I have. It vibrates again and I stare at it for a few moments. I can't ignore him forever. My stomach clenched with nerves, I lift it to my ear and press TALK.

"Hi." My voice is scratchy. "It's . . . it's me."

"Samantha?" His incredulous voice blasts down the line. "Is that *you*? Where *are* you?"

"I don't know. I had to get away. I . . . I went into shock. . . ."

"Samantha, I don't know if you got my messages. But . . ." He hesitates. "Everyone knows."

"I know." I lean against an old crumbling wall and squeeze my eyes shut.

"How did it *happen*?" He sounds as shocked as I feel. "How the hell did you make a simple error like that? I mean, Christ, Samantha—"

"I don't know," I say numbly.

"You never make mistakes!"

"Well, I do now!" I feel tears rising and fiercely blink them down. "What's . . . what's happened?"

"It's not good." He exhales. "Ketterman's been having damage limitation talks with Glazerbrooks' lawyers and talking to the bank—and the insurers, of course."

The insurers. The firm's professional indemnity insurance. I'm suddenly gripped by an almost exhilarating hope. If the insurers pay up without making a fuss, maybe things won't be as bad as I thought. . . .

But even as I feel my spirits lift I know I'm like some traveler seeing the mirage through the haze. Insurers never cough up the whole amount. Sometimes they don't cough up anything. Sometimes they pay up but raise their premiums to unfeasible levels.

"What did the insurers say? Will they—"

"They haven't said anything yet."

"Right." I wipe my sweaty face, screwing up my courage to ask the next question. "And what about . . . me?"

Guy is silent.

There's my answer. I open my eyes to see two small boys on bikes staring at me.

"It's over, isn't it? My career's over."

"I . . . I don't know that. Listen, Samantha, you're freaked out. It's natural. But you can't hide. You have to come back—"

"I can't." Ketterman's face looms in my mind. And what will Arnold think of me now? "I can't face everyone."

"Samantha, be rational!"

"I need some time!"

"Saman—" I flip my phone shut.

I feel a bit faint. I must get some water. But I can't face going into a noisy pub, and I can't see any shops.

I totter along the road until I reach a pair of tall carved pillars decorated with lions. Here's a house. I'll ring the bell and ask for some aspirin and a glass of water. And ask if there's a hotel nearby.

I push open the elaborate wrought-iron gate and crunch over the gravel toward the heavy oak front door.

It's a rather grand old house made out of honey-colored stone, set well back from the road, with steep gables and tall chimneys and two Porsches on the drive. I raise a hand and tug the bellpull.

There's silence. The whole house seems dead. I'm about to give up and trudge back down the drive—when all of a sudden the door swings open.

Before me stands a woman with blond lacquered hair to her shoulders and long, dangly earrings. She has lots of makeup, long silk trousers in a weird shade of peach, a cigarette in one hand and a cocktail in the other.

"Hello." She drags on her cigarette and looks at me a bit suspiciously. "Are you from the agency?"

Six

I have no idea what this woman's talking about. My head's hurting so much, I can barely look at her, let alone take in what she's saying.

"Are you all right?" She peers at me. "You look terrible!"

"I've got a rather bad headache," I manage. "Could I possibly have a glass of water?"

"Of course! Come in!" She waves her cigarette in my face and beckons me into a huge, impressive hall with a vaulted ceiling. There's a circular oak table in the middle, bearing a vase of huge lilies, and a medieval-style bench at the side. "You'll want to see the house, anyway. *Eddie*?" Her voice rises to a shriek. "Eddie, another one's here! I'm Trish Geiger," she adds to me. "You may call me Mrs. Geiger. This way . . ."

She leads me down a short passage into a luxurious maple kitchen and tries a few drawers, apparently at random, before crying "Aha!" and pulling out a plastic box. She opens it to reveal about fifty assorted bottles of pain-relief tablets, vitamins, and bottles of something called Hollywood Skin Glow Supplement, and starts rootling about with her lacquered fingernails.

"I've got aspirin...paracetamol...ibuprofen...*very* mild Valium..." She holds up a livid red pill. "This one's from America," she says brightly. "Illegal in this country."

"Um...lovely."

She hands me three green tablets and after a few attempts locates a cupboard full of glasses. "Here we are. Migraine relief. They'll zap any headache. *Eddie!*" She runs me some iced water from the fridge. "Drink that up."

"Thanks," I say, swallowing the tablets down with a wince. "I'm so grateful. My head's just so painful. I can barely think straight."

"Your English is very good." She gives me a close, appraising look. "Very good indeed!"

"Oh," I say, thrown. "Right. Well, I'm English. That's... you know, probably why."

"You're *English*?" Trish Geiger seems galvanized by this news. "Well! Come and sit down. Those'll kick in, in a minute. If they don't we'll get you some more."

She sweeps me out of the kitchen and back through the hall. "This is the drawing room," she says, pausing by a door. She gestures around the large, grand room, dropping ash on the carpet. It's decorated with what look like antiques, several big velvet sofas, and lots of lamps and ornaments everywhere. "As you'll see, there's quite a lot of hoovering...dusting...silver to be kept clean..." She looks at me expectantly.

"Right." I nod. I have no idea why this woman is telling me about her housework, but she seems to be waiting for a reply.

"That's a beautiful table," I offer at last, gesturing at a shiny mahogany side table.

"It needs polishing." Her eyes narrow. "Regularly. I do notice these things."

"Of course." I nod, bemused.

"We'll go in here..." She's leading me through another huge, grand room into an airy glassed conservatory furnished with opulent teak sun-loungers, frondy plants, and a well-stocked drinks tray.

"Eddie! Come in here!" She bangs on the glass and I look up to see a dark-haired man in golfing slacks walking over the large, well-manicured lawn. He's tanned and affluent-looking, probably in his late forties.

Trish is probably in her late forties too, I think, glimpsing her crow's feet as she turns away from the window.

"Lovely garden," I say.

"Oh." Her eyes sweep over it without much interest. "Yes, our gardener is very good. Has all sorts of ideas. Now, sit down!" She makes a flapping motion with her hands and, feeling a little awkward, I sit down on a lounger. Trish sinks into a basket chair opposite and drains her cocktail.

"Can you make a good Bloody Mary?" she asks abruptly.

I stare at her, bewildered.

"No matter." She drags on her cigarette. "I can teach you."

"Teach me...?"

"How's your head?" she demands before I'm able to finish. "Better? Ah, here's Eddie!"

"Greetings!" The door opens and Mr. Geiger comes into the conservatory. He doesn't look quite as impressive close up as he did striding over the lawn. His blue eyes are a little bloodshot, and he has the beginnings of a beer belly.

"Eddie Geiger," he says, holding out his hand jovially. "Master of the house."

"Eddie, this is . . ." Trish looks at me in surprise. "What's your name?"

"Samantha," I explain. "I'm so sorry to bother you, but I had the most terrible headache . . ."

"I gave Samantha some of those wonderful migraine tablets!" puts in Trish.

"Good choice!" Eddie unscrews a Scotch bottle and pours himself a drink.

"I'm very grateful, really." I manage a half smile. "You've been very kind, letting me trespass on your evening."

"Her English is good, isn't it?" Eddie raises his eyebrows at Trish.

"She's English!" says Trish triumphantly, as though she's pulled a rabbit out of a hat. "Understands everything I say!"

I am really not getting something here. Do I *look* foreign?

"Shall we do the tour of the house?" Eddie turns to Trish.

"Really, it's not necessary," I begin. "I'm sure it's absolutely beautiful—"

"Of course it's necessary!" Trish stubs out her cigarette. "Come on . . . bring your glass!"

This woman cannot have a life. All she seems interested in is housework. As we trail round the first floor, viewing one splendid room after another, she keeps pointing out things that need special dusting and polishing, and

how careful you have to be with the soft furnishings.
I'm sure silk drapes *do* need special treatment—but why
tell me?

"Now upstairs!" She sweeps out of the dining room.
Oh, God. There's more?

"You come from London, Samantha?" says Eddie
Geiger as we head up the stairs. A huge oil painting of
Trish in a long blue evening dress with astonishingly
sparkly eyes and teeth gazes down at us, and I can see
the real Trish waiting for a reaction.

"Yes, I do. That's a . . . lovely painting," I add. "So
vivid!"

"We were rather pleased with it." Trish looks com-
placent.

"And you have a full-time job there?" I'm sure Eddie's
only asking to be polite—but for a few moments I can't
bring myself to answer. Do I have a job?

"I did," I say at last. "To be honest . . . I don't know
what my situation is at the moment."

"What sort of hours did you work?" Trish seems suddenly interested in the conversation.

"All hours." I shrug. "I'm used to working all day and
into the night. Through the night, sometimes."

The Geigers look absolutely stunned at this revela-
tion. People just have no idea what the life of a lawyer is
like.

"You used to work *through the night*?" Trish seems
stupefied. "On your own?"

"Me and the other staff. Whoever was needed."

"So you come from . . . a big setup?"

"One of the biggest in London."

Trish and Eddie are darting glances at each other.
They really are the oddest people.

"Well, we're *far* more relaxed, you'll be glad to hear!"

Trish pushes open a door. "This is the master bedroom... the second bedroom..."

As we walk down the corridor she opens and closes doors and shows me four-poster beds and swishy curtains and matching upholstered ottomans, until my head swims. I don't know if it's too much floral wallpaper or whatever was in those migraine pills—but I'm feeling more lightheaded by the minute.

"The green bedroom... As you will know, we don't have children or pets.... Are you a smoker?" Trish suddenly demands.

"Um... no. Thanks."

"Not that we mind either way."

We descend a small flight of stairs and I grab on to the wall to keep myself steady.

"Are you all right?" Eddie catches my arm.

"I think those tablets were a bit strong..." I mumble.

"They can be." Trish gives me a considering look. "You haven't drunk any *alcohol* today, have you?"

"Er... well, yes..."

"Aaah." She pulls a face. "Well, maybe you should have a little rest before you leave. What a good thing we've come to the staff accommodation!" She opens the last door with a flourish.

All the rooms in this house are huge. This one is about the size of my flat, with pale walls and stone mullioned windows overlooking the garden. It has the plainest bed I've seen yet in this house, vast and square and made up with crisp white bed linen.

I fight a sudden, almost overwhelming urge to lie down on it and sink into oblivion.

"Lovely," I say politely. "It's... a gorgeous room."

"Good!" Eddie smacks his hands together. "Well, Samantha. I'd say you've got the job!"

I look at him dumbly.

Job?

"Eddie!" snaps Trish. "You can't just *offer her the job*! We haven't finished the interview!"

Interview?

"We haven't even given her a full job description!" Trish is still laying into Eddie. "We haven't been through any of the details!"

"Well, go through the details, then!" retorts Eddie. Trish shoots him a look of fury and clears her throat.

"So, Samantha," she says in formal tones. "Your role as full-time housekeeper will comprise—"

"I'm sorry?"

Trish clicks her tongue in exasperation. "Your role as full-time housekeeper," she says, more slowly, "will comprise all cleaning, laundry, and cooking. You will wear a uniform and maintain a courteous and respectful . . . ."

My role as—

These people think I'm applying to be their *housekeeper*?

I'm too dumbfounded to speak.

" . . . full board and lodging," Trish is saying, "and four weeks holiday a year."

"What's the salary?" says Eddie with interest. "Are we paying her more than the last girl?"

I think Trish might murder him, there and then.

"I'm so sorry, Samantha!" Before I can even open my mouth she's dragged Eddie out of the room and banged the door, whereupon a furious, muted argument breaks out.

I look around the room, trying to gather my wits.

They think I'm a housekeeper. A housekeeper! This is ridiculous. I have to put them right. I have to explain the misunderstanding.

Another wave of wooziness engulfs me and I sit

down on the bed. Then, before I can stop myself, I lie back on the cool white cover and close my eyes. It's like sinking into a cloud. It's been a long day. A long, exhausting, painful nightmare of a day. I just want it to be over.

"Samantha, I'm sorry about that." I open my eyes and struggle up to see Trish coming back in, followed by a pink-faced Eddie. "Before we continue, did you have any questions about the post?"

I stare back at her, my head swirling. This is the moment where I have to explain there's been a big mistake. That I'm not a housekeeper, I'm a lawyer.

But . . . nothing comes out of my mouth.

I could stay here one night, flashes through my brain. *Just one night. I could sort out the misunderstanding tomorrow.*

"Um . . . would it be possible to start tonight?" I hear myself saying.

"I don't see why not—" begins Eddie.

"Let's not jump ahead of ourselves," Trish interrupts pointedly. "We have had *quite* a few promising applicants for this post, Samantha. Several quite dazzling. One girl even had a diploma in French Cordon Bleu cookery!"

Something inside me stiffens, like an automatic reflex.

Is she suggesting—

Is she implying that I might not *get* this job?

I regard Trish silently. Somewhere, down inside my bruised state of shock, I can feel a tiny flicker of the old Samantha returning. I can beat some French Cordon Bleu cookery girl.

I have never failed an interview in my life.

I'm not about to start now.

"So." Trish consults her list. "You're experienced in all forms of laundry?"

"Naturally." I nod.

"And are you Cordon Bleu trained?" It's clear from her expression that nothing less will pass the test.

"I trained under Michel de la Roux de la Blanc." I pause. "His name obviously speaks for itself."

"Absolutely!" says Trish, glancing uncertainly at Eddie.

We're sitting in the conservatory again, ten minutes later, and I'm sipping a cup of coffee, which Eddie made for me. Trish is firing a series of questions at me that sound like they come from a how-to-hire-your-housekeeper pamphlet. And I'm answering every single one with total confidence.

Deep down in my brain I can hear a little voice calling out, *What are you doing? Samantha, what the hell are you DOING?*

But I'm not listening. I don't want to listen. Somehow I've managed to block out real life, the mistake, my ruined career, the whole nightmare of a day—everything else in the world except this interview.

"Could you give us a sample menu?" Trish lights another cigarette. "For a dinner party, say?"

Food . . . impressive food . . .

Suddenly I remember Maxim's last night. The souvenir birthday menu.

"I'll just consult my . . . notes." I unzip my bag and surreptitiously scan the Maxim's menu. "For a formal dinner, I would serve . . . er . . . seared foie gras with an apricot glaze . . . lamb with minted hummus . . . followed by orange-chocolate soufflé with two homemade sorbets."

Take *that*, Cordon Bleu girl.

"Well!" Trish looks astounded. "I must say, that's ... very impressive."

"Marvelous!" Eddie looks like he's salivating. "Seared foie gras! You couldn't knock some up for us now?"

Trish shoots him an annoyed look. "I'm assuming you have a reference, Samantha?"

A reference?

"We *will* need a reference...." Trish begins to frown.

"My reference is Lady Freya Edgerly," I say, in sudden inspiration.

"*Lady* Edgerly?" Trish's eyebrows rise and a pink flush starts slowly creeping up her neck.

"I have been associated with Lord and Lady Edgerly for many years," I reply gravely. "I know Lady Edgerly will vouch for me."

Trish and Eddie are both staring at me, agog.

"You cooked for them, did you?" inquires Eddie. "Breakfasts and so forth?"

"Naturally. Lord Edgerly was very fond of my signature dish, eggs Benedict." I take a sip of water.

I can see Trish pulling what she clearly imagines are cryptic faces at Eddie, who is surreptitiously nodding back. They might as well have *Let's Have Her!* tattooed on their foreheads.

"One final thing." Trish takes a deep drag on her cigarette. "You will be answering the phone when Mr. Geiger and myself are out. Our image in society is very important. Please, would you demonstrate how you will do it?" She nods at a phone on a nearby table.

They cannot be serious. Except ... I think they are.

"You should say, 'Good afternoon, the Geiger residence,' " prompts Eddie.

Obediently I get up, walk across the room, and lift the receiver.

"Good afternoon," I say in my most charming, head-school-prefect tones. "The Geiger residence. How may I help?"

Eddie and Trish look like all their Christmases have come at once.

Seven

I wake the next morning to an unfamiliar, smooth white ceiling above me. I frown in puzzlement, then lift my head a little. The sheets make a strange rumpling sound as I move. What's going on? My sheets don't sound anything like that.

But of course. They're the Geigers' sheets.

I sink comfortably back into my pillows—until another thought strikes me.

Who are the Geigers?

I screw up my face, trying to remember. I feel as though I'm both hungover and still drunk. Snatches of yesterday are vivid in my mind, amid a dense fog. I'm not sure what's real and what's a dream. I came on the train...yes...I had a headache...Paddington Station... walking out of the office...

Oh, God. Oh, please, no.

With a sickening whoosh the whole nightmare comes rushing back. The memo. Third Union Bank. Fifty million pounds. Asking Guy if I had a job left...

His silence...

My career is wrecked. My life as I knew it is over.

At last I push back the covers and get out of bed, feeling weak and spacey. This time yesterday I was in my kitchen, getting ready for work, blissfully unaware of what was about to happen. In another world—in a parallel universe to this one—I would be waking up today a partner of Carter Spink. I'd be surrounded by messages of congratulation.

I squeeze my eyes tight, trying to escape the sickening if-only thoughts. If I'd seen the memo earlier—if I had a tidier desk—if Arnold hadn't given me that loan agreement—

But there's no point. I walk to the window and take deep gulps of fresh air. What happened happened. All I can do is deal with it. Until this moment in time my whole life has been mapped out to the hour. Through exams, through holiday internships, the rungs of the career ladder... I thought I knew exactly where I was headed. And now I find myself in a strange room in the middle of the countryside, my career in ruins.

Plus... there's something else. Something's nagging at me. A final piece of the jigsaw still missing in my dazed brain. It'll come to me in a minute.

I lean against the windowsill and watch a man on the distant horizon walking his dog. Maybe things are salvageable. Maybe it's not all as bad as I thought. Guy didn't actually *say* I'd lost my job. I have to call him—and find out just how bad it is. I take a deep breath and run my hands through my tangled hair. God, I flipped out yesterday. When I consider the way I acted, running out of the office, jumping on a train... I was really on another planet. If it weren't for the Geigers being so understanding—

My train of thought halts abruptly.

The Geigers.

Something about the Geigers. Something I'm not remembering...something that's ringing slight alarm bells...

I turn round and focus on a blue dress hanging on the wardrobe door. Some kind of uniform, with piping. Why would there be a—

The alarm bells are getting louder. They're starting to clang wildly. It's coming back to me like some kind of terrible, drunken dream.

Did I take a job as a housekeeper?

For a few instants I cannot move. Oh, God. What have I done? What have I *done*?

My heart starts to thump as I take in my situation properly for the first time. I am staying in a strange couple's house under completely false pretenses. I've slept in their bed. I'm wearing one of Trish's old T-shirts. They even gave me a toothbrush, after I invented a suitcase-stolen-on-the-train story. The last thing I remember is hearing Trish gloating on the phone. "She's English!" she was saying. "Yes, speaks English perfectly! *Super* girl. Cordon Bleu trained!"

I'll have to tell them it was all lies.

There's a rapping at my bedroom door and I jump in fright.

"Samantha?" Trish's voice comes through the door. "May I come in?"

"Oh! Um...yes!"

The door opens and Trish appears, wearing pale pink exercise clothes with a diamanté logo.

"I've made you a cup of tea," she says, handing me the mug with a formal smile. "Mr. Geiger and I would like you to feel very welcome in our house."

"Oh!" I swallow nervously. "Thanks."

Mrs. Geiger, there's something I need to tell you. I'm not a housekeeper.

Somehow the words don't make it out of my mouth.

Trish's eyes have narrowed as though she's already regretting her kind gesture. "Don't think you'll be getting this every day, of course! But since you weren't feeling well last night . . ." She taps her watch. "Now you'd better get dressed. We'll expect you down in ten minutes. We only have a light breakfast as a rule. Toast and coffee. Then we can discuss the menu for the week."

"Er . . . OK," I say feebly.

She closes the door and I put the tea down. Oh, fuck. What am I going to do?

OK. Prioritize. I need to call the office. Find out exactly how bad the situation is. With a spasm of apprehension I reach inside my bag for my mobile phone.

The display is blank.

I tap it in frustration, but the battery must have run out. I must have been so spaced out yesterday I forgot to charge it. I pull out my charger, plug it into the wall, and attach the phone. At once it starts charging up.

I wait for the signal to appear . . . but there's no bloody signal. How am I going to call the office? How am I going to do *anything*? I cannot exist without my mobile phone.

Suddenly I remember passing a telephone on the landing. It was on a table in a little window bay. Maybe I could use that. I open my bedroom door and look up and down the corridor. No one's about. Cautiously I creep into the bay and lift the receiver. The dial tone rings in my ear. I take a deep breath—then dial the direct line for Arnold. It isn't nine yet, but he'll be in.

"Arnold Saville's office," comes the cheerful voice of Lara, his secretary.

"Lara," I say nervously. "It's Samantha. Samantha Sweeting."

"*Samantha?*" Lara sounds so gobsmacked, I wince. "Oh, my God! What happened? Where *are* you? Everyone's been—" She draws herself up.

"I . . . I'm out of London right now. May I speak with Arnold?"

"Of course. He's right here. . . ." She disappears briefly into chirpy Vivaldi, before the line clears again.

"Samantha." Arnold's friendly, assured voice booms down the line. "My dear girl. You've got yourself in a pickle, haven't you?"

Only Arnold could describe the loss of a client's £50 million as a "pickle." In spite of everything, I feel the beginning of a smile. I can just picture him, in his waistcoat, his woolly eyebrows knitting together.

"I know," I say, trying to match his understated tones. "It's . . . not great."

"I'm obliged to point out that your hasty departure yesterday did not help matters."

"I know. I'm so sorry. I just . . . panicked."

"Understandable. However, you left a bit of a mess behind."

Beneath Arnold's jolly veneer I can hear unfamiliar levels of stress. Arnold never gets stressed. Things must be really bad. I want to fall to the floor in a groveling heap, crying, "I'm so sorry!" But that wouldn't help. I've already been unprofessional enough.

"So—what's the latest situation?" I'm trying to sound matter-of-fact. "Is there anything the receivers can do?"

"I think it unlikely. They say their hands are tied."

"Right." His response is like a hammer blow to the stomach. So that's it. The fifty million is gone for good. "And . . . the insurers?"

"That is the next step, of course. The money will be

recovered eventually, I'm sure. But not without complications. As I think you will appreciate."

"I know," I whisper.

There's no good news. There's no silver lining. I've fucked up.

"Arnold . . ." I say, my voice quivering. "I have no idea how I could have made such a . . . a *stupid* mistake. I don't understand how it happened. I don't even remember seeing the memo on my desk—"

"Where are you now?" Arnold breaks in.

"I'm . . ." I look helplessly out the window at the Geigers' gravel drive. "To be honest, I don't even know exactly where I am."

"You don't know?"

"I'm in the country somewhere. But I can come back right now!" My words tumble out. "I'll get on the first train . . . I'll only be a few hours. . . ."

"I don't think that's a good idea." There's a new edge to Arnold's voice, which pulls me up short.

"Have I . . . have I been fired?"

"There have been slightly more pressing matters to consider, Samantha." He sounds testy.

"Of course." I feel the blood rush back into my head. "I'm sorry. I just . . . I've been with Carter Spink all my working life. All I ever, ever wanted was . . ."

I can't even say it.

"Samantha, I know you're a very talented lawyer." Arnold sighs. "No one is in any doubt of that."

"But I made a mistake."

I can hear tiny crackles down the line; my own pulse beating in my ears.

"Samantha, I'll do everything I can," he says at last. "I might as well tell you, a meeting has been arranged this morning to discuss your future."

"And you honestly don't think I should come in?" I bite my lip.

"It might do more harm than good at the moment. Stay where you are. Leave the rest to me." Arnold hesitates, his voice a little gruff. "I'll do my best, Samantha. I promise."

"Thank you so much..." I say quickly. But he's gone. Slowly I put down the phone.

I have never felt so powerless in my life. I have a sudden vision of them all sitting gravely round a conference table. Arnold. Ketterman. Maybe even Guy. Deciding whether to give me another break.

There's still a chance. If Arnold is on my side, others might be too....

"*Super* girl."

I jump at the sound of Trish's approaching voice. "Well, of course I'll check her references, but, Gillian, I am a *very* good judge of character. I'm not easily fooled...."

Trish rounds the corner, holding a mobile to her ear, and I quickly move away from the telephone.

"Samantha!" she says in surprise. "What are you doing? Still not dressed? Buck up!" She heads off again and I scuttle back to my room.

I suddenly feel bad.

In fact... I feel terrible. How are the Geigers going to react when I tell them I'm a total fraud? That I'm not a trained Cordon Bleu housekeeper at all, I just wanted a place to stay for the night?

I have a sudden image of them bundling me furiously out of the house. Feeling totally used. Maybe they'll even call the police and file charges. Oh, God. This could get really nasty.

But, I mean, it's not like I have any other option. It's not like I could actually...

... Could I?

I pick up the blue uniform and finger it, my mind whirling round and round.

They've been so kind, putting me up. It's not like I'm doing anything else right now. It's not like I have anywhere else to go. Maybe it'll even take my mind off things, doing a little light housework—

Abruptly I come to a decision.

I'll busk it for a morning. It can't be that hard. I'll make their toast and dust the ornaments or whatever. I'll think of it as my little thank-you to them. Then as soon as I hear from Arnold I'll find a convincing excuse to leave. And the Geigers will never know I wasn't a proper housekeeper.

Hurriedly I put on my uniform and run a comb through my hair. Then I stand to face myself in the mirror.

"Good morning, Mrs. Geiger," I say to my reflection. "And...er...how would you like the drawing room dusted?"

The Geigers are standing at the bottom of the stairs looking up at me as I descend. I have never felt more self-conscious in my life.

I'm a housekeeper. I must behave like a housekeeper.

"Welcome, Samantha!" says Eddie as I arrive down in the hall. He's wearing a polo shirt with some crested logo, and golfing trousers. "Sleep all right?"

"Very well, thank you, Mr. Geiger," I reply demurely.

"That's good!" Eddie rocks back and forth on the soles of his feet. He seems just a little awkward. In fact... they both seem awkward. Underneath the makeup, the tans, the expensive clothes...there seems a hint of uncertainty about the Geigers.

I walk over to the bench seat and straighten a cushion, trying to look as though I know what I'm doing.

"You'll be wanting to get to know your new kitchen!" says Trish brightly.

"Of course!" I say with a confident smile. "I'm . . . looking forward to it!"

It's only a kitchen. It's only one morning. I can do this.

Trish leads the way into the vast maple kitchen, and this time I try to take in the details. There's a huge hob set into the granite counter to my left. A bank of ovens built into the wall. Everywhere I look I can see shiny chrome gadgets plugged into sockets. Racks of saucepans and implements of all descriptions are hanging overhead in a jumble of stainless steel.

"You'll want to get it the way you like it, of course," says Trish, gesturing around. "Just change anything you like. Knock it into shape. You're the professional!"

They're both looking at me expectantly.

"Absolutely," I say in a businesslike way. "Obviously I have my own . . . um . . . systems. That shouldn't be there, for example." I point randomly at a small metal gadget resembling a torpedo. "The . . . um . . ."

"Juice extractor," supplies Trish.

"Exactly. I'll have to move it."

"Really?" Trish looks fascinated. "Why's that?"

There's a beat of silence. Even Eddie looks interested.

"Kitchen . . . ergonomic . . . theory," I improvise. "So, you'd like toast for breakfast?" I add quickly.

"Toast for both of us," says Trish. "Whole wheat. And coffee with skim milk."

"Coming up." I smile, feeling slight relief.

I can make toast. And the bread bin is helpfully marked *Bread*.

"So, I'll just bring that through in a moment," I add,

trying to chivvy them out. "Would you like to eat in the dining room?"

There's a small crash from the hall.

"That'll be the newspaper," says Trish. "Yes, you may serve breakfast in the dining room." She hurries out, but Eddie loiters in the kitchen.

"You know, I've changed my mind." He gives me a jovial smile. "Forget the toast, Samantha. I'll have your famous eggs Benedict. You whetted my appetite last night!"

Last night? What did I say last—

Oh, Jesus. Eggs Benedict. My famous signature dish as beloved by Lord Edgerly.

What was I *thinking*?

I don't even know what eggs Benedict *is*.

"Are you . . . sure that's what you want?" I try to sound relaxed.

"I wouldn't miss your specialty!" Eddie rubs his stomach in anticipation. "It's my favorite breakfast. The best eggs Benedict I've ever tasted were at the Carlyle in New York, but I'll take a bet yours are even better!"

"I don't know about that!"

OK, think. It must be simple enough. Eggs and . . . something.

Eddie leans against the counter with an expectant look. I have a nasty suspicion he's waiting for me to start cooking. Hesitantly, I get down a gleaming pan from the rack, just as Trish bustles in with the newspaper. She eyes me with bright curiosity.

"How will you be using the asparagus steamer, Samantha?"

Shit.

"I just wanted to . . . examine it. Yes." I nod briskly, as though the pan has confirmed my suspicions, then carefully hang it back on the rack again.

Could I quickly look it up in a cookbook?

But it's supposed to be my specialty. Why would I need a cookbook?

I'm feeling hotter and hotter. I have no idea even how to begin. Do I . . . crack the eggs? Boil them?

"Here you are." Eddie takes a huge box of eggs out of the fridge, plonks them on the counter, and lifts the lid. "Should be enough there, I'd imagine!"

Before me are rows and rows of brown eggs. What do I think I'm doing? I can't make bloody eggs Benedict. I can't make these people breakfast. I'm going to have to confess.

I turn round and take a deep breath.

"Mr. Geiger . . . Mrs. Geiger . . ."

"Eggs?" Trish's voice cuts across mine. "Eddie, you can't have eggs! Remember what the doctor said!" Her eyes bore into me. "What did he ask you for, Samantha? Boiled eggs?"

"Er . . . Mr. Geiger ordered eggs Benedict. But the thing is—"

"You're not eating eggs Benedict!" Trish practically shrieks at Eddie. "It's full of cholesterol!"

"I'll eat what I like!" Eddie protests.

"The doctor gave him an eating plan." Trish is dragging furiously on her cigarette as she speaks. "He's already had a bowl of cornflakes this morning!"

"I was hungry!" says Eddie, defensive. "You had a chocolate muffin!"

Trish gasps as though he's hit her. Small red dots appear in her cheeks.

"We will have a cup of coffee each, Samantha," she announces at last in a dignified voice. "You may serve it in the lounge. Use the pink china. Come along, Eddie." And she sweeps out before I can respond.

I'm not sure if I want to laugh or cry. This is ridiculous. I can't carry on with this charade. I have to tell the Geigers the truth. Now. I walk decisively out of the kitchen into the hall, but then behind the closed door of the sitting room I can hear the shrill, indistinct voice of Trish angrily berating Eddie, and Eddie's defensive rumbles in return. Hastily I back away again into the kitchen and switch the kettle on.

A quarter of an hour later I've arranged a silver tray with a French press coffeepot, pink cups, creamer, sugar, and a sprig of pink flowers I snipped from a hanging basket outside the kitchen window. Fifteen minutes, just to make a cup of coffee. At Carter Spink I would have earned the firm £125 in that time.

Of course, I would have been quicker if I hadn't had to work out how to use the French press first. And if my first batch of coffee hadn't tasted like dishwater.

I approach the sitting-room door, put the tray down on the table in the hall, and knock cautiously.

"Come in!" Trish calls.

As I enter, she's sitting in an overstuffed striped velvet chair by the window, holding a magazine at a rather artificial angle. Eddie is on the other side of the room, examining a wooden carving.

"Thank you, Samantha." Trish inclines her head graciously as I pour out the coffee. "That will be all for the moment."

I feel as though I've stumbled into some bizarre Merchant Ivory costume drama, except the costumes are pink yoga wear and golfing sweaters.

"Er . . . very good, madam," I say, playing my part. Then, without meaning to, I bob a curtsy.

There's a staggered pause. Both Geigers just gape at me in astonishment.

"Samantha...did you just...*curtsy*?" says Trish at last.

I stare back, frozen.

What was I *thinking*? Why did I curtsy? Housekeepers don't bloody curtsy. This isn't *Gosford Park*.

They're still goggling at me. I have to say something.

"The Edgerlys liked me to...curtsy." My face is prickling all over. "It's a habit I got into. I'm sorry, madam, I won't do it again."

Trish is squinting at me as though she's trying to make me out. She must realize I'm a fake, she *must*....

"I like it," she pronounces at last, and nods her head in satisfaction. "Yes, I like it. You can curtsy here too."

What?

This is the twenty-first century. And I am being asked to curtsy to a woman called Trish?

I take a breath to protest—then close my mouth again. It doesn't matter. It's not real. I can curtsy for a morning.

Eight

As soon as I'm out of the room, I dash upstairs, along the corridor, and into my bedroom to check my mobile. But it's only half charged and I have no idea where I'm going to find a signal. If Trish could get one, I must be able to. I wonder what network she's on—

"Samantha?"

Trish's voice rises from the ground floor.

"Samantha?" She sounds annoyed. Now I can hear her footsteps coming up the stairs.

"Madam?" I hurry back along the corridor.

"There you are!" She frowns slightly. "Kindly do *not* disappear to your room while on duty. I don't want to have to be calling you like that."

"Er . . . yes, Mrs. Geiger," I say. As we arrive down in the hall my stomach flips over. Beyond Trish, I can see the *Times* lying on the table. It's open at the business pages and a headline reads GLAZERBROOKS CALLS IN RECEIVERS.

My eyes run down the text as Trish starts rootling around in a huge white Chanel bag—but I can't see any mention of Carter Spink. Thank God for that. The PR department must have managed to keep a lid on the story.

"Where are my keys?" Trish sounds fretful. "Where *are* they?" She rummages more and more violently in her Chanel bag. A gold lipstick goes flying through the air and lands at my feet. "Why do things *disappear*?"

I pick up the lipstick and hand it to her. "Do you remember where you lost them, Mrs. Geiger?"

"I didn't *lose* them." She inhales sharply. "They've been stolen. It's obvious. We'll have to change all the locks. Our identities will be taken." She clutches her head. "This is what these fraudsters do, you know. There was a huge article about it in the *Mail*—"

"Is this them?" I've suddenly noticed a Tiffany key fob glinting on the windowsill. I pick it up and hold out the bunch of keys.

"Yes!" Trish looks utterly amazed. "Yes, that's them! Samantha, you're marvelous! *How* did you find them?"

"It was . . . no trouble." I shrug modestly.

"Well! I'm very impressed!" She gives me a significant look. "I will be telling Mr. Geiger."

"Yes, madam," I say, trying to inject the right note of overwhelming gratitude into my voice. "Thank you."

"Mr. Geiger and I will be going out in a minute," she continues, producing a scent spray and spritzing herself. "Kindly prepare a light sandwich lunch for one o'clock, and get on with the downstairs cleaning. We'll talk about dinner later." She swivels round. "I might tell you, we were both very impressed by your seared foie gras menu."

"Oh . . . um . . . good!"

It's fine. I'll be gone by dinnertime.

"*Now*." Trish pats her hair one final time. "Come in the drawing room, Samantha."

I follow her into the room and over to the fireplace.

"Before you start dusting in here," Trish says, "I wanted to show you the arrangement of the ornaments." She gestures to a row of china figurines on the mantelpiece. "This can be tricky to remember. For some reason, cleaners never get it right. So kindly *pay attention*."

Obediently, I turn with her to face the mantelpiece.

"It's very important, Samantha, that these china dogs face each other." Trish points to a pair of King Charles spaniels. "Do you see? They don't face out. They face *each other*."

"Each other," I echo, nodding. "Yes. I see."

"And the shepherdesses face very slightly *out*. You see? They face *out*."

She's speaking slowly and clearly, as though I have the IQ of a rather thick three-year-old.

"Out," I repeat dutifully.

"Now, have you got that?" Trish steps back from the fireplace. "Let's see. Which way do the china dogs go?" She lifts an arm to block my view of the mantelpiece.

I don't believe it. She's testing me.

"The china dogs," she prompts. "Which way?"

Oh, God, I cannot resist this.

"Er . . ." I ponder hard for a few moments. "They face . . . out?"

"*Each other!*" Trish cries in exasperation. "They face *each other!*"

"Oh, right," I say apologetically. "Yes. Sorry. I've got that now."

Trish has closed her eyes and is holding two fingers to her forehead as though the stress of stupid help is too much to bear.

"Never mind," she says at last. "We'll try again to-morrow."

"I'll take the coffee tray out," I suggest humbly. As I

pick it up I glance again at my watch. Ten twelve. I wonder if they've started the meeting.

By eleven-thirty my nerves are really beginning to fray. My mobile's charged and I've finally found a signal in the kitchen, but it hasn't rung. And there are no messages. I've checked it every minute.

I've stacked the dishwasher and at last managed to turn it on. And I've dusted the china dogs with a tissue. Other than that all I've done is pace up and down the kitchen.

I gave up on the "light sandwich lunch" almost straightaway. At least, I briefly tried sawing away at two loaves of bread—and ended up with huge, wonky slices, each one more misshapen than the last, lying in a sea of crumbs.

All I can say is, thank God for yellow pages and caterers. And American Express. It's only going to cost me £45.50 to provide Trish and Eddie with a "gourmet sandwich lunch" from Cotswold Caterers. Less than six minutes of my time at Carter Spink.

Now I'm just sitting on a chair, my hand clasped tight over the mobile in my pocket, desperately willing it to ring.

At the same time I'm utterly terrified that it will.

This tension is unbearable. I need something to relieve it. *Anything*. I wrench open the door of the Geigers' enormous fridge and pull out a bottle of white wine. I pour myself a glass and take an enormous gulp. I'm about to take another when I feel a tingling on the nape of my neck.

As if . . . I'm being watched.

I swivel round and nearly jump out of my skin. There's a man at the kitchen door.

He's tall and broad, and deeply tanned, with intense

blue eyes. His wavy hair is golden brown with bleached-blond tips. He's wearing old jeans and a torn T-shirt and the muddiest boots I've ever seen.

His eyes run doubtfully over the ten wonky, crumbly bread slices on the side, then onto my glass of wine.

"Hi," he says at last. "Are you the new Cordon Bleu cook?"

"Er . . . yes! Absolutely." I smooth my uniform down. "I'm the new housekeeper, Samantha. Hello."

"I'm Nathaniel." He holds out his hand and after a pause I take it. His skin is so hard and rough, it's like shaking a piece of tree bark. "I do the garden for the Geigers. You'll be wanting to talk to me about vegetables."

I look at him uncertainly. Why would I want to talk to him about vegetables?

As he leans against the door frame and folds his arms, I can't help noticing how massive and strong his forearms are. I've never *seen* a man with arms like that before.

"I can supply pretty much anything," he continues. "Seasonal, of course. Just tell me what you want."

"Oh, for *cooking*," I say, suddenly realizing what he means. "Er . . . yes. I'll be wanting some of those. Definitely."

"They told me you trained with some Michelin-starred chef?" He gives a small frown. "I don't know what kind of fancy stuff you use, but I'll do my best." He produces a small, mud-stained notebook and a pencil. "Which brassicas do you like to use?"

Brassicas?

What are brassicas? They must be some kind of vegetable. I search my mind frantically but all I can see is images of brassieres, waving on a washing line.

"I'd have to consult my menus," I say at last with a businesslike nod. "I'll get back to you on that one."

"But just generally." He looks up. "Which do you use most? So I know what to plant."

I daren't risk naming a single vegetable in case I get it totally wrong.

"I use . . . all sorts, really." I give him an airy smile. "You know how it is with brassicas. Sometimes you're in the mood for one . . . sometimes another!"

I'm really not sure how convincing that sounded. Nathaniel looks baffled.

"I'm about to order leeks," he says slowly. "What variety do you prefer? Albinstar or Bleu de Solaise?"

I fiddle with a button on my uniform, my face prickling. I didn't catch either of those. Oh, God, *why* did this guy have to come into the kitchen right now?

"The . . . um . . . first one," I say at last. "It has very tasty . . . qualities."

Nathaniel puts down his notebook and surveys me for a moment. His attention shifts to my wineglass again. I'm not sure I like his expression.

"I was just about to put this wine in a sauce," I say hastily. With a nonchalant air, I take a saucepan down from the rack, put it on the hob, and pour the wine in. I shake in some salt, then pick up a wooden spoon and stir.

Then I dart a glance at Nathaniel. He's regarding me with something approaching incredulity.

"Where did you say you trained?" he says.

I feel a twinge of alarm. He's not stupid, this man.

"At . . . Cordon Bleu school." My cheeks are growing rather hot. I shake more salt into the wine and stir it briskly.

"You haven't turned the hob on," Nathaniel observes.

"It's a cold sauce," I reply, without lifting my head. I

keep stirring for a minute, then put down my wooden spoon. "So. I'll just leave that to . . . marinate now."

At last I look up. Nathaniel is still leaning against the door frame, calmly watching me. There's an expression in his blue eyes that makes my throat tighten.

He knows.

He knows I'm a fake.

Please don't tell the Geigers, I silently transmit to him. *Please. I'll be gone soon.*

"Samantha?" Trish's head pops round the door and I start nervously. "Oh, you've met Nathaniel! Did he tell you about his vegetable garden?"

"Yes." I can't look at him. "He did."

"*Marvelous!*" She pushes her sunglasses up onto her head. "Well, Mr. Geiger and I are back now, and we'd like our sandwiches in twenty minutes."

Twenty *minutes*? But it's only ten past twelve. The caterers aren't coming till one o'clock.

"Would you like a drink first, maybe?" I suggest.

"No, thanks!" she says. "Just the sandwiches. We're both rather famished, actually, so if you could hurry up with them . . ."

"Right." I swallow. "No problem!"

I automatically bob a curtsy as Trish disappears, and I hear a kind of snorting sound from Nathaniel.

"You curtsy," he says.

"Yes, I curtsy," I say defiantly. "Anything wrong with that?"

Nathaniel's eyes move to the misshapen bread slices lying on the breadboard.

"Is that lunch?"

"No, that's not lunch!" I snap, flustered. "And please could you get out of my kitchen? I need a clear space to work in."

He raises his eyebrows. "See you around, then. Good luck with the sauce." He nods toward the pan of wine.

As he closes the kitchen door behind him I whip out my phone and speed-dial the caterers. But they've left their machine on.

"Hi," I say breathlessly after the bleep. "I ordered some sandwiches earlier? Well, I need them *now*. As soon as you can. Thanks."

Even as I put the phone down I realize it's fruitless. The caterers are never going to turn up in time. The Geigers are waiting.

OK. I can do this. I can make a few sandwiches.

Quickly I pick up the two least wonky of my bread slices and start cutting off the crusts until they're about an inch square but presentable. There's a butter dish on the side and I gouge some out with a knife. As I spread butter on the first slice of bread, it tears into two pieces.

Fuck.

I'll patch them together. No one'll notice.

I fling open a cupboard door and frantically root through pots of mustard . . . mint sauce . . . strawberry jam. Jam sandwiches it is. An English classic. I hastily smother one piece of bread with jam, spread some more butter on the other, and sandwich the two together. Then I stand back and consider the result.

Total disaster. Jam is oozing out of the cracks and it still isn't completely square. I've never seen a more revolting sandwich in my life.

Slowly I put the knife down in defeat. So this is it. Time for my resignation. Two jobs potentially lost in one day. As I stare at the jammy mess I feel strangely disappointed in myself. I would have thought I could last a morning.

The sound of someone knocking breaks me out of

my reverie and I whip round to see a girl in a blue velvet hair band peering through the kitchen window.

"Hi!" she calls. "Did you order sandwiches for twenty?"

It all happens so fast. One minute I'm standing there looking at my botch of jam and crumbs. The next, two girls in green aprons are trooping into the kitchen with plate after plate of professionally made sandwiches.

Clean-cut white and brown sandwiches, stacked in neat pyramids, garnished with sprigs of herbs and slices of lemon. They even have little handwritten paper flags describing the fillings.

Tuna, mint, and cucumber. Smoked salmon, cream cheese, and caviar. Thai chicken with wild rocket.

"I'm *so* sorry about the numbers mix-up," the girl in the hair band says as I sign for them. "It honestly looked like a twenty. And we don't often get an order for sandwiches for just two people—"

"It's fine!" I say, edging her toward the door. "Really. Whatever. Just put it on my card. . . ."

The door finally closes and I look around the kitchen, totally dazed. I've never *seen* so many sandwiches. There are plates of them everywhere. On every surface. I've even had to put some on the cooker.

"Samantha?" I can hear Trish approaching. .

"Um . . . hold on!" I hurry to the door, trying to block her view.

"It's already five past one," I can hear her saying a little sharply. "And I did ask, *most* clearly, for . . ."

Her voice trails off into silence as she reaches the kitchen door, and her whole face sags in astonishment. I turn and follow her gaze as she surveys the endless plates of sandwiches.

"My goodness!" At last Trish finds her voice. "This is . . . this is very impressive!"

"I wasn't sure what fillings you'd prefer," I say. "Obviously next time I won't make quite so many. . . ."

"Well!" Trish appears totally at a loss. She picks up one of the little flags and reads it out loud. *"Rare beef, lettuce, and horseradish."* She looks up in astonishment. "I haven't bought any beef for weeks! Where did you find it?"

"Er . . . in the freezer?"

I looked in the freezer earlier. The amount of food crammed into it would probably feed an entire small African country for a week.

"Of course!" Trish clicks her tongue. "And you thawed it in the microwave! Aren't you clever!"

"I'll put a selection on a plate for you," I suggest. "And bring it out to the conservatory."

"*Mar*velous. Nathaniel!" Trish raps on the kitchen window. "Come in and have a sandwich!"

I stop dead. No. Not him again.

"We don't want to waste them, after all." She arches her eyebrows. "If I did have a criticism, Samantha, it would be that you were a *little* profligate—Not that we're *poor,*" she adds suddenly. "It isn't *that.*"

"Er . . . no, madam."

"I don't like to talk about money, Samantha." Trish lowers her voice a little. "It's very vulgar. However—"

"Mrs. Geiger?"

Nathaniel has appeared in the kitchen doorway again, holding a muddy garden spade.

"Have one of Samantha's delicious sandwiches!" exclaims Trish, gesturing around the kitchen. "Just look! Isn't she clever?"

There's total silence as Nathaniel surveys the endless mounds of sandwiches. I can't bring myself to meet his eye. I feel I could be losing my grip on sanity here. I'm standing in a kitchen in the middle of nowhere. In a blue nylon uniform. Masquerading as a housekeeper who can magically make sandwiches out of thin air.

"Extraordinary," he says at last.

I finally risk looking up. He's gazing at me, his brow deeply furrowed as if he really can't make me out.

"That didn't take you long," he says, a slight question in his voice.

"I'm . . . pretty quick when I want to be," I say blandly.

"Samantha's wonderful!" says Trish, biting greedily into a sandwich. "And such a tidy worker! Look at this immaculate kitchen!" She shoves another sandwich in her mouth and practically swoons. "This Thai chicken is divine!"

Surreptitiously I pick up one from the pile and take a bite into it, feeling suddenly ravenous.

Bloody hell, that's good. Though I say it myself.

By half past two the kitchen is empty. Trish and Eddie devoured over half the sandwiches and have now gone out. Nathaniel is back in the garden. I'm pacing up and down, fiddling with a spoon.

Arnold will call soon. The meeting must have broken up by now.

I look out the window at a small brown bird pecking at the ground, then turn away and sink into a chair, staring down at the table, running my thumbnail obsessively round the fine grain of the polished wood.

I made one mistake. One. People are allowed to make one mistake in life. It's in the rules.

Or . . . maybe it's not. I just don't know.

Suddenly I feel my mobile vibrate. I grab the phone out of my uniform pocket with a trembling hand.

The caller ID tells me it's Guy.

"Hi, Guy?" I try to speak confidently—but my voice sounds tiny and scared to my own ears.

"Samantha? Is that *you*?" Guy's voice rushes through the phone in an urgent torrent. "Where the hell *are* you? Why aren't you here? Didn't you get my e-mails?"

"I haven't got my BlackBerry," I say, taken aback. "Why didn't you call?"

"I tried early today, but your phone seemed out of order. Then I was in meetings, but I've been sending you e-mails all morning. . . . Samantha, where on earth *are* you? You should be here at the office! Not hiding out, for Christ's sake!"

Hiding out? What does he mean?

"But . . . but Arnold said don't come in! He said it would be best! He told me to stay away and he would do what he could—"

"Do you have any idea how this *looks*?" Guy cuts across me. "First you freak out, then you disappear. People are saying you're unhinged, you've had a breakdown . . . There's a rumor you've skipped the country. . . ."

As the truth hits me, I feel a hot, choking panic. I can't believe how wrong I've played this. I can't believe how stupid I've been. What am I doing still sitting in this kitchen, miles from London?

"Tell them I'm coming straight in," I stammer. "Tell Ketterman I'll be there at once. . . . I'm getting on a train . . ."

"It might be too late." Guy sounds heavy and reluctant. "Samantha . . . all sorts of stories are going round."

"Stories?" My heart is thudding so hard I can barely say the word. "What . . . what stories?"

I can't take all this in. I feel like my car has suddenly lurched off the road and I can't stop it.

"Apparently people have said you're...unreliable," Guy says at last. "That this isn't the first time. That you've made errors before."

"*Errors?*" I leap to my feet, my voice as sharp as though I've been scalded. "Who's saying that? I've never made any errors! What are they talking about?"

"I don't know. I wasn't in the meeting. Samantha... think back carefully. Have you made any other mistakes?"

Think back carefully?

I'm stunned. He doesn't believe me?

"I've never made any mistakes," I say, trying and failing to keep my voice level. "None. Never! I'm a good lawyer. I'm a *good* lawyer." To my dismay I realize tears are pouring down my cheeks. "I'm steady! You *know* that, Guy."

In the tense little silence that follows, the unsaid is there between us. Like a conviction. I lost a client £50 million.

"Guy, I don't know how I didn't see the Glazerbrooks documentation." My words tumble out faster and faster. "I don't know how it happened. It doesn't make any sense. I know my desk is messy, but I have my systems, for God's sake. I don't miss things like that. I just don't—"

"Samantha, calm down—"

"How can I calm down?" I almost yell. "This is my life. My *life*. I don't have anything else!" I wipe the tears away from my cheeks. "I'm not losing this. I'm coming in. Now."

I cut the phone dead and get to my feet, bubbling with panic. I should have gone back. I should have gone back straightaway, not wasted time here. I don't know what times the trains will be, but I don't care. I have to get out of here.

I grab a piece of paper and a pencil and scrawl,

Dear Mrs. Geiger,
   I am afraid I must resign as your housekeeper.
While I have enjoyed my time

Come on. I haven't got time to write any more, I have to leave now. I put the paper down on the table and head for the door. Then I stop. I can't leave the letter unfinished in the middle of a sentence.

   While I have enjoyed my time with you, I feel I
   would like a fresh challenge. Many thanks for your
   kindness.

                              Yours sincerely
                              Samantha Sweeting

I put the pen down and push my chair back with a scrape. As I reach the door my mobile vibrates again.

Guy, I instantly think. I reach for it—and am already flipping it open when I see the caller ID. It's not Guy.

It's Ketterman.

Something cold grips my spine. As I stare at his name I feel real fear in a way I never have before. Childish, nightmarish fear. Every instinct in my body is telling me not to answer.

But my phone's already open. It's too late. Slowly I lift it up to my ear.

"Hello."

"Samantha. John Ketterman here."

"Right." My voice is scratchy with nerves. "Hello."

There's a long pause. I know this is my moment to speak, but my throat feels wadded by cotton wool.

No words seem adequate. Everyone knows how much Ketterman despises apologies and excuses and explanations.

"Samantha, I'm ringing to tell you that your contract with Carter Spink has been terminated."

I feel all the blood drain from my face.

"A letter is on its way to you giving the reasons." His tone is distant and formal. "Gross negligence compounded by your subsequent unprofessional behavior. Your P45 will be sent to you. Your pass has been disabled. I don't expect to see you at the Carter Spink offices again."

He's going too fast. This is all happening too fast.

"Please don't . . ." I blurt out. "Please give me another chance. I made one mistake. One."

"Lawyers at Carter Spink don't make mistakes, Samantha. Nor do they run away from their mistakes."

"I know it was wrong to run away." I'm shaking all over. "But it was such a shock. . . . I wasn't thinking straight. . . ."

"You've disgraced the reputation of the firm and yourself." Ketterman's voice sharpens as though he, too, might be finding this difficult. "You have lost fifty million pounds of a client's money through your own negligence. And subsequently absconded with no explanation. Samantha, you cannot have expected any other outcome, surely."

There's a long silence. My forehead is pressed hard against the heel of my hand. I try to focus on just breathing. In and out. In and out.

"No," I whisper at last.

It's over. My entire career is really over.

Ketterman starts on a preprepared speech about meeting with the human-resources department, but I don't listen.

Everything I've worked for since I was twelve years old. Gone. Everything ruined. In twenty-four hours.

At last I realize Ketterman has disappeared from the line. I get to my feet and stagger over to the shiny fridge. My eyes are huge, burning holes.

For a long time I just stand there, staring at my own face until the features blur.

I've been fired. The phrase echoes round my mind. *I've been fired.* I could collect the dole. I imagine myself with the men from *The Full Monty.* Standing in the un-employment queue, moving my hips back and forth to "Hot Stuff."

Suddenly I hear the sound of a key in the front door. I can't be found in this condition. I can't face any prob-ing, any sympathy. Otherwise I'm afraid I might just collapse into sobs and never stop.

Distractedly, I reach for a cloth and start sweeping it in meaningless circles over the table. Then I glimpse my note to Trish, still lying there. I crumple it up and throw it in the bin. Later. I'll do it later. I feel as though I can barely function right now, let alone give a convincing resignation speech.

"There you are!" Trish comes tripping into the kitchen on her high-heeled clogs, holding three burst-ing shopping bags. "Samantha!" She stops at the sight of me. "Are you all right? Is your headache back?"

"I'm . . . fine. Thanks."

"You look *dreadful!* Goodness me! Have some more pills!"

"Really . . ."

"Now, sit down . . . and I'll make *you* a cup of tea!"

She plonks the bags down and switches on the ket-tle, then rootles around for the green painkillers.

"These are the ones you like, aren't they?"

"I'd rather just have an aspirin," I say quickly. "If that's OK?"

"Are you quite sure?" She runs me a glass of water and gives me a couple of aspirin. "Now. You just sit there. Relax. Don't even *think* of doing anything else! Until it's time to make the supper," she adds as an after-thought.

"You're . . . very kind," I manage.

As I say the words I have the dim realization that I mean them. Trish's kindness may be a bit warped, but it's real.

"Here we are . . ." Trish puts a cup of tea down and scrutinizes me. "Are you *home*sick?" She sounds triumphant, as though she may have cracked the mystery. "Our girl from the Philippines did get rather blue from time to time . . . but I used to say to her, cheer up, Manuela!" Trish pauses thoughtfully. "Then I found out her name was Paula. Extraordinary."

"I'm not homesick," I say, gulping my tea.

My mind is beating like a butterfly's wings. What am I going to do?

Go home.

But the thought of returning to that flat, with Ketterman living two floors above, makes me sick. I can't face him. I can't do it.

Phone Guy. He'll have me to stay. He and Charlotte have that huge house in Islington with all those spare rooms. I've stayed the night before. Then I'll . . . sell my flat. Find a job.

What job?

"This will cheer you up." Trish's voice breaks my thoughts. She pats the shopping bags with suppressed glee. "After your *stunning* performance at lunch . . . I've been shopping. And I've got a surprise for you! This will make your day!"

"A surprise?" I look up, bewildered, as Trish starts producing packets from the bag.

"Foie gras ... chickpeas ... shoulder of lamb ..." She hefts a joint of meat onto the table and looks at me expectantly. Then she clicks her tongue at my bewildered expression. "It's *ingredients*! Your dinner-party menu! We'll eat at eight, if that's OK?"

Nine

It'll be all right.

If I say it often enough to myself, it must be true.

I've opened my phone several times to call Guy. But each time, humiliation has stopped me. Even though he's my friend, even though he's the person closest to me in the company. I'm the one who's fired. I'm the one in disgrace. And he's not.

At last I sit up and rub my cheeks, trying to get my spirits back. Come on. This is *Guy*. He'll want to hear from me. He'll want to help. I flip open my phone and dial his direct line. A moment later I hear footsteps clopping along the wooden floor of the hall.

Trish.

I shut the phone, pocket it, and reach for a clump of broccoli.

"How are you getting on?" Trish's voice greets me. "Making progress?"

As she enters the kitchen she looks a little surprised

to see me still sitting in the exact same spot she left me. "Everything all right?"

"I'm just . . . assessing the ingredients," I improvise. "Getting the feel of them."

Just then a thin red-haired woman appears round the door, next to Trish. She's wearing diamanté sunglasses on her head and regards me with an avid interest.

"I'm Petula," she announces. "How do you do."

"Petula's just eaten some of your sandwiches," puts in Trish. "She thought they were *marvelous*."

"And I've heard about the foie gras with an apricot glaze!" Petula raises her eyebrows. "Very impressive!"

"Samantha can cook anything!" boasts Trish, pink with pride. "She trained with Michel de la Roux de la Blanc! The master himself!"

"So how exactly will you be glazing the foie gras, Samantha?" asks Petula with interest.

The kitchen is silent. Both women are waiting, agog.

"Well." I clear my throat several times. "I expect I'll use the . . . usual method. The word *glaze,* obviously, comes from the transparent nature of the . . . er . . . finish . . . and complements the . . . gras. Foie," I amend. "De gras. The . . . blend of the flavors."

I am making absolutely no sense here, but neither Trish nor Petula seems to have noticed. In fact they both seem totally impressed.

"Where on earth did you find her?" says Petula to Trish in what she clearly imagines to be a discreet undertone. "My girl is *hopeless*. Can't cook *and* doesn't understand a word I say."

"She just applied out of the blue!" Trish murmurs back, still flushed with pleasure. "Cordon Bleu! English! We couldn't believe it!"

They both eye me as though I'm some rare animal

with horns sprouting out of my head. I can't bear this anymore.

"Shall I make you some tea and bring it through to the conservatory?" I ask. Anything to get them out of the kitchen.

"No, we're popping out to have our nails done," says Trish. "I'll see you later, Samantha."

There's an expectant pause. Suddenly I realize Trish is waiting for my curtsy. I start to prickle all over in embarrassment. Why did I curtsy? *Why* did I curtsy?

"Very good, Mrs. Geiger." I bow my head and make an awkward bob. When I look up, Petula's eyes are like saucers.

As the two women leave, I can hear Petula hissing, "She *curtsies*? She *curtsies* to you?"

"It's a simple mark of respect," I hear Trish replying airily. "But very effective. You know, Petula, you should really try it with your girl...."

Oh, God. What have I started?

I wait until the sound of tapping heels has completely disappeared. Then, moving into the larder to be on the safe side, I flip open my phone and redial Guy's number. After three rings he answers.

"Samantha." He sounds guarded. "Hi. Have you..."

"It's OK, Guy. I've spoken to Ketterman. I know."

"Oh, Christ, Samantha. I'm so sorry this has happened. *So* sorry..."

I cannot stand his pity. If he says anything else I'll burst into tears.

"It's fine," I say, cutting him off. "Really. Let's not talk about it. Let's just...look forward. I have to get my life on track."

"Jesus, you're focused!" There's a note of admiration in his voice. "You don't let anything faze you, do you?"

I push my hair back off my face. "I just have to...get

on with things." Somehow I keep my voice even and steady. "I need to get back to London. But I can't go home. Ketterman bought a flat in my building. He *lives* there."

"Ouch. Yes, I heard about that." There's a wince in his voice. "That's unfortunate."

"I just can't face him, Guy." I feel the threat of tears again and force myself to hold them back. "So . . . I was wondering. Could I come and stay with you for a while? Just for a few days?"

There's silence. I wasn't expecting silence.

"Samantha . . . I'd love to help," says Guy at last. "But I'll have to check with Charlotte."

"Of course," I say, a little taken aback.

"Just stay on the line for a sec. I'll call her."

The next moment I've been put on hold. I sit waiting, listening to the tinny harpsichord music, trying not to feel discomfited. It was unreasonable to expect him to say yes straightaway. Of course he has to clear it with his girlfriend.

At last Guy comes onto the line again. "Samantha, I'm not sure it's possible."

I feel slammed. "Right." I try to sound natural, as though this is no big deal. "Well . . . never mind. It doesn't matter . . ."

"Charlotte's very busy right now . . . we're having some work done to the bedrooms . . . it's just not a good time. . . ."

He sounds halting, as if he wants to get off the line. And suddenly I realize. This isn't about Charlotte. This is all about him. He doesn't want to be near me. It's as though my disgrace is contagious, as though his career might get blighted too.

Yesterday I was his best friend. Yesterday, when I was about to become a partner, he was hanging around my desk, full of smiles and quips. And today he doesn't want to be associated with me at all.

I know I should stay quiet, keep my dignity, but I just can't contain myself.

"You don't want to be associated with me, do you?" I burst out.

"Samantha!" His voice is defensive. "Don't be ridiculous."

"I'm still the same *person*. I thought you were my friend—"

"I am your friend! But you can't expect me to...I have Charlotte to consider...we don't have *that* much space...Look, call me in a couple of days, maybe we can meet up for a drink—"

"Really, don't worry." I try to control my voice. "I'm sorry to have bothered you."

"Wait!" he exclaims. "Don't go! What are you going to do?"

"Oh, Guy." I manage a little laugh.

I switch off my phone. Everything's changed. Or maybe he hasn't changed. Maybe this was what Guy was always like and I just never realized it.

I stare down at the tiny display of my phone, watching the seconds of each minute tick by. Wondering what to do next. When it suddenly vibrates in my hand, I nearly jump out of my skin. *Tennyson*, my display reads.

Mum.

I feel a clutch of dread. She can only be ringing for one thing. She's heard the news. I guess I should have known this was coming. I could go and stay with her, it occurs to me. How weird. I didn't even think of that before. I open up the phone and steel myself.

"Hi, Mum."

"Samantha." Her voice pierces my ear with no preamble. "Exactly how long were you going to wait before you told me about your debacle? I have to find out about my own daughter's disgrace from an *Internet joke*." She utters the words with revulsion.

"An . . . Internet joke?" I echo faintly. "What do you mean?"

"You didn't know? Apparently in certain legal circles the new term for fifty million pounds is 'a Samantha.' Take it from me, I was not amused."

"Mum, I'm so sorry—"

"At least the story has been contained within the legal world. I've spoken to Carter Spink and they assure me that it won't be going further. You should be grateful for that."

"I . . . I suppose so . . ."

"Where are you?" she cuts across my faltering words. "Where are you right now?"

I'm standing in a larder, surrounded by packets of cereal.

"I'm . . . at someone's house. Out of London."

"And what are your plans?"

"I don't know." I rub my face. "I need to . . . get myself together. Find a job."

"A job," she says scathingly. "You think any top law firm is going to touch you now?"

I flinch at her tone. "I . . . I don't know. Mum, I've only just heard about being fired. I can't just—"

"You can. Thankfully, I have acted for you."

She's *acted* for me?

"What do you—"

"I've called in all my favors. It wasn't an easy job. But the senior partner at Fortescues will see you tomorrow at ten."

I'm almost too stupefied to reply. "You've . . . organized me a job interview?"

"Assuming all goes well, you will enter at senior associate level." Her voice is crisp. "You're being given this chance as a personal favor to me. As you can imagine, there are . . . reservations. So if you want to progress, Samantha, you are going to have to perform. You're going to give this job every hour you have."

"Right." I shut my eyes, my thoughts whirling. I have a job interview. A fresh start. It's the solution to my nightmare.

Why don't I feel more relieved?

"You will have to give more than you did at Carter Spink," Mum continues in my ear. "No slacking. No complacency. You will have to prove yourself *doubly*. Do you understand?"

"Yes," I say automatically.

More hours. More work. More late nights.

It's almost as if I can feel the concrete blocks being loaded onto me again. More and more of them. Heavier and heavier.

"I mean . . . no," I hear myself saying. "No. It's too much. I . . . don't want that now. I need some time."

The words come out of my mouth all by themselves. I wasn't planning them; I've never even thought them before. But now that they're out in the air they somehow feel . . . true.

"I'm *sorry*?" Mum's voice is sharp. "Samantha, what on earth are you saying?"

"I don't know." I'm kneading my forehead, trying to make sense of my own confusion. "I was thinking . . . I could take a break, maybe."

"A break would finish your legal career." Her voice snaps dismissively. "*Finish* it."

"I could . . . do something else."

"You wouldn't last more than two minutes in anything else!" She sounds affronted. "Samantha, you're a *lawyer*. You've been trained as a *lawyer*."

"There are other things in the world than being a lawyer!" I cry, rattled.

There's an ominous silence. I can't believe I'm standing up to her. I don't think I've ever challenged my mother in my life. I feel shaky as I grip the phone. But at the same time, I know I can't do what she wants.

"Samantha, if you're having some kind of breakdown like your brother—"

"I'm not having a breakdown!" My voice rises in distress. "I never *asked* you to find me another job. I don't know what I want. I need a bit of time . . . to . . . to think . . ."

"You will be at that job interview, Samantha." Mum's voice is like a whip. "You will be there tomorrow at ten o'clock."

"I won't!"

"Tell me where you are! I'm sending a car straight-away."

"No! Leave me alone."

I switch off my phone, come out of the larder, and almost savagely throw it down onto the table. She's my mother. And she didn't express one word of sympathy. Not one jot of kindness. My face is burning and tears are pressing hotly at the back of my eyes. The phone starts vibrating angrily on the table, but I ignore it. I'm not going to answer it. I'm not going to talk to anyone. I'm going to have a drink. And then I'm going to cook this bloody dinner.

I slosh some white wine into a glass and take several gulps. Then I address myself to the pile of raw ingredients waiting on the table.

I can cook. I can cook this stuff. Even if everything else in my life is in ruins, I can do this. I have a brain, I can work it out.

Without delay I rip the plastic coverings off the lamb.

This can go in the oven. In some kind of dish. Simple. And the chickpeas can go in there too. Then I'll mash them and that will make the hummus.

I open a cupboard and pull out a whole load of gleaming baking dishes and trays. I select a baking tray and scatter the chickpeas onto it. Some bounce onto the floor, but I don't care. I grab a bottle of oil from the counter and drizzle it over the top. Already I'm feeling like a cook.

I shove the tray into the oven and turn it on full blast. Then I put the lamb in an oval dish and shove that in too.

So far so good. Now all I need to do is leaf through all Trish's recipe books and find instructions for seared foie gras with an apricot glaze.

OK. I didn't find a single recipe for seared foie gras with an apricot glaze. I found apricot and raspberry flan, turkey with chestnut and apricot stuffing, and almond pithivier with apricot filling and Prosecco sabayon.

I stare at the page blindly. I have just turned down what may be my only opportunity to start over. I'm a lawyer. That's what I *am*. What else am I going to do? What's happened to me?

Oh, God. Why is smoke coming out of the oven?

By seven o'clock I'm still cooking.

At least I think that's what I'm doing. Both ovens are roaring with heat. Pots are bubbling on the hob. The electric whisk is whirring busily. I've burned my right hand twice taking things out of the oven. Eight recipe books are open around the kitchen, one drenched with spilled oil and another with egg yolk. I'm puce in the face, sweating hard, and trying every so often to run my hand under cold water.

I've been going for three hours. And I haven't yet made anything that could actually be eaten. So far I've discarded a collapsed chocolate soufflé, two pans of burned onions, and a saucepan of congealed apricots that made me feel sick just to look at them.

I can't work out what's going wrong. I haven't got *time* to work out what's going wrong. There's no scope for analysis. Every time there's a disaster I just dump it and start again, quickly thawing food from the freezer, changing tack, trying to cobble *something* together.

The Geigers meanwhile are drinking sherry in the drawing room. They think everything is going splendidly. Trish tried to come into the kitchen about half an hour ago, but I managed to head her off.

In less than an hour she and Eddie are going to be sitting down at the table expecting a gourmet meal. Shaking out their napkins with anticipation, pouring out their mineral water and wine.

A kind of frenzied hysteria has come over me. I know I cannot do this, but somehow I can't give up either. I keep thinking a miracle will happen. I'll pull it all together. I'll manage it somehow—

Oh, God, the gravy's bubbling over.

I shove the oven door shut, grab a spoon, and start stirring it. It looks like revolting lumpy brown water. Frantically I start searching in the cupboards for something to chuck in. Flour. Cornstarch. Something like that. This'll do. I grab a small pot and shake in vigorous amounts of the white powder, then wipe the sweat off my brow. OK. What now?

Suddenly I remember the egg whites, still whisking up in their bowl. I grab the recipe book, running my finger down the page. I changed the dessert course to pavlova after I chanced upon the line in a recipe book: *Meringues are so easy to make.*

So far so good. What next? *Form the stiff meringue mixture into a large circle on your baking parchment.*

I peer at my bowl. *Stiff* meringue mixture? Mine's liquid.

It has to be right, I tell myself feverishly. It has to be. I followed the instructions. Maybe it's thicker than it looks. Maybe once I start pouring it out, it'll stiffen up by some weird culinary law of physics.

Slowly I start to pour it onto the tray. It doesn't stiffen up. It spreads in a white oozing lake and starts dripping off the tray onto the floor.

Something tells me this is not going to make white chocolate pavlova for eight.

A splodge lands on my foot and I give a frustrated cry, near tears. Why didn't it work? I followed the sodding recipe and everything. A pent-up rage is rising inside me: rage at myself, at my defective crappy egg whites, at cookery books, at cooks, at food . . . and most of all at whoever wrote that meringues were *so easy to make.*

"They're not!" I hear myself yelling. "They're bloody not!" I hurl the book across the kitchen, where it smashes against the kitchen door.

"What the hell—" a male voice exclaims in surprise.

The door flies open and Nathaniel is standing there, a rucksack hefted over his shoulder; he looks like he's on his way home. "Is everything OK?"

"It's fine," I say, rattled. "Everything's fine. Thank you. Thank you so much." I make a dismissive motion with my hand, but he doesn't move.

"I heard you were cooking a gourmet dinner tonight," he says slowly, surveying the mess.

"Yes. That's right. I'm just in the . . . most complex

stage of the...um..." I glance down at the hob and give an involuntary scream. "Fuck! The gravy!"

I don't know what's happened. Brown bubbles are expanding out of my gravy saucepan, all over the cooker, and down the sides on the floor. It looks like the porringer in the story of the magic pot that wouldn't stop making porridge.

"Get it off the heat, for God's sake!" exclaims Nathaniel, throwing his rucksack aside. He snatches up the pan and moves it to the counter. "What on earth is in that?"

"Nothing!" I say. "Just the usual ingredients..."

Nathaniel has noticed the little pot on the counter. He grabs it and takes a pinch between his fingers. "*Baking soda?* You put baking soda in gravy? Is that what they taught you at—" He breaks off and sniffs the air. "Hang on. Is something burning?"

I watch helplessly as he opens the bottom oven, grabs an oven glove with a practiced air, and hauls out a baking tray covered in what look like tiny black bullets.

Oh, no. My chickpeas.

"What are *these* supposed to be?" he says incredulously. "Rabbit droppings?"

"They're chickpeas," I retort. My cheeks are flaming but I lift my chin, trying to regain some kind of dignity. "I drizzled them in olive oil and put them in the oven so they could...melt."

Nathaniel stares at me. "*Melt?*"

"Soften," I amend hurriedly.

Nathaniel puts down the tray and folds his arms. "Do you know *anything* about cooking?"

Before I can answer, there's the most almighty BANG from the microwave.

"Oh, my God!" I shriek in terror. "Oh, my *God!* What was that?" Nathaniel is peering through the glass door.

"What the hell was in there?" he demands. "Something's exploded."

My mind races frantically. What on earth did I put in the microwave? It's all a blur.

"The eggs!" I suddenly remember. "I was hard-boiling the eggs for the canapés."

"In a *microwave*?" he expostulates.

"To save time!" I practically yell back. "I was being efficient!"

Nathaniel yanks the plug of the microwave from the wall socket and turns round to face me, his face working with disbelief. "You know bugger all about cooking! You're not a housekeeper. I don't know what the hell you're up to—"

"I'm not up to anything!" I reply, in shock.

"The Geigers are good people." He faces me square on. "I won't have them exploited."

Oh, God. What does he think? That I'm some kind of confidence trickster?

"Look . . . please." I rub my sweaty face. "I'm not trying to rip anyone off. OK, I can't cook. But I ended up here because of . . . a misunderstanding."

"What kind of misunderstanding?"

I sink down onto a chair and massage my aching lower back. I hadn't realized how exhausted I was. "I was running away from . . . something. I needed a place to stay for the night. I stopped here for some water and directions to a hotel and the Geigers assumed I was a housekeeper. And then this morning I felt terrible. I thought I'd do the job for the morning. But I'm not planning to stay. And I won't take any money from them, if that's what you're thinking."

Nathaniel is leaning against the counter, his arms folded. His wary frown has eased a little. He reaches into his rucksack and takes out a bottle of beer. He offers it to me and I shake my head.

"What were you running from?" he says, cracking the bottle open.

I feel a painful wrench inside. I cannot face telling the whole dreadful story.

"It was . . . a situation." I look down.

He takes a drink of beer. "A bad relationship?"

For a moment I'm silenced. I think back over all my years at Carter Spink. All the hours I gave them, everything I sacrificed. Finished in a three-minute phone call.

"Yes," I say slowly. "A bad relationship."

"How long were you in it?"

"Seven years." To my horror I can feel tears seeping out of the corners of my eyes. I have no idea where they came from. "I'm sorry," I gulp. "It's been quite a stressful day."

Nathaniel tears off a piece of kitchen towel from the wall-mounted roll behind him and hands it to me. "If it was a bad relationship, you're well out of it," he says in calm tones. "No point staying. No point looking back."

"You're right." I wipe my eyes. "Yes. I just have to decide what to do with my life. I can't stay here." I reach for the bottle of Cointreau, which was supposed to go in the chocolate-orange soufflé, pour some into a handy eggcup, and take a gulp.

"The Geigers are good employers," says Nathaniel with a tiny shrug. "You could do worse."

"Yeah." I raise a half smile. "Unfortunately, I can't cook."

He puts his bottle of beer down and wipes his mouth. His hands look scrubbed clean, but I can still see the traces of earth ingrained around his nails, in the seams of his weather-beaten skin.

"I could speak to my mum. She can cook. She could teach you the basics."

I look at him in astonishment, almost laughing. "You think I should *stay*? I thought I was supposed to be a confidence trickster." I shake my head, wincing at the taste of the Cointreau. "I have to go."

"Shame." He shrugs. "It would have been nice to have someone around who speaks English. And makes such great sandwiches," he adds, totally deadpan.

I can't help smiling back. "Caterers."

"Ah. I wondered."

A faint rapping at the door makes us both look up.

"Samantha?" Trish's voice outside is hushed and urgent. "Can you hear me?"

"Er . . . yes?"

"Don't worry, I won't come in. I don't want to disturb anything! You're probably at a very *crucial* stage."

"Kind of . . ."

I catch Nathaniel's eye and a sudden wave of hysteria rises through me.

"I just wanted to ask," Trish's voice continues, "if you will be serving any kind of *sorbet* between the courses?"

I look at Nathaniel. His shoulders are shaking with silent laughter. I can't stop a tiny snort escaping. I clamp my hand over my mouth, trying to get control of myself.

"Samantha?"

"Er . . . no," I manage at last. "There won't be any sorbet."

Nathaniel has picked up one of my pans of burned onions. He mimes taking a spoonful and eating it. *Yummy,* he mouths.

"Well! See you later!"

Trish tip-taps away and I collapse into helpless

laughter. I've never laughed so hard in my life. My ribs hurt; I'm coughing; I almost feel like I'll be sick.

At last I wipe my eyes and blow my runny nose on the kitchen towel. Nathaniel's stopped laughing too and is looking around the bombshelled kitchen.

"Seriously," he says. "What are you going to do about this? They're expecting a fancy dinner."

"I know. I know they are. I'll just have to . . . think of something."

There's silence in the kitchen. Nathaniel is curiously eyeing the white splodges of meringue on the floor. I cast my mind back to all the times I've had to go into a room at Carter Spink and bluff my way out of a tricky spot. There *has* to be a way.

"OK." I take a deep breath and push back my damp hair. "I'm going to rescue the situation."

"You're going to rescue the situation?" He looks skeptical.

"In fact, I think this might solve everyone's problems." I get to my feet and start busily sweeping packets into the bin. "First I need to clear up the kitchen a bit. . . ."

"I'll help." Nathaniel stands up. "This I have to see."

Companionably, we empty pans and pots and packets into the bin. I scrub all the smeared surfaces while Nathaniel mops up the meringue.

"How long have you worked here?" I ask as he rinses out the mop in the sink.

"Three years. I worked for the people who lived here before the Geigers, the Ellises. Then Trish and Eddie moved in two years ago and kept me on."

I digest this. "Why did the Ellises move? It's such a beautiful house."

"The Geigers made them an offer they couldn't refuse." Nathaniel's mouth is twitching with . . . amusement?

"What?" I say, intrigued. "What happened?"

"Well . . ." He puts the mop down. "It was fairly comical. The house was used as a location in a BBC period drama, all set in the Cotswolds. Two weeks after it was aired, Trish and Eddie arrived on the doorstep waving a check. They'd seen it on television, decided they wanted it, and tracked it down."

"Wow." I laugh. "Presumably they paid a good price."

"God knows what they paid. The Ellises would never say."

"Do you know how the Geigers made all their money?"

"They built up a road haulage company from nothing and sold it off. Made a bundle." He starts mopping up the final patch of meringue.

"And how about you? Before the Ellises?" I tip the congealed apricots down the waste disposal with a shudder.

"I was working at Marchant House," Nathaniel replies. "It's a stately home near Oxford. Before that, university."

"University?" I say, my ears pricking up. "I didn't know—"

I halt, reddening. I was about to say, "I didn't know gardeners went to university."

"I did natural sciences." Nathaniel gives me a look that makes me think he knew exactly what I was thinking.

I open my mouth to ask him where and when he was at university—then on second thought, close it and switch the waste disposal on. I don't want to start getting into details, going down the "do we know anyone in common?" road. Right now, I could do without remembering the particulars of my life.

At last the kitchen looks a bit more normal. I pick up the eggcup, drain the rest of the Cointreau, and take a deep breath.

"OK. Showtime."

"Good luck." Nathaniel raises his eyebrows.

I open the kitchen door to see Trish and Eddie loitering in the hall, holding their sherry glasses.

"Ah, Samantha! Everything ready?" Trish's face is all lit up with anticipation, and I feel a huge twinge of guilt for what I'm about to do.

But I can't see any other way.

I take a deep breath and put on my best breaking-bad-news-to-a-client face.

"Mr. and Mrs. Geiger." I look from one face to the other, making sure I have their attention. "I am devastated."

I close my eyes and shake my head.

"Devastated?" echoes Trish nervously.

"I have done my best." I open my eyes. "But I'm afraid I cannot work with your equipment. The dinner I created was not up to my own professional standards. I could not allow it out of the kitchen. I will of course reimburse all your costs—and offer my resignation. I will leave in the morning."

There. Done. And no casualties.

I can't help glancing at Nathaniel, standing in the doorway of the kitchen. He gives me the thumbs-up.

"*Leave?*" Trish puts her sherry glass down on a side table with a little crash. "You can't leave! You're the best housekeeper we've ever had! Eddie, *do* something!"

"Mrs. Geiger, after tonight's performance, I feel I have no choice," I say. "To be frank, the dinner was inedible."

"That wasn't your fault!" she says in consternation. "It was *our* fault! We'll order you new equipment at once."

"But—"

"Just give us a list of what you need. Spare no expense!

And we'll give you a pay rise!" She's suddenly gripped by a new idea. "How much do you want? Name your price!"

This is not going the way I planned. Not at all.

"Well . . . we never discussed pay," I begin. "And really I can't accept—"

"Eddie!" Trish rounds on him savagely. "This is *your* fault! Samantha's leaving because you're not paying her enough!"

"Mrs. Geiger, that's not the case—"

"And she needs new kitchen pots and pans. From the best place." She digs Eddie in the ribs with her elbow and mutters, "Say something!"

"Ah . . . Samantha." Eddie clears his throat awkwardly. "We'd be very happy if you would consider staying with us. We've been delighted with your performance, and whatever your salary expectations are . . . we'll match them." Trish digs him in the ribs again. "Exceed them."

"And health care," adds Trish.

They're both gazing at me with a kind of eager hope.

I glance over at Nathaniel, who cocks his head as though to say, "Why not?"

The strangest feeling is coming over me. Three people. All telling me they want me within the space of ten minutes.

I could stay. It's as simple as that. For however long it takes to . . . work myself out. I'm miles away from London. No one knows I'm here. I'll be safe.

I can't cook, a little voice reminds me. *I can't clean. I'm not a housekeeper.*

But I could learn. I could learn it all.

The silence is growing in tension. Even Nathaniel is watching me closely from the door.

"Well . . . OK." I feel a smile coming to my lips. "OK. If you want me to . . . I'll stay."

Later that night, after we've all eaten a Chinese take-away, I take out my mobile phone, call my mother's office, and wait till I'm put through to voice mail.

"It's all right, Mum," I say. "You don't need to call in any favors. I've got a job." And I click the mobile shut.

Ten

The only thing is, now I actually have to be a house-keeper.

The next morning my alarm goes off at six fifteen and I arrive downstairs in the kitchen before seven, in my uniform. The garden is misty and there are no sounds, except a couple of magpies chacking at each other on the lawn. I feel as though I'm the only person awake in the world.

As quietly as I can, I empty the dishwasher and put everything away in the cupboards. I straighten the chairs under the table. I make a cup of coffee. Then I look around at the gleaming granite counters.

My domain.

It doesn't feel like my domain. It feels like someone else's scary kitchen.

So . . . what do I do now? I feel twitchy, just standing here. I should be occupied. My mind flashes back to London before I can stop it, to my regular routine. If I were still at Carter Spink, I would be queuing for a cappuccino by now. Or maybe on the tube, answering e-mails. I wonder how many e-mails are stacked up, unanswered, in my BlackBerry? The thought makes me feel slightly ill.

No. Don't think about it. There's an old copy of *The Economist* in the magazine rack by the table and I pick it up. I flip through and start reading a piece on international monetary controls, sipping my coffee.

Then, as I hear a sound from upstairs, I hastily put it down again. Housekeepers aren't supposed to read articles on international monetary controls. They're supposed to be making breakfast. But how can I do that until I know what the Geigers want?

Then all of a sudden I remember yesterday morning. Trish made me a cup of tea.

Maybe today I'm supposed to make *her* a cup of tea. Maybe they're waiting upstairs, tapping their fingers impatiently, saying "Where's the damn tea?"

Quickly I boil the kettle and make a teapot full. I put it on a tray with cups and saucers and after a moment's thought add a couple of biscuits. Then I head upstairs, venture along the silent corridor to Trish and Eddie's bedroom . . . and stop outside the door.

Now what?

What if they're asleep and I wake them up?

I lift a hand to knock—but the tray's too heavy to hold in one hand and there's an alarming chinking as the whole thing starts tilting sideways. In horror, I grab it just before the teapot slides off. Sweating, I put the whole lot on the ground, raise a hand, and knock very quietly, then pick up the tray again.

There's no answer.

Hesitantly I tap again.

"Eddie! Stop that!" Trish's raised voice filters faintly through the door.

Oh, God. Why can't they hear me?

I'm hot all over. This tray is bloody heavy. I can't stand outside their room with a cup of tea all morning. Shall I just . . . retreat?

I'm about to turn round and creep away. Then determination comes over me. No. Don't be so feeble. I've made the tea. They can always tell me to leave.

I grip the tray tightly and bang the corner hard against the door. They *have* to have heard that.

After a moment, Trish's voice rises up. "Come in!"

I feel a swell of relief. They're expecting me. I knew they would be. Somehow I turn the doorknob while balancing the tray against the door. I push the door open and walk into the room.

Trish looks up from the canopied mahogany bed, where she's sprawled on a pile of lace pillows, alone. She's wearing a silky nightie, her hair is disheveled, and makeup is smudged about her eyes. For a moment she looks startled to see me.

"Samantha," she says sharply. "What do you want? Is everything all right?"

I have an immediate, horrible feeling I've done the wrong thing. My gaze doesn't move from hers, but my peripheral vision starts to register a few details in the room. I can see a book called *Sensual Enjoyment* on the floor. And a bottle of musk-scented massage oil. And . . .

A well-worn copy of *The Joy of Sex*. Right by the bed. Open at "Turkish Style."

OK. So they weren't expecting tea.

I swallow, trying to keep my composure, desperately pretending I haven't seen anything.

"I . . . brought you a cup of tea," I say, my voice cracking with nerves. "I thought you might . . . like one."

Do not look at *The Joy of Sex*. Keep your eyes *up*.

Trish's face relaxes. "Samantha! You treasure! Put it down!" She waves an arm vaguely at a bedside table.

I'm just starting to move toward it when the bathroom door opens and Eddie emerges, naked except for a pair of too-tight boxer shorts, displaying a quite staggeringly hairy chest.

Somehow I manage not to drop the entire tray on the floor.

"I'm . . . I'm sorry," I stammer, backing away. "I didn't realize . . ."

"Don't be silly! Come *in*!" exclaims Trish gaily. She now seems completely reconciled to me being in her bedroom. "We're not *prudish*."

OK, I'm really wishing they were. Cautiously I edge further toward the bed, stepping over a mauve lace bra. I find a place for the tray on Trish's bedside cabinet by pushing aside a photo of her and Eddie sitting in a Jacuzzi, holding up glasses of champagne.

I pour out the tea as fast as I can and hand a cup to each of them. I cannot look Eddie in the eye. In what other job do you see your boss naked?

Only one other occupation springs immediately to mind. Which isn't that encouraging.

"Well . . . I'll go now," I mumble, head down.

"Don't rush off!" Trish sips her tea with relish. "Mmm. Now you're here, I wanted to have a little chat! See where we *are* with things."

"Er . . . right." Her nightie is gaping and I can see the edge of her nipple. I hastily look away and find myself catching the eye of the bearded guy in *The Joy of Sex* as he contorts himself.

I can feel my face flaming with embarrassment. What kind of surreal weirdness is this, that I am standing in the bedroom of two people, pretty much strangers to me, being practically *shown* how they have sex? And they don't seem remotely bothered. . . .

And then it comes to me. Of course. I'm staff. I don't count.

"So, is everything all right, Samantha?" Trish puts her cup down and gives me a beady look. "You've got your routine sorted? All under control?"

"Absolutely." I grope for a competent-sounding phrase. "I'm pretty much . . . on top of everything." Aaargh. "I mean . . . getting to grips with it all."

Aaaargh.

She takes a sip of tea. "I expect you'll be tackling the laundry today."

The laundry. I hadn't even thought about the laundry.

"Only I'd like you to change the sheets when you make the beds," she adds.

Make the beds?

I feel a slight twinge of panic.

"Obviously I have my own . . . er . . . established routine," I say, trying to sound casual. "But it might be an idea if you give me a list of duties."

"Oh." Trish looks a little irritated. "Well . . . if you really think you need it . . ."

"And I, Samantha, must go through your terms and conditions later on," says Eddie. He's standing in front of the mirror, holding a dumbbell. "Let you know what you've got yourself into." He guffaws, then with a slight grunt lifts the weight above his head. His stomach is rippling with the effort. And not in a good way.

"So . . . I'll get on with . . . things." I start backing toward the door.

"See you later, then, at breakfast." Trish gives me a cheery little wave from the bed. "Ciao ciao!"

I cannot keep up with Trish's mood shifts. We seemed

to have lurched straight from employer-employee to people-enjoying-a-luxury-cruise-together.

"Er...bye then!" I say, matching her chirpy tone. I bob a curtsy, step over her bra again, and exit the room as quickly as I can.

Breakfast is a bit of a nightmare. It takes me three failed attempts before I realize how you're supposed to cut a grapefruit in half. You'd think they'd make it clearer. They could draw guidelines round them, or have perforations, or something. Meanwhile the milk for the coffee boils over—and when I plunge down the cafetière, the coffee explodes everywhere. Luckily Trish and Eddie are so busy arguing about where to go on their next holiday, they don't seem to notice what's going on in the kitchen.

When they've finished, I stack the dirty dishes in the dishwasher and am desperately trying to remember how I made it work yesterday, when Trish comes into the kitchen.

"Samantha, Mr. Geiger would like to see you in his study," she says. "To discuss your pay and conditions. Don't keep him waiting!"

"Er...very good, madam." I curtsy, then smooth down my uniform and head out into the hall. I approach the door of Eddie's study and knock twice.

"Come in!" replies a jovial voice. I walk in to find Eddie sitting behind his desk—a huge affair of mahogany and tooled leather—with an expensive-looking laptop in front of him. He's fully clothed by now, thank God, in tan trousers and a sports shirt.

"Ah, Samantha. Ready for our little meeting?" Eddie gestures to an upright wooden chair, and I sit down. "Here we are! The document you've been waiting for!"

With a self-important air he hands me a folder marked HOUSEKEEPER'S CONTRACT. I open it up to find a title sheet on cream vellum paper.

CONTRACT OF AGREEMENT
Between Samantha Sweeting and
Mr. and Mrs. Edward Geiger,
this first day of July in the year of our Lord
two thousand and four.

"Wow," I say in surprise. "Did a lawyer draw this up?"

"I didn't need a lawyer." Eddie chuckles knowingly. "Downloaded it from the Internet. And obviously amended it slightly. All you need is a bit of common sense."

I turn over the title sheet and run my eyes down the printed clauses. I have to bite my lip as I take in phrases here and there, presumably Eddie's "amendments."

"Now, I know it looks frightening!" says Eddie, misinterpreting my silence. "But don't be intimidated by all these long words. Did you have a chance to look at the pay?"

My eye flicks to the figure quoted in bold under *Weekly Salary*. It's slightly less than I charged per hour as a lawyer.

"It seems extremely generous," I say after a pause. "Thank you very much, sir."

"Is there anything you don't understand?" He beams jovially. "Just say!"

"Um...this bit." I point to *Clause 7: Hours*. "Does this mean I have the whole weekend off? Every weekend?"

"Unless we're entertaining." Eddie nods. "In which case you'll have two days off in lieu...You'll see in clause nine..."

I'm not listening. Every weekend free. I can't get my head around this idea. I don't think I've had a totally free weekend since I was about twelve.

"That's great." I look up, unable to stop myself smiling. "Thanks very much!"

"Didn't your previous employers give you weekends off?" Eddie looks taken aback.

"Well, no," I say truthfully. "Not really."

"They sound like slave drivers!" He beams. "Now, I'll leave you alone for a while to study the agreement before you sign."

"I've pretty much read it—" I halt as Eddie raises a hand in reproof.

"Samantha, Samantha, Samantha," he says in avuncular tones, shaking his head. "I'm going to give you a little tip that will stand you in good stead in life. Always read legal documents *very carefully*."

"Yes, sir," I say, my nose twitching with the effort of staying deadpan. "I'll try to remember that."

As Eddie disappears from the room, I look down at the contract again, rolling my eyes. I pick up a pencil and automatically start correcting the text, rephrasing, scoring out, and adding queries in the margin.

What am I doing?

I grab an eraser and hastily erase all my amendments. I reach for a Biro and turn to the bottom of the page.

Name: Samantha Sweeting.

Occupation:

I hesitate for a moment . . . then put *Domestic Help*.

I'm really doing this. I'm really committing to this job, miles away from my former life in every sense. And no one knows what I'm doing.

I have a sudden flash on my mother's face, on the expression she'd have if she knew where I was right now . . . if she could see me in my uniform . . . her reaction. . . . It would be as though some seismic world catastrophe had occurred. I'm almost tempted to call her up and tell her what I'm doing.

But I'm not going to. And I haven't got time to think about her. I have laundry to do.

It takes me two trips to bring down all the washing to the laundry room, just off the kitchen. I dump the overflowing baskets on the tiled floor and look at the hi-tech washing machine. This should be simple enough. Experimentally, I open the door of the machine and at once an electronic display starts flashing at me. *WASH? WASH?*

Immediately I feel flustered. *Obviously* I want you to wash, I feel like snapping back. Just give me a chance to get the bloody clothes in.

Stay calm. One thing at a time. First step: sort the clothes. Feeling pleased with myself for having thought of this, I start sorting out the dirty clothes into piles on the floor, consulting the labels as I go. As I'm peering at one marked *Wash with GREAT CARE*, I hear Trish coming into the kitchen, clearly on the phone.

"You're right," she's saying, her voice trembling. "You're right! But *he* doesn't see it like that! And let me tell you, I've tried!"

I freeze in embarrassment. Does Trish know I'm in here? Should I cough?

"I don't *want* to play golf! Is there nothing *else* we can do together?" I glance out of the laundry door into the kitchen and to my horror see Trish at the table, dabbing at her eyes with a pink tissue. "It's all right for him! He has no idea what it's like for me!"

Hastily I duck back into the laundry and start busily

shoving clothes into the drum at random. If Trish comes in, she'll see me dutifully at work, impervious to her conversation. I shake some washing powder into the little tray at the top and close the door firmly. Now what?

WASH? the machine is still flashing at me. *WASH?*

"Er ... yes!" I mutter. "Wash them." I jab randomly at a button.

ENTER PROGRAM? it flashes back.

My eyes dart about for clues, and I spot a manual tucked behind a spray bottle. I grab it and start leafing through.

The half-load option for small washes is only available for prewash programs A3-E2 and superrinse programs G2-L7 not including H4.

... What?

OK, let's forget the manual. Let's just use common sense. I briskly press at the keypad in my best house-keeper manner.

PROGRAM K3? the machine flashes at me. *PRO-GRAM K3?*

I don't like the sound of program K3. It sounds sinister. Like a cliff face or secret government plot.

"No," I say aloud, jabbing at the machine. "I want something else."

YOU HAVE CHOSEN K3, it flashes back. *HEAVY-DUTY UPHOLSTERY PROGRAM.*

Heavy duty? *Upholstery?*

"Stop it," I say under my breath, and start banging all the buttons. "Stop!" I kick the machine in desperation. *"Stop!"*

"Everything all right, Samantha?" Trish appears at the laundry door. All signs of tears are gone and she's applied fresh lipstick. I wonder what she was so upset about. But it's hardly my place to ask.

"Er ... fine! Just ... getting some washing on."

"Well done." She holds out a stripy shirt to me. "Now, Mr. Geiger needs a button sewn on this shirt, if you would be so kind."

"Absolutely!" I take it from her, praying my trepidation doesn't show on my face.

"And here's your list of duties!" She hands me a sheet of paper. "It's by no means complete, but it should get you *started.*"

As I run my eyes down the endless list, I feel a bit faint.

Make beds . . . sweep and clean front steps . . . arrange flowers . . . polish all mirrors . . . store cupboards tidy . . . laundry . . . clean bathrooms daily . . .

"Now, there's nothing here that should present you with a *problem,* is there?" adds Trish.

"Er . . . no!" My voice is a little strangled. "No, it should all be fine!"

"But make a stab at the ironing *first,*" she continues firmly. "There is quite a lot, I'm afraid, as you'll have seen. It does tend to mount *up* rather . . ." For some reason, Trish is looking upward. With a slight foreboding, I follow her gaze. There, above us, is a mountain of crumpled shirts hanging on a wooden drying rack. At least thirty.

As I stare up at them, I feel wobbly. I can't iron a shirt. I've never used an iron in my life. What am I going to do?

"I expect you'll whip through these in no time!" she says gaily. "The ironing board's just there," she adds with a nod.

"Um, thanks!" I manage.

I reach for the ironing board, trying to look matter-of-fact, as if I do this all the time. I tug briskly at one of the metal legs, but it won't move. I try another one with no luck. I'm pulling harder and harder, till I'm hot with the effort, but the bloody thing won't budge. How am I supposed to open it up?

"It's got a catch," Trish says, watching me in surprise. "Underneath." She takes the board from me, and in two movements has opened it up to exactly the right height. "I expect you're used to a different model," she adds wisely as she clicks it shut. "They all have their own little tricks."

"Absolutely!" I say, seizing on this excuse in relief. "Of course! I'm far more used to working with a . . . a . . . a Nimbus 2000."

Trish peers at me in surprise. "Isn't that the broomstick out of *Harry Potter*?"

Damn. I knew I'd heard it somewhere.

"Yes . . . it is," I say at last, my face flaming. "And also a well-known ironing board. In fact, I think the broomstick was named . . . er . . . *after* the ironing board."

"Really?" Trish looks fascinated. "I never knew that!" To my horror she leans expectantly against the door and lights a cigarette. "Don't mind me!" she adds, her voice muffled. "Just carry on!"

Carry on?

"There's the iron," she adds with a gesture. "Behind you."

"Er . . . great! Thanks!" I take the iron and plug it in, as slowly as possible, my heart banging in fright. I cannot do this. I need a way out. But I can't think of one. My brain is totally blank.

"I expect the iron's hot enough now!" says Trish helpfully.

"Right!" I give her a sick smile.

I have no choice. I reach for one of the shirts overhead and spread it out awkwardly on the ironing board. Unable to believe what I'm doing, I pick up the iron. It's far heavier than I imagined and emits a terrifying cloud of steam. Very gingerly, I start lowering it toward the cotton fabric. I have no idea which bit of the shirt I'm aiming for. I think my eyes might be shut.

Suddenly there's a trilling from the kitchen. The phone. Thank God . . . thank God . . . thank God . . .

"Oh, who's *that*?" says Trish, frowning. "Sorry, Samantha. I should get this . . ."

"That's fine!" My voice is shrill. "No worries! I'll just get on—"

As soon as Trish is out of the room I put the iron down with a crash and bury my head in my hands. I must have been mad. This isn't going to work. I'm not made to be a housekeeper. The iron puffs steam in my face and I give a little scream of fright. I switch it off and collapse against the wall. It's only nine twenty and I'm already a total wreck.

And I thought being a lawyer was stressful.

Eleven

By the time Trish comes back into the kitchen I'm a little more composed. I can do this. Of course I can. It's not quantum physics. It's *housework*.

"Samantha, I'm afraid we're going to *desert* you for the day," says Trish, looking concerned. "Mr. Geiger is off to golf and I'm going to see a *very* dear friend's new Mercedes. Will you be all right on your own?"

"I'll be fine!" I say, trying not to sound too joyful. "Don't you worry about me. Really. I'll just get on with things. . . ."

"Is the ironing done already?" She glances at the laundry room, impressed.

Done?

"Actually, I thought I'd leave the ironing for now and tackle the rest of the house," I say, trying to sound matter-of-fact. "That's my normal routine."

"Absolutely." She nods vigorously. "Whatever suits you. Now, I won't be here to answer any questions, I'm afraid, but Nathaniel will!" She beckons out the door. "You've met Nathaniel, of course?"

"Oh," I say as he walks in, wearing ripped jeans, his hair disheveled. "Er . . . yes. Hi, again."

It feels a bit strange seeing him this morning, after all the dramas of last night.

"Hi," he says. "How's it going?"

"Great!" I say lightly. "Really well."

"Nathaniel knows *all* there is to know about this house," puts in Trish, who is doing her lipstick. "So if you can't find anything—need to know how a door unlocks or whatever—he's your man."

"I'll bear that in mind," I say. "Thanks."

"But, Nathaniel, I don't want you *disturbing* Samantha," adds Trish, giving him a severe look. "Obviously she has her own established routine."

"Obviously," says Nathaniel. As Trish turns away, he raises an eyebrow in amusement and I feel my color rise.

What's that supposed to mean? How does he know I don't have a routine? Just because I can't cook, it doesn't follow I can't do *anything*.

"So you'll be OK?" Trish picks up her handbag. "You've found all the cleaning stuff?"

"Er . . ." I look around uncertainly.

"In the laundry room!" She disappears through the doorway for a moment, then reappears, holding a gigantic blue tub full of cleaning products. "There you are!" she says, dumping it on the table. "And don't forget your Marigolds!" she adds merrily.

My what?

"Rubber gloves," says Nathaniel. He takes a huge pink pair out of the tub and hands them to me with a little bow.

"Yes, thank you," I say with dignity. "I knew that."

I have never worn a pair of rubber gloves in my life. Trying not to flinch, I slowly pull them onto my hands.

Oh, my God. I've never felt anything quite so rubbery and . . . *revolting*. Must I wear these all *day*?

"Toodle-oo!" calls Trish from the hall, and the front door bangs shut.

"Right!" I say. "Well . . . I'll get on."

I wait for Nathaniel to leave, but he leans against the table and looks at me quizzically. "Do you have any idea how to clean a house?"

I'm starting to feel quite insulted here. Do I *look* like someone who can't clean a house?

"Of course I know how to clean a house."

"Only I told my mum about you last night." He smiles, as though remembering the conversation. What could he have said about me? "Anyway. She's willing to teach you cooking. And I said you'd probably need cleaning advice too—"

"I do not need cleaning advice!" I retort. "I've cleaned houses loads of times. In fact, I need to get started."

"Don't mind me." Nathaniel shrugs.

I'll show him. In a businesslike manner, I pick a can out of the tub and spray it onto the counter.

"So you've cleaned lots of houses," says Nathaniel, watching me.

"Yes. Millions."

The spray has solidified into crystalline little gray droplets. I rub them briskly with a cloth—but they won't come off.

I look more closely at the can. DO NOT USE ON GRANITE. *Shit.*

"Anyway," I say, hastily putting the cloth down to hide the droplets. "You're in my way." I grab a feather duster from the blue tub and start brushing crumbs off the kitchen table. "Excuse me . . ."

"I'll leave you, then," says Nathaniel, his mouth twitching. He looks at the feather duster. "Don't you want to be using a dustpan and brush for that?"

I look uncertainly at the feather duster. What's wrong with this one? Anyway, what is he, the duster police?

"I have my methods," I say, lifting my chin. "Thank you."

"OK." He grins. "See you."

I'm not going to let him faze me. I just need . . . a plan. Yes. A time sheet, like at work.

I grab a pen and the pad of paper by the phone and start scribbling a list for the day. I have an image of myself moving smoothly from task to task, brush in one hand, duster in the other, bringing order to everything. Like Mary Poppins.

9:30–9:36 Make Geigers' bed

9:36–9:42 Take laundry out of machine and put in dryer

9:42–10:00 Clean bathrooms

I get to the end and read it over with a fresh surge of optimism. At this rate I should be done easily by lunchtime.

9:36 Fuck. I cannot make this bed. Why won't this sheet lie flat?

9:42 And why do they make mattresses so *heavy*?

9:54 This is sheer torture. My arms have never ached so much in my entire life. The blankets weigh a ton, and the sheets won't go straight and I have no idea how to do the wretched corners. How do chamber-maids do it?

10:16 At last. Forty minutes of hard work and I have made precisely one bed. I'm already way behind. But never mind. Just keep moving. Laundry next.

10:26 No. Please, no.

I can hardly bear to look. It's a total disaster. Everything in the washing machine has gone pink. Every single thing.

What *happened*?

With trembling fingers I pick out a damp cashmere cardigan. It was cream when I put it in. It's now a sickly shade of candy floss. I knew K3 was bad news. I *knew* it—

There must be a solution, there must be. Frantically I scan the cans of products stacked on the shelves. Stain Away. Vanish. There has to be a remedy. . . . I just need to think. . . .

10:38 OK, I have the answer. It may not totally work—but it's my best shot.

11:00 I've just spent £852 replacing all the clothes in the machine as closely as possible. Harrods personal-shopping department was very helpful and will send them all tomorrow, Express Delivery. I just hope to heaven Trish and Eddie won't notice that their wardrobe has magically regenerated.

11:06 And . . . oh. The ironing. What am I going to do about that?

11:12 I have a solution, via the local paper. A girl from the village will collect it, iron it all overnight at £3 a shirt, and sew on Eddie's button.

So far this job has cost me nearly a thousand pounds. And it's not even midday.

11:42 I'm doing fine. I'm doing well. I've got the Hoover on, I'm cruising along nicely—

What was that? What just went up the Hoover? Why is it making that grinding noise?

Have I *broken* it?

11:48 How much does a Hoover cost?

12:24 My legs are in total agony. I've been kneeling on hard tiles, cleaning the bath, for what seems like hours. There are little ridges where the tiles have dug into my knees, and I'm boiling hot and the cleaning chemicals are making me cough. All I want is a rest. But I can't stop for a moment. I am *so* behind . . .

12:30 What is wrong with this bleach bottle? Which way is the nozzle pointing, anyway? I'm turning it round in confusion, peering at the arrows on the plastic . . . Why won't anything come out? OK, I'm going to squeeze it really, really hard—

That nearly got my eye.

12:32 FUCK. What has it done to my HAIR?

By three o'clock I am utterly knackered. I'm only halfway down my list and I can't see myself ever making it to the end. I don't know how people clean houses. It's the hardest job I've ever done, ever.

I am not moving smoothly from task to task like Mary Poppins. I'm darting from unfinished job to unfinished job like a headless chicken. Right now I'm standing on a chair, cleaning the mirror in the drawing room. But it's like some kind of bad dream. The more I rub, the more it smears.

I keep catching glances of myself in the glass. I have never looked more disheveled in my life. My hair is sticking out wildly, with a huge grotesque streak of greeny-blond where I splashed the bleach. My face is bright red and shiny, my hands are pink and sore from scrubbing, and my eyes are bloodshot.

Why won't it get clean? Why?

"Get clean!" I cry, practically sobbing in frustration. "Get clean, you bloody . . . bloody—"

"Samantha."

Abruptly I stop rubbing, to see Nathaniel standing in the doorway. "Have you tried vinegar?"

"*Vinegar?*"

"It cuts through the grease," he adds. "It's good on glass."

"Oh. Right." I put my cloth down, trying to regain my cool. "Yes, I knew that."

Nathaniel shakes his head. "No, you didn't."

I look at his adamant face. There's no point pretending anymore. He knows I've never cleaned a house in my life.

"You're right," I admit at last. "I didn't."

As I get down off the chair, I feel wobbly with fatigue.

"You should have a break," says Nathaniel firmly. "You've been at it all day; I've seen you. Did you have any lunch?"

"No time."

I collapse onto a chair, suddenly too drained to move. Every single muscle in my body is in pain, including muscles I never even knew I had. I feel like I've run a marathon, and I still haven't polished the woodwork or beaten the mats.

"It's . . . harder than I thought," I say at last. "A lot harder."

"Uh-huh." He's peering at my head. "What happened to your hair?"

"Bleach," I say shortly. "Cleaning the loo."

He gives a muffled snort of laughter, but I don't respond. To be honest, I'm beyond caring.

"You're a hard worker," he says. "I'll give you that. And it'll get easier—"

"I can't do it." The words come out before I can stop them. "I can't do this job. I'm . . . hopeless."

"Sure you can." He rifles through his rucksack and produces a can of Coke. "Have this. You can't work on no fuel."

"Thanks," I say, taking it gratefully. I crack open the can and take a gulp, and it's the most delicious thing I've ever tasted.

"The offer still stands," he adds after a pause. "My mother will give you lessons if you like."

"Really?" I wipe my mouth, push back my sweaty hair, and look up at him. "She'd . . . do that?"

"She likes a challenge, my mum." Nathaniel gives a little smile. "She'll teach you your way around a kitchen. And . . . anything else you need to know."

I feel a sudden burn of humiliation and look away. I don't want to be useless. I don't want to need lessons. That's not who I am. I want to be able to do this on my own, without asking assistance from anyone.

But . . . the truth is, I need help.

Apart from anything else, if I keep on going like today I'll be bankrupt in two weeks.

I turn back to Nathaniel.

"That would be great," I say. "I really appreciate it. Thanks."

Twelve

I **wake up** the next morning, heart pounding, leaping to my feet, my mind racing with everything I have to do...

And then it stops, like a car screeching to a halt. For a moment I can't move. Then, hesitantly, I sink back into bed, overcome by the most extraordinary feeling.

It's Saturday. I have nothing to do.

No contracts to go over, no e-mails to reply to, no emergency meetings at the office. Nothing.

I try to remember the last time I had nothing to do. But I'm not sure I can. It seems like I've *never* had nothing to do, ever since I was about seven. I get out of bed, walk to the window, and stare out at the early morning translucent blue sky, trying to get my head around my situation. It's my day off. No one has any hold over me. No one can call me up and demand my presence. This is my own time. *My own time.*

As I stand there at the window, contemplating this

fact, I start to feel an odd feeling inside. Light and giddy, like a helium balloon. I'm free. A smile of exhilaration spreads across my face. For the first time ever, I can do whatever I like.

I check the time—and it's only 7:15 a.m. The whole day stretches before me like a fresh sheet of paper. What shall I do? Where do I *start*?

I'm already sketching out a timetable for the day in my head. Forget six-minute segments. Forget hurrying. I'm going to start measuring time in *hours*. An hour for wallowing in the bath and getting dressed. An hour for lingering over breakfast. An hour for reading the paper, cover to cover. I'm going to have the laziest, most indolent, most enjoyable morning I've ever had in my adult life.

As I head into the bathroom, I can feel muscles twinging with pain all over my body. They really should market housecleaning as a workout. I run a deep warm bath and slosh in some of Trish's bath oil, then step into the scented water and lie back happily.

Delicious. I'm just going to stay here for hours and hours and hours.

I close my eyes, letting the water lap my shoulders, and time wafts past in great swathes. I think I even fall asleep for a while. I have never spent so long in a bath in my entire life.

At last I open my eyes, reach for a towel, and get out. As I'm starting to dry myself off I reach for my watch, just out of curiosity.

7:30 a.m.

What?

I was only fifteen minutes?

How can I have only taken fifteen minutes? I stand, dripping, in indecision for a moment, wondering if I should get back in and do it all again, more slowly.

But no. That would be too weird. It doesn't matter. So I had my bath too quickly. I'll just make sure I take my time properly over breakfast.

At least I have some clothes to put on. Trish took me out last night to a shopping center a few miles away so I could stock up on underwear and shorts and summer dresses. She told me she'd leave me to it—then ended up bossing me about and picking everything out for me...and somehow I ended up with not a single item in black.

I cautiously put on a pink slip dress and a pair of sandals and look at myself. I've never worn pink before in my life. My entire closet at home is filled with black suits for work—and I've got into the habit of wearing black at the weekends too. It just makes life easy. But to my amazement I don't look too bad! Apart from the huge streak of bleach in my hair.

As I make my way along the corridor, there's no sound from the Geigers' bedroom. I move silently past the door, feeling suddenly awkward. It'll be a bit strange, spending all weekend in their house, with nothing to do. I'd better go out later. Get out of their way.

The kitchen is as silent and gleamy as ever, but it's starting to feel slightly less intimidating. I know my way around the kettle and the toaster, if nothing else. I'll have toast for breakfast, with orange and ginger marmalade, and a nice cup of coffee. And I'll read the paper from cover to cover. That'll take me to about eleven o'clock and then I can think about what else to do. . . .

I wonder how the Fallons deal is progressing.

The thought pops into my mind with no warning. I can't help picturing my last scribbled amendments on the draft agreement—all my work, left half done.

And Ketterman's due diligence report. I never finished that.

My grip on the kettle tightens as I remember all the projects I've left behind. I wonder who's taken over all my unfinished deals. Edward Faulkner, maybe? He's a year or two younger than me, but pretty sharp. With a wince I imagine him taking the files off my desk, flipping through all my work, introducing himself to the Fallons people. The team could be there right now, finishing up an all-nighter—sitting around the table, Edward Faulkner in my place . . .

Stop.

Just stop. I mustn't think about it. I've *left* Carter Spink. It's nothing to do with me anymore. I'm going to relax and enjoy my free time, like any normal person.

Forcing the images out of my mind, I head out into the hall, where I find a copy of the *Times* on the doormat. I bring it back to the kitchen just as my toast is popping up.

This is the life.

I sit by the window, crunching toast, sipping coffee, and leafing through the paper in a leisurely way. At last, after devouring three slices, two cups of coffee, and all the Saturday sections, I stretch my arms in a big yawn and glance at the clock.

I don't believe it. It's only seven fifty-six.

What is wrong with me? I was supposed to take *hours* over breakfast. I was supposed to be sitting there all morning. Not get everything finished in twenty minutes flat.

OK . . . never mind. I'll soon get the hang of it.

I put my crockery away in the dishwasher and wipe away my toast crumbs. Then I sit down at the table again and look about. I wonder what to do next.

Abruptly I realize I'm tapping the table with my fingernails. I stop myself and survey my hands for a moment. This is ridiculous. I'm having my first true day off in about ten years. I should be *relaxed*. Come on, I can think of something nice to do, surely.

What do people do on days off? My mind scrolls through a series of images from TV. I could make another cup of coffee, but I've already had two. I could read the paper again, but I have an almost photographic memory. So rereading things I already know is a bit pointless.

My gaze drifts to the garden, where a squirrel is perched on a stone pillar, looking around with bright eyes. Maybe I'll go outside. Enjoy the garden and the wildlife and the early morning dew. Good idea.

Except the trouble with early morning dew is it gets all over your feet. As I pick my way over the damp grass, I'm already wishing I hadn't put on open-toed sandals. Or that I'd waited till later for my little stroll.

The garden is a lot bigger than I'd appreciated. I walk down the lawn toward an ornamental hedge where the land seems to finish, only to realize there's a whole section beyond it, with an orchard at the end and some sort of walled garden to my left.

It's a stunning garden. Even I can see that. The flowers are vivid without being garish; every wall is covered with some beautiful creeper or vine. As I walk toward the orchard I can see little golden pears hanging from the branches of trees. I don't think I've ever seen an actual pear growing on a tree before in my life. I grew up in a town house with a small paved courtyard containing nothing but a few nondescript shrubs.

I walk through the fruit trees toward a huge, square, brown patch of earth with vegetation growing in serried rows. These must be the vegetables. I prod one of them cautiously with my foot. It could be a cabbage or a lettuce. Or the leaves of something growing underground, maybe.

To be honest, it could be an alien. I have no idea.

I sit down on a mossy wooden bench and look at a nearby bush covered in white flowers. Mm. Pretty.

Now what? What do people *do* in their gardens?

I feel I should have something to read. Or someone to call. My fingers are itching to move. I look at my watch. Still only eight sixteen. Oh, God.

Come on, I can't give up yet. I'll just sit here for a bit and enjoy the peace. I lean back and watch a little speckled bird pecking the ground nearby for a while.

Then I look at my watch again: eight seventeen.

I can't do this.

I can't do nothing all day. It's going to drive me crazy. I'll have to go and buy another paper from the village shop. If they've got *War and Peace,* I'll buy that too. I get up and head briskly back across the lawn when a bleep from my pocket makes me stop still.

It's my mobile. It's received a text. Someone's just texted me, early on a Saturday morning. I pull out my mobile, feeling edgy. I haven't had any contact with the outside world for two days. Is it from Carter Spink?

I know there are other texts in my phone—but I haven't read any of them. I know there are messages in my voice mail—but I haven't listened to a single one. I don't want to know.

I finger my mobile, telling myself to put it away. But now my curiosity has been sparked. Someone texted me a few seconds ago. Someone, somewhere, has been holding a mobile phone, punching in a message to me. I have a sudden vision of Guy, in his off-duty chinos and blue shirt. Sitting at his desk, frowning as he texts. Apologizing. Or giving me some news. Some kind of development I couldn't have guessed at yesterday—

I can't help it. Despite all, I feel a sudden flicker of hope. As I stand there on the early morning lawn, I can feel my mental self being dragged out of this garden, back to London, back to the office. Two whole days have gone on there without me. A lot can happen in forty-eight hours. Things can change for the better.

Or . . . become even worse. They're suing me. They're prosecuting me. There's some obscure piece of negligence law I don't know about. . . .

I'm gripping my phone more and more tightly. I have to know. Good or bad. I flip open the phone and find the text. It's from a number I don't even recognize.

Who? Who on earth is texting me?

Feeling a little sick, I press OK to read.

hi samantha, nathaniel here.

Nathaniel?
Nathaniel?
My relief is so huge, I laugh out loud. Of course! I gave him my mobile number yesterday for his mother. I scroll down to read the rest of the message.

if you're interested, mum could start cooking lessons today. nat

Cooking lessons. I feel a spark of delight. What a perfect way to fill the day! I press REPLY and quickly text:

would love to. thanks. sam

I send it with a little smile. This is fun. A minute or two later, the phone bleeps again.

what time? is 11 too early? nat

I look at my watch. Eleven o'clock is still two and a half hours away.

Two and a half hours with nothing to do except avoid Trish and Eddie. I press REPLY.

shall we make it 10? sam

At five to ten I'm ready in the hall. Nathaniel's mother's house is nearby but apparently tricky to find, so the plan is to meet here and he'll walk me over. I check my reflection in the hall mirror and wince. The streak of bleach in my hair is as obvious as ever. Am I really going out in public like this? I push my hair backward and forward a few times—but I can't hide it. Maybe I could walk along with my hand carelessly positioned at my head, as if I'm thinking hard. I attempt a few casual, pensive poses in the mirror.

"Is your head all right?"

I swivel round in shock to see Nathaniel at the open door, wearing a plaid shirt and jeans.

"Er . . . fine," I say, my hand still glued to my head. "I was just . . ."

Oh, there's no point. I bring my hand down from my hair and Nathaniel regards the streak for a moment.

"It looks nice," he says. "Like a badger."

"A *badger*?" I say, affronted. "I don't look like a badger."

"Badgers are beautiful creatures," says Nathaniel with a shrug. "I'd rather look like a badger than a stoat."

Hang on. Since when was my choice between badger and stoat? How did we get onto this subject, anyway?

"Perhaps we should go," I say with dignity, then pick up my bag and give one last glance in the mirror.

OK. Maybe I look a little bit like a badger.

The summer air is already warming up outside, and as we walk down the gravel drive I sniff appreciatively. There's some sort of nice flowery smell that I definitely recognize. . . .

"Honeysuckle and jasmine!" I exclaim in sudden recognition. I have the Jo Malone bath oil at home.

"Honeysuckle on the wall." Nathaniel points to a tangle of tiny pale-yellow flowers on the old stone wall bordering the drive. "Put it in a year ago."

I peer up at the delicate flowers with interest. That's what real honeysuckle looks like?

"There's no jasmine around here, though," he says, curiously. "Can you smell it?"

"Er . . ." I spread my hands vaguely. "Maybe not."

I don't think I'll mention my Jo Malone bath oil at this point. Or, in fact, at any point.

As we turn out of the drive I realize this is the first time I've been out of the Geigers' grounds since I arrived here—apart from the shopping trip with Trish, when we turned in the opposite direction. And anyway, I was too busy scrabbling for her Celine Dion CD to notice my surroundings. Nathaniel has turned left and is striding easily along the road—but I can't move. I'm gazing at the sight in front of me, my jaw wide open. This village is absolutely *stunning*.

I had no idea.

I look around, taking in the old, honey-colored stone walls, the rows of ancient cottages with steeply pitched roofs, the little river lined with willow trees. Up ahead is the pub I noticed on the first night, decorated with hanging baskets. I can hear the distant clip-clop of horses' hooves. Nothing jars. Everything is soft and mellow and feels like it's been here for hundreds of years.

"Samantha?"

Nathaniel has finally noticed I'm pinned to the spot.

"I'm sorry." I hurry to join him. "It's just such a beautiful place!"

"It's nice." I can hear a note of pride in his voice. "Gets too many tourists, but . . ."

"I had no idea!" We continue to walk along the street, but I can't stop looking around, wide-eyed. "Look at the river! Look at the little *church*!"

I feel like a child discovering a new toy. I've hardly ever been to the English countryside, I suddenly realize. We always stayed in London or went abroad. I've been to Tuscany more times than I can remember, and I once spent six months in New York when Mum was working there. But I've never been to the Cotswolds in my life.

We walk over the river on an old arched stone bridge. At the top I stop to look at the ducks and swans.

"It's just . . . gorgeous." I exhale. "Absolutely beautiful."

"Didn't you see any of this as you arrived?" Nathaniel looks amused. "Did you just appear in a bubble?"

I think back to that panicked, dazed, desperate journey.

"Kind of," I say at last. "I didn't really notice where I was going."

We both watch as a pair of swans sail regally under

the little bridge. Then I glance at my watch. It's already five past ten.

"We should get going," I say with a little start. "Your mother will be waiting."

"There's no rush," Nathaniel calls as I hasten down the other side of the bridge. "We've got all day." He lopes down the bridge. "It's OK. You can slow down."

I try to match his relaxed pace. But I'm not used to this easy rhythm. I'm used to striding along crowded pavements, fighting my way, pushing and elbowing.

"So, did you grow up here?" I ask.

"Yup." He swings into a little cobbled lane. "I came back when my dad got ill. Then he died and I had to sort things out. Take care of Mum. It's been tough on her. The finances were in a mess—everything was in a mess."

"I'm . . . sorry," I say awkwardly. "Do you have any other family?"

"My brother, Jake. He came back for a week." Nathaniel hesitates. "He runs his own computer business. Very successful."

"Didn't you mind?" I say. "That he only stayed a week?"

"Jake's a busy man. He has other priorities."

Nathaniel's voice is as easy as ever, but I can detect a thread of . . . something. Maybe I won't ask any more about his family.

"Well, *I'd* live here," I say with enthusiasm.

"You do live here," he reminds me.

I feel a tweak of surprise. I suppose he's right. Technically, I do.

I try to process this new thought. I've never lived anywhere except London before, apart from my three years at Cambridge and those six months in New York when I was eight. I'm a city person. That's who I am. That's who I . . . was.

But already the old me is feeling more distant. When I think back to myself even last week, it's as if I'm seeing myself through tracing paper. Everything I once prized has been destroyed. I'm still feeling sore and bruised. But at the same time . . . my rib cage expands widely as I breathe in the country air, and I suddenly feel a wave of optimism. On impulse, I stop by a huge tree and gaze up into the green-laden branches. As I do so, a memory from English A Level suddenly comes into my mind.

"There's a wonderful Walt Whitman poem about an oak tree." I lift a hand and tenderly stroke the cool, rough bark. *"I saw in Louisiana a live-oak growing. All alone stood it, and the moss hung down from the branches."*

I glance over at Nathaniel, half-expecting him to look impressed.

"That's a beech," he says, nodding at the tree.

Oh. Right.

I don't know any poems about beeches.

"Here we are." Nathaniel pushes open an old iron gate and gestures me to go up a stone path toward a little cottage with blue flowered curtains at the windows. "Come and meet your cooking teacher."

Nathaniel's mother is nothing like I expected. I was picturing some cozy Mrs. Tiggywinkle character with gray hair in a bun and half-moon spectacles. Instead, I'm looking at a wiry woman with a vivid, pretty face. Her eyes are bright blue, and her graying hair is in plaits on either side of her face. She's wearing an apron over jeans, T-shirt, and espadrilles, and is vigorously kneading some kind of dough on the kitchen table.

"Mum." Nathaniel grins and pushes me forward into the kitchen. "Here she is. This is Samantha. Samantha—my mum. Iris."

"Samantha. Welcome." Iris looks up, and I can see her taking me in, head to foot. "Just let me finish this."

Nathaniel gestures to me to sit down, and I cautiously take a seat on a wooden chair. The kitchen is at the back of the house and is filled with light and sun. Flowers in earthenware jugs are everywhere. There's an old-fashioned range and a scrubbed wooden table and a stable door open to the outside. As I'm wondering whether I should be making conversation, a chicken wanders in and starts scratching at the ground.

"Oh, a chicken!" I exclaim before I can stop myself.

"Yes, a chicken." I can see Iris looking at me with wry amusement. "Never seen a chicken before?"

Only in the supermarket chill counter. The chicken comes pecking toward my open-toe-sandaled feet and I quickly tuck them under my chair, trying to look as though I meant to do that anyway.

"There." Iris picks up the dough, shapes it efficiently into a round shape on a tray, opens the heavy oven door, and pops it in. She washes her floury hands at the sink, then turns to face me.

"So. You want to learn how to cook." Her tone is friendly but businesslike. I sense this is a woman who doesn't waste words.

"Yes." I smile. "Please."

"Cordon Bleu fancy stuff," chimes in Nathaniel, who's leaning against the range.

"And how much cooking have you done before?" Iris dries her hands on a red-checked towel. "Nathaniel said none. That can't be right." She folds the towel and smiles at me for the first time. "What can you make? What are your basics?"

Her intent blue gaze is making me feel a little nervous. I rack my brains, trying to think of something I can make.

"Well...I can...I can make...um...toast," I say. "Toast would be my basic."

"*Toast?*" She looks taken aback. "Just toast?"

"And crumpets," I add quickly. "Tea cakes...anything that goes in a toaster, really."

"But what about *cooking*?" She drapes the towel over a steel bar on the range and looks at me more carefully. "What about...an omelet? Surely you can cook an omelet."

I swallow. "Not really."

Iris's expression is so incredulous I feel my cheeks flame. "I never really did home economics at school," I explain. "I never really learned how to make meals."

"But your mother, surely...or your grandmother—" She breaks off as I shake my head. "*Anyone?*"

I bite my lip. Iris exhales sharply as though taking in the situation for the first time.

"So you can't cook anything at all. And what have you promised to make for the Geigers?"

Oh, God.

"Trish wanted a week's worth of menus. So I...um... gave her one based on this." Sheepishly, I get the crumpled Maxim's menu out of my bag and hand it to her.

"Braised lamb and baby onion assemblé with a fondant potato and goat's cheese crust, accompanied by cardamom spinach puree," she reads out, in tones of disbelief.

I hear a snort and look up to see Nathaniel in fits of laughter.

"It was all I had!" I exclaim defensively. "What was I going to say, fish fingers and chips?"

"*Assemblé* is just flannel." Iris is still perusing the sheet. "That's souped-up shepherd's pie. We can teach you that. And the braised trout with almonds is straightforward enough...." She runs her finger further down the page, then at last looks up, frowning. "I can teach you these dishes, Samantha. But it isn't going to be easy. If you've really never cooked before." She glances at Nathaniel. "I'm really not sure..."

I feel a flicker of alarm. Please don't say she's going to back out.

"I'm a quick learner." I lean forward. "And I'll work hard. I really, really want to do this."

Please. I need this.

"All right," says Iris at last. "Let's get you cooking."

She reaches into a cupboard for a set of weighing scales, and I take the opportunity to reach into my bag for a pad of paper and a pen.

"What's that for?" She raises her chin toward the paper.

"So I can take notes," I explain. I write down the date and *Cooking lesson no. 1,* underline it, then stand at the ready. Iris is slowly shaking her head.

"Samantha, cooking isn't about writing down. It's about tasting. Feeling. Touching. Smelling."

"Right." I nod.

I must remember that. I quickly uncap my pen and scribble down *Cooking = all about tasting, smelling, feeling, etc.* I cap my pen again, only to see Iris regarding me with incredulity.

"Tasting," she says, removing my pen and paper from my hands. "Not writing. You need to use your senses. Your instincts."

She lifts the lid off a pot gently steaming on the cooker and dips a spoon into it. "Taste this."

Gingerly I take the spoon in my mouth. "Gravy," I say at once. "Delicious!" I add politely. Iris shakes her head.

"Don't tell me what you think it is. Tell me what you can taste."

This is a trick question, surely.

"I can taste . . . gravy."

Her expression doesn't change. She's waiting for something else.

"Er . . . meat?" I hazard.

"What else?"

My mind is blank. I can't think of anything else. I mean, it's gravy. What else can you say about gravy?

"Taste it again." Iris is relentless. "You need to try harder."

My face is growing hot as I struggle for words. I feel like the dumb kid at the back of the class who can't do the two-times table.

"Meat . . . water . . ." I try desperately to think what else is in gravy. "Flour!" I say in sudden inspiration.

"You can't taste flour. There's none in there. Samantha, don't think about identifying the taste. Just tell me what the sensation is." Iris holds the spoon out a third time. "Taste it again—and this time close your eyes."

Close my eyes?

"OK." I take a mouthful and close my eyes obediently.

"Now. What can you taste?" Iris's voice is in my ear. "Concentrate on the flavors. Nothing else."

Eyes shut tight, I block out everything and focus all my attention on my mouth. All I'm aware of is the warm salty liquid on my tongue. *Salt.* That's one flavor. And sweet . . . and . . . there's another taste as I swallow it down. . . .

It's almost like colors appearing. First the bright,

obvious ones, and then the gentler ones you'd almost miss.

"It's salty and meaty..." I say slowly, without opening my eyes. "And sweet...and...and almost fruity? Like cherries?"

I open my eyes, feeling a bit disoriented. There is Iris, smiling. Behind her I suddenly notice Nathaniel, scrutinizing me intently. I feel a tad flustered. Tasting gravy with your eyes closed is a fairly intimate thing to do, it turns out. I'm not sure I want anyone watching me.

Iris seems to understand. "Nathaniel," she says briskly. "We're going to need ingredients for all these dishes." She scribbles a long list and hands it to him. "Run down and get these for us, love."

As he leaves the room, she looks at me with kindness. "That was much better."

"By George, she's got it?" I say hopefully, and Iris throws back her head in laughter.

"Not yet, sweetie, by a long chalk. Here, get a pinny on." She hands me a red-and-white striped apron and I tie it around my waist, feeling self-conscious.

"It's so good of you to help me," I venture. Iris is pulling onions and some orange vegetable I don't recognize out from a bin by the door. "I'm really grateful."

"I like a challenge." She takes a knife from a block on the counter. "I get bored. Nathaniel does everything for me. Too much sometimes."

"But still. You'd never even met me—"

"I liked the sound of you." Iris draws down a heavy wooden chopping board from a shelf above. "Nathaniel told me how you got yourself out of your mess the other night. That took some spirit."

"I had to do something," I say ruefully.

"And they offered you a pay rise as a result. Wonderful." As she smiles, fine lines appear round her eyes like starbursts. "Trish Geiger is a very foolish woman."

"I like Trish," I say, feeling a stab of loyalty.

"So do I." Iris nods. "She's been very supportive to Nathaniel. But I do sometimes wonder—" She pauses, her hand resting on an onion.

"What?" I say tentatively.

"*Why* she needs quite so much help. *Why* the full-time housekeeper? What does she do with her time?" She looks genuinely interested.

"I don't know," I say truthfully. "I haven't quite worked it out."

"Intriguing." Iris seems lost in thought for a moment. Then she focuses on me again. "So you've taken the Geigers in completely."

"Yes." I smile. "They have no idea who I am."

"And who are you?"

Her question takes me completely by surprise.

"Is your name really Samantha?"

"Yes!" I say in shock.

"That was a little blunt," Iris acknowledges. "But a girl arrives in the middle of the countryside out of nowhere and takes a job she can't do . . ." She pauses, clearly choosing her words with care. "Nathaniel tells me you've just got out of a bad relationship?"

"Yes," I mumble, my head bowed, hoping she won't start probing for details.

"You don't want to talk about it, do you?"

"Not really. No. I don't."

As I look up there's a thread of understanding in her eyes.

"That's fine by me." She picks up a knife. "Now let's start. Roll up your sleeves, tie back your hair, and wash your hands. I'm going to teach you to chop an onion."

We spend all weekend cooking.

I learn to slice an onion finely, turn it the other way, and produce tiny dice. As I first watch Iris wielding her knife I can't imagine doing the same without chopping off a finger—but after two ruined onions I just about crack it. I learn to chop herbs with a rounded blade. I learn how to rub flour and ground ginger into chunks of meat, then drop them into a spitting hot, cast-iron pan. I learn that pastry has to be made with quick, cold hands, by an open window. I learn the trick of blanching French beans in boiling water before sautéing them in butter.

A week ago I didn't know what *blanching* even meant.

In between cooking I sit on the back step with Iris. We watch the chickens scratch in the dirt, and sip freshly brewed coffee accompanied by a pumpkin muffin or salty, crumbly cheese sandwiched with lettuce in homemade bread.

"Eat and enjoy," Iris says each time, handing me my share. My impulse is to gobble down my food—but Iris always shakes her head in dismay. "Not so fast. Take your time! *Taste* the food!"

As we're stirring risotto on Saturday afternoon, Iris puts on a CD of Puccini and tells me how she spent a year in Italy at the age of twenty, learning to cook and speak the language. She tells me how she came home for a holiday, intending to return to Italy after a month. She'd been offered a cooking job there. But she met Benjamin, Nathaniel's father—and never took the job.

"He must have been an extraordinary person for you to do that." I look up from the risotto.

"Yes, he was," says Iris, her face softening. "He was

funny and warm...and full of life. And kind. Most of all, kind." Then she notices my stationary spoon. "Keep stirring!"

On Sunday afternoon, under Iris's calm guidance, I make roast chicken with sage and onion stuffing, steamed broccoli, cumin-scented carrots, and roast potatoes. As I heave the huge roasting tin out of the oven, I pause for a moment and let the warm, chicken-scented air rise over me. I have never smelled a more homey smell in my life. The chicken is golden, its crisp, crackly skin speckled with the pepper I ground on earlier, the juices still sizzling in the tin.

"Gravy time," Iris calls from the other side of the kitchen. "Take the chicken out and put it on the dish—and cover it up. We need to keep it warm. Now tilt the roasting tin. Can you see those globules of fat floating on the surface? You need to spoon those out."

She's finishing the topping on a plum crumble as she speaks. She dots it with butter and pops it into the oven, then seamlessly reaches for a cloth and wipes down the surface. I've watched her all day, moving swiftly and precisely around the kitchen, tasting as she goes, fully in control.

"That's right." She's by my side, watching as I whisk the gravy. "Keep going...it'll thicken in a minute..."

I cannot believe I'm making gravy. *Making gravy.*

And—like everything I've learned to make in this amazing kitchen—it's working. The ingredients are obeying. The mishmash of chicken juices, stock, and flour is somehow turning into a smooth, fragrant broth.

"Very good!" says Iris. "Now pour it into this nice warm jug...sieve out any bits...See how easy that was?"

"I think you're magic," I say bluntly. "That's why everything works in here. You're a cooking witch."

"A cooking witch! Ha! I like that. Now come on. Pinny off. Time to enjoy what we've made." She takes off her apron and holds out a hand for mine. "Nathaniel, have you finished the table?"

Nathaniel has been in and out of the kitchen all weekend, and I've got used to his presence. In fact, I've been so taken up with cooking I've barely noticed him. Now he's laying the wooden table with rush mats, old bone-handled cutlery, and soft checked napkins.

"Wine for the cooks," says Iris, producing a bottle from the fridge and uncorking it. She pours me a glass, then gestures to the table. "Sit, Samantha. You've done enough for one weekend. You must be shattered."

"I'm fine!" I say automatically. But as I sink down into the nearest chair, I realize for the first time quite how exhausted I am. And how much my feet hurt. I close my eyes and feel myself relax for the first time that day. My arms and back are aching from all the chopping and mixing. My senses have been bombarded with smells and tastes and new sensations.

"Don't fall asleep!" Iris's voice jolts me back to the present. "This is our reward! Nathaniel love, put Samantha's roast chicken down there. You can carve."

I open my eyes to see Nathaniel carrying over the serving dish bearing the roast chicken, and feel a fresh glow of pride. My first roast chicken. I almost want to take a photo.

"You're not telling me you *made* this?" says Nathaniel.

Ha ha. He knows full well I made it.

"Just something I rustled up earlier." I wink at him. "As we Cordon Bleu chefs do."

Nathaniel carves the chicken with an expert ease, and Iris dishes out the vegetables. When we're all served she sits down and raises her glass.

"To you, Samantha. You've done splendidly."

"Thanks." I smile and am about to sip my wine when I realize the other two aren't moving.

"And to Ben," Iris adds softly.

"On Sundays we always remember Dad," Nathaniel explains.

"Oh." I hesitate, then raise my glass.

"And now." Iris reaches for her knife and fork. "The moment of truth." She takes a bite of chicken while I try to hide my nerves.

"Very good." She nods at last. "Very good indeed."

I can't stop beaming. "Really? It's . . . good?"

Iris lifts her glass to me. "By George. She's got roast chicken, at any rate."

I sit in the glow of the evening light, not talking much but eating and listening to Iris and Nathaniel chat. They tell me stories about Eddie and Trish, about when they tried to buy the local church and turn it into a guest cottage, and I can't help laughing. Nathaniel outlines his plans for the Geigers' garden and draws a sketch of the avenue of limes he created at Marchant House. When he gets animated he draws more and more quickly, his hand dwarfing the stub of pencil he's using. Iris notices me watching in admiration and points out a watercolor of the village pond, hanging on the wall.

"Ben did that." She nods toward Nathaniel. "He takes after his father."

The atmosphere is so relaxed and easy, so different from any meal I've ever had at home. No one's on the phone. No one's rushing to get anywhere else. I could sit here all night.

As the meal is finally drawing to a close I clear my throat. "Iris, I just want to say thank you again."

"I enjoyed it." Iris takes a forkful of plum crumble. "I always did enjoy bossing people about."

"But really. I'm so grateful. I don't know what I would have done without your help. Is there any way I can repay you?"

"Don't be ridiculous!" Iris takes a sip of wine and dabs her mouth. "Next weekend we'll make lasagne. And gnocchi!"

"*Next* weekend?" I stare at her. "But—"

"You don't think you've finished? I've only just started on you!"

"But . . . I can't take up all your weekends . . ."

"I'm not graduating you yet," she says with a cheerful asperity. "So you have no choice. Now, what else do you need help with? Cleaning? Washing?"

I feel a twinge of embarrassment. She clearly knows exactly how much of a mess I got myself into the other day.

"I'm not really sure how to use the washing machine," I admit at last.

"We'll cover that." She nods. "I'll pop up to the house when they're out and have a look at it."

"And I can't sew on buttons."

"Buttons . . ." She reaches for a piece of paper and a pencil, and writes it down, still munching on the crumble. "I suppose you can't hem either."

"Er . . ."

"Hemming . . ." She scribbles it down. "What about ironing?" She looks up, suddenly alert. "You must have had to iron. How did you wriggle out of that one?"

"I'm sending the clothes out to Stacey Nicholson," I confess. "In the village. She charges three pounds a shirt."

"Stacey Nicholson?" Iris puts her pencil down. "That flibbertigibbet?"

"In her ad she said she was an experienced laundress."

"She's fifteen years old!" Galvanized, Iris pushes back her chair. "Samantha, you are *not* paying Stacey Nicholson to do your ironing. You're going to learn how to do it yourself."

"But I've never—"

"I'll teach you. Anyone can iron." She reaches into a little side room, pulls out an old ironing board covered in flowery material, and sets it up, then beckons me over. "What do you have to iron?"

"Mr. Geiger's shirts, mainly," I say, nervously joining her at the ironing board.

"All right." She plugs in an iron and turns the dial. "Hot, for cotton. Wait for the iron to heat up. No point beginning till it's at the right temperature. Now, I'll show you the right way to tackle a shirt. . . ."

She rootles, frowning, in a pile of clean laundry in the little room. "Shirts . . . shirts . . . Nathaniel, take off your shirt a moment."

I stiffen. As I glance at Nathaniel I see he has stiffened too.

"Mum!" He gives an awkward laugh.

"Oh, don't be ridiculous, love," says Iris impatiently. "You can take off your shirt for a moment. No one's embarrassed. You're not embarrassed, are you, Samantha?"

"Um . . ." My voice is a little grainy for some reason. "Um . . . no, of course not."

"Now, this is your steam." She presses a button on the iron and a jet of steam shoots into the air. "Always check that your steam compartment has water. . . . Nathaniel! I'm waiting!"

Through the steam I can see Nathaniel slowly unbuttoning his shirt. I catch a flash of smooth tanned skin and hastily lower my gaze.

Let's not be adolescent about this. So he's taking off his shirt. It's no big deal.

He tosses the shirt to his mother, who catches it deftly. My eyes are studiously fixed downward.

I'm *not* going to look at him.

"Start with the collar." Iris is smoothing the shirt out on the ironing board. "Now, you don't have to press hard." She guides my hand as the iron glides over the fabric. "Keep a smooth touch . . ."

This is ridiculous. I'm an adult, mature woman. I can look at a man with no shirt on without falling to bits. What I'll do is . . . take a casual peek. And get this out of my mind.

"Now the yoke . . ." Iris turns the shirt around on the board and I start pressing again. "Very good . . . onto the cuffs now . . ."

I lift the shirttail to flip it over—and as I do so, accidentally-on-purpose raise my eyes.

Sweet Jesus.

I'm not sure the whole getting-it-out-of-my-mind plan is going to work after all.

"Samantha?" Iris grabs the iron from my hand. "You're scorching the shirt!"

"Oh!" I come to. "Sorry. I . . . I lost concentration for a moment."

"Your cheeks seem very flushed." Iris puts a curious hand to my cheek. "Are you all right, sweetie?"

"Must be the . . . um . . . steam." I start ironing again, my face like a furnace. "I'm fine. Thanks."

At last I shake out his ironed shirt, perfectly done with all the creases in the right places.

"Very good!" says Iris, applauding. "After some practice you'll be able to do that in four minutes flat."

"Looks great." Nathaniel smiles, holding out a hand. "Thanks."

"That's OK!" I manage in a strangled squawk, and hastily look away again, my heart thumping.

Great. Just great. One glimpse of his body and I have a full-blown crush.

I honestly thought I was a bit deeper than that.

Thirteen

He doesn't have a girlfriend.

I managed to get that information out of Trish on Sunday night, under the guise of asking about all the neighbors. There was some girl in Gloucester, apparently—but that was all over months ago. The way is clear. I just need a strategy.

As I shower and get dressed the next morning, I'm totally fixated by thoughts of Nathaniel. I'm aware I've reverted to the behavior of a fourteen-year-old, that next I'll be doodling *Samantha loves Nathaniel* with a love heart dotting the i. But I don't care. It's not as though being a mature, levelheaded professional was working out so great for me.

I brush my hair, looking out at the misty green fields, and feel inexplicably lighthearted. I have no reason to feel this way. On paper, everything is still catastrophic. My fast-track career is over. My family has no idea where I am. I'm earning a fraction of what I used to, for a job that involves picking up other people's dirty underwear off the floor.

And yet I find myself humming as I straighten my bed.

My life has changed, and I'm changing with it. It's as if the old conventional monochrome Samantha has faded away into a paper doll. I've thrown her into the water and she's melting away to nothing. And in her place is a new me. A me with possibilities.

I've never gone after a man before. But then, until yesterday I'd never basted a chicken before. If I can do that, I can ask a man out, surely? The old Samantha would have sat back and waited to be approached. Well, not the new Samantha. I've seen the dating shows on TV; I know the rules. It's all about looks and body language and flirty conversation.

I walk over to the mirror and, for the first time since I've arrived here, examine my appearance with an honest, unflinching eye.

At once I regret it. Ignorance was better.

For a start, *how* can anyone look good in a blue nylon overall? I reach for a belt, fasten it around my middle, and hitch up my overall till the skirt is about three inches shorter, like we used to at school.

"Hi," I say to my reflection, and casually toss back my hair. "Hi, Nathaniel. Hi, Nat."

All I need now is lots of black eyeliner badly applied, and I'll be back to my fourteen-year-old self in every single way.

I reach for my makeup bag and spend about ten minutes alternately applying and removing makeup, until I've got something that looks natural and subtle, yet defined. Or else like I've wasted ten minutes. I have no idea.

Now to the body language. I wrinkle up my fore-head, trying to remember the rules from TV. If a woman is attracted to a man, her pupils will dilate. Also, she will unconsciously lean forward, laugh at his jokes, and expose her wrists and palms.

Experimentally I lean toward my reflection, holding out my hands as I do so.

I look like Jesus.

I try adding a flirty laugh. "Ha ha ha!" I exclaim aloud. "You just crack me up!"

Now I look like a cheerful Jesus.

I'm really not sure this is adding to my chances.

I head downstairs and draw back the curtains, letting in the bright morning sunshine. I'm picking up the post from the doormat when the doorbell rings. A guy in uniform, holding a clipboard, is standing outside, a van behind him in the drive. "Delivery from Professional Chef's Equipment Direct," he says. "Where shall I put the boxes?"

"Oh, right," I say apprehensively. "In the kitchen, please. Thanks."

Professional Chef's Equipment. I guess that would be for me, the Professional Chef.

"What's that van, Samantha?" calls Trish, tottering down the stairs in a dressing gown and high-heeled mules. "Is it flowers?"

"It's the cookery equipment you ordered for me!" Somehow I summon up an enthusiastic front.

"Oh, *good*!" Trish is delighted. "Now you'll be able to stun us with your cooking! It's roasted sea bream with julienned vegetables tonight, isn't it?"

"Er . . . yes!" I gulp. "I suppose it is."

"Mind your backs!"

We both jump aside as two deliverymen troop past with boxes stacked high in their arms. I follow them into the kitchen and watch the growing pile in disbelief.

"Now, we bought you *everything*," says Trish, as though reading my mind. "Go on! Open them! I'm sure you can't wait!"

I fetch a knife and start unpacking the first box, while Trish slits the plastic on another. Out of the profusion of foam peanuts and bubble wrap, I lift a gleaming stainless-steel...something. What on earth is this? I glance quickly at the label on the side of the box. *Savarin Mold.*

"A...savarin mold!" I exclaim. "How marvelous. Just what I...wanted."

"We only got *eight* of those," says Trish, with concern. "Is that enough?"

"Er..." I look at it helplessly. "That should be plenty."

"Now, the saucepans." Trish has ripped open a box of shiny aluminum pans and holds out one to me expectantly. "We were told these were the very *best* quality. Would you agree? As a trained chef?"

"Let's just have a look," I say, trying to sound professional. I heft the saucepan appraisingly, then study the bottom and, for good measure, ping the surface with my fingernail.

"Yes, that's a nice-quality pan," I say at last. "You chose well."

"Oh, *good*!" Trish beams, delving into another box. "And look at *this*!" She scatters foam to reveal a weird-shaped gadget with a wooden handle. "I've never even *seen* one of these! What is it, Samantha?"

Yikes. What's that? It looks like a cross between a sieve, a grater, and a whisk. I glance quickly at the box for clues, but the label has been torn off.

"What is it?" says Trish again.

"This is used for a highly specialized cooking technique," I say at last. "Highly specialized."

"What do you *do* with it? Show me!" She thrusts the handle at me.

"Well." I take the thing from her. "It's a kind of . . . whisking . . . circular motion . . . keep the wrist light . . ." I beat the air briskly a few times. "Kind of like that. It's difficult to show properly without the . . . um . . . truffles."

"So what's it called?" says Trish, agog.

"I've always known it as a . . . truffle beater," I say at last. "But it could have some . . . other name as well. Why don't I make you a cup of coffee?" I add quickly. "And I'll unpack everything else later."

I switch on the kettle, reach for the coffeepot, and glance out the window. Nathaniel is striding across the lawn.

Oh, God. Full crush alert. Full, one hundred percent, old-fashioned adolescent crush.

I cannot take my eyes off him. The sunlight is catching the ends of his tawny hair and he's wearing ancient, faded jeans. As I watch, he picks up some huge sack of something, swings it round easily, and throws it onto something that might be a compost heap.

My mind is suddenly filled with a fantasy of him picking me up in exactly the same way. Swinging me round easily in his big strong arms. I mean, I can't be *that* much heavier than a sack of potatoes—

"So, how was your weekend off, Samantha?" Trish breaks my thoughts. "We barely saw you! Did you go into town?"

"I went to Nathaniel's house," I reply without thinking.

"Nathaniel?" Trish sounds astonished. "The *gardener*? Why?"

Immediately I realize my huge mistake. I can't exactly say, "To have cooking lessons." I try to fabricate an instant, convincing reason.

"Just . . . to say hello, really," I say at last, aware that I sound tongue-tied. And also that my cheeks are turning pink.

Trish's face suddenly snaps in comprehension and her eyes open very wide.

"Oh, I *see*," she says. "How *adorable*!"

"No!" I say quickly. "It's not . . . Honestly—"

"Don't worry!" Trish cuts me off emphatically. "I won't say a *word*. I am discretion itself." She puts a finger to her lips. "You can rely on me."

Before I can say anything else she picks up her coffee and heads out of the kitchen. I sit down amid all the kitchen stuff and packaging and fiddle with the truffle beater.

That was awkward. But I suppose it doesn't really matter. As long as she doesn't say anything inappropriate to Nathaniel.

Then I realize I'm being stupid. Of *course* she'll say something inappropriate to Nathaniel. She'll make some oh-so-subtle innuendo, and then who knows what he'll think. This could be really embarrassing. This could ruin everything.

I must go and make the situation quite clear to him. That Trish misunderstood me, and I do *not* have a crush on him.

While, obviously, making it clear that I do.

I force myself to wait until I've done breakfast for Trish and Eddie, tidied the new kitchen equipment away, mixed up some olive oil and lemon zest, and put tonight's sea bream fillets into it, just as Iris taught me.

Then I hitch up my uniform a bit more, add some more eyeliner for luck, and head out into the garden, holding a basket I found in the larder. If Trish wants to know what I'm doing, I'm gathering herbs for cooking.

I find Nathaniel in the orchard behind the old wall, standing on a ladder, tying some rope round a tree. As I make my way toward him I'm ridiculously nervous. My mouth feels dry—and did my legs just *wobble*?

God, you'd think I'd have some poise. You'd think being a lawyer for seven years would have prepared me a bit better. Ignoring my jitters as best I can, I walk up to the ladder, toss back my hair, and wave up to him, trying not to squint in the sun.

"Hi!"

"Hi." Nathaniel smiles back. "How's it going?"

"Fine, thanks! Much better. No disasters yet . . ."

There's a pause. I suddenly realize I'm gazing a little too hard at his hands as they tighten the rope. "I was just after some . . . rosemary." I gesture to my basket. "If you have any?"

"Sure. I'll cut you some." He jumps down off the ladder and we walk along the path toward the herb garden.

It's totally silent, down here away from the house, apart from the odd buzzing insect and the crunch of gravel on the path. I try to think of something light and easy to say, but my brain is blank.

"It's . . . hot," I manage at last.

"Uh-huh." Nathaniel nods, and steps up easily over the stone wall into the herb garden. I try to follow him with a light springing step and catch my foot on the wall. Ow. Fuck.

"All right?" Nathaniel turns.

"Fine!" Even though my foot is throbbing with agony. "Wow. This is amazing!" I look around the garden in genuine admiration. It's laid out in a hexagonal shape, with little paths between the sections. Tiny dark green hedges act as borders, and topiary spheres mark the corners. Lavender stems are gently waving in old stone planters, interspersed with tubs of some tiny white flower that smells of honey.

"Did you do all this?" I peer at a bed of plants that I think might be oregano. "It's absolutely stunning!"

"Thanks. I'm pleased with it." Nathaniel sounds off-hand but I can tell he's gratified. "Anyway. Your rosemary."

He pulls out a pair of secateurs from an old leather holster-type thing and starts clipping at a dark green, spiky bush.

OK. I have to say what I've come to say.

"So . . . um . . . it's really weird," I begin as lightly as I can, fingering the scented leaves of some bushy plant. "But Trish seems to have got the wrong idea about us! She seems to think we're . . . you know."

"Ah." He nods, his face averted.

"Which is obviously . . . ridiculous!" I add.

"Mm-hmm." He clips some more rosemary sprigs and holds them up. "This enough for you?"

Mm-hmm? That's it? That's all he has to say on the subject?

"Actually, I'd like some more," I say, and he turns back to the bush. "So . . . isn't it ridiculous?" I add, trying to prod him into a proper answer.

"Well, of course." At last Nathaniel looks at me properly. "You won't be wanting to get into anything for a while. Not so soon after a bad relationship."

I look at him blankly. What on earth—

Oh, yes. My bad relationship.

"Right," I say after a pause. "Yes, that."

Dammit.

Why did I go along with the bad relationship story? What was I *thinking*?

"Here's your rosemary." Nathaniel puts a fragrant bundle into my arms. "Anything else?"

"Um . . . yes!" I say quickly. "Could I have some mint?"

I watch as he moves carefully over the rows of herbs to where mint is growing in large stone containers.

"Actually . . ." I force myself to sound careless. "Actually, the relationship wasn't *that* bad. In fact, I think I've pretty much got over it."

Nathaniel looks up, shading his eyes against the sun. "You've got over a seven-year relationship in a week?"

Now that he puts it like that, it does sound a bit implausible. I cast around quickly in my mind.

"I have great reserves of resilience," I say at last. "I'm like . . . rubber."

"Rubber," he echoes, his expression unreadable.

Was *rubber* a bad choice of word? No. Come on, rubber is sexy.

Nathaniel adds the mint to the rosemary in my arms. "Mum said . . ." He pauses awkwardly.

"What?" I say, a little breathless. They've been talking about me?

"Mum wondered if you'd been . . . badly treated." He shifts his gaze away. "You're so tense and twitchy."

"I'm not tense and twitchy!" I retort at once.

Well, maybe that was a little tense and twitchy.

"I'm naturally twitchy," I explain. "But I wasn't badly treated or anything like that. I was just . . . I always felt . . . trapped."

The word comes out to my own surprise. I have a flash of my life at Carter Spink. Constantly at the beck and call of senior partners. Practically living at the office some weeks. Taking piles of work home with me.

Answering e-mails at every hour. Maybe I did feel a little bit trapped.

"But I'm fine now." I shake back my hair. "Ready to move on...and start a new relationship...or something more casual...whatever."

I gaze up at him, trying as hard as I can to dilate my pupils and casually lifting my hand to my ear for good measure. There's a still, tense silence, broken only by the buzzing of insects.

"You probably shouldn't rush into anything new," Nathaniel says. He moves away without meeting my eye and starts examining the leaves on a shrub.

There's a stiffness in his back. I feel a rush of blood to my face. He's letting me down lightly. He doesn't want to go out with me.

Aargh. This is hideous. Here I am, with my hitched-up skirt and eyeliner, employing all the body language I know, basically just *offering* myself to him. And he's trying to let me know he's not interested.

I'm mortified. I have to get away from here. From him.

"You're right," I say, flustered. "It's...far too soon to think about anything like that. In fact, it would be a terrible idea. I'm just going to focus on my new job. Cooking and...and...so forth. I must get on. Thanks for the herbs."

"Anytime," says Nathaniel.

"Yes. Well. I'll see you."

Clasping the bundle more tightly, I turn on my heel, step over the wall, managing not to bash my foot this time, and stride back along the gravel path up to the house.

I am *beyond* embarrassed. So much for a whole new Samantha.

That is the last time I ever go after a man, ever. My

original strategy of waiting politely, being ignored, and then being passed over for someone else was a million times better.

Anyway. I don't care. It's for the best, really. Because I *do* have to concentrate on my work. As soon as I get back to the house I set up the ironing board, plug in the iron, turn on the radio, and make a nice strong cup of coffee. This is going to be my focus from now on. Getting my tasks for the day done. Not some ridiculous crush on the gardener. I'm being paid to do a job here and I'm going to do it.

By midmorning I've ironed ten shirts, put a load of laundry on, and hoovered the conservatory. By lunchtime, I've dusted and hoovered all the downstairs rooms and polished all the mirrors with vinegar. By teatime, I've put on another load of laundry, shredded my vegetables in the food processor, measured out the wild rice to be steamed, and carefully prepared four filo pastry cases for my *tartes de fruits,* as Iris taught me.

By seven o'clock I've thrown away one lot of burned filo cases, baked another four, topped them with strawberries, and finished with heated-up apricot jam. I've pan-fried the vegetable shreds in olive oil and garlic till they're soft. I've blanched my French beans. I've put the sea bream in the oven. I've also taken more than a few sips of vermouth meant for the coulis, but that's neither here nor there.

My face is bright red and my heart is beating fast and I'm moving round the kitchen in a kind of speeded-up reality—but I kind of feel OK. In fact, I almost feel exhilarated. Here I am, actually cooking a meal all on my own—and I'm just about on top of it! Apart from the mushroom fiasco. But they're safely in the bin.

I've laid the dining table with the Minton china and put candles in the silver candlesticks. I've got a bottle of Prosecco waiting in the fridge and heated plates waiting in the oven, and I've even put Trish's CD of Enrique Iglesias love songs in the player. I feel like I'm throwing my first dinner party.

With a pleasant flutter in my stomach, I smooth down my apron and push open the kitchen door. "Mrs. Geiger? Mr. Geiger?"

What I need is a big gong.

"Mrs. Geiger?" I try again.

There's absolutely no reply. I would have thought they'd be hovering around the kitchen by now. I fetch a glass and a fork and tinkle one loudly in the other.

Nothing. Where *are* they?

I investigate the rooms on the ground floor, but they're all empty. Cautiously, I advance up the stairs.

Maybe they're having a *Joy of Sex* moment. Should I retreat?

"Er . . . Mrs. Geiger?" I call hesitantly. "Dinner's served."

I can hear voices from the end of the corridor, as I take a few more steps forward. "Mrs. Geiger?"

Suddenly the bedroom door is violently flung open.

"What's money *for*?" comes Trish's shrill voice. "Just tell me that!"

"I don't need to tell you what money's for!" Eddie is yelling back. "Never have!"

"If you understood *anything*—"

"I understand!" Eddie sounds apoplectic. "Don't tell me I don't understand!"

Ooooookay. So probably not a *Joy of Sex* moment. I start backing away silently on tiptoe—but it's too late.

"What about *Portugal*?" Trish shrieks. "Do you remember *that*?" She strides out of the room in a whirlwind of pink and stops short as she sees me.

"Um . . . dinner's ready," I mumble, my eyes fixed on the carpet. "Madam."

"If you mention *bloody* Portugal one more *bloody* time—" Eddie comes marching out of the room.

"Eddie!" Trish cuts him off savagely, then gives a tiny nod toward me. *"Pas devant."*

"What?" says Eddie, scowling.

"Pas devant! Les . . . les . . ." She wheels her hands, as though trying to conjure the missing word.

"Domestiques?" I offer awkwardly.

Trish shoots me a flinty look, then draws herself up with dignity. "I shall be in my room."

"It's my bloody room too!" says Eddie furiously, but the door has already banged shut.

"Erm . . . I've made dinner . . ." I venture, but Eddie stalks to the stairs, ignoring me.

I feel a swell of dismay. If the sea bream isn't eaten soon it'll get all shriveled.

"Mrs. Geiger?" I knock on her door. "I'm just worried the dinner will spoil—"

"So what?" comes back her muffled voice. "I'm not in the mood for eating."

I stare at the door in disbelief. I've spent all bloody day cooking dinner for them. It's all ready. The candles are lit, the plates are in the oven. They can't just not eat it.

"You *have* to eat!" I cry out, and Eddie stops, halfway down the stairs. The bedroom door opens, and Trish looks out in astonishment.

"What?" she says.

OK. Play this one carefully.

"Everyone has to eat," I improvise. "It's a human need. So why not discuss your differences over a meal? Or put them on hold! Have a glass of wine and relax and agree not to mention . . . er . . . Portugal."

As I say the word, I can feel their hackles rising.

"I'm not the one who mentioned it," growls Eddie. "I thought the subject was closed."

"I only mentioned it because you were so *insensitive*." Trish brushes a sudden tear from her eye. "How do you think *I* feel, being your . . . trophy wife?"

Trophy?

I must not laugh.

"Trish." To my astonishment, Eddie is hurrying up the stairs. "Don't you *ever* say that." He grips her shoulders and looks her fiercely in the eye. "We've always been a partnership. You know that. Ever since Sydenham."

First Portugal, now Sydenham. One day I have to sit Trish down with a bottle of wine and coax her entire life history out of her.

"I know," whispers Trish.

She's gazing up at Eddie as though no one else exists, and I suddenly feel a little pang. They really are in love. I can see the antagonism slowly melting away in their eyes. It's like witnessing a chemical reaction in a test tube.

"Let's go and eat," says Eddie finally. "Samantha was right. We should have a nice meal together. Sit down and talk it over."

Thank God for that. The sea bream will still be just about OK. . . . I only need to put the sauce in a jug.

"All right, let's." Trish sniffs. "Samantha, we'll be out to dinner tonight."

My smile freezes on my face.

"Don't worry about cooking for us," puts in Eddie, giving me a jovial pat. "You can have a night off!"

What?

"But . . . I've cooked!" I say quickly. "It's done!"

"Oh. Well . . . never mind." Trish makes a vague dismissive gesture with her hand. "Eat it yourself."

No. No. They cannot do this to me.

"But it's all ready for you downstairs! Roasted fish . . . and julienned vegetables . . ."

"Where shall we go?" says Trish to Eddie, not listening to a word. "Shall we try and get in at The Mill House?"

As I stand there in stupefaction, she disappears into the bedroom, followed by Eddie. The door closes and I'm left on the landing.

My dinner party's ruined.

When they've roared out of the drive in Eddie's Porsche, I go into the dining room and slowly clear everything up. I put away the crystal glasses and fold up the napkins and blow out the candles. Then I head back into the kitchen and look for a moment at all my dishes, set out ready for action. My sauce, bubbling away on the hob. My carved lemon-slice garnishes. I was so proud of everything.

Well, there's nothing I can do about it.

My sea bream are looking pretty sorry for themselves, but I slip one onto a plate anyway and pour myself a glass of wine. I sit at the table, cut myself a piece, and raise it to my mouth. Then I put my knife and fork down without even tasting it. I'm not hungry.

A whole wasted afternoon. And tomorrow I've got to do it all over again. The thought makes me feel like sinking my head down onto my arms and never looking up again.

What am I doing here?

I mean, really. What am I doing? Why am I not walking out right now and getting on a train back to London?

As I'm slumped there I become aware of a faint tapping at the open door, and I look up to see Nathaniel leaning in the door frame, holding his rucksack. Remembering this morning's encounter, I feel a flash of embarrassment. Without quite meaning to, I swivel my chair away slightly and fold my arms.

"Hi," I say, with a tiny If-you-think-I'm-interested-in-you-you're-*much*-mistaken shrug.

"I thought I'd come and see if you needed any help." His eyes travel around the kitchen, at the dishes of untouched food. "What happened?"

"They didn't eat it. They went out to dinner."

Nathaniel stares at me for a moment, then shakes his head. "After you spent all day cooking for them?"

"It's their food. Their house. They can do what they like."

I'm trying to sound careless and matter-of-fact. But the disappointment remains heavy inside me. Nathaniel puts down his rucksack and inspects the sea bream. "Looks good."

"It looks like congealed, overcooked fish," I correct him.

"My favorite." He grins, but I'm not in the mood for his good humor.

"Have some, then." I gesture at the dish. "No one else is going to eat it."

"Well, then. Shame to waste it." He helps himself to everything, piling his plate ludicrously high, then pours himself a glass of wine and sits down opposite me at the table.

"To you." Nathaniel raises his glass. "Congratulations."

"Yeah, right."

"Seriously, Samantha." He waits patiently until I drag my eyes up from the floor. "Whether they ate it or not, this is a real achievement. I mean, bloody hell. Remember the last dinner you cooked in this kitchen?"

I give a reluctant smile. "The lamb of doom, you mean."

"The *chickpeas*. I'll never forget those." He takes a bite of fish. "This is good, by the way."

An image comes to me of those tiny blackened bullets; myself running around in a frenzy; the meringue dripping on the floor...and in spite of everything I want to giggle. I've already learned so much since then.

"Well, of course, I'd have been OK that night," I say nonchalantly. "If you hadn't insisted on *helping* me. I had it all under control till you got in my way."

Nathaniel puts his fork down, still munching, his blue eyes crinkled up with something—amusement, maybe. I can feel the telltale heat rising in my cheeks, and as I glance downward I notice that my hands are resting on the table, palms up.

And I'm leaning forward, I realize in sudden horror. My pupils are probably half a mile wide too. My body language could not be any clearer if I wrote *I fancy you* in felt-tip on my forehead.

I hastily remove my hands to my lap, sit up straight, and adopt a stony expression. I haven't got over this morning's mortification. In fact, I might take the opportunity to regain my equilibrium.

"So—" I begin, just as Nathaniel starts speaking too.

"Go on." He takes another bite of fish. "After you."

"Well." I clear my throat. "After our...conversation this morning. I was just going to say that you're quite right about relationships. Obviously I'm not ready for anything new yet. Or even interested. At all."

There. At least I've salvaged my dignity a little.

"What were you going to say?" I ask, pouring more wine into his glass.

"I was going to ask you out," says Nathaniel, and I nearly flood the table with wine.

He what?

The body language *worked*?

"But not to worry." He takes a gulp of wine. "I understand."

Backtrack. I need to backtrack, very, very quickly. Yet subtly, so he doesn't actually *notice* I'm backtracking.

Oh, bugger it, I'll just be inconsistent. I'm a woman, I'm allowed to be.

"Nathaniel," I force myself to say calmly. "I'd love to go out with you."

"Good." He looks unperturbed. "How's Friday night?"

"Perfect."

As I grin back, I suddenly realize I'm hungry. I pull my plate of sea bream toward me, pick up my knife and fork, and begin to eat.

Fourteen

I get to Friday morning without any major calamities. At least, none that the Geigers know about.

There was the vegetable-risotto disaster on Tuesday— but thank God I managed to get a last-minute substitute from the caterers. There was a peach camisole that, in hindsight, should have been ironed on a lower setting. There was the Dartington vase that I broke while trying to dust with the vacuum-cleaner attachment. But no one seems to have noticed it's gone yet. And the new one should arrive tomorrow.

So far, this week has cost me only two hundred pounds, which is a vast improvement on last week. I may even start making a profit before too long.

I'm putting Eddie's damp underwear in the dryer, averting my eyes as best I can, when I hear Trish calling me.

"Samantha! Where *are* you?" She doesn't sound pleased. What's she discovered? "I *can't* have you walking around like that anymore." Trish arrives at the door of the utility room, shaking her head vigorously.

"I'm sorry?" I peer at her.

"Your *hair*." She makes a face.

"Oh, right." I touch the bleached patch with a grimace. "I meant to get it done at the weekend—"

"You're having it done now," she cuts across me. "My *super* hairdresser's here."

"Now?" I stare at her. "But . . . I've got vacuuming to do."

"I'm not having you walk around like a fright anymore. You can make up the hours later. Come on. Annabel's waiting!"

I guess I have no choice. I dump the rest of Eddie's underpants in the dryer, switch it on, and follow her up the stairs.

"Now, I've been meaning to mention my cashmere cardigan," Trish adds sternly as we reach the top. "The cream one?"

Shit. Shit. She's found out I replaced it. Of course she has. I should have known she couldn't be that stupid—

"I don't know what you've done to it." Trish pushes open her bedroom door. "But it looks *marvelous*. That little ink stain on the hem has completely disappeared! It's like new!"

"Right." I give a smile of relief. "Well . . . all part of the service!"

I follow Trish into the bedroom, where a thin woman with big blond hair, white jeans, and a gold chain belt is setting up a chair in the middle of the floor.

"Hello!" She looks up, cigarette in hand, and I realize that she's about sixty years old. "Samantha. I've heard *all* about you."

Her voice is gravelly, her mouth is pursed with lines,

and her makeup looks like it's been welded to her skin. She comes forward, surveys my hair, and winces.

"What's all this? Thought you'd try the streaky look?" She gives a raucous laugh at her own joke.

"It was a . . . bleach accident."

"Accident!" She runs her fingers through my hair, tsking all the while. "Well, it can't stay this color. We'd better go a nice blond. You don't mind going blond, do you, dear?"

Blond?

"I've never been blond," I say in alarm. "I'm not really sure—"

"You've got the coloring for it." She's brushing my hair out.

"Well, as long as it's not *too* blond," I say hurriedly. "Not . . . you know, that fake, tarty, platinum blond . . ."

I trail off as I realize that the other two women in the room have fake, tarty, platinum-blond hair.

"Or . . . um . . ." I swallow. "Whatever you think. Really."

I sit down on the chair, wrap a towel around my shoulders, and try not to flinch as Annabel briskly pastes some chemical-smelling goo on my head and layers in what feels like a thousand bits of silver foil.

Blond. Yellow hair. Barbie dolls.

Oh, God. What am I *doing*?

"I think this was a mistake," I say abruptly, trying to get out of my chair. "I don't think I'm a natural blonde—"

"Relax!" Annabel clamps down on my shoulders, forcing me back into my seat, and puts a magazine in my hand. Behind, Trish is opening a bottle of champagne. "You'll look lovely. Pretty girl like you should *do* something with her hair. Now, read us our signs."

"Signs?" I say in bewilderment.

"Horoscopes!" Annabel tsks again. "Not the brightest penny, is she?" she adds in an undertone to Trish.

"She is a little dim," Trish murmurs back discreetly. "But *marvelous* at laundry."

So this is what being a lady of leisure is like. Sitting with foil in your hair, drinking Buck's Fizz, and reading glossy magazines. I haven't read any magazines except *The Lawyer* since I was about thirteen. Normally I spend my hairdresser's appointments typing e-mails or reading contracts.

But I simply can't relax. By the time Annabel is blow-drying my hair, my entire body is seized up in fear.

I can't be blond. It's just not who I am.

"There we are!" Annabel gives a final blast and switches the hair dryer off. There's silence. I can't open my eyes.

"*Much* better!" Trish says approvingly.

I slowly open one eye. Then the other.

My hair isn't blond. It's caramel. It's warm caramel with streaks of honey and the tiniest threads of gold. As I move my head it shimmers.

I think I might cry.

"You didn't believe me, did you?" Annabel raises her eyebrows at me in the mirror, a satisfied smile at her lips. "Thought I didn't know what I was doing?"

She can so obviously read my mind, I feel abashed.

"It's wonderful," I say, finding my voice. "I'm . . . Thank you so much."

I'm entranced by my reflection, by my new, glowing, caramel, honey self. I look alive. I look *colorful*.

I'm never going back to the way I looked before. Never.

My pleasure doesn't fade. Even when I've gone downstairs again and am pushing the Hoover round the drawing room, I'm totally preoccupied by my new hair. As I pass any shiny surface, I stop to admire myself and flick up my hair so it cascades back down in a caramelly shower.

Vacuum under the rug. *Flick*. Vacuum under the coffee table. *Flick. Flick*.

It never even *occurred* to me to dye my hair before. What else have I been missing out on?

"Ah, Samantha." I look up to see Eddie coming into the room, wearing a navy jacket and tie. "I'm having a meeting in the dining room. I'd like you to make some coffee and bring it in to my guests."

"Yes, sir." I curtsy. "How many of you are there?"

"Four altogether. And some biscuits. Snacks. Whatever."

"Of course."

Huh. He didn't even *notice* my hair. In fact, he looks hyped up and red in the face. I wonder what this meeting is. As I head to the kitchen I glance curiously out the front window and see an unfamiliar red Mercedes Series 5 parked in the drive, next to a silver convertible BMW and a dark green Rover.

Hmm. Probably not the local vicar, then. Maybe it's something to do with his company.

I make a pot of coffee, put it on a tray, add a plate of biscuits and some muffins I bought for tea. Then I head to the dining room and knock.

"Come in!"

I push the door open to see Eddie sitting with three men in suits, around the dining-room table, each with a thick, open file before him. Sitting beside Eddie is a plumpish man in a soft brown jacket and horn-rimmed glasses. Directly opposite him is a guy with chiseled, good-looking features, wearing an expensive-looking suit.

"So just a few amendments," the chiseled man is saying as I approach the table. "Nothing that should concern anyone!"

"Your coffee," I murmur in deferential tones.

"Thank you, Samantha." Eddie looks puffed up, like the lord of the manor. "If you could serve it out?"

I put the tray down on the sideboard and distribute the cups among the men. As I'm doing so I can't help glancing at the papers on the table—and immediately recognize them as contracts.

"Er . . . white or black?" I say to a burly, red-haired guy in a blazer.

"White, thanks." He doesn't even acknowledge me. While I pour the coffee, I have another casual look. It looks like some kind of property investment deal. Is Eddie sinking his money into something?

"Biscuit?" I offer.

"I'm sweet enough." The red-haired man bares his teeth in a grin. What an asshole.

"So, Eddie. You understand that point now?" The chiseled-looking man is speaking, his voice dripping with concern.

I recognize this man. Not his face—but I know him. I worked with people like this for seven years. And I know instinctively that this man doesn't care two jots whether Eddie understands.

"Yes!" says Eddie. "Yes, of course." He peers at the contract uncertainly, then looks at the man in the brown jacket next to him. "Martin?"

"Let's just have a look," replies Martin. He starts

perusing the document, nodding every so often. I guess he must be Eddie's lawyer.

"We're as concerned about security as you are," says the chiseled man, with a smile.

"When it comes to money, who isn't?" quips the red-haired guy.

OK. What exactly is going on here? Why am I suspicious?

As I move round to the chiseled-looking man and pour his coffee, the contract is clearly visible and I run my eyes down it with a practiced speed. It's a property-development partnership. Both sides putting up money... residential development... so far so standard... It looks fine.

I pour out coffee for Eddie and have another quick scan, just to be sure.

And then I see something that makes me freeze in shock. A carefully worded, innocuous-looking little clause at the bottom of the page that commits Eddie to funding any shortfall. In one line. With no reciprocity.

If things go wrong... Eddie has to foot the bill. Does he *realize*?

Does his *lawyer* realize?

I'm totally aghast. My urge to reach for the contract and rip it up is almost overpowering. If this were at Carter Spink, these guys would not last two minutes. Not only would I throw their contract out, but I would recommend to my client that—

"Samantha?" I jerk back to reality to see Eddie frowning slightly at me. "Could you please serve Martin?"

I'm not at Carter Spink. I'm in a housekeeper's uniform and I have refreshments to serve.

I move round the table and pour out coffee for Martin, who is reading through the contract with not one sign of alarm. Hasn't he seen the clause?

"Chocolate biscuit?" I offer him the plate. "Or a muffin?"

"Ah!" His fleshy face lights up. "Now . . . let me see . . . they all look so good. . . ." His hand hovers over the plate.

I don't believe this. He's paying more attention to the muffins than he is to the contract. What kind of lawyer is this guy?

"So. Enough talk. The adventure begins." Mr. Chiseled is unscrewing the lid of a smart pen. "Ready?" He hands it to Eddie.

He's about to sign? *Now?*

"Everything OK by you?" says Eddie to Martin, whose mouth is now stuffed full of muffin.

"Take your time," Mr. Chiseled adds with a perfect-toothed smile. "If you'd like to read it through again . . ."

I feel a surge of sudden fury at these guys, with their flash cars and sharp suits and smooth voices. They are not going to rip off my boss. I'm not going to let it happen.

"Mr. Geiger," I say urgently. "Could I see you for a minute please? In private?"

Eddie looks up in annoyance.

"Samantha," he says with heavy humor. "I'm in the middle of rather important business here. Important to me, at any rate!" He glances round the table, and the three men laugh sycophantically.

"It's very urgent," I say. "It won't take long."

"Samantha—"

"Please, Mr. Geiger. I *need* to speak to you."

At last Eddie exhales in exasperation and puts down the pen.

"All right." He gets up and ushers me out of the room. "What is it?" he demands.

I stare back at him dumbly. Now I've got him out here I have no idea how to bring up the subject. What can I say?

Mr. Geiger, I would recommend reviewing clause 14.

Mr. Geiger, your liabilities are not sufficiently protected.

It's impossible. Who takes legal advice from their housekeeper?

His hand is on the doorknob. This is my last chance.

"Do you take sugar?" I blurt out.

"What?"

"I couldn't remember," I mumble. "And I didn't want to draw attention to your sugar consumption in public."

"Yes, I take one lump," says Eddie testily. "Is that all?"

"Well . . . yes, there was something else. It looks like you're signing some papers in there."

"That's right." He frowns. "Private papers."

"Of course!" I swallow. "I was just . . . remembering. You told me always to be very careful with legal documents."

Eddie laughs jovially.

"You don't need to worry. I'm not a fool. I do have a lawyer!"

"Um . . . yes, sir." I think quickly for another way. "Only I couldn't help thinking of a time that Lady Edgerly signed up to some kind of investment, I think it was. And afterward she said to me that she wished she'd got a second opinion."

I look into his eyes, willing the message to get through. *Consult a decent lawyer, you stupid schmuck.*

"Very thoughtful of you to be concerned, Samantha." Eddie gives me a pat on the shoulder, then opens the door and strides back in. "Where were we, gentlemen?"

I watch in dismay as he picks up the pen again. He's going to get fleeced.

But not if I can help it.

"Your coffee, Mr. Geiger," I murmur, hurrying into the room. I pick up the pot, start pouring, then accidentally-on-purpose drop it on the table.

"Aaargh!"

"Jesus!"

There's total mayhem as the coffee spreads in a dark brown lake over the table, soaking into papers and dripping onto the floor.

"The contracts!" shouts Mr. Chiseled in annoyance. "You stupid woman!"

"I'm really sorry," I say in my most flustered voice. "I'm really, really sorry. The coffeepot just . . . slipped." I start mopping the coffee with a tissue, making sure to spread it over all the remaining paperwork.

"Do we have any copies?" asks the red-haired man, and I look up, alert.

"They were all on the bloody table," says Mr. Chiseled in exasperation. "We'll have to get them printed out again." He looks at Eddie. "Can you make tomorrow?"

"Actually . . ." Eddie clears his throat. "Not tomorrow. I think I want a little more time. Just want to make sure it's all shipshape. Might even get another opinion, to be on the safe side. No offense, Martin!"

"None taken," said Martin amiably, reaching for a chocolate biscuit.

The visitors exchange looks.

"Of course," says the chiseled-looking man after a long pause. "No problem."

Ha! Something tells me this deal may not be happening after all.

"Your jacket, sir?" I say with a smile, handing it to him. "And again, I'm dreadfully, dreadfully sorry."

The great thing about legal training is it *really* teaches you to lie.

It also teaches you to put up with being yelled at by your boss. Which is handy, because as soon as Trish hears what I've done, I'm forced to stand in the kitchen for twenty minutes while she strides around, haranguing me.

"Mr. Geiger is putting together a very important business deal! That meeting was crucial!"

"I'm very sorry, madam," I say, eyes downcast.

"I know you have no understanding of these things, Samantha. But a lot of money is at stake! Money that you probably have no conception of."

Stay calm. Stay humble.

"A lot of money," Trish repeats, impressively.

She's *itching* to tell me more. I can see the urge to show off and the urge to remain discreet fighting it out on her face.

"*Seven figures,*" she says at last.

"Um . . . gosh." I do my best to look awestruck.

"We've been very good to you, Samantha. We've made *every* effort." Her voice throbs with resentment. "And we expect you to make every effort in return."

"I'm very sorry," I say for the millionth time, but Trish still seems dissatisfied.

"Well, I'll expect far more care tonight."

"Tonight?"

"At dinner." Trish raises her eyes skyward.

"But . . . I've got tonight off," I say in alarm. "You said it would be OK, I could leave you a cold supper . . ."

Trish has clearly forgotten all about our conversation.

"Well," she says querulously. "That was before you *threw* coffee over our guests. That was before you spent all morning sitting about, having your hair done."

What? That is so unfair I can't even find a response.

"Frankly, Samantha, I expect a little better. You will stay in tonight and serve dinner." She picks up a magazine and strides out of the kitchen.

I stare after her, a familiar, heavy resignation creeping over me. This has happened so many times in my life, I'm used to it. I'll have to call off my date with Nathaniel. Another date . . . another cancellation.

And then my thoughts stop mid-track. I'm not at Carter Spink anymore. I don't have to put up with this.

I stalk out of the kitchen and find Trish in the living room.

"Mrs. Geiger," I say as forcefully as I can. "I'm sorry about the coffee and I'll make every effort to do better. But I have to have tonight off. I've made arrangements—and I'm going to stick to them. I'll be going out at seven as planned."

My heart is beating fast as I finish. I've never asserted myself like that before in my life. If I'd ever spoken like that at Carter Spink I'd have been dead meat.

For a moment Trish looks livid. Then, to my astonishment, she gives an irritated click with her tongue and turns a page.

"Oh, very well. If it's *that* important—"

"Yes." I swallow. "It's important. My personal life is important."

As I say the words, I feel stirred up. I almost want to say something more to Trish. Something about priorities, about balance.

But Trish is already engrossed in an article on "The Red Wine Diet—How It Can Work for You." I'm not sure she'd appreciate being disturbed.

I'm putting the finishing touches to a cold roasted-vegetable salad for the Geigers' supper when Trish comes into the kitchen. She opens the fridge, peers into it, then closes the door, looking dissatisfied. She leans against the counter, watching me work, until I start feeling twitchy.

"Er . . . can I get you anything, Mrs. Geiger?"

"No, you just carry on." She picks up a vegetable parer and twirls it around in her hands.

"Um . . . Mrs. Geiger . . ." I gesture that I need the parer, and she hands it over with a tsk of irritation.

"You have such a simple life, Samantha," she says, with a sigh. "So . . . untroubled."

"Yes, madam," I say after a pause. *If you only knew . . .*

Trish moves to the window and gives another gusty sigh.

"Mr. Geiger will be out this evening. So you only need to make one cold supper."

"Um . . . right." I have the feeling that if I point out I've already made a salad for two, she'll bite my head off.

She definitely looks out of sorts, standing there, running her finger up and down the windowpane. Maybe I should make conversation.

"Nathaniel told me that you used to run a business, Mrs. Geiger," I say, carving strips off a huge chunk of Parmesan. "Road haulage? That must have been interesting."

"Oh, yes. It was our life."

"You must have worked hard," I prompt.

"We built it up from scratch, you know. Mr. Geiger and I." She suddenly looks animated. "By the end we had a staff of thirty. Contracts with every major supermarket chain in the country. You'll have seen our lorries on the road. Red with a black flash."

"Those are yours?" I feel a flash of genuine interest. "I've seen them on the motorway!"

"They *were* ours," corrects Trish. "We were made an extremely generous offer a few years ago. Which naturally . . . we took." All the animation has waned from her voice.

As I sprinkle torn basil over the plate, she gazes out the window again, her face rigid.

"And you don't ever think about . . . doing another job?" I venture.

"Samantha," says Trish, in her explaining-things-to-a-three-year-old voice. "Mr. Geiger and I have *made* our money. I am fortunate enough not to need to work."

"No, of course not," I say deferentially.

I grind black pepper onto the salad, remembering Trish's tears that day by the washing machine. I can't help feeling a bit sorry for her. She obviously has no idea what to do with all her time. And Eddie doesn't help, being out on the golf course all day.

"You know, Lady Edgerly didn't have a job either," I say casually as I put cling wrap over the salad dish and place it in the fridge. "But of course she kept busy with her charity work."

"Charity work?" echoes Trish after a pause. "What sort of charity work?"

"All sorts! Fund-raisers . . . charity lunches . . . She said if she hadn't had those to occupy her, she would have gone stir-crazy, doing nothing all day except filing her nails and having her hair done—although obviously that's nothing like you!" I backtrack as Trish turns around. "You've got . . . er . . . loads going on!"

"Absolutely." Trish lifts her chin defensively. "I have

many interests and . . . and . . . occupations. People envy me my full life, you know, Samantha."

"I'm . . . sure they do, madam. It was just a thought." I bob a curtsy and head out of the kitchen. At the door I glance back. Trish is still standing in exactly the same place.

Fifteen

By seven o'clock that evening, Trish's mood has un-
accountably transformed. Or maybe not so unaccount-
ably. I arrive downstairs in the hall to see her wandering
out of the living room with a cocktail glass, bloodshot
eyes, and a high color.

"So!" she says benevolently. "You're going out with
Nathaniel tonight."

"That's right." I glance at myself in the mirror. I've
gone for a fairly informal outfit. Jeans, nice simple top,
sandals.

"He's a very attractive young man." She eyes me in-
quisitively over the top of her glass. "Very *muscular*."

"Er . . . yes. I suppose so."

"Is that what you're wearing?" She runs her eyes over
my outfit. "It's not very *jazzy*, is it? Let me lend you a little something."

"I don't mind not being jazzy—" I begin, feeling a
few qualms, but Trish has already disappeared up the

stairs. A few moments later she appears, holding a jewel box.

"Here we are. You need a bit of *glitz*." She produces a diamanté clip in the shape of a sea horse. "I got this in Monte Carlo!"

"Er . . . lovely!" I say, eyeing it in horror. Before I can stop her, she sweeps my hair to one side and plonks it on. She looks at me appraisingly. "No . . . I think you need something *larger*. Here." She fishes out a large jeweled beetle and clips it to my hair. "*Now*. You see how the emerald brings out your eyes?"

I gaze at myself speechlessly. I cannot go out with a sparkly beetle on my head.

"And this is very glam!" Now she's garlanding a gilt chain around my waist. "Let me just hang the charms on . . ."

Charms?

"Mrs. Geiger . . ." I begin, flustered, as Eddie appears out of the study.

"Just got the quote in for the bathroom," he says to Trish.

"Isn't this twinkly elephant *gorgeous*?" says Trish, hooking it on the gilt belt. "And the frog!"

"Please," I say desperately. "I'm not sure I need any elephants—"

"Seven thousand." Eddie cuts across me. "Seems quite reasonable. Plus VAT."

"Well, how much is it with VAT?" says Trish, rifling in her box. "Where's that monkey gone?"

I feel like a Christmas tree. She's hanging more and more glittery baubles off the belt, not to mention the beetle. And Nathaniel will arrive any moment—and he'll *see* me.

"I don't know!" retorts Eddie impatiently. "What's seventeen and a half percent of seven thousand?"

"One thousand, two hundred, and twenty-five," I respond absently.

There's a stunned silence.

Shit. That was a mistake.

I look up to see Trish and Eddie goggling at me.

"Or . . . something." I laugh, hoping to distract them. "Just a guess. So . . . have you got any more charms?"

Neither of them takes the slightest notice of me. Eddie's eyes are fixed on the paper he's holding. Very slowly he looks up, his mouth working strangely.

"She's right," he announces. "She's bloody right. That's the correct answer." He jabs the paper. "It's here!"

"She's *right*?" Trish breathes in sharply. "But how . . ."

"You saw her! She did it in her head!" They both swing round to goggle at me again.

"Is she *autistic*?" Trish seems beside herself.

Oh, for God's sake. *Rain Man* has a lot to answer for, if you ask me.

"I'm not autistic!" I say. "I'm just . . . I'm just quite good with numbers. It's no big deal . . ."

To my huge relief the doorbell rings, and I rush to answer it. Nathaniel is standing on the doorstep, looking a little smarter than usual in tan jeans and a green shirt.

"Hi," I say hurriedly. "Let's go."

"Wait!" Eddie blocks my way. "Young lady, you may be a lot brighter than you realize."

Oh, no.

"What's going on?" asks Nathaniel.

"She's a mathematical genius!" says Trish wildly. "And we discovered it! It's just extraordinary!"

I shoot Nathaniel an agonized she's-talking-nonsense look.

"What formal education have you had, Samantha?" Eddie demands. "Other than cooking."

Oh, God. What did I say in my interview? I honestly can't remember.

"I...um...here and there." I spread my hands vaguely. "You know..."

"It's the schools today," Trish declares. "Tony Blair should be *shot*."

"Samantha," Eddie says self-righteously. "I will take on your education. And if you're prepared to work hard—hard, mind—I'm sure we can get you some qualifications."

This is getting worse.

"I don't really want any qualifications, sir," I mumble. "I'm happy as I am. Thanks anyway—"

"I won't take no for an answer!" insists Eddie.

"Aim higher, Samantha!" says Trish with sudden passion, gripping my arm. "Give yourself a chance in life! Reach for the stars!"

As I look from face to face I can't help feeling touched. They only want the best for me.

"Um...well...maybe." I surreptitiously divest myself of all the jeweled creatures and slip them back into the jewelry box. Then I turn to Nathaniel, who has been waiting patiently on the doorstep. "Shall we go?"

"So, what was all that about?" asks Nathaniel as we start walking along the village road. The air is soft and warm and my new hair is bouncing lightly, and with every step I can see my toes, painted in Trish's pink nail polish. "You're a mathematical genius?"

"No." I can't help laughing. "Of course not! I can just...do sums in my head. It's no big deal."

"Must be useful."

"It can be. But I'd rather be able to cook like your

mum. She's wonderful." I think back to the serene, homey atmosphere of the cottage, sitting at Iris's table, feeling sated and sleepy and secure. "You must have had a really happy childhood."

"We were pretty happy," Nathaniel assents. "Of course, Dad was alive then."

"It sounds like they had a fantastic marriage."

"It wasn't all hearts and flowers." Nathaniel grins. "Mum can speak her mind, and so could Dad. But it was . . . grounded. They knew they belonged together and that was more important than anything else in life." He smiles, reminiscently. "When they got really mad with each other, Dad would go and chop wood in the barn, and Mum would chop vegetables in the kitchen. The two of them would be at it furiously. Jake and I would be creeping around, not daring to make a sound."

"Then what happened?"

"One of them would crack," he says, laughing. "Usually Dad." He turns his head. "How about your parents?"

I tense up with apprehension. I'm not sure if I'm ready to start talking about myself yet.

"They split up when I was little," I say at last. "And my mum works hard. . . . It wasn't really the same."

"People do what they have to do," says Nathaniel after a pause. "It's tough for a single woman bringing up a family on her own, having to make ends meet."

"Um . . . yes."

Somehow I sense he might have formed a slightly different idea of Mum from the reality.

We walk on, passing an old stone wall covered with a profusion of climbing roses, and as I breathe in the delicious scent, I feel a sudden buoyancy. The street is dappled with soft evening light and the last rays of sun are warm on my shoulders.

"Nice hair, by the way," says Nathaniel.

"Oh, thanks," I say nonchalantly. "It's nothing, really." *Flick.* "So . . . where are we heading?"

"The pub. If that's OK?"

"Perfect!"

We walk over the bridge and pause to look at the river. Moorhens are diving for weed and the sunlight is like amber puddles on the water. Some tourists are taking pictures of each other, and I feel a glow of pride. I'm not just visiting this beautiful place, I want to tell them. I *live* here.

"And what about you?" says Nathaniel. "Before you came here? What's your background?"

"Oh . . . you don't want to know." I give him a brush-off smile. "Very boring."

"I don't believe that for a minute." His tone is light but persistent. "Did you have a career?"

I walk for a few paces without responding, trying to think what to say. I can feel Nathaniel's eyes on me, but I twist my head away from his scrutiny.

"You don't want to talk about it," he says at last.

"It's . . . it's hard."

Nathaniel exhales sharply. "You've had a bad time of it?"

Oh, God, he still thinks I'm an abused wife.

"No! It's not that. It's just . . . a long story."

Nathaniel doesn't look put off. "We've got all evening."

As I meet his steady gaze I feel a sudden pull, like a hook inside my chest. Although it'll be painful, I want to tell him. I want to unburden everything. Who I am, what happened, how hard it's been. Of all people, I could trust him. He wouldn't tell anyone. He'd understand. He'd keep it secret.

"So." He stops still in the street, his thumbs in his pockets. "Are you going to tell me who you are?"

"Maybe." We're only a few yards away from The Bell, and there's a small crowd outside. A couple of people greet Nathaniel and he waves back; the atmosphere is casual and happy. I don't want to puncture the mood.

"But . . . not right now." I smile at him. "It's too nice an evening to spoil with all my problems. I'll tell you later."

We make our way through the crowd. Some are standing by the door, others sitting at the wooden tables.

"What are they doing?" I ask.

"Waiting," he says. "Landlord's late."

"Oh," I say. I look around but all the tables are already taken. "Well, never mind. We can sit here."

I perch on an old barrel—but Nathaniel has already headed for the door of the pub.

And . . . that's odd. Everyone is standing back to let him through. I watch in astonishment as he reaches in his pocket and produces a big bunch of keys, then looks around to find me.

"Come on." He beckons with a grin. "Opening time."

"You own a pub!" I say in wonderment, as the initial melee of the evening dies down.

I've watched for fifteen minutes as Nathaniel has pulled pints, bantered with customers, given instructions to the bar staff, and made sure everyone is happy. Now the initial rush is over, he's come round to where I'm perched on a bar stool with a glass of wine.

"Three pubs," he corrects me. "And it's not just me.

It's our family business. The Bell, The Swan over in Bingley, and The Two Foxes."

Every seat seems to be full, with people spilling outside into the tiny garden and onto the forecourt. The chatter is tremendous. "How on earth do you keep the pubs running and have time to be a gardener?" I ask.

"OK, I'll come clean." Nathaniel lifts his hands. "I don't serve very often. We have a great bar staff. But I thought it might be fun tonight."

"So you're not really a gardener!"

"I am really a gardener." He straightens a bar mat. "This is . . . business."

There's the same tone in his voice as before. As though I've trodden on something sensitive. I look away—and my attention is caught by a picture on the wall of a fair-haired middle-aged man. He has Nathaniel's strong jaw and blue eyes, and the same crinkles around his eyes as he smiles.

"That's your dad?" I say cautiously. "He looks wonderful."

"He was the life and soul." Nathaniel's eyes soften. "Everyone here, they all loved him." He takes a deep slug of beer, then puts his glass down. "But listen. We don't have to stay. If you'd rather go somewhere else, somewhere nicer . . ."

The pub is bustling. Some song I vaguely recognize as a current hit is playing above the noise of talk and laughter. A group of regulars are greeting each other by the bar with cheerful insults. A pair of elderly American tourists in Stratford T-shirts are being advised on local beers by a barman with red hair and twinkling eyes. Across the room a darts game has started. I can't remember the last time I was in such an easy, friendly atmosphere.

"Let's stay. And I'll help!" I slip off my bar stool and head behind the bar.

"Have you ever pulled a pint before?" Nathaniel follows me.

"No." I pick up a glass and put it under one of the beer taps. "But I can learn."

Nathaniel comes round the bar. "You tilt the glass like this. . . . Now pull."

I pull the tap, and a burst of foam splutters out. "Damn!"

"Slowly . . ." He puts his arms around me, guiding my hands. "That's better."

Mmm, this is nice. I'm in a blissful happy haze, enveloped in his strong arms. Maybe I'll pretend I'm very slow at learning how to pull pints. Maybe we can stand like this all evening.

"You know—" I begin, turning my head toward him. And then I stop as my eyes focus on something. There's an old wooden notice on the wall, stating NO MUDDY BOOTS, PLEASE and NO WORKING CLOTHES. Underneath, another notice has been pinned. It's printed on yellowing paper in faded marker pen—and it reads: NO LAWYERS.

I'm dumbfounded. No lawyers?

"There we are." Nathaniel holds up the glass, full of gleaming amber liquid. "Your first ever pint."

"Er . . . great!" I say. I pretend to examine the pump, then gesture casually at the sign. "What's this?"

"I don't serve lawyers," he replies.

"Nathaniel! Get over here!" someone calls from the other end of the bar, and he clicks in annoyance.

"I'll only be a moment." He touches my hand, then moves away. Immediately I take a deep gulp of wine. He doesn't serve lawyers. Why doesn't he serve lawyers?

OK . . . just calm down, I instruct myself firmly. It's a

joke. Obviously it's a joke. Everyone hates lawyers, just like everyone hates estate agents and tax collectors. It's an accepted fact of life.

But they don't all put up signs about it in their pubs, do they?

As I'm sitting there, the red-haired barman comes up to where I'm standing and scoops some ice out of the tank.

"Hi," he says, holding out his hand. "I'm Eamonn."

"Samantha." I shake it with a smile. "I'm here with Nathaniel."

Eamonn nods. "Welcome to Lower Ebury!"

I watch him serving for a moment, my mind working. This guy will know something about the sign.

"So!" I say when he comes back over. "That sign about lawyers. It's a . . . joke, right?"

"Not really," Eamonn replies cheerfully. "Nathaniel can't stand lawyers."

"Right!" Somehow I manage to keep on smiling. "Um . . . why's that?"

"Ever since his dad died." Eamonn hefts a crate of orange mixers onto the bar and I shift round on my stool so I can see him properly.

"Why? What happened?"

"There was some lawsuit between him and the council." Eamonn pauses in his work. "Nathaniel says it should never have been started in the first place, but Ben got talked into it by the lawyers. He got more and more stressed by it and couldn't think about anything else—then he had a heart attack."

"God, how awful," I say in horror.

Eamonn resumes hefting crates. "Worst thing was, after Ben died they had to sell off one of the pubs. To pay the legal bills."

I'm aghast.

"The last lawyer came in this pub . . ." Eamonn leans conspiratorially across the bar. "Nathaniel punched him."

"He *punched* him?" My voice comes out a petrified squeak.

"It was on the day of his dad's funeral." Eamonn lowers his voice. "One of his dad's lawyers came in here and Nathaniel socked him one. We tease him about it now."

He turns away to serve someone and I take another drink of wine, my heart hammering with nerves.

Let's not freak out here. So he doesn't like lawyers. That doesn't mean *me*. Of course it doesn't. I can still be honest with him. I can still tell him about my past. He won't take it against me. Surely.

But . . . what if he does?

What if he punches me?

"Sorry about that." All of a sudden Nathaniel is in front of me. "Are you OK?"

"I'm fine!" I say over-brightly. "Having a lovely time!"

"Hey, Nathaniel," says Eamonn, polishing a glass. He winks at me. "What do you call five thousand lawyers at the bottom of the ocean?"

"A start!" The words jump out of my mouth before I can stop them. "They should all . . . rot. Away. Into hell."

There's a surprised silence. I can see Eamonn and Nathaniel exchanging raised eyebrows.

OK. Change the subject. Now.

"So! Er . . ." I quickly turn to a group standing by the bar. "Can I serve anyone?"

By the end of the evening I've pulled about forty pints. I've had a plate of cod and chips and half a dish of sticky toffee pudding—and beaten Nathaniel at darts, to loud cheers and whoops from everyone watching around.

"You said you hadn't played before!" he says in disbelief after I nail my winning triple eight.

"I haven't," I say innocently. There's no need to mention that I did archery at school for five years.

At last Nathaniel rings Last Orders with a resounding clang of the bell, and a good hour later the last few stragglers make it to the door, each pausing to say goodbye as they leave. He must know every single person in this village.

"We'll clear up," says Eamonn firmly, as Nathaniel starts picking up glasses, five at a time. "Give those here. You'll want to be enjoying the rest of the evening."

"Well...OK." Nathaniel claps him on the back. "Thanks, Eamonn." He looks at me. "Ready to go?"

Almost reluctantly I slide down off my bar stool. "It's been an amazing evening," I say to Eamonn. "Brilliant to meet you."

"Likewise." He grins. "Send us your invoice."

I'm still buoyed by the atmosphere; by my win at darts; by the satisfaction of having spent the evening actually *doing* something. I've never had an evening out like this in my life.

No one in London ever took me to a pub for a date—let alone to the other side of the bar. On my first evening out with Jacob he took me to *Les Sylphides* at Covent Garden, then left after twenty minutes to take a call from the States and never returned. The next day he said he was so bound up in a point of commercial contract law, he "forgot" I was there.

And the worst thing is, instead of saying "You bastard!" and punching him, I asked what point of commercial contract law.

After the beery warmth of the pub, the summer night feels fresh and cool. I can hear the faint laughter of pub-goers up ahead, and a car starting in the distance. There are no street lamps; the only light comes from a big full moon and curtained cottage windows.

"I really, really loved tonight," I say with enthusiasm. "It's a great pub. And I can't get over how friendly it is. The way everyone knows you! And the village spirit. Everyone cares about each other. You can tell."

"How can you tell that?"

"From the way everyone claps each other on the back," I explain. "Like, if someone were in trouble, everyone would rally round in a heartwarming way. You can just see it."

I hear Nathaniel stifle a laugh.

"We did get the 'Most Heartwarming Village' award last year," he says.

"You can laugh," I retort. "But in London, no one's heartwarming. If you fell over dead in the street they'd just push you into the gutter. After emptying your wallet and stealing your identity. That wouldn't happen here, would it?"

"Well, no," says Nathaniel, straight-faced. "If you die here, the entire village gathers round your bed and sings the village lament."

My mouth twists into a smile. "I knew it. Strewing flower petals?"

"Naturally." He nods. "And making ceremonial corn dollies."

A small animal runs across the road, stops, and regards us with two tiny yellow headlamps, then skitters into the hedgerow.

"How does the lament go, then?" I say.

"It goes something like this." Nathaniel clears his

throat, then sings in a low, mournful monotone. " 'Oh, no. He's gone.' "

"What about if it's a woman?" I match his deadpan manner.

"Good point. Then we sing a different lament." He draws a deep breath and sings again, on exactly the same tuneless note: " 'Oh, no. She's gone.' "

I can't help but laugh. "Well . . . we don't have laments in London. We move on. Big on moving, Londoners. Big on staying ahead."

"I know about Londoners." Nathaniel runs his hand along a hedge. "I lived in London for a time."

Nathaniel lived in London? I try, and fail, to picture him straphanging on the tube, reading *Metro*.

"When?"

"I was a waiter on my year off before uni. My flat was opposite a twenty-four-hour supermarket. It was lit up all night, with these bright fluorescent strips. And the noise . . ." He winces. "In ten months of living there, I never had a single moment of total darkness or total quiet. I never heard a bird. I never saw the stars."

Instinctively I tilt my head back to look up at the clear night sky. Slowly, as my eyes adjust to the blackness, the tiny pinpricks begin to appear, forming whorls and patterns that I can't begin to decipher. He's right. I never saw the stars in London either.

"My dad taught me the constellations," Nathaniel says, looking up too. "He had a telescope up in the attic."

"Nathaniel . . . what happened with your dad?" I speak tentatively. "Eamonn told me there was a court case with the council?"

"Yes." His voice tightens. "There was."

"Was he suing them? Or . . . or . . ." I trail off.

"It was all so bloody *pointless*." He exhales. "It started when the council dug up the road outside one of our pubs for eight months. They ruined access to it, and business went down. So Dad sued them. And lost. That's when he had his first heart attack. That should have been the end of it."

I bite my lip. "So . . . what went wrong?"

"Then some other lawyers made contact. More expensive." I can hear the bitterness in Nathaniel's voice. "They persuaded Dad he would win on appeal. They kept whipping him up, pressing the right buttons. They *knew* he was ill. Mum and I tried to talk him out of it . . . but he just called us negative. Dad always believed he was in the right. He kept saying justice would prevail. He *trusted* those bastards." Nathaniel is silent for a moment, then adds, "He had the next heart attack a week after they lost the second appeal. It killed him."

"Nathaniel . . . I'm really sorry. That's awful."

"Thanks," he says after a pause. "It was a pretty bad time."

I feel chastened after hearing his story. This is a side of the law I have no experience of. Genuine concerns and people. At Carter Spink the deals may have been huge—but I was pretty much cushioned from real life.

"How about you?" His voice brings me back to earth. "You were going to tell me how you came to be here."

"Oh." I feel a spasm of nerves. "Yes, right. So I was."

This is impossible. I want to tell him. But . . . how on earth can I now? How can I admit that I'm a lawyer?

"Well," I say at last. "I was in London. In this . . . this . . ."

"Relationship," he prompts.

"Er . . . yes." I pause, racking my brains for a way to continue. "Well. Things went wrong. I got on a train . . . and I ended up here."

There's an expectant silence. "That's it," I add.

"That's *it*?" Nathaniel sounds incredulous. "That's the long story?"

Oh, God.

"Look." I turn to face him in the moonlight. "I know I was going to tell you more. But are the details really important? Does it matter, what I used to do . . . or be? The point is, I'm here. And I've just had the best evening of my life. Ever."

I can see he wants to challenge me; he even opens his mouth to speak. Then he relents and turns away.

I feel a plunge of despair. Maybe I've ruined everything. Maybe I should have told the truth anyway. Or made up some convoluted story about a nasty boyfriend.

We walk on again into the night without speaking. Nathaniel's shoulder brushes against mine. Then I feel his hand. His fingers graze against my own casually at first, as though by accident—then, slowly, entwine round mine.

I feel an arching inside as my entire body responds, but somehow force myself not to catch my breath. There's no sound except our footsteps on the road and the hooting of an owl. Nathaniel's hand is sure and firm round my own. I can feel the roughened calluses on his skin, his thumb rubbing over mine.

We come to a stop at the entrance to the Geigers' drive. He looks down at me silently, his expression almost grave. I can feel my breath thickening. I don't care if it's obvious I want him.

I was never any good at the rules, anyway.

He releases my hand and puts both hands round my waist. Now he's slowly pulling me toward him. I close my eyes.

"For goodness sake!" comes an unmistakable voice. "Aren't you going to *kiss* her?"

I jump backward. Nathaniel looks equally shocked; his arms have dropped to his sides. I turn round—and to my utter horror, Trish is leaning out of an upstairs window, holding a cigarette.

"I'm not a *prude,* you know," she says. "You are allowed to kiss!"

I shoot furious daggers at her. Has she never heard the word *privacy*?

"Carry on!" Her cigarette end glows as she waves it. "Don't mind me!"

Don't mind her? I'm sorry, but Nathaniel and I are not having our first kiss with Trish as a spectator. I glance uncertainly at Nathaniel, who looks as nonplussed as I feel.

"Should we—" I'm not even sure what I'm about to suggest.

"Isn't it a lovely summer's night?" adds Trish conversationally.

"Lovely," calls back Nathaniel politely.

This is disastrous. The mood is totally broken.

"Um . . . thanks for a great evening," I say, trying to keep a straight face. "I had a great time."

"Me too." His eyes are almost indigo in the shadows. "So. Are we going to give Mrs. Geiger her kicks? Or leave her in an unbearable frenzy of frustration?"

Trish is still leaning avidly out the window, as if we're the floor show.

"Oh . . . I think she probably deserves the unbearable frenzy of frustration," I say with a tiny smile.

"So I'll see you tomorrow?"

"I'll be at your mum's at ten o'clock."

He holds out his hand and we barely brush fingertips

before he turns and walks away. I watch him disappear into the darkness, then turn and head down the drive to the house, my whole body still pulsating.

It's all very well, getting one over on Trish. But what about *my* unbearable frenzy of frustration?

Sixteen

I'm woken the next day by Trish banging sharply on my door. "Samantha! I need to speak to you! Now!"

It's not even eight o'clock on a Saturday morning. Where's the fire?

"OK! Hang on a sec!" I call blearily.

I get out of bed and put on a dressing gown, my head filled with delicious memories of last night. Nathaniel's hand in mine... Nathaniel's arms around me...

"Yes, Mrs. Geiger?" I open my door to see Trish standing there in a white robe. She puts her hand over the cordless phone in her hand.

"Samantha." There's a strange note of triumph in her voice. "You've fibbed to me, haven't you?"

I feel a white flash of shock. How did she—how could she—

"Haven't you?" She gives me a penetrating look. "I'm sure you know what I'm talking about?"

My mind frantically runs over all the fibs I've ever told Trish, up to and including "I'm a housekeeper." It could be anything. It could be something small and insignificant. Or she could have found out the whole lot.

"I don't know what you're referring to," I say in a throaty voice. "Madam."

"Well." Trish walks toward me, swishing her silk dressing gown crossly. "As you can imagine, I'm *rather* upset that you never told me you'd cooked paella for the Spanish ambassador."

My mouth hangs open.

"I specifically asked in your interview if you had cooked for any notable persons." Trish arches her eyebrows in reproof. "You never even *mentioned* the banquet for three hundred at the Mansion House."

OK, has she been bipolar all this time? That would explain a lot.

"Mrs. Geiger," I say, a little nervous. "Would you like to sit down?"

"No, thank you!" she says crisply. "I'm still on the phone with Lady Edgerly."

Freya's on the phone?

"Lady Edgerly..." Trish lifts the phone to her ear. "You're quite right, *far* too unassuming..." She looks up. "Lady Edgerly would like to have a word with you."

She hands me the phone and in a blur of incredulity I lift it to my ear.

"Hello?"

"Samantha?" Freya's familiar, raspy voice erupts into my ear through a sea of static. "Are you OK? What the *fuck* is going on?"

"I'm...fine!" I glance at Trish, who is standing approximately two meters away. "I'll just...go somewhere a bit more..."

Ignoring Trish's laserlike eyes, I hurry into my bedroom and close the door tight. Then I lift the phone to my ear again.

"I'm fine!" I feel a rush of joy to be talking to Freya again. "It's so amazing to hear from you!"

"What on earth's going on?" she demands again. "I got this message but it made no sense! You're a *house-keeper*? Is this some huge windup?"

"No." I glance at the door, then move into the bathroom and turn the fan on. "I'm a full-time house-keeper," I say in a lower voice. "I've left my job at Carter Spink."

"You've *quit*?" says Freya. "Just like that?"

"I didn't quit. I was . . . thrown out. I made a mistake and they fired me."

It's still hard to say it. Or even to think about it.

"You were thrown out for a simple *mistake*?" Freya sounds outraged. "Jesus H. Christ, these people—"

"It wasn't a simple mistake," I cut her off in mid-flow. "It was . . . a really big, important mistake. Anyway, that's what happened. And I decided to do something differ-ent. Become a housekeeper for a bit."

"You decided to become a housekeeper," echoes Freya slowly. "Samantha, did you totally lose your mind?"

"Why not?" I say defensively. "You were the one who said I should have a break."

"But a *housekeeper*? You can't cook!"

"Well, I know."

"I mean, you *really* can't cook!" She's giggling now. "I've seen your cooking. And your nonexistent cleaning."

"I know! It was a bit of a nightmare to begin with. But I'm kind of . . . learning. You'd be surprised."

"Do you have to wear an apron?"

"I've got this hideous nylon uniform." I'm snuffling with laughter now. "And I call them Madam . . . and Sir . . . and I curtsy."

"Samantha, this is insane," says Freya. "Absolutely insane. You cannot stay there. I'm going to rescue you. I'll fly back tomorrow—"

"No!" I say with more vehemence than I intended. "No! I'm . . . having a good time. I've met—"

I halt abruptly. But Freya's too quick off the mark for me.

"A *man*?" she exclaims in delight.

"Well . . . yes."

"That's fantastic! About time too. Only he'd better not be another dreary lawyer—"

"Don't worry." I feel an unwilling grin come to my face. "He's not."

"Details?"

"It's early days. But he's . . . you know. Nice."

"Well, even so. If you want to escape, you know I'm only a phone call away. You can stay at our place."

"Thanks, Freya." I feel a tug of affection for her.

"No problem. Samantha?"

"Yes?" There's a long silence, until I think the line must have cut out.

"What about the law?" says Freya at last. "What about partnership? I know I gave you a hard time about it. But it was your dream. Are you just going to abandon it?"

I push down a twinge of deep, buried grief.

"That dream's over," I say shortly. "Partners don't make fifty-million-quid mistakes."

"Fifty million quid?"

"Uh-huh."

"Jesus." I hear her sharp intake of breath. "I had no idea. I can't imagine how you've coped with all this—"

"It's fine." I cut her off. "I've got over it."

Freya sighs. "You know, I had a feeling something was up. I tried to send you an e-mail the other day via the Carter Spink Web site. But your page was gone."

"Really?" I feel an odd tweak inside.

"And then I thought—" She breaks off, and I can hear some kind of mayhem in the background. "Oh, bugger. Our transport's here. Listen, I'll call again soon—"

"Wait!" I say urgently. "Before you go, Freya, what on *earth* did you say to Trish about the Spanish ambassador? And the Mansion House?"

"Oh, that! Well, she kept asking questions, so I thought I'd better make some stuff up. I said you could fold napkins into a scene from *Swan Lake* . . . and make ice sculptures . . . and David Linley once asked for your cheese-straw recipe."

"Freya . . ." I close my eyes.

"I made quite a lot up, actually. She lapped it up! I have to go, babe. Love you."

"Love you too."

The phone goes dead and I stand motionless for a moment, the bathroom suddenly very silent without Freya's husky voice in my ear.

I look at my watch. It's still early. I've got time to have a look.

Three minutes later I'm sitting at Eddie's desk, tapping my fingers as I wait for the Internet connection to work. I asked Trish if I could possibly send an e-mail of thanks to Lady Edgerly, and she was only too eager to open up the study for me and loiter behind the chair, until I politely asked her for some privacy.

Eddie's home page opens and I immediately type in www.carterspink.com.

As the familiar purple logo appears and describes a 360-degree circle on the screen, I can feel all the old tensions rising, like leaves from the bottom of a pond. Taking a deep breath, I click swiftly past the introduction, straight to Associates. The list comes up—and Freya's right. The names segue straight from *Snell* to *Taylor*. No *Sweeting*.

I tell myself to be rational. Of course they've taken me off. I've been fired, what else did I expect? That was my old life and I'm not concerned with it anymore. I should just close down, go to Iris's house, and forget about it. That's what I should do. Instead, I find myself reaching for the mouse and tapping *Samantha Sweeting* into the search box. *No result* pings up a few moments later.

No result? Nowhere on the whole *Web site*? But . . . what about in the Media section? Or News Archives?

I quickly click onto the Done Deals box, and search for *Euro-Sal, merger, DanCo*. That was a big European deal last year, and I handled the financing. The report appears on the screen, with the headline CARTER SPINK ADVISES ON £20BN MERGER. My eyes run down the familiar text. *The Carter Spink team was led from London by Arnold Saville, with associates Guy Ashby and Jane Smilington.*

I stop in disbelief, then go back and read the text more carefully, searching for the missing words: *and Samantha Sweeting,* it should read. But the words aren't there. I'm not there. Quickly I click onto another deal, the Conlon acquisition. I *know* I'm in this report. I've read it, for Christ's sake. I was on the team, I've got a tombstone to prove it.

But I'm not mentioned here either.

My heart is thudding as I click from deal to deal, tracking back a year. Two years. Five years. They've wiped me out. Someone has gone painstakingly through the entire Web site and removed my name. I've been erased from every deal I was involved with. It's as if I never even existed.

I try to stay calm, but anger is bubbling up, hot and

strong. How dare they change history? How dare they wipe me out? I gave them seven years of my *life*. They can't just blot me out, pretend I was never even on the payroll.

Then a new thought hits me. Why have they bothered doing this? Other people have left the firm and haven't disappeared. Am I *such* an embarrassment? I look at the screen silently for a moment. Then, slowly, I type in www.google.com and enter *Samantha Sweeting* in the box. I add *lawyer* to be on the safe side, and press ENTER.

A moment later the screen fills with text. As I scan the entries I feel as though I've been hit over the head.

> . . . the Samantha Sweeting debacle . . .
> . . . discovery, Samantha Sweeting went AWOL, leaving colleagues to . . .
> . . . heard about Samantha Sweeting . . .
> . . . Samantha Sweeting jokes. What do you call a lawyer who . . .
> . . . Samantha Sweeting fired from Carter Spink . . .

One after another. From lawyers' Web sites, legal news services, law students' message boards. It's as if the whole legal world has been talking about me behind my back. In a daze, I click to the next page—and there are still more. And on the next page, and the next.

I feel as though I'm surveying a wrecked bridge. Looking at the damage, realizing for the first time quite how bad the devastation is.

I can never go back.

I knew that.

But I don't think I really *knew* it. Not deep down in the pit of my stomach. Not where it counts.

I feel a wetness on my cheek and jump to my feet,

shutting all the Web pages down; clearing History in case Eddie gets curious. I shut down the computer and look around the silent room. This is where I am. Not there. That part of my life is over.

Iris's cottage is looking as idyllic as ever as I dash up to the front door, out of breath. In fact, even more idyllic, as a goose is now wandering about with her hens.

"Hello." Iris is sitting on the front step with a mug of tea. "You seem in a hurry."

"I just wanted to get here on time." I glance around the garden, but there's no sign of Nathaniel.

"Nathaniel had to go and sort out a leaking pipe at one of the pubs," says Iris, as though reading my mind. "But he'll be back later. Meanwhile, we're going to make bread."

"Great!" I say. I follow her into the kitchen and put on the same stripy apron as last time.

"I've started us off already," says Iris, going over to a large, old-fashioned mixing bowl on the table. "Yeast, warm water, melted butter, and flour. Mix together and you have your dough. Now, you're going to knead it."

"Right," I say, looking blankly at the dough. She shoots me a curious glance.

"Are you all right, Samantha? You seem...out of sorts."

"I'm fine." I will myself to concentrate. "Sorry."

"I know people have machines to do this for them," she says, hefting the dough onto the table. "But this is how we make it the old-fashioned way. You'll never taste better."

She kneads it briskly a couple of times. "You see? Fold it over, make a quarter turn. You need to use a bit of energy."

Cautiously I plunge my hands into the soft dough and try to imitate her.

"That's it," says Iris, watching carefully. "Get into a rhythm and really *work* it. Kneading's very good for releasing stress," she adds with wry humor. "Pretend you're bashing all your worst enemies."

"I'll do that!" I manage a cheerful tone.

But there's a knot of tension in my chest, which doesn't dwindle away as I knead. In fact, the more I fold and turn the dough, the worse it seems to get. I can't stop my mind flipping back to that Web site.

I did good things for that firm. I won clients. I negotiated deals. I was not nothing.

I was *not* nothing.

"The more you work the dough, the better the bread will be," says Iris, coming over to the table with a smile. "Can you feel it becoming warm and elastic in your hands?"

I look at the dough in my fingers, but I can't connect with it. I can't feel what she wants me to. My senses aren't plugged in. My mind is skittering about like a squirrel on ice.

I start kneading again, harder than before, trying to capture it. I want to find that contentment I had last time I was here, that feeling of simplicity and earthiness. But I keep losing my rhythm, cursing in frustration as my fingers catch on the dough. My upper arms are aching; my face is sweating. And the turmoil inside me is only getting worse.

How dare they wipe me out? I was a good lawyer.

I was a good fucking lawyer.

"Would you like a rest?" Iris comes over and touches my shoulder. "It's hard work when you're not used to it."

"What's the point?" My words shoot out before I can stop them. "I mean, what's the point of all this? Making bread. You make it and you eat it. And then...it's gone."

I break off abruptly, not quite knowing what's come over me. I don't feel totally on top of myself.

Iris gives me a careful look.

"You could say the same of all food," she points out gently. "Or life itself."

"Exactly." I rub my forehead with my apron. "Exactly."

I don't know what I'm saying. Why am I picking a fight with Iris? I must calm down.

"I think that's enough kneading," she says, taking the dough from me and patting it into a round shape.

"Now what?" I say, trying to speak more normally. "Shall I put it in the oven?"

"Not yet." Iris places the dough back in the bowl and puts it on top of the stove. "Now we wait."

"Wait?" I stare at her. "What do you mean, wait?"

"We wait." She pops a tea towel over the bowl. "Half an hour should do it. I'll make a cup of tea."

"But...what are we waiting *for*?"

"For the yeast to rise and work its magic on the dough." She smiles. "Underneath that towel, a small miracle is happening."

I look at the bowl, trying to think miracles. But it isn't working. I can't feel calm or serene. My body is wound up too far; every nerve is hopping with tension. I used to be in control of my time to the minute. To the second. And now I'm supposed to wait for yeast? I'm supposed to stand here, in an apron, waiting for a... *fungus*?

"I'm sorry," I hear myself say. "I can't do it." I head for the kitchen door and out into the garden.

"What?" Iris comes after me, wiping her hands on her apron. "Sweetie, what's wrong?"

"I can't do this!" I wheel round. "I can't just . . . just sit around patiently, waiting for *yeast* to get its act together."

"Why not?"

"Because it's such a waste of time!" I clutch my head in frustration. "It's such a waste of time. All of it!"

"What do you think we should be doing instead?" she asks with interest.

"Something . . . *important*. OK?" I walk to the apple tree and back again, unable to keep still. "Something constructive."

I glance at Iris, but she doesn't seem offended.

"What's more constructive than making bread?"

Oh, *God*. I feel an urge to scream. It's OK for her, with her hens and her apron and no wrecked career on the Internet.

"You don't understand anything," I say, close to tears. "I'm sorry, but you don't. Look . . . I'll just leave."

"Don't leave." Iris's voice is surprisingly firm. The next moment she's in front of me, placing her two hands on my shoulders, looking at me with her penetrating blue eyes.

"Samantha, you've had a trauma," she says in kind, even tones. "And it's affected you very deeply—"

"I *haven't* had a trauma!" I wheel away, out of her grasp. "I just . . . I can't do this, Iris. I can't pretend to be this. I'm not a bread maker, OK? I'm *not* a domestic goddess." I look around the garden desperately, as though searching for clues. "I don't know who I am anymore. I have no bloody idea."

A single tear rolls down my cheek and I wipe it away roughly. I'm not going to cry in front of Iris.

"I don't know who I am." I exhale, more calmly. "Or what my goal is . . . or where I'm headed in life. Or anything."

My energy's gone and I sink down on the dry grass. A few moments later Iris comes and squats down beside me.

"It doesn't matter," she says, her voice soft. "Don't beat yourself up for not knowing all the answers. You don't always have to know who you are. You don't have to have the big picture, or know where you're heading. Sometimes it's enough just to know what you're going to do next."

For a while I let her words run through my head, like cool water on a headache.

"And what am I going to do next?" I say at last, with a hopeless shrug.

"You're going to help me shell the beans for lunch." She's so matter-of-fact that I half smile in spite of myself.

Meekly, I follow Iris into the house, then collect a big bowl of broad beans and start splitting the pods as she shows me. Pods into a basket on the floor. New broad beans into the basin. Over and over and over.

I become a little calmer as I immerse myself in my task. I never even knew broad beans came from pods like this. To be honest, my total experience of broad beans has been picking them up in a plastic-covered packet from Waitrose, putting them in my fridge, taking them out a week after the sell-by date, and throwing them away.

But this is the real thing. This is what they're like, dug straight out of the ground. Or . . . picked off the bush. Whatever it is.

Each time I split one open it's like finding a row of pale green jewels. And when I put one in my mouth, it's like—

Oh, OK. It needs to be cooked.

Yuck.

When I've finished the beans we return to the dough, kneading it into loaves. We put the loaves into special tins and then have to wait another half hour for them to rise again. But somehow this time I don't mind. I sit at the table with Iris, hulling strawberries and listening to the radio until it's time to put the tins into the oven. Then Iris loads a tray with Cheshire cheese, bean salad, biscuits, and strawberries and we take it outside to a table set under the shade of a tree.

"There," she says, pouring some iced tea into a tumbler made of bubbled glass. "Better?"

"Yes. Thanks," I say awkwardly. "I'm sorry about earlier. I just . . ."

"Samantha, it's all right." She cuts a piece of cheese and puts it on my plate. "You don't have to apologize."

"But I do." I take a deep breath. "You've been so wonderful . . . and Nathaniel . . ."

"He took you to the pub, I heard."

"It was amazing!" I say with enthusiasm. "You must be so proud, to have that in your family."

Iris nods. "Those pubs have been run by Blewetts for generations." She sits down and helps us both to bean salad, dressed with oil and speckled with herbs. I take a bite—and it's absolutely delicious.

"It must have been hard when your husband died," I venture cautiously.

"Everything was in a mess." Iris sounds matter-of-fact. A chicken wanders over to the table and she shoos it away. "There were financial difficulties. I wasn't well. If it hadn't been for Nathaniel we might have lost all of the pubs. He made sure they got back on track. For his father's memory." Her eyes cloud a little and she hesitates. "You never know how things are going to turn out, however much you plan. But you already know that."

"I always thought my life would be a certain way," I say, gazing down at my plate. "I had it all mapped out."

"But . . . it didn't happen like that?"

For a few seconds I can't answer. I'm remembering the moment I heard I was going to be partner. That instant of undiluted, dazzling joy. When I thought my life had finally fallen into place, when I thought everything was perfect.

"No," I say, trying to keep my voice level. "It didn't happen like that."

Iris is watching me with such clear, empathetic eyes I almost believe she's able to read my mind.

"Don't be too hard on yourself, chicken," she says. "We all flounder."

I can't imagine Iris ever floundering. She seems so put-together.

"Oh, I floundered," she says, reading my expression. "After Benjamin went. It was so sudden. Everything I thought I had, gone overnight."

"So . . . what did you . . ." I spread my hands helplessly.

"I found another way," she says. "But . . . it took time." For a moment she holds my gaze, then looks at her watch. "Speaking of which, I'll make some coffee. And see how that bread's getting on."

I get up to follow her, but she bats me down again.

"Sit. Stay. Relax."

So I sit in the dappled sunlight, sipping my iced tea, trying to relax. Trying to enjoy the present, just sitting here in a beautiful garden. But emotions are still darting around me like unsettled fish.

Another way.

But I don't know any other way. I feel like the light's gone out and I'm feeling my way forward, one step at a time. And all I know is I can't go back to what I was.

I clench my eyes shut, trying to clear my mind. I should never have looked at that Web site. I should never have read those comments.

"Hold out your arms, Samantha." Iris's voice is suddenly behind me. "Close your eyes. Go on."

I have no idea what she's up to, but I keep my eyes closed and hold out my arms. The next moment I feel something warm being put into them. A yeasty smell is rising up. I open my eyes to see a loaf of bread in my arms.

Proper bread. Real, proper bread like you'd see in a baker's window. Fat and plump and golden-brown, with faint striations and a crusty, almost flaky top. It smells so delicious I can feel my mouth watering.

"Tell me that's nothing," says Iris, squeezing my arm. "You made that, sweetie. And you should be proud of yourself."

Something hot is wadding my throat as I clutch the warm loaf. I made this bread. I made it. I, Samantha Sweeting, who couldn't even microwave a packet of soup. Who gave up seven years of her life to end up with nothing, to be wiped out of existence. Who has no idea who she even is anymore.

I made a loaf of bread. Right now I feel like this is the only thing I have to hold on to.

To my horror a tear suddenly rolls down my cheek, followed by another. This is ridiculous. I must get a grip on myself.

"Looks good," comes Nathaniel's easy voice behind me, and I wheel round in shock to see him standing next to Iris.

"Hi," I say, flustered. "I thought you were . . . fixing a pipe or something."

"Still am." He nods. "I just popped home."

"I'll go and get the other loaves out," says Iris, patting me on the shoulder and disappearing over the grass toward the house.

I stand up. Just the sight of Nathaniel is adding all sorts of new emotions into the mix: more fish darting around my body.

Although now I think about it, they're mainly varieties of the same fish.

"Are you all right?" he says, acknowledging my tears.

"I'm fine. It's just been a strange day." I brush them away in embarrassment. "I don't usually get so emotional about . . . bread."

"Mum said you got a bit frustrated." He raises his eyebrows. "All that kneading?"

"It was the rising." I raise a rueful smile. "Having to wait. I've never been good at waiting."

"Uh-huh." Nathaniel's steady blue eyes meet mine.

"For anything." Somehow I seem to be edging closer and closer to him, I'm not entirely sure how. "I have to have things *now*."

"Uh-huh."

We're inches apart, and as I gaze up at him, breathing hard, all the frustrations and shocks of the last couple of weeks are distilling inside me. A huge block of pressure is growing, until I can't bear it. Unable to stop myself, I reach up and pull his face down toward mine.

I haven't kissed like this since I was a teenager. Arms wrapped around each other, oblivious of anything else in the world. Completely lost. Trish could be standing there with a video camera, issuing directions, and I wouldn't notice.

It seems hours later that I open my eyes and we draw

apart. My lips feel swollen; my legs are staggery. Nathaniel looks equally shell-shocked.

The bread is totally squashed, I suddenly notice. I try to reshape it as best I can, putting it on the table like a deformed pottery exhibit while I gather my breath.

"I don't have long," Nathaniel says. "I have to get back to the pub." His hand runs lightly down my back and I feel my body curving toward his.

"I don't take long," I say, my voice husky with desire. When did I become so brazen, exactly?

"I *really* don't have long." He glances at his watch. "About six minutes."

"I only take six minutes," I murmur with an enticing glance, and Nathaniel smiles back, as though I'm joking.

"Seriously," I say, trying to sound modest yet sexy. "I'm fast. Six minutes, give or take."

There's silence for a few moments. An incredulous expression is coming over Nathaniel's face. Somehow he doesn't look as impressed as I thought he would.

"Well...round here we take things a bit slower," he says at last.

"Right," I say, trying not to look at all disappointed. "Er...well...I'm sure..." I trail off.

I should not have started that sentence.

He looks at his watch again. "I must be off. I have to drive over to Gloucester tonight."

I feel an inward drop at his businesslike tone. He's barely looking at me anymore. I should never have mentioned timing, I realize in dismay. Everyone knows, you never bring up any kind of numerical measurement during sex with a man. It's the most basic rule.

"So...I'll see you," I say, trying to sound casual yet encouraging. "What are you doing tomorrow?"

"I'm not sure yet." He shrugs noncommittally. "Are you around?"

"I guess so. Maybe."

"Well . . . I may see you."

And with that he's striding away again over the grass, and I'm left with nothing but a misshapen loaf of bread and total confusion.

Seventeen

Like I said. There should be a different system. There should be some kind of universal arrangement that leaves no room for misunderstanding. It could involve hand signals, perhaps. Or small, discreet stickers placed on the lapel, color-coded for different messages:

AVAILABLE/NOT AVAILABLE
RELATIONSHIP ON/RELATIONSHIP OFF
SEX IMMINENT/SEX CANCELED/SEX MERELY
    POSTPONED.

How else are you supposed to know what's going on? How?

By the next morning I've thought long and hard and have got nowhere. Either: a) Nathaniel was offended by my references to sex and isn't interested anymore. Or b) he's fine, it's all still on, he was just being a man and not saying much, and I should stop obsessing.

Or somewhere in between.

Or some other option I haven't even considered. Or . . .

Actually, I think that might cover it. But still. I'm totally confused just thinking about it.

I stumble downstairs in my robe at around nine, to find Eddie and Trish in the hall, dressed up very smartly. Eddie is in a blue blazer with shiny gold buttons, and Trish is in a white slub silk suit, with the biggest corsage of fake red roses I've ever seen. She also seems to be having the teeniest problem doing up the buttons of her jacket. At last she edges the last one into its buttonhole and stands back to look at herself in the mirror, panting slightly.

Now she looks as though she can't move her arms.

"What do you think?" she says to Eddie.

"Yes, very nice," he says, frowning at a copy of *Road Map of Britain 1994*. "Is it the A347? Or the A367?"

"Um . . . I think it looks nice with the jacket unbuttoned," I venture. "More . . . relaxed."

Trish looks as though she suspects me of deliberately sabotaging her appearance.

"Yes," she says at last. "Maybe you're right." She makes to undo her buttons—but she's so trussed up, she can't get her hands near enough. And now Eddie's wandered off into the study.

"Shall I . . ." I offer.

"Yes." Her neck flames red. "If you would be so kind."

I move forward and undo the buttons as gently as I can, which is not very, given how stiff the fabric is. When I've finished she takes a step backward and regards herself again, looking slightly dissatisfied, plucking at her silky shirt thing.

"Tell me Samantha," she says casually. "If you saw me now for the first time ... what *word* would you use to describe me?"

Oh, bloody hell. I'm sure this wasn't in my job description. I rack my brains hastily for the most flattering word I can come up with.

"Um ... um ... elegant," I say at last, nodding as though to add conviction to what I'm saying. "I'd say you were elegant."

"Elegant?" Something tells me I got it wrong.

"I mean, thin!" I amend, in sudden realization.

How could I have overlooked thin?

"Thin." She looks at herself a few moments, turning from side to side. "Thin."

She doesn't sound entirely happy. What's wrong with being thin and elegant, for God's sake?

Not that she's either, let's be honest.

"What about ..." She shakes back her hair, deliberately avoiding my eye. "What about ... young?"

For a moment I'm too flummoxed to answer. Young? Young compared to what?

"Er ... absolutely," I say at last. "That ... goes without saying."

Please don't say, "How old do you think I—"

"How old would you say I am, Samantha?"

She's moving her head from side to side, flicking dust off her jacket, as though she's not really interested in the answer. But I know her ears are ready and waiting, like two giant microphones ready to pick up the slightest sound.

My face is prickling. What am I going to say? I'll say ... thirty-five. No. Don't be ridiculous. She can't be *that* self-deluded. Forty? No. I can't say forty. It's too near the truth.

"Are you about . . . thirty-seven?" I hazard at last. Trish turns round—and from her smug expression of pleasure I reckon I hit the note of flattery about right.

"I'm actually . . . thirty-nine!" she says, two spots of color appearing on her cheeks.

"No!" I exclaim, trying not to look at her crow's-feet. "That's . . . amazing!"

She is such a liar. She was forty-six last February. And if she doesn't want people to know, she shouldn't leave her passport out on her dressing table.

"Now!" she says, clearly cheered up. "We'll be out *all day* at my sister's party. Nathaniel will be coming over to work in the garden, but I expect you know that—"

"Nathaniel?" I feel an electric jolt. "He's coming here?"

"He called this morning. The sweet peas need . . . stringing or looping or something?" She gets out a lip pencil and begins outlining her already lined lips.

"Right. I didn't realize." I'm trying to stay collected, but tentacles of excitement are creeping through me. "So . . . he's working on a Sunday?"

"Oh, he often does. He's *very* dedicated." She stands back to look at her reflection, then starts shading in her lips with yet more lipstick. "I heard he took you to his little pub?"

His *little* pub. She is so patronizing.

"Er . . . yes. He did."

"I was *so* glad about that, really." She takes out a mascara wand. "We nearly had to look for another gardener, can you *imagine*. Although of course it was a great shame for him. After all his plans."

I must have missed a beat or three. What's she talking about?

"What was a shame?" I say.

"Nathaniel. His nursery. Plant thing." She frowns at

her reflection. "Organic something or other. He showed us the business proposition. In fact, we even considered backing him. We are very *supportive* employers, Samantha." She fixes me with a blue gaze as though daring me to disagree.

"Of course!"

"All set?" Eddie comes out of the study wearing a Panama hat. "It's going to be bloody sweltering, you know."

"Eddie, don't start," snaps Trish, shoving her mascara wand back in the tube. "We are going to this party and that's final. Have you got the present?"

"And what happened?" I ask, trying to haul the conversation back on track. "With Nathaniel's plans?"

Trish makes a small, regretful moue at herself in the mirror. "Well, his father passed away very suddenly, and there was all that dreadful business with the pubs. And he changed his mind. Never bought the land." She gives herself another dissatisfied look. "Should I wear my *pink* suit?"

"*No,*" Eddie and I say in unison. I glance at Eddie's exasperated face and stifle a laugh.

"You look lovely, Mrs. Geiger," I say. "Really."

Somehow, between us, Eddie and I manage to chivvy her away from the mirror, out the front door, and across the gravel to Eddie's Porsche. Eddie's right, it's going to be a boiling day. The sky is already a translucent blue, the sun a dazzling ball.

"What time will you be back?" I ask as they get in.

"Not until late this evening," says Trish. "Eddie, where's the *present*? Ah, Nathaniel, here you are."

I look over the top of the car. There he is, coming down the drive, in jeans and an old gray T-shirt, his rucksack over his shoulder. And here I am, in my dressing gown with my hair all over the place.

And still not sure how things have been left between us. Although certain bits of my body are already responding to the sight of him. They don't seem to be in any confusion at all.

"Hi," I say as he gets near.

"Hi." Nathaniel's eyes crinkle in a friendly way, but he doesn't make any attempt to kiss me or even smile. Instead, he just comes to a halt. There's something about his intent, purposeful gaze that makes me feel a bit wobbly around the legs.

"So." I wrench my eyes away. "You're ... working hard today."

"I could do with some help," he says casually. "If you're at a loose end. Mum told me you weren't cooking today."

I feel a huge leap of delight, which I attempt to hide with a cough.

"Right." I shrug slightly, almost frowning. "Well ... maybe."

"Great." He nods to the Geigers and saunters off toward the garden.

Trish has been watching this exchange in increasing dissatisfaction.

"You're not very *affectionate* with each other, are you?" she says. "You know, in *my* experience—"

"Leave them alone, for God's sake!" retorts Eddie, starting the engine. "Let's get this bloody thing over with."

"Eddie Geiger!" Trish shrills. "This is my sister's party you're talking about! Do you realize—"

Eddie revs the engine, drowning out her voice, and with a spattering of gravel the Porsche disappears out of the drive, leaving me alone in the silent, baking sunshine.

Right.

So ... it's just Nathaniel and me. Alone together. Until eight o'clock this evening. That's the basic scenario.

A pulse is starting to thud somewhere deep inside me. Like a conductor setting the beat, like an introduction.

Deliberately nonchalant, I turn on the gravel and start to make my way back toward the house. As I pass a flower bed I even pause and study a random plant for a moment, holding the green leaves between my fingers.

I guess I could wander down and offer a helping hand. It would be polite.

I force myself not to rush. I take a shower and get dressed and have breakfast, consisting of half a cup of tea and an apple. Then I go upstairs and put on a little makeup.

I've dressed low-key. A T-shirt, a cotton skirt, and flip-flops. As I look in the mirror I feel almost shivery with anticipation. But other than that my mind is weirdly blank. I seem to have lost all my thought processes.

After the cool house, the garden feels scorching, the air still and almost shimmery. I keep to the shade, heading down the side path, not knowing where he's working, where I'm heading. And then I see him, in the midst of a row of lavender and lilac-colored flowers, knotting a length of twine.

"Hi," I say.

"Hi." He looks up and wipes his brow. I'm half-expecting him to drop what he's doing, come forward, and kiss me. But he doesn't. He just carries on knotting, then cuts the twine off with a knife.

"I came to help," I say after a pause. "What are we doing?"

"Tying up the sweet peas." He gestures at the plants, which are growing up what look like cane wigwams. "They need support, otherwise they just flop." He throws me a ball of twine. "Have a go. Just tie them gently."

He's not joking. I really *am* helping with the gardening. Cautiously I unwind a length of twine and follow what he's doing, cutting with a pair of secateurs he passes to me. The soft leaves and petals tickle me as I work and fill the air with an amazing sweet scent.

Nathaniel comes over to take a look. "You could tie a little tighter." His hand brushes briefly against mine as he turns away. "Let's see you do the next one."

My hand tingles at his touch. Did he mean to do that? Uncertain, I tie up the next plant, knotting tighter than before.

"Yeah, that's good." Suddenly Nathaniel's voice is behind me and I feel his fingers on the back of my neck, tracing around my earlobe. "You need to do the whole row."

He definitely meant to do that. No question. I turn round, wanting to reciprocate, but he's already on the other side of the row, intent on a sweet pea plant, as though nothing happened.

He has a game plan, I suddenly realize.

Now I really am turned on.

The pulse is growing stronger inside me as I move from plant to plant. There's silence except for the rustling of leaves and faint snap of twine as I cut. Three more plants and I'm at the end of the row.

"Done," I say without turning round.

"Great, let's see." He comes over to inspect my knotted twine. I can feel his other hand edging up my thigh, pushing up my skirt. I can't move. I'm transfixed. Then suddenly he breaks away, businesslike again, picking up a pair of trugs.

"What—" I can't even frame a sentence properly.

He kisses me briefly, hard on the mouth. "Let's move on. Raspberries need picking."

The raspberry cages are further down the garden, like rooms of green netting, with dry, earthy floors and rows of plants. As we enter there's no sound except that of buzzing insects and the flapping of a trapped sparrow, which Nathaniel shoos away through the netting.

We work the first row wordlessly, picking the fruit off the plants. By the end of the row my mouth is tangy with the taste of them, my hands are scratched and aching from the constant plucking, and I'm sweating all over. The heat seems more intense in this raspberry cage than anywhere else in the garden.

We meet at the end of the row. Sweat is pouring down our faces.

"Hot work," he says. He puts his basket down and strips off his T-shirt.

"Yes." There's a still beat between us. Then, almost defiantly, I do the same. I'm standing there in my bra, inches from him, my skin pale and milky next to his.

"Have we done enough?" I gesture at the basket, but Nathaniel doesn't even glance down.

"Not yet."

His expression makes me damp and prickly behind my knees. I meet his eyes and it's like we're playing truth or dare.

"I couldn't reach those ones." I point at a high cluster of fruit just out of reach.

"I'll help." He leans over me, skin against skin, and I feel his mouth on my earlobe as he picks the fruit. My entire body responds. I can't bear this; I need it to stop. And I need it not to stop.

But it goes on. We move up and down the rows like two performers in a courtly dance. Outwardly concentrating on our moves yet aware only of each other. At the end of every row, he brushes some part of me with his mouth or fingers. One time he feeds me raspberries and I graze his fingers with my teeth. I want to get at him, I want my hands all over him, but every time he turns away before anything can progress.

I'm starting to shiver all over with desire. He unhooked my bra two rows ago. I've discarded my knickers. He's unbuckled his belt. And still, *still* we're picking raspberries.

The baskets are full and heavy and my arms are aching, but I'm barely aware of them. All I'm aware of is that my whole body is throbbing, that I can't stand this for much longer. As I reach the end of the last row I put the basket down and face him, unable to hide how desperate I am.

"Are we done?"

My breath is coming in short, hot bursts. I have to have him. He has to realize.

"We've done pretty well." His gaze drifts toward the other fruit cages. "There's still more to do . . ."

"No," I hear myself saying. "No more."

I stand there in the heat and the dusty earth, panting and aching. And just as I think I might explode, he comes forward and bends his mouth down to my nipple, and I nearly swoon. And this time he doesn't move away. This time is for real. His hands are moving over my body, my skirt is falling to the ground, his jeans are sliding off. Then I'm shuddering, and clutching him, and crying out. And the raspberries are forgotten, scattered on the ground, squashed, crushed beneath us.

We seem to lie still for hours afterward. I feel numb with euphoria. There are stones and dust embedded in my back and knees and hands and raspberry stains all over my skin. I don't mind. I can't even bring myself to lift a hand and remove the ant that is crawling up my stomach like a tickling dot.

My head is on Nathaniel's chest, his heart beating like a deep, comforting clock. The sun is hot on my skin. I have no idea what time it is. I don't care what time it is. I've lost all sense of minutes and hours.

At last Nathaniel shifts his head slightly. He kisses my shoulder, then smiles. "You taste of raspberry."

"That was—" I break off, almost too stupefied to frame any sensible words. "You know . . . normally I . . ." A huge yawn suddenly overcomes me and I clap my hand over my mouth. I want to go to sleep now, for days.

Nathaniel traces lazy circles around my back.

"Six minutes isn't sex," I hear him saying as my eyes crash shut. "Six minutes is a boiled egg."

By the time I wake up, the raspberry cages are in partial shade. Nathaniel has moved from underneath me, given me a pillow constructed from my crumpled, raspberry-stained skirt, put on his jeans, and brought down some beer from the Geigers' fridge. I sit up, my head still groggy, to see him leaning against a tree on the grass.

"Slacker," I say. "The Geigers think you're tying up sweet peas."

He turns toward me with a flicker of amusement. "Sleep well?"

"How long was I asleep?" I put my hand to my face and remove a small stone. I feel totally disoriented.

"Couple of hours. You want some of this?" He gestures to the bottle. "It's cold."

I get to my feet, brush myself down, put on my skirt and bra as a good compromise outfit and join him. I sink back against the tree trunk, my bare feet in the cool grass.

"God, I feel so . . ." I lift a hand and let it drop down with a heavy thump.

"You're not as twitchy as you were," says Nathaniel. "You used to jump a mile whenever I spoke to you."

"No, I didn't!"

"Uh-huh, you did." He nods. "Like a rabbit."

"I thought I was a badger."

"You're a rabbit–badger cross. Very rare breed." He grins at me. For a while neither of us speaks. I watch a tiny plane high above, leaving a white trail in the sky.

"Mum says you've changed too. She said she reckons whoever you've run away from . . . whatever happened . . . they're losing their grip on you."

The question is there in his voice, but I don't respond. I'm thinking of Iris yesterday. Letting me take all my frustrations out on her. It's not like she's had it easy herself.

"Your mum's amazing," I say at last. I put the bottle down and roll onto the grass, staring up at the blue sky. I can smell the earth beneath my head and feel grass stems against my ears and hear a grasshopper chirruping nearby.

I have changed. I can feel it in myself. I feel . . . stiller.

"Who would you be?" I say, twisting a grass stem round my finger. "If you could just run away. Become a different person."

"I'd be me," he says at last. "I'm happy as I am. I like living where I live. I like doing what I do."

I roll over onto my front and look up at him, squinting in the sunlight. "There must be something else you'd like to do. Some dream you've got."

He shakes his head, smiling. "I'm doing what I want to do."

"But what about the nursery you were going to set up?"

I see the surprise on his face. "How did you—"

"Trish told me about it this morning. She said you had business plans and everything. What happened?"

For a moment he's silent, his eyes averted from mine. I can't tell what's going on inside.

"It was just an idea," he says finally.

"You gave it up for your mum. To run the pubs."

"Maybe." He reaches for a low-growing branch and starts stripping it of leaves. "Everything changed."

"But do you really want to run the pubs?" I edge forward on the grass, trying to intercept his gaze. "You said it yourself, you're not a landlord. You're a gardener."

"It's not a question of *want*." Nathaniel's voice has a sudden edge of frustration. "It's a family business. Someone has to run it."

"Why you?" I persist. "Why not your brother?"

"He's . . . different. He does his own thing."

"*You* could do your own thing!"

"I have responsibilities." His frown grows heavier. "My mum—"

"She'd want you to do whatever you want to do," I

insist. "I know she would. She'd want you to be happy in your life, not give it up for her."

"I am happy. It's ridiculous to say—"

"But couldn't you be *happier*?"

There's silence in the garden. Nathaniel's shoulders are bent round as if he wants to shut out what I'm saying.

"Don't you ever want to ditch your responsibilities?" I throw my arms out wide in sudden abandon. "Just . . . walk out into the world and see what happens?"

"Is that what you did?" he demands, wheeling round.

"I—We're not talking about me. We're talking about you."

"Samantha. . . ." He rubs his cheek. "I know you don't want to talk about the past. But I want you to tell me one thing. And be truthful."

I feel a deep tremor of alarm. What's he going to ask me?

"I'll . . . try. What is it?"

Nathaniel looks me directly in the eye and takes a deep breath.

"Do you have kids?"

I'm so dumbfounded, I can't speak for a moment. He thinks I have *kids*? A gurgle of relieved laughter rises through me before I can stop it.

"No, I don't have kids! What, you think I've left five starving little mouths behind?"

"I don't know." He frowns, looking sheepish but defensive. "Why not?"

"Because . . . I mean . . . do I *look* like I've had five kids?" I can't help a note of indignation, and he starts to laugh too.

"Maybe not *five* . . ."

"What's that supposed to mean?" I'm about to hit him with his shirt when a voice pierces the air.

"Samantha?"

It's Trish. Coming from the house. They're *home*?

"Samantha?" her voice trills again. "Are you outside?"

Oh, fuck. I'm naked except for a skirt and a bra, and covered in dust and raspberry stains. Nathaniel is much the same, except in jeans.

"Quick! My clothes!" I hiss, scrabbling to my feet.

"Where are they?" says Nathaniel, looking around.

"I don't *know*!" I'm trying to control my laughter. "We're going to get the sack."

"Samantha?" I can hear the clunk of the conservatory doors being opened.

"Shit!" I squeak. "She's coming!"

"It's fine," says Nathaniel, retrieving his T-shirt from the raspberry cage. He pops it over his head and at once looks pretty together. "I'll create a diversion. You sneak up the side, behind the shrubs, go in the kitchen door, run upstairs, and get changed. OK?"

"OK," I say breathlessly. "And what's our story?"

"Our story is . . ." He pauses as though thinking. "We didn't shag in the garden or help ourselves to beers from the fridge."

"Right." I can't help giggling. "Good plan."

"Go swiftly, Brown Rabbit." He kisses me, and I dart across the lawn to the cover of a huge rhododendron bush.

I sneak up the side of the garden, keeping behind the shrubs, trying not to give myself away. My bare feet are cool on the damp, shaded earth; I step on a sharp pebble and wince in total silence. I feel about ten years old, playing hide-and-seek, the same mixture of terror and delight pounding in my heart.

When I'm only ten yards from the house I crouch behind a shrub and wait. After a minute or two I see

Nathaniel firmly leading the Geigers down the lawn toward the lily pond.

"I think we could have a case of powdery mildew," he's saying. "I thought you should see it for yourselves."

I wait until they're well past, then sprint to the conservatory, in through the house, and up the stairs. When I'm in my room and the door is safely closed, I collapse on the bed, wanting to laugh at my own relief, at the hilarity, at the *silliness* of it all. Then I get up and look out the window. I can just see them all down by the pond. Nathaniel is pointing at something with a stick.

I hurry into the bathroom, turn on the shower full blast, and stand under it for thirty seconds. I pull on clean underwear, a pair of fresh jeans, and a demure long-sleeved top. I even add fresh lipstick. Then, slipping on a pair of espadrilles, I head downstairs and out into the garden.

Nathaniel and the Geigers are by now making their way back up to the house. Trish's heels are sinking into the lawn and both she and Eddie look hot and irritated.

"Hi," I say casually as they approach.

"*There* you are," says Nathaniel. "I haven't seen you all afternoon."

"I was studying recipes," I say innocently, and turn to Trish with a polite smile. "Did you enjoy the party, Mrs. Geiger?"

Too late I see Nathaniel making deathlike, finger-across-the-throat gestures behind their backs.

"Thank you for asking, Samantha." Trish snaps her purse shut and dabs her nose with a tissue. "I'd rather not talk about the party, thank you."

Eddie makes an incensed spluttering sound. "You won't bloody give up, will you? All I said was—"

"It was the *way* you said it!" shrieks Trish. "Sometimes I think your *sole* purpose in life is to embarrass me!"

Eddie stalks off toward the house, his Panama hat lopsided on his head.

Uh-oh. I raise my eyebrows at Nathaniel, who grins back over Trish's head.

"Would you like a nice cup of tea, Mrs. Geiger?" I say soothingly. "Or . . . a Bloody Mary?"

"Thank you, Samantha," she replies, lifting her chin in a dignified manner. "A Bloody Mary would be very nice."

As we walk up to the conservatory, Trish seems to calm down a little. She even mixes her own Bloody Mary instead of bossing me around as I do it, and makes one each for me and Nathaniel too.

"*Now,*" she says, after we've each taken a sip and sat down among the frondy plants. "There was something I needed to tell you, Samantha. We're having a visitor."

"Oh, right," I say, trying not to smile. Nathaniel is sitting next to me and is edging off my espadrille with his foot under the coffee table.

"My niece is coming to stay tomorrow for a few weeks. She's coming to get some peace and quiet in the country. She has some work to do, and it's *very* important she isn't disturbed, so Mr. Geiger and I offered her a place here. I'd like you to get the spare room ready for her."

"Very good." I nod dutifully.

"She'll need a bed made up and a desk—I believe she's bringing a laptop computer with her."

"Yes, Mrs. Geiger."

"She's a very bright girl, Melissa." Trish lights up a cigarette with a Tiffany lighter. "*Extremely* high-powered. One of these City girls."

"Oh, right," I say, trying to stay composed as Nathaniel finally manages to push my espadrille off. "What does she do?"

"She's a lawyer," says Trish—and I look up, speechless. A lawyer?

A lawyer is coming to stay in this house?

Nathaniel is tickling the sole of my foot, but I can only respond with a weak smile. This could be bad.

What if I *know* this lawyer?

As Trish mixes herself another Bloody Mary, I'm racking my brains frantically. *Melissa.* It could be Melissa Davis from Freshwater. It could be Melissa Christie from Clark Forrester. It could be Melissa Taylor who worked on the DeltaCo merger. We spent hours in the same room together. She'd recognize me straightaway.

"So . . . is she a niece on your side, Mrs. Geiger?" I ask casually as Trish sits down. "Is she called Geiger too?"

"No, she's called Hurst."

Melissa Hurst. Doesn't ring any bells.

"And where does she work?" *Please let it be abroad. . . .*

"Oh, she's at some high-powered place in London." Trish gestures vaguely with her glass.

OK, so I don't know her. But if she's at any of the big law firms she's bound to have heard about me. She's bound to know about the Carter Spink lawyer who lost fifty million and ran away. She'll know every humiliating detail of my disgrace.

I'm feeling cold all over at the thought of it. All it takes is for her to recognize my name, to put two and two together . . . and the whole story will come out. I'll be as humiliated here as I was in London. Everyone will know what happened at Carter Spink. Everyone will know my lies. I glance at Nathaniel and feel a spike of dread.

I *can't* let things be spoiled. Not now.

Eighteen

The crucial thing is that this lawyer doesn't recognize me. So the following afternoon, after I've prepared the spare room, I hurry to my own room and pin my hair up on top of my head, allowing large tendrils to escape artistically and conceal my face. Then I find myself adding a pair of old tinted glasses I discovered in the dressing table drawer, which look like they date from the 1980s. As disguises go, this isn't exactly the most subtle job in the world—but at least I look nothing like my old self.

As I come downstairs, Nathaniel is heading out of the kitchen, looking pissed off. He looks up at me and stops dead in surprise.

"Samantha . . . what have you done?"

"Oh, my hair?" I touch it casually. "I just wanted it in a different style."

"Are those *your* sunglasses?"

"I've got a bit of a headache. So . . . what's up?" I add, hastily changing the subject.

"Trish." He scowls. "She's been lecturing me on noise. I can't mow the lawn between the hours of ten and two. I can't use the trimmer without giving warning. Could I please tiptoe on the gravel. *Tiptoe.*"

"Why?"

"Because of this blasted visitor. We all have to dance around her. A bloody *lawyer.*" He shakes his head in disbelief. "*Her* work's important? *My* work's important!"

"She's coming!" Trish's voice suddenly shrills from the kitchen and she comes hurrying out. "Are we all ready?" She flings open the front door and I hear the sound of a car door opening in the drive.

This is it. I pull a few more strands of hair over my face and clench my fists by my sides. If I recognize this woman I'll just keep my eyes down, mumble my words, and play my part. I'm a housekeeper. I have never been anything but a housekeeper.

"Now, you should get *lots* of peace here, Melissa," I can hear Trish saying. "I've instructed the staff to look after you with *extra* special care. . . ."

I exchange looks with Nathaniel, who rolls his eyes.

"Here we are! Let me hold the door open . . ."

I hold my breath. A moment later Trish enters the house, followed by a girl in jeans and a tight white top, dragging a suitcase.

This is the top, high-powered lawyer?

She has long dark hair and a pert, pretty face, and can't be much out of her teens.

"Melissa, this is our *wonderful* housekeeper, Samantha—" Trish breaks off in surprise. "Samantha . . . what on earth are you wearing? You look like Elton John!"

"Hello," I say awkwardly, removing the sunglasses. "It's very nice to meet you."

"It's *fab* to be here." Melissa has a boarding-school drawl. "London was, like, sooo getting me down."

"Mrs. Geiger said you're a lawyer at some...big place in London?"

"Yah." She gives me a smug smile. "I'm at Chelsea Law School."

What?

She's not even a qualified lawyer. She's a law student. She's a *baby*. I cautiously raise my head and meet her eyes—but there's not a blink of recognition. Oh, for God's sake. I have nothing to worry about from this girl. I almost want to laugh.

"And who's this?" Melissa bats her mascaraed eyelashes alluringly at Nathaniel, whose scowl deepens.

"This is Nathaniel, our gardener," says Trish. "But don't worry, he's under *strict* instructions not to disturb you. I've told him, you need absolute quiet for your work."

"It's true. I've got *loads* of revision to do." Melissa gives a world-weary sigh and pushes a hand through her hair. "You wouldn't believe the workload, Auntie Trish. I've been *soooo* stressed."

"I don't know how you do it!" Trish puts an arm around her shoulders and squeezes tight. "Now, what would you like to do first? We're *all* at your disposal."

"Could you unpack all my things?" Melissa turns to me. "They'll be creased, so they'll all need ironing."

She's not going to do her own unpacking? I'm to be this girl's personal *maid*?

"I might take my books out in the garden," she adds airily. "Maybe the gardener could set up a table for me in the shade?"

Trish is watching in total admiration as Melissa rummages in a backpack full of textbooks.

"*Look* at all those books, Samantha!" she exclaims as Melissa retrieves *Beginner's Guide to Litigation*. "Look at all those long words!"

"Er ... wow," I say politely.

"Why don't you make us all some coffee first?" Trish turns to me. "We'll take it on the terrace. Bring some biscuits out too."

"Of course, Mrs. Geiger," I say, bobbing an automatic curtsy.

"Could you make mine half caffeinated, half decaf?" Melissa adds over her shoulder. "I, like, don't want to get too wired."

No, I bloody couldn't, you pretentious little cow.

"Of course." I smile through gritted teeth. "My pleasure."

As I carry the coffee out to the terrace ten minutes later, Trish and Melissa are ensconced in chairs under a parasol along with Eddie.

"You've met Melissa, have you?" he says as I set down the tray on a wrought-iron table. "Our little star? Our legal eagle?"

"Yes, I have. Your coffee," I add, handing the cup to Melissa. "Just as you asked for it."

"Melissa's under a great deal of pressure," says Eddie. "It's up to us to make things easy for her."

"You can't *imagine* what the strain's like," says Melissa seriously. "I've been working into the evenings and everything. My social life's, like, gone out the window." She takes a sip of coffee, then turns to me. "By the way, I meant to say ..." She frowns. "What's your name again?"

"Samantha."

"Yes, Samantha. Be really careful with my red beaded top, OK?" She takes another gulp of coffee.

"I'll do my best," I reply. "Will that be all, Mrs. Geiger?"

"Wait!" Eddie puts his cup down. "I've got something

for you. I haven't forgotten our little conversation the other day!" He reaches under his chair and produces a brown paper bag. I can see a couple of shiny books poking out of the top. "Now, you're not going to get out of this one, Samantha. This can be our little project!"

Oh, no. Please do not let this be what I think it is.

"Mr. Geiger," I begin quickly. "It's really nice of you, but—"

"I won't hear another word!" he interrupts with a raised hand. "You'll thank me one day!"

"What are you talking about?" Melissa wrinkles her nose in curiosity.

"Samantha's going to take some qualifications!" With a flourish Eddie pulls two workbooks from the bag. Both are brightly colored, with big jazzy letters and illustrations. I can see the words *Math* and *English* and *Adult Learning*.

I'm totally speechless.

"I'm sure Melissa will be delighted to help with anything tricky," chips in Trish. "Won't you, love?"

"Of course," says Melissa with a patronizing smile. "Well done you, Samantha! It's never too late." She pushes her full cup of coffee toward me. "Make me another coffee, will you? This one's too weak."

By the middle of the following day I have had just about enough of Melissa. I've made her about fifty cups of coffee, half of which she hasn't bothered to drink. I've brought her chilled water. I've rustled up sandwiches. I've washed all the dirty laundry, which it turned out her suitcase contained. I've ironed her a white shirt to wear in the evening. Every time I try to start on one of my regular jobs I hear Melissa's high-pitched voice summoning me.

Meanwhile, Trish is tiptoeing around as though we have Cherie Blair herself in the garden, working on some vital human-rights case. As I dust the living room, she's watching Melissa, sitting at a table set up on the lawn.

"She's working so hard. Such an *intelligent* girl, Melissa."

"Mmm," I grunt, noncommittally.

"You know, it's not easy to get into law school, Samantha. Especially the best one! Melissa had to beat hundreds of people just to get the place!"

"Fantastic." I flick my cloth roughly over the TV. "That's great. So . . . how long is she staying?" I try to ask the question casually.

"It depends," replies Trish. "Her exams are in a few weeks, and I've said she's welcome to stay as long as she likes!"

A few *weeks*? It's only been one day, and already she's driving me mad.

I spend the afternoon in the kitchen, pretending to have selective deafness. Whenever Melissa calls me, I turn the blender on, or the radio up, or clatter around with baking trays. If she wants me she can find me herself.

At last, she appears at the kitchen door, her cheeks flushed with annoyance. "Samantha, I've been calling you!"

"Really?" I look up innocently from the butter I'm chopping to make pastry. "I didn't hear."

"We need a bell system or something." She exhales in impatience. "This is ridiculous, me having to stop what I'm doing."

"What did you want?"

"My water jug is empty. And I need some kind of snack. To keep my energy levels up."

"You could have brought your jug into the kitchen," I suggest mildly. "Or made your own snack?"

"Look, I don't have time to be making snacks, OK?" snaps Melissa. "I'm under a great deal of time pressure right now. I have piles of work, I have exam deadlines . . . you have no *idea* what my life is like."

I'm silent for a moment, trying to get my resentment under control.

"I'll bring you out a sandwich," I say at last.

"*Thank* you," she says sarcastically, then stands with her arms folded, as though she's waiting for something.

"What?" I say.

"Go on." She gestures with her head. "Curtsy."

What? She can't _be serious. "I'm not curtsying to *you*!" I say, almost laughing.

"You curtsy to my aunt. And my uncle."

"They're my employers," I retort tightly. "It's different." *And believe me, if I could turn back the clock, curtsying would not be featured in any of our lives.*

"I'm living in this house. So I'm your employer too. You should show me the same respect."

I want to *slap* this girl. If she was my junior at Carter Spink I would . . . annihilate her.

"Right." I put my knife down. "I'll go and ask Mrs. Geiger, shall I?" Before she can reply I stride out of the kitchen. I cannot tolerate this. If Trish takes her side, that's it. I'm leaving.

I can't see Trish anywhere downstairs, so I head upstairs, heart racing. I arrive outside her room and knock. "Mrs. Geiger? I'd like a word."

A few moments later, Trish opens the door a crack and pokes her head out, looking a little ruffled. "Samantha! What do you want?"

"I'm not happy with the current situation," I say,

attempting a calm, civilized voice. "I'd like to discuss it, please."

"What situation?" She wrinkles her brow.

"With Melissa. And her . . . her constant needs. I'm being taken away from my regular duties. The house-keeping will suffer if I have to keep attending to her."

Trish doesn't seem to have heard a word.

"Oh, Samantha . . . not now." She waves a distracted, dismissive hand. "We'll talk about this later."

I can hear Eddie mumbling something from inside the room. Great. They were probably having sex. She probably wants to get back to Turkish style.

"Right." I try to control my frustration. "So I'll just . . . get on, then, shall I?"

"Wait." Trish suddenly seems to focus on me. "Samantha, we'll be having champagne on the terrace in half an hour with some . . . ahm . . . friends. I'd like you to wear something other than your uniform." Her eyes run over it with slight distaste. "It's not the most *flattering* garment you possess."

You bloody chose it! I want to yell back at her. But instead, I curtsy, turn away, and walk to my room, fuming.

Bloody Trish. Bloody Melissa. If she's waiting for a sandwich, she can just wait.

I close the door, slump down on my bed, and look down at my hands, red and raw from hand-washing Melissa's delicate garments.

What am I doing here?

I can feel disappointment and disillusionment spreading through me. Maybe I was being naive—but I honestly thought Trish and Eddie had come to respect me. Not just as their housekeeper but as a person. But the way Trish behaved just now . . . it's plain I'm just "staff" to them. Like some sort of useful object, one notch above the Hoover. I almost feel like packing my bags and walking out.

I have a sudden vision of myself flouncing down the stairs, flinging open the door, shooting over my shoulder to Melissa, "And by the way, I've got a law degree too, and mine is *better* than yours."

But that would be petulant. No, worse. It would be pathetic.

I massage my temples, gradually getting things in perspective.

I chose to do this. No one forced me. And maybe it wasn't the most rational move in the world, and maybe I won't stay here forever. But it's up to me to make the most of it while I am here. It's up to me to be professional.

Or at least . . . as professional as I can be, bearing in mind I still haven't a clue what a savarin mold is.

At last I summon some energy and get up off the bed. I change out of my uniform, into a dress, and brush out my hair. I even add some lipstick for good measure. Then I reach for my mobile and text Nathaniel:

hi! RU there? sam

I wait for a reply but none comes. He hasn't been around all afternoon, I realize. I wonder what he's up to.

As I descend the stairs into the hall, the house is still and silent. I don't know what time Trish's friends are coming, but there's no sign of them yet. Maybe I've got time to finish my pastry quickly. I might even get the vegetables peeled.

I'm hurrying toward the kitchen when Nathaniel appears out the door.

"*There* you are." He puts his arms round me and kisses me, pulling me under the stairs, which we've discovered is quite a convenient hiding place. "Mmm. I've missed you."

"Nathaniel—" I protest, but his grip around me only gets tighter. After a few moments I manage to wriggle free.

"Nathaniel, I've got pastry to make. I'm already behind schedule, and apparently I've got to serve drinks to some people—"

"Wait." Nathaniel tugs me back, glancing at his watch. "One more minute. Then we can go."

I peer at him uncertainly.

"Nathaniel, what are you talking about?"

"Samantha..." He shakes his head in amusement. "Did you really think you could fool us? Sweetheart, your secret's out. We *know*."

I feel a plunging dread. They know? What do they know?

"What exactly—" I begin, but Nathaniel puts a finger to my lips.

"No, no, no. You're going to get your surprise."

"Surprise?" I falter.

"Now come out. They're waiting for you. Close your eyes..." He puts one arm around my waist and the other hand over my eyes. "Come this way...I'll lead you...."

As I walk forward in darkness, guided only by Nathaniel's arm, I feel almost sick with fear. My mind is ranging wildly about, trying to work out what might have been going on behind my back. Who's waiting for me out there?

Please, please, don't say they've tried to fix my life up. Please don't say they've arranged some kind of reunion. I have a sudden image of Ketterman standing on the lawn, his steel glasses glinting in the sunlight. Or Arnold. Or my mother.

"Here she is!" Nathaniel guides me out of the French doors and down the steps into the garden. I can feel sun on my face and hear some kind of flapping sound and . . . jazz? "All right! Open your eyes!"

I can't open my eyes. Whatever it is, I don't want to know.

"It's OK!" Nathaniel's laughing. "No one's going to eat you! Open them!"

I open my eyes and blink several times, wondering if I'm dreaming.

What . . . what's going on?

An enormous banner reading HAPPY BIRTHDAY, SAMANTHA! is tied between two trees. That's what's making the flapping noise. The garden table is laid with a white tablecloth, a bouquet of flowers, several bottles of champagne, and a bowl of strawberries. A bunch of shiny helium balloons reading *Samantha* is tethered to a chair. Eddie and Trish are standing on the grass, together with Iris, Eamonn, and Melissa—and they're all beaming at me, apart from Melissa, who's pouting.

I feel as though I've lurched into some parallel universe.

"Surprise!" they all cry out in unison. "Happy birthday!"

I open my mouth but no sound comes out. I'm too poleaxed to speak. Why do the Geigers think it's my birthday?

"Look at her," says Trish. "She's stunned! Aren't you, Samantha?"

"Um . . . yes," I stutter.

"She had no idea," confirms Nathaniel with a grin.

"Happy birthday, sweetie." Iris comes over, clasps me tightly, and gives me a kiss.

"Eddie, open the champagne!" I can hear Trish exclaiming impatiently behind me. "Come on!"

What do I do? What do I say? How do you break it to the people who have organized your surprise birthday party that actually . . . it's not your birthday?

Why would they think it's my birthday? Did I give them some made-up date of birth at the interview? But I don't remember doing that—

"Champagne for the birthday girl!" Eddie pops open a bottle and the champagne froths into a glass.

"Many happy returns!" Eamonn proffers the bowl of strawberries. "Ah, you should have seen your face just now!"

"Priceless!" agrees Trish. "Now, let's have a toast!"

I can't let this go on any longer.

"Um . . . Mr. and Mrs. Geiger . . . everyone . . . this is lovely, and I'm really touched." I swallow hard, screwing myself up to say it. "But . . . it's not my birthday."

Everyone bursts into laughter.

"I told you this would happen!" Trish says in delight. "She *said* you'd deny it!"

"It's not *that* bad, getting a year older," teases Nathaniel. "Now, face it, we know. So have your champagne and enjoy yourself."

I'm totally confused. "Who said I'd deny it?"

"Lady Edgerly, of course!" says Trish. "She's the one who gave away your little secret!"

Freya? Freya is behind this?

"What—what exactly did she say? Lady Edgerly."

"She told me that your birthday was coming up," says Trish, looking pleased. "And she warned me you'd try to keep it secret. Naughty, naughty!"

I do not believe Freya. I do not *believe* her.

"She also told me," Trish lowers her voice sympathetically, "your last birthday was rather a *letdown*? She said we simply had to make it up to you. In fact, she was the one who suggested we should do it as a big surprise!" Trish raises her glass. "So here's to Samantha! Happy birthday!"

"Happy birthday!" the others echo, lifting their glasses.

I'm not sure if I want to laugh or cry. Or both. I look around at the banner and silvery balloons, bobbing in the breeze; at the champagne bottles; at everyone's smiling faces. There's nothing I can say. I'll have to go with it.

"Well...thank you," I say, looking around. "I...I really appreciate it."

"I'm sorry I was a little *short* with you this afternoon," says Trish cheerfully. "We were rather *struggling* with the helium balloons. We'd already lost one bunch this afternoon." She darts a baleful glance at Eddie.

"Have you ever tried to get helium balloons into a car boot?" Eddie retorts hotly. "I'd like to see you do it! I haven't got three bloody hands, you know."

An image comes to me of Eddie battling with a load of shiny balloons, trying to stuff them into the Porsche, and I bite my lip hard.

"We didn't put your *age* on the balloons, Samantha," Trish adds in a breathy whisper. "As one woman to another, I thought you'd appreciate that gesture."

I look from her vivid, over-made-up face to Eddie's fleshy pink one and suddenly feel so moved I don't know what to say. All the time, they were planning this. They were doing a banner. They were ordering balloons.

"Mr. Geiger, Mrs. Geiger, I'm...I'm so bowled over..."

"It's not over yet!" says Trish, nodding over my shoulder.

"Happy birthday to you..." A voice behind me is singing and after a moment the others join in. I look over my shoulder to see Iris coming forward over the lawn, holding the most enormous, two-tier birthday cake. It's iced all over in palest pink, with sugar roses and raspberries and one elegant white candle. As she gets near I see, in silver writing: *Happy Birthday Dear Samantha From Us All.*

It's the most beautiful thing I've ever seen. My throat is tight. No one's ever made a cake for me in my life before.

"Blow out your candle!" calls out Eamonn as the singing comes to an end. Somehow I puff feebly at the flame, and everyone cheers.

"You like it?" Iris smiles.

"It's . . . wonderful," I manage to say. "I've never seen anything like it."

"Happy birthday, chicken." She pats my hand. "You deserve it, if anyone does."

As Iris sets the cake down and begins to slice it up, Eddie tinkles his glass with the end of a pen.

"If I could have your attention." He takes a step up onto the terrace and clears his throat. "Samantha, we're all very glad you've come into our family. You're doing a marvelous job and we all appreciate it." Eddie raises his glass to me. "Er . . . well done."

"Thank you, Mr. Geiger," I falter. I look around at all the friendly faces, framed by blue sky and summer leaves. "I'm . . . I'm glad I've come here too. You've all been really welcoming and kind to me." Oh, God, I'm starting to well up. "I couldn't wish for better employers—"

"Oh, stop!" Trish flaps her hands and dabs her eye with a napkin.

"For she's a jolly good fellow," Eddie begins gruffly. "For she's a jolly good fellow—"

"*Eddie!* Samantha doesn't want to hear your stupid singing!" interrupts Trish shrilly, still dabbing her eyes. "Open some more champagne, for goodness sake!"

It's one of the warmest evenings of the year. As the sun slowly lowers in the sky, we all loll on the grass, drinking champagne and talking. Eamonn tells me about his girlfriend, Anna, who works in a hotel in Gloucester. Iris produces tiny feather-light tarts filled with chicken and herbs. Nathaniel rigs up a set of fairy lights in a tree. Melissa announces loudly several times that she can't sit around, she has to get back to work—then accepts just one more champagne refill.

The sky is an endless, evening blue and there's the smell of honeysuckle in the air. Music is burbling away gently in the background and Nathaniel's hand is resting casually on my thigh. I have never felt so content in my life.

"Presents!" says Trish suddenly. "We haven't done presents!"

I'm pretty sure she's drunk more champagne than anyone else. She lurches unsteadily over to the table, searches in her bag, and produces an envelope. "This is a little *bonus*, Samantha," she says, handing it to me. "To spend on a treat for yourself."

"Thank you!" I say, taken aback. "That's . . . incredibly kind of you!"

"We're not increasing your *pay*," she adds, eyeing me with slight mistrust. "You do understand this isn't a *raise* or anything. It's just a one-off."

"I understand," I say, trying not to smile. "It's very generous of you, Mrs. Geiger."

"I've got something too." Iris reaches into her basket and produces a parcel wrapped in brown paper. Inside I find four shiny new bread tins and a rose-sprigged, goffered apron. I can't help laughing out loud.

"Thank you," I say. "I'll put these to good use."

Trish is peering at the bread tins. "But...surely Samantha has loads of bread tins already?" she says, picking one up in her manicured hand. "And aprons?"

"I took a chance," Iris says, her eyes twinkling at me.

"Here you are, Samantha." Melissa hands me a Body Shop shampoo gift set, which I know for a fact has been sitting in Trish's bathroom cupboard since I got here.

"Thanks," I say politely. "You shouldn't have."

"And, Melissa," chimes in Trish, abruptly abandoning interest in the bread tin, "stop making extra work for Samantha! She can't spend all her time running after you! We can't afford to lose her, you know."

Melissa opens her mouth to retort.

"And this is from me," says Nathaniel, stepping in quickly. He hands me a tiny present wrapped in white tissue paper, and everyone turns to see what it is.

I unwrap the little parcel, and a pretty silver charm bracelet falls into my hand. There's only one charm on it: a tiny wooden spoon. I give another snuffle of laughter. A frilly apron, and now a wooden spoon.

Neither Nathaniel nor Iris knows the details of my real life—and yet in some ways I feel they know me better than anyone else in the world. They've seen me frazzled and incompetent, at my most vulnerable. I haven't had to put on a front or act efficient or pretend I know everything.

"It reminded me of the first time we met," says Nathaniel, his mouth curving into a smile.

"It's...fantastic." I put my arms round him and kiss him. "Thank you so much," I murmur into his ear.

Trish is watching with avid eyes as we draw apart.

"Well, it's obvious what drew *you* to Samantha," she says to Nathaniel. "It was her cooking, wasn't it?"

"It was her chickpeas," agrees Nathaniel gravely.

Eamonn has been up on the terrace. Now he bounds

down the steps and hands me a bottle of wine. "This is from me," he says. "It's not much, but—"

"Oh, that's lovely!" I say, touched. "Thanks, Eamonn."

"And I was going to ask, would you be interested in waitressing ever?"

"At the pub?" I say in surprise, but he shakes his head.

"Private functions. We have a little concern going in the village. It's not really a business, more like passing on work to friends. Make a little extra money, that kind of thing."

Passing on work to friends. I suddenly feel a little warm glow inside.

"I'd love to. Thanks for thinking of me."

Eamonn grins. "And there's a drink or two waiting for you behind the bar if you want to come along?"

"Well . . . er . . ." I glance at Trish. "Maybe later . . ."

"You go!" says Trish. "Enjoy yourselves! Don't *think* about work! We'll put the dirty glasses in the kitchen," she adds, "and you can deal with them tomorrow."

"Thanks, Mrs. Geiger." I force myself to remain straight-faced. "That's very . . . good of you."

"Oh, and Samantha." She beckons me over with her glass. "I was thinking about what you said to me the other day. About finding myself a little project of my own. Not that my life isn't *extremely* busy already . . ."

"Of course." I nod.

"Anyway." She pauses momentously. "I've decided I'm going to hold a charity lunch for Save The Children."

"Good idea!" I say with enthusiasm.

"And you can help me organize it! After all your experience running such events for Lady Edgerly, you must be an expert!"

"Absolutely," I gulp. "I look forward to it!"

The only experience I have with charity events is attending them with clients and being forced to watch drunken, highly paid bankers outbid each other in the auction.

"I must go too," says Iris, getting up. "Good night, and thanks."

"We can't tempt you to the pub, Iris?" says Eamonn.

"Not tonight." She smiles, her face illuminated by the twinkling fairy lights. "Good night, Samantha. Night, Nathaniel."

"Good night, Mum."

"Night, Eamonn."

"Night, Iris."

"Night, Grandpa," I say.

It comes out before I can stop myself. I'm hot with embarrassment, hoping no one picked it up. But Nathaniel is slowly swiveling toward me. *Trust* him to have heard.

"Good night, Mary Ellen." He lifts his eyebrows.

"Good night, Jim Bob," I retort nonchalantly.

"I see myself as more of a John Boy."

"Hmmm." I look him up and down. "OK, you can be John Boy."

I had a total crush on John Boy when I was a child. Not that I'll mention this fact to Nathaniel.

"C'mon." Nathaniel holds out his hand. "Let's get to Ike's Tavern."

"Ike had the *store*." I roll my eyes. "Do you know nothing?"

As we head up to the house we pass Melissa and Eddie on the terrace, sitting at the garden table, which is covered in papers and brochures.

"It's just sooo difficult," Melissa is saying. "I mean, this is a decision that will affect my whole life. It's, like, how are you supposed to know?"

"Mr. Geiger?" I interrupt awkwardly. "I just wanted to

thank you very much for this evening. It's been absolutely incredible."

"It was fun!" says Eddie.

"Have a nice evening," says Melissa, heaving an enormous sigh. "I've still got work to do."

"It'll be worth it, love." Eddie pats her hand reassuringly. "When you're at . . ." He picks up a brochure from the table and peers at it through his reading glasses. "Carter Spink."

Melissa is going for a job at Carter Spink?

"Is that . . ." I try to speak naturally. "Is that the name of the law firm where you're applying?"

"Oh, I don't know," says Melissa, looking sulky. "It's the top one. But it's *incredibly* competitive. Hardly anyone gets a place."

"Looks very swanky!" says Eddie, flipping over the glossy pages, each illustrated with a photograph. "Look at these offices!"

As he flips through, I'm transfixed. There's a picture of the foyer. There's one of the floor I used to work on. I can't tear my eyes away—but at the same time I don't want to look. That's my old life. It doesn't belong here. And then suddenly, as Eddie flips another page over, I feel a jolt of disbelief.

It's a picture of me. Me.

I'm in my black suit, my hair pinned up, sitting at a meeting-room table along with Ketterman, David Elldridge, and a guy who was over from the States. I remember that picture being taken. Ketterman was absolutely livid at being disturbed.

I look so *pale*. I look so *serious*.

"And it's like . . . do I *want* to give up all my time?" Melissa is jabbing the page. "These people work every night! What about a social life?"

My face is right there in full view. I'm just waiting for

someone to frown in recognition, to say, "*Hang* on a moment..."

But no one does. Melissa is still rabbiting on, gesturing to the brochure; Eddie is nodding. Nathaniel is staring upward, obviously bored.

"Although, you know, the money *is* really good...." Melissa sighs, and flips the page.

The picture's gone. I'm gone.

"Shall we go?" Nathaniel's warm hand tugs mine and I clasp it tightly back.

"Yes." I smile up at him. "Let's."

Nineteen

I don't see the Carter Spink brochure again for two weeks, when I'm drifting into the kitchen to make lunch.

I don't know what happened to time. I barely recognize it anymore. The minutes and hours don't march past in rigid chunks, they ebb and flow and swirl around. I don't even wear a watch anymore. Yesterday I lay in a hay field all afternoon with Nathaniel, watching dandelion seeds float by, and the only ticking sound came from the crickets.

I barely recognize myself anymore either. I'm tanned from lying in the sun at lunchtimes. There are golden streaks in my hair. My cheeks are full. My arms are gaining muscles from all the polishing and kneading and carting heavy saucepans around.

The summer is in full throttle and each day is hotter than the last. Every morning, before breakfast, Nathaniel walks me back through the village to the Geigers' house from his flat above the pub—and even at that hour the air is already warming up. I stay there most nights now, and it's almost got to feel like home. It's surprisingly spacious, with old sofas covered with cotton throws, and a tiny roof terrace that Nathaniel built himself.

We often sit up there as evening turns into night, listening to the babble of pub-leavers down below. Sometimes Nathaniel's doing the pub accounts, but he talks to me as he works: about the backgrounds of everyone in the village, about the plants he wants to put into the Geigers' garden, once explaining the entire geology of the local landscape. I tell him about the day I've had with the Geigers and entertain him with stories about the latest catering job I've done for Eamonn. It's become quite a regular event for me—driving off in his scruffy Honda with a couple of other girls from the village, changing into black waitress outfits and serving canapés at some posh party or other.

Everything seems slow and lazy, these days. Everyone's in holiday mood—except Trish, who is in full frenzy. She's holding her charity lunch next week, and from the fuss she's making, you'd think it was a royal wedding.

I'm tidying away the papers that Melissa has left littered on the table when I spot the Carter Spink brochure underneath a folder. I can't resist picking it up and leafing through the familiar pictures. There are the steps I went up every day of my life for seven years. There's Guy, looking as dazzling as ever. There's that girl Sarah from the litigation department, who was up for partnership too. I never even heard if she got it.

"What are you doing?" Melissa has come into the kitchen without me hearing. She eyes me suspiciously. "That's mine."

Right. Like I'm going to steal a brochure.

"Just tidying your things," I say pointedly, putting the brochure down. "I've got to use this table."

"Oh. Thanks." Melissa rubs her face. She looks haggard. There are shadows under her eyes, and her cheeks seem sunken. Could I have looked that stressed out even at her age?

"You're working hard," I volunteer.

"Yah, well." She lifts her chin. "It'll be worth it in the end. They work you really hard to start, but after you qualify, it calms down."

I look at her tired, pinched, arrogant little face. Even if I could tell her what I know, she wouldn't believe me.

"Yup," I say after a pause. "I'm sure you're right." The Carter Spink brochure is open at a picture of Arnold. He's wearing a bright blue spotted tie and matching handkerchief and is beaming out at the world. Of all the people at Carter Spink, he's the one I'd like to see again.

"So are you applying to this law firm?" I ask, stacking the papers on the counter.

"Yup. They're the best." Melissa is getting a Diet Coke from the fridge. "That's the guy who was supposed to be interviewing me." She points to the picture of Arnold. "But he's leaving."

I'm astonished. Arnold's leaving Carter Spink?

"Are you sure?" I say before I can stop myself.

"Yes." Melissa regards me quizzically. "What's it to you?"

"Oh, nothing," I say, throwing down the brochure. "I just meant . . . he doesn't look old enough to retire."

"Well, he's going." She grabs the brochure and wanders out of the kitchen.

Arnold is leaving Carter Spink? But he's always said he'd never retire. He's always boasted about lasting another twenty years. Why would he be leaving now?

I'm totally out of touch. For more than a month I've been living in a bubble. I haven't seen *The Lawyer*, I've barely even seen a normal paper. I don't know any of the gossip, and I haven't cared a bit. But now, as I look at Arnold's familiar face, I can feel my curiosity rise.

So that afternoon, when I've cleared up lunch, I slip into Eddie's study, switch on the computer, and click on Google. I search for *Arnold Saville*—and sure enough on the second page I come across a little diary item about his early retirement. I read the fifty-word piece over and over, trying to glean clues. Why would Arnold retire early? Is he ill?

I search for further items, but that's the only one I can find. Next I go to the search box and—telling myself I shouldn't—type in *Samantha Sweeting*. Immediately a zillion stories about me pop up again on the screen. I don't feel so freaked out this time, though. The person in these stories doesn't feel like me anymore.

I scan entry after entry, seeing the same details replayed. After clicking through about five pages I add *Third Union Bank* to my search, and scan the resulting entries. Then I type in *Third Union Bank, BLLC Holdings*, then *Third Union Bank, Glazerbrooks*. Then, with a beat of apprehension, I type in *Samantha Sweeting, £50 million, career over*, and wait for all the really nasty stories to appear. It's like watching my own car crash on action replay.

God, Google is addictive. I sit there, totally absorbed, clicking and typing and reading, gorging on endless Web pages, automatically using the Carter Spink password wherever I need to. After an hour I'm slumped in Eddie's chair like a zombie. My back is aching and my neck is stiff, and the words are all running into another. I'd forgotten what it was like to sit at a computer. Did I really used to do this all day?

I rub my tired eyes and glance at the Web page open

in front of me, wondering how I even got to it. It's some obscure list of guests at a lunch held earlier this year at the Painters Hall. About halfway down is the name BLLC Holdings, which must have been the link. On autopilot, I move the cursor along the page—and into view comes the name *Nicholas Hanford Jones, Director.*

Something chimes inside my addled brain. *Nicholas Hanford Jones.* Why do I know that name? Why am I somehow associating it with Ketterman?

Is BLLC Holdings a client of Ketterman? No. It can't be. I'd have heard of it before.

I screw my eyes up tight and concentrate as hard as I can. *Nicholas Hanford Jones.* I can almost see it in my mind's eye. I'm grasping at an association . . . an image . . . come on, think . . .

This is the trouble with having a nearly photographic memory. People think it must be useful, when in fact all it does is drive you insane.

And then suddenly it comes to me. The swirly writing of a wedding invitation. It was stuck up on the pin board in Ketterman's office about three years ago. It was there for weeks. I used to see it every time I went in.

Mr. and Mrs. Arnold Saville
request the pleasure of your company
at the wedding of their daughter Fiona
to Mr. Nicholas Hanford Jones

Nicholas Hanford Jones is Arnold Saville's son-in-law? Arnold has a family connection with BLLC Holdings?

I sit up in my chair, totally disconcerted. How come he never mentioned that?

And then another thought strikes me. I was on the

BLLC Holdings Companies House page a minute ago. Why wasn't Nicholas Hanford Jones listed as a director? That's illegal, for a start.

I rub my brow, then out of curiosity type in *Nicholas Hanford Jones*. A moment later the screen is full of entries, and I lean forward.

Oh, for God's sake. The Internet is crap. I'm looking at other Nicholases and other Hanfords and other Joneses, mentioned in all sorts of different contexts. I peer at them in total frustration. Doesn't Google *realize* that's not what I'm interested in? Why would I want to read about some Canadian rowing team list containing a Greg Hanford, a Dave Jones, and a Chip Nicholas?

I'm never going to find anything here.

Even so, I start picking my way down, skimming each chunk of text, clicking onto the next page and the next. And then, just as I'm about to give up, my eye falls on an entry tucked away at the bottom of the page. *William **Hanford Jones**, Finance Director of Glazerbrooks, thanked **Nicholas** Jenkins for his speech . . .*

This is incredible. The finance director at Glazerbrooks is called Hanford Jones too? Are they from the same *family*? Feeling like some kind of private detective, I log onto FriendsReunited, and two minutes later I have my answer. They're brothers.

I feel a bit dazed. This is a pretty huge connection. The finance director of Glazerbrooks, which went bust owing Third Union Bank £50 million. A director of BLLC Holdings, which lent it £50 million three days before. And Arnold, representing Third Union Bank. All related; all in the same extended family.

I'm almost certain nobody else knows. Arnold's never mentioned it. No one at Carter Spink has ever mentioned it. Nor have I seen it brought up in any of the reports on the whole affair. Arnold's kept all of this very quiet.

I rub my shoulders, trying to gather my jumbled thoughts. Isn't this a potential conflict of interest? Shouldn't he have disclosed the information straight-away? Why on earth would Arnold keep such an important thing secret? Unless—

No. *No.*

I feel a bit light-headed, as though I've suddenly swum over the ledge into mile-deep water. My mind is flying ahead, careening onto possibilities and shearing away again in disbelief.

Did Arnold discover something? Is he hiding something?

Is this why he's leaving?

I get up and thrust my hands through my hair. OK, let's just . . . stop all this, right now. This is Arnold I'm talking about. *Arnold.* I'm turning into some nutty conspiracy theorist. Next I'll be typing in *aliens, Roswell, they live among us.*

With sudden resolution I get out my phone. I'll call Arnold. I'll wish him well in his retirement. Then maybe I can get rid of all these ridiculous ideas floating round my head.

It takes me about six failed attempts before I muster the courage to dial the entire number and wait for a reply. The idea of talking to anyone at Carter Spink—let alone Arnold—makes me feel slightly sick. I keep bottling out before being connected, thrusting the phone down as though I've had a narrow escape.

But at last I steel myself to press the digits and hold the line. I'm never going to know unless I do this. I can talk to Arnold. I can hold my head up.

After three rings the phone is picked up by Lara. "Arnold Saville's office."

I have a sudden vision of her, plump and shiny-haired, sitting at her pale wooden desk, in the burgundy jacket she always wears, tapping on the computer. It all seems a million miles away now.

"Hi, Lara," I say. "It's . . . Samantha. Samantha Sweeting."

"*Samantha?*" Lara sounds poleaxed. "Bloody hell! How are you? What are you up to?"

"I'm fine, thanks. Really good." I quell a spasm of nerves. "I just rang because I've heard that Arnold's leaving? Is it true?"

"It's true!" says Lara with relish. "I was gobsmacked! Apparently, Ketterman took him out to dinner and tried to get him to stay, but he'd made up his mind. Get this, he's moving to the Bahamas."

"The *Bahamas*?" I say in astonishment.

"He's bought a house there! Looks lovely. His retirement party's next week," Lara continues. "I'll be transferring to Derek Green's office—you remember him? Taxation partner? Very nice guy, though apparently he can have a bit of a temper—"

"Er . . . great!" I cut her off, suddenly remembering her ability to gossip for hours. "Lara, I just wanted to give Arnold my best wishes. If you could possibly put me through?"

"Really?" Lara sounds surprised. "That's incredibly . . . generous of you, Samantha. After what happened."

"Well, you know," I say awkwardly. "It wasn't Arnold's fault, was it? He did what he could."

There's a strange silence.

"Yes," says Lara after a pause. "Well. I'll put you through."

After a few moments Arnold's familiar voice is booming down the line.

"Samantha, dear girl! Is it really you?"

"It's ... really me." I manage a smile. "I haven't *quite* disappeared off the face of the earth."

"I should hope not! Now, you're all right, are you?"

"I'm ... fine," I say awkwardly. "Thanks. I was just surprised to hear you're retiring."

"I was never a glutton for punishment!" He gives an easy laugh. "Thirty-three years at the coal face of law. That's enough for any human. Let alone any lawyer!"

Just his jovial voice is reassuring me. I must be crazy. Arnold couldn't be involved in anything untoward. He couldn't be hiding anything. He's *Arnold*.

I'll mention it to him, I decide. Just to prove it to myself.

"Well ... I hope it all goes well," I say. "And I ... I guess you'll be seeing more of your family?"

"I'll be lumbered with the blighters, yes!" He booms with laughter again.

"I never knew your son-in-law was a director of BLLC Holdings!" I attempt an easy tone. "Quite a coincidence!"

There's a beat of silence.

"I'm sorry?" says Arnold. His voice is still as charming as ever, but the warmth has disappeared.

"BLLC Holdings." I swallow. "You know, the other company involved with the Third Union Bank loan? The one that registered a charge? I just happened to notice—"

"I have to go now, Samantha!" Arnold cuts me off smoothly. "Delightful to chat, but I'm leaving the country next week, and there's a lot to do. It's exceedingly busy here, so I wouldn't ring again if I were you."

The line goes dead before I can say any more. I

slowly put down the phone and stare at a butterfly fluttering outside the window.

That wasn't right. That wasn't a natural reaction. He got rid of me as soon as I mentioned his son-in-law.

Something is going on. Something is definitely going on.

I have totally abandoned the housework for the afternoon and am sitting on my bed with a pad of paper and pencil, trying to work out the possibilities.

Who stands to gain? I stare at my scribbled facts and arrows of connection yet again. Two brothers. Millions of pounds being transferred between banks and companies. Think. *Think* . . .

With a small cry of frustration I rip out the page and crumple it. Let's start again. Let's get everything in logical order. Glazerbrooks went into receivership. Third Union Bank lost their money. BLLC Holdings jumped ahead in the queue. . . .

I tap my pencil impatiently on the paper. But so what? They only get back the money they loaned. They don't get any advantage, they don't get any benefit, it's pointless.

Unless—unless they never paid over anything in the first place.

The thought comes to me out of nowhere. I sit bolt upright, unable to breathe. What if that's it? *What if it's a scam?*

My mind starts to race. Suppose there are two brothers. They know that Glazerbrooks is in serious financial trouble. They know that the bank has just paid in fifty million but the bank's charge wasn't registered. That means there's a fifty-million unsecured loan swilling around in the company, up for grabs by anyone else who registers a charge....

I can't sit anymore. I'm pacing backward and forward, feverishly gnawing my pencil, my brain sparking like an electrical circuit. It works. It works. They fiddle the figures. BLLC Holdings gets the money that Third Union Bank paid over, Carter Spink's insurers foot the bill—

I pause in my striding. No. It doesn't work. I'm being stupid. The insurers are only covering the fifty million because I was negligent. That's the crucial element. The whole plan would have depended on me, Samantha Sweeting, making that particular mistake.

But I mean . . . how on earth could they have planned that? It makes no sense. It's impossible. You can't plan a mistake in advance. You can't *make* someone forget to do something, you can't *make* someone fuck up—

And then I stop dead. My skin suddenly feels clammy. The memo.

I never saw that memo on my desk until it was too late. I know I didn't.

What if—

Oh, my God.

I sink onto the window seat, my legs like rubber. What if someone planted that memo on my desk? Slipped it into a pile of papers after the deadline had passed?

What if I didn't make a mistake?

I feel like everything is cracking and reshaping around me. What if Arnold deliberately didn't register the bank charge—and made it look like my fault?

Like a looped tape, my conversation with Arnold that day is playing over and over in my mind. When I said I couldn't remember seeing the memo on my desk. And he immediately changed the subject.

I assumed the memo was there all the time. I assumed it was my error. My inefficiency. But what if it wasn't? Everyone at Carter Spink knew I had the messiest desk in the firm. It would be easy to slip it into a pile of papers. Make it look as if it had been there for weeks.

I'm breathing harder and harder, till I'm almost hyperventilating. For the first time I'm realizing the huge strain I've been under. I have lived with that mistake for more than a month. It's been there every morning when I wake up and every day when I go to bed. Like a constant background ache that I've gotten used to, like a chorus in my head: *Samantha Sweeting ruined her life. Samantha Sweeting fucked up.*

But . . . what if I was used? What if it wasn't my fault? *What if I didn't make a mistake after all?*

I have to know. I have to know the truth. Right now. With a shaking hand I reach for my mobile phone and punch in the number again.

"Lara, I need to speak to Arnold again," I say as soon as I'm connected.

"Samantha . . ." Lara sounds awkward. "I'm afraid Arnold won't take any more calls from you. And he asked me to tell you that you're not to pester him about your job anymore."

I'm in shock. What has he been saying about me?

"Lara, I'm not pestering him about my job," I say, trying to keep my voice steady. "I just need to talk to him about a . . . matter. If he won't talk to me, I'll come to the office. Can you make me an appointment, please?"

"Samantha." She sounds even more embarrassed than before. "Arnold told me to inform you . . . if you try to come here to the offices, Security will eject you."

"*Eject* me?" I stare at the phone in disbelief.

"I'm sorry. I really am. And I don't blame you!" she

adds fervently. "I thought what Arnold did to you was really shocking! A lot of us do."

What he *did* to me? Does Lara know the memo was planted?

"What—what do you mean?" I stammer.

"The way he got you fired!" says Lara.

"What?" I feel like all the breath has been squeezed from my chest. "What are you talking about?"

"I *did* wonder if you knew." She lowers her voice. "He's leaving now, so I can say it. I took the minutes at that meeting, after you ran off. And Arnold talked round all the other partners. He said you were a liability and they couldn't risk taking you back and all sorts. A lot of them wanted to give you another chance, you know." She clicks her tongue. "I was appalled. Of course, I couldn't *say* anything to Arnold."

"Of course not," I manage. "Thanks for telling me, Lara. I . . . had no idea."

Everything is distorted. Arnold didn't fight in my corner at all. He got me fired. I don't know this man at all. All that genial, affable charm—it's an act. It's a bloody act.

With a sickening lurch I suddenly recall him the day after it happened, insisting I should stay where I was, not come back. That's why. He wanted me out of the way so I couldn't fight for myself. So he could stitch me up.

And I trusted him. Totally and utterly. Like a stupid, *stupid* gullible fool.

My chest is heaving painfully. All my doubts have disappeared. Arnold is in on something crooked. I know it. He planted that memo, knowing it would destroy my career.

And in a week he'll have disappeared to the Bahamas. I feel a stab of panic. I need to take action now.

"Lara," I say, trying to sound calm. "Could you put me through to Guy Ashby?"

I know Guy and I had a row. But he's the only person I can think of right now who'll be able to help me.

"Guy's in Hong Kong," says Lara in surprise. "Didn't you know?"

"Right," I say, my heart plummeting. "No. I . . . didn't know."

"But he'll have his BlackBerry with him," she adds helpfully. "You could send him an e-mail."

"Yes." I take a deep breath. "Yes, maybe I'll do that."

Twenty

I can't do it. I just can't. There is no way of writing this
e-mail without sounding like a paranoid crazy.

I look in despair at my tenth attempt.

```
Dear Guy,
    I need you to help me. I think I
have been set up by Arnold. I think he
planted that memo on my desk. Something
is going on. He has family links with
both BLLC Holdings and Glazerbrooks,
did you know that?? Why did he never
tell anyone? And now he's banned me
from the building, which in itself
is suspicious—
```

I sound delusional. I sound like some bitter, twisted
ex-employee with a grudge.

Which of course is what I am.

As I run my eyes over my words, I'm reminded of

nothing more than the wild-eyed old woman who used to stand at the corner of our street, muttering, "They're coming to GET me."

I have total sympathy for that old woman now. They probably *were* coming to get her.

Guy will just laugh. I can see him now. Arnold Saville a crook? It sounds insane. Maybe I *am* insane. It's only a theory. I don't have evidence; I don't have anything solid. I lean forward and rest my head hopelessly on my hands. No one's ever going to believe me. Or even listen to me.

If I only had some proof. But where am I supposed to get that from?

A bleeping from my mobile phone makes me jump, and I look up blearily. I'd almost forgotten where I was. I pick it up and see that I've got a text.

> I'm downstairs. have a surprise to show
> you. nat

As I head downstairs, I'm really not with it. Flashes of anger keep overwhelming me as I think of Arnold's jocular smile, the way he encouraged my messy desk, the way he told me he'd do his very best for me, the way he listened as I blamed myself, as I apologized and groveled...

The worst thing is, I never even tried to defend myself. I never questioned the fact that I couldn't remember seeing the memo. I immediately assumed the worst of myself, assumed it was my fault for having such a messy desk.

Arnold knows me pretty well. Maybe that's what he was counting on.

Bastard. *Bastard.*

"Hi." Nathaniel waves a hand in front of my face. "Earth to Samantha."

"Oh . . . Sorry. Hi!" Somehow I muster a smile.

"Come this way." He grins and ushers me out to his car, which is an ancient Beetle convertible. As usual, rows of seed pots are crowding the backseat and an old wooden spade is sticking out of the back.

"Madam." He opens the door gallantly.

"So what are you showing me?" I ask as I get in.

"Magical mystery tour." He smiles enigmatically and starts up the engine.

We drive out of Lower Ebury and take a route I don't recognize, through a tiny neighboring village and up into the hills. Nathaniel seems in a cheerful mood and tells me stories about each farm and pub that we pass. But I barely hear a word. My mind is still churning.

I don't know what I can do. I can't even get into the building. I have no credibility. I'm powerless. And I only have three days. Once Arnold disappears off to the Bahamas that'll be it.

"Here we are!" Nathaniel turns off the road into a gravel drive. He maneuvers the car into place by a low brick wall, then stops the engine. "What do you think?"

With an effort I wrench my mind back to the present time. "Um. . . ." I peer around blankly. "Yes. Lovely."

What am I supposed to be looking at?

"Samantha, are you OK?" Nathaniel shoots me a curious glance. "You seem on edge."

"I'm fine." I try to smile. "Just a bit tired."

I open the car door to get out, away from his gaze. I shut the door behind me and look around.

We're in some kind of courtyard. There's a ramshackle old stone house to the right, with a FOR SALE post. Ahead are banks of greenhouses, glinting in the low sunlight.

There are plots filled with rows of vegetables, there's a Portakabin marked GARDEN CENTER . . .

Hang on.

I turn to see that Nathaniel has got out of the car too and is holding a sheaf of papers in his hand.

"*A horticultural business opportunity,*" he reads aloud. "*Four acres of land, with ten more available, subject to negotiation. Ten thousand square feet of glasshouses. Four-bedroom farmhouse, needs work . . .*"

"You're *buying* this?" I say, my attention fully grabbed.

"I'm thinking about it. I wanted to show you first." He spreads an arm around. "It's a pretty good concern. Needs building up, but the land's there. We can get some polytunnels going, extend the offices . . ."

I can't take all this in.

"But what about the pubs? How come you're suddenly—"

"It was you. What you said in the garden that day." He pauses, the breeze ruffling his hair. "You're right, Samantha. I'm not a landlord, I'm a gardener. I'd be happier doing what I really want to do. So . . . I had a long talk with Mum and she understood. We both reckon Eamonn can take over. Not that he knows yet."

"Wow." I look around again, taking in a pile of wooden crates, stacks of seed trays, a tattered poster advertising Christmas trees. "So you're really going to do it?"

I can see the excitement in his face. "You only get one chance at life."

"Well, I think it's fantastic!"

"And there's a house." He nods toward it. "Or at least, there will be a house. It's a bit run-down."

"Right." I take in the old stone house again. The paintwork is peeling and there's a shutter hanging off one hinge. "It does look a bit of a mess."

"I wanted you to see it first," says Nathaniel. "Get your approval. I mean, one day you might—" He stops.

All of a sudden my relationship sensors are swiveling round madly, like the Hubble spotting an alien ship. What did they just pick up? What was he going to say?

"I might . . . stay over?" I supply at last.

"Exactly." Nathaniel rubs his nose. "Shall we have a look?"

The house is bigger than it seems from the outside, with bare boards and old fireplaces and a creaking wooden staircase. One room has practically no plaster, and the kitchen is totally old-fashioned, with 1930s cupboards.

"Great kitchen." I shoot him a teasing look.

"I'm sure I could refit it to your Cordon Bleu standards," he returns.

We make our way upstairs and into a huge bedroom overlooking the rear of the house. From above, the vegetable plots look like an orderly patchwork quilt, stretching away into the green meadow. I can see a little terrace down below and a tiny private garden belonging to the house, all clematis and tangled roses.

"It's a beautiful place," I say, leaning on the windowsill. "I love it."

Standing here, looking out at the view, I feel like London is on another planet. Carter Spink and Arnold and all of them suddenly seem part of another life.

But even as I'm gazing out at the restful country scene, I can't relax. All it would take is one phone call to the right person . . .

If I had some proof . . .

Anything . . .

My mind starts turning over the facts again, like a bird turning over empty snail shells. I'm going to drive myself crazy like this.

"What I was wondering is . . ."

Suddenly I become aware that Nathaniel is speaking. In fact I think he could have been speaking for a while—and I haven't heard a word. I hastily turn round, to see him facing me. His cheeks are flushed and he has an unfamiliar awkwardness about him. It looks like whatever he's been saying has required some effort.

" . . . do you feel the same way, Samantha?"

He coughs, and breaks off into an expectant silence.

I stare back at him dumbly. Do I feel the same way about what?

Oh, shit. *Bollocks.* The man I'm secretly falling in love with just made a romantic speech to me—probably the only one I'll get in my whole life—and *I wasn't listening*? I *missed* it?

I want to shoot myself for being so *rubbish.*

And now he's waiting for me to reply. What am I going to do? He's just spilled his heart to me. I can't say, "Sorry, I didn't quite catch that."

"Um . . ." I push my hair back, playing for time. "Well . . . you've given me quite a lot to think about."

"But do you agree?"

OK, this is Nathaniel. I'm sure I agree with it, whatever it is.

"Yes." I give him the most sincere look I can muster. "Yes, I agree. Wholeheartedly. In fact . . . I've often thought so myself."

Nathaniel is scrutinizing me. "You agree," he says, as though to make sure. "With everything?"

"Er . . . yes!" I'm starting to feel a bit nervous now. What have I agreed to?

"Even about the chimpanzees?"

"The *chimpanzees*?" I suddenly see Nathaniel's mouth twitching. He's on to me.

"You didn't listen to a word I was saying, did you?" he says, in matter-of-fact tones.

"I didn't realize you were saying something important!" I wail, hanging my head. "You should have warned me!"

Nathaniel looks at me incredulously. "That took some nerve, you know, saying all that."

"Say it again," I beg. "Say it all again! I'll listen!"

"Uh-uh." He laughs, shaking his head. "Maybe one day."

"I'm sorry, Nathaniel. Really I am." I turn away to press my head against the window glass. "I was just . . . distracted."

"I know." He comes over and puts his arms around me, over my own. I can feel his steady heartbeat against me, calming me down. "Samantha, what's up? It's your old relationship, isn't it?"

"Yup," I mutter after a pause.

"Why won't you tell me about it? I could help."

I turn round to face him. The sun is glowing in his eyes and on his burnished face. He's never looked more handsome.

I know I can't hide my past forever. I could tell Nathaniel the whole story, right here, right now. But at the same time, I know that the minute I tell him who I was, he'll look at me differently. Everything will change between us. I won't be Samantha anymore. I'll be a lawyer.

And it's all so perfect as it is. I can't bear to rock the boat just yet.

"I don't want to bring that world into this one," I say at last. "I just don't." Nathaniel opens his mouth again, but I turn away before he can speak. I stare out at the idyllic view, blinking against the rays of the sun, my mind in total turmoil.

Maybe I should just give up on the whole nightmare.

Forget about it. Let it go. The chances are I'll never be able to prove anything. Arnold has all the power; I have none. The chances are if I try to stir things up again all I'll get is more humiliation and disgrace.

I could so easily do nothing. I could just put it from my mind, as I've tried to do all this time. Close the door on my old life and leave it behind forever. I have a job. I have Nathaniel. I have a possible future here.

But even as I'm thinking it—I know that's not what I'm going to do. I can't forget about it. I can't let go.

Twenty-one

The city isn't the way I remember it. I can't believe
how dirty it is. How *rushed* it is. As I arrived at Paddington Station this afternoon I felt almost bewildered by the
commuter crowds moving like a swarm of ants over
the concourse. I could smell the fumes. I saw the litter.
Things I never even noticed before. Did I just filter them
out? Was I so used to them, they faded into the background?

But at the same time, the minute my feet hit the
ground I felt the buzz. By the time I reached the Underground station I'd already picked up my pace: matching
the stride of everyone else; feeding my travel card into
the machine at exactly the right angle; whipping it out
with not a second to spare.

And now I'm in the Starbucks around the corner
from Carter Spink, sitting at the counter in the window,
watching City-suited businesspeople walking past, talking and gesticulating and making phone calls. The

adrenaline is catching. My heart's already beating more quickly—and I haven't even got inside the building yet.

I glance at my watch yet again. Nearly time. The last thing I want to do is arrive early. The less time I spend in there, the better.

As I drain my latte, my phone bleeps, but I ignore it. It'll be yet another message from Trish. She was livid when I told her I had to go away for a couple of days; in fact, she tried to stop me. So I told her I had a foot complaint that needed urgent attention from my specialist in London.

In hindsight this was a huge mistake, as she wanted to know every single gory detail. She even demanded I take off my shoe and show her. I had to spend ten minutes improvising about "bone misalignment" while she peered at my foot and said, "It looks perfectly normal to me," in tones of great suspicion.

She looked at me with mistrust for the rest of the day. Then she left a copy of *Marie-Claire* casually open at the *Pregnant? Need Confidential Advice?* advertisements. Honestly. I have to knock that one on the head or it'll be all over the village and Iris will be knitting booties.

I told Nathaniel in private that I had a situation to sort out with my old relationship. I could tell he wanted to know more details, that he was finding it hard being shut out, but he didn't press me. I think he saw how strained I was already.

I look at my watch again. Time to go. I head for the Ladies, face the mirror, and check my appearance. Unfamiliar blond hair: check. Tinted glasses: check. Magenta lipstick: check. I look nothing like my former self.

Apart from the face, of course. If you looked really closely.

But the point is, no one's going to look closely at me. This is what I'm counting on, anyway.

"Hi," I practice in a low, guttural voice. "Pleased to meet you."

I sound like a drag queen. But never mind. At least I don't sound like a lawyer.

Keeping my head down, I leave Starbucks and walk along the street, until I round the corner and see the distinctive granite steps and glass doors of Carter Spink. I feel unreal being back here. The last time I saw those doors I was pushing my way out of them, gibbering with panic, convinced I'd wrecked my own career, convinced my life was over.

Fury starts boiling up again and I close my eyes briefly, trying to keep my emotions in line. I don't have any proof yet. I have to stay focused on what I'm doing. Come on. I can do this.

I know my plan is slightly insane; I know my chances aren't great. It's unlikely Arnold has left proof of his misdemeanors just lying about. But I couldn't just give up, tamely stay in Lower Ebury, and let him get away with it. My anger is like a huge driving force inside me. I had to come here and at least try to find out what I can.

And if they won't let me in the building as a lawyer . . . then I'll just have to go in as something else.

I cross the road and resolutely head up the steps. I can almost see myself that day, a ghostlike figure, running down them in a state of bewildered shock. It all seems like a lifetime ago now. I don't just look like a different person, I *feel* like a different person. I feel like I've been rebuilt.

With a deep breath, I pull my mac around me and push open the glass doors. As I step into the foyer I feel a sudden giddy wave of disbelief. Am I actually doing this? Am I actually trying to blag my way, incognito, into the Carter Spink offices?

My legs are wobbling and my hands feel damp, but

I'm walking steadily forward over the shiny marble floor, my eyes fixed downward. I head toward the new receptionist, Melanie, who started only a couple of weeks before I left.

"Hi," I say in my drag-queen voice.

"Can I help you?" Melanie smiles at me. There's not a glimmer of recognition in her face. I can't believe this is so easy.

In fact, I feel a tad insulted. Was I *so* nondescript before?

"I'm here for the party?" I mumble, my head down. "I'm waitressing. Bertram's Caterers," I add for good measure.

"Oh, yes. That's all happening up on the fourteenth floor." She taps on her computer. "What's your name?"

"It's . . . Trish," I say. "Trish Geiger." Melanie peers at the computer screen, frowning and tapping her pen on her teeth.

"You're not on my list," she says at last.

"Well, I should be there." I keep my head well down. "There must be a mistake."

"Let me call up. . . ." Melanie taps on her phone and has a brief conversation with someone called Jan, then looks up.

"She'll be down to see you." She gestures to the leather sofas with a smile. "Please take a seat."

I head toward the seating area—then veer in a sharp U-turn as I see David Spellman from Corporate sitting on one of the sofas with a client. Not that he seems to have recognized me. I walk toward a rack of glossy leaflets on Carter Spink's philosophy and bury my head in one on Dispute Resolution.

I've never actually read any of these leaflets before. God, they really are a load of meaningless crap.

"Trish?"

"Er . . . yes?" I swivel round to see a woman in a tuxedo with a raddled face. She's holding some typed sheets and regarding me with a frown.

"Jan Martin, head of waiting staff. You're not on my list. Have you worked for us before?"

"I'm new," I say, keeping my voice low. "But I've worked for Ebury Catering. Down in Gloucestershire."

"Don't know it." She consults her paper again and flips to the second page, her brow creased in impatience. "Love, you're not on the list. I don't know what you're doing here."

"I spoke to a guy," I say without flickering. "He said you could do with extra."

"A guy?" She looks perplexed. "Who? Tony?"

"I don't remember his name. But he said to come here."

"He couldn't have said—"

"This is Carter Spink, isn't it?" I look around. "95 Cheapside? A big retirement party?"

"Yes." I see the beginnings of doubt on the woman's face.

"Well, I was told to come here." I allow just the faintest belligerence into my voice.

I can see the calculation going on in this woman's head: if she turns me away I might cause a scene, she's got other pressing stuff to think about, what's one extra waitress . . .

"All right!" she says at last, with an irritated noise. "But you'll have to change. What's your name again?"

"Trish Geiger."

"That's right." She scribbles it down. "Well you'd better come up, Trish."

I feel almost elated as I travel up in the service elevator with Jan, a plastic label reading *Trish Geiger* attached to my lapel. Now all I need is to keep my head down, bide my time, and, when the moment is right, get onto the eleventh floor.

We come out in the kitchens attached to the executive function rooms, and I look around in surprise. I had no idea there was all this back here. It's like going backstage at a theater. Chefs are working busily at the cooking stations, and waiting staff are milling around in distinctive green and white striped uniforms.

"The outfits are in there." Jan points to a huge wicker basket full of folded uniforms. "You'll need to get changed."

"OK." I rummage around for an outfit in my size and take it off to the Ladies to change. I touch up my magenta lipstick and pull my hair further round my face, then look at my watch.

It's five-forty now. The party's at six. By about ten past, the eleventh floor should be clearing. Arnold is a very popular partner; no one's going to miss his farewell speech if they can help it. Plus, at Carter Spink parties, the speeches always happen early on, so people can get back to work if they need to.

And while everyone's listening I'll slip down to Arnold's office. It should work. It *has* to work. As I stare at my own bizarre reflection, I feel a grim resolve hardening inside me. He's not going to get away with everyone thinking he's a cheery, harmless old teddy bear. He's not going to get away with it.

At ten to six we all gather in one of the kitchens and receive our orders. Hot canapés . . . cold canapés . . . I barely listen to any of it. It's not like I'm intending to do any actual waiting. After Jan's lecture is over, I follow the herd of waiting staff out of the kitchen. I'm given a tray of champagne glasses to carry, which I put down as soon as I can, then head back to the kitchen and grab an open bottle of champagne and a napkin. As soon as I'm sure no one's looking, I escape to the Ladies.

OK. This is the difficult bit. I lock myself in a cubicle and wait for fifteen minutes in utter silence. I don't clatter anything and I don't sneeze and I don't giggle when I hear a girl rehearsing her breakup speech to someone called Mike. It's the longest fifteen minutes of my life.

At last I cautiously unbolt the door, make my way out, and peer round the corner. From where I'm standing I can see the entrance to the big function room. A crowd has already gathered and I can hear laughter and lots of loud talking. People are still coming down the corridor in a steady stream. I recognize the girls from PR...a couple of trainees...Oliver Swan, a senior partner. They all head into the party, taking a glass as they do so.

The corridor's clear. Go.

With trembling legs I walk straight past the entrance to the function room, toward the lifts and the door to the stairwell. Within thirty seconds I'm safely through the door and walking as quietly as I can down the stairs. No one ever uses the stairs at Carter Spink, but still.

I reach the eleventh floor and peer out of the glass panel in the door. I can't see anyone. But that doesn't mean there's no one there. There could be a whole crowd of them, just out of my line of vision.

Well, that's a risk I'll have to take. I take a few deep breaths, trying to psych myself up. No one will ever recognize me in my green-and-white waitress gear. And I even have a story if anyone challenges me: I'm on this floor to place this bottle of champagne in Mr. Saville's room as a surprise.

Come on. I can't waste any more time.

Slowly I push the door open, step out onto the blue carpeted corridor, and exhale in relief. It's empty. The whole floor is pretty much dead. Everyone must have gone up to the party. I can hear someone on the phone a few yards away—but as I start nervously walking toward Arnold's office, all the surrounding workstations are empty. All my senses are on red alert.

The crucial thing is to use my time efficiently. I'll start with the computer and take it from there. Or maybe I should start with the filing cabinet. Have a quick look while the computer is warming up. Or I'll search his desk drawers. His BlackBerry could be in there. I hadn't thought of that.

Suddenly I can hear voices behind me, coming out of the lifts. In panic, I pick up my pace. I reach Arnold's office, wrench the door open, slam it behind me, and duck down underneath the glass panel. I can hear the voices getting closer. David Elldridge and Keith Thompson and someone I don't recognize. They pass by the door, and I don't move a muscle. Then they're receding into the distance. Thank God.

I let out my breath, slowly rise to my feet, and peep through the glass. I can't see anyone. I'm safe. Only then do I turn around and survey the office.

It's *empty*.

It's been cleared out.

Bewildered, I take a few steps into the room. The desk is empty. The shelves are empty. There are faint squares on the walls where framed photos have been taken down. There's nothing in this office apart from one piece of industrial tape on the floor and some drawing pins still stuck into the pin board.

I can't believe it. After all this effort. After making it this far. There's nothing to bloody *search*?

There must be boxes, I think in sudden inspiration. Yes. It's all been put into boxes to be moved, and they'll all be stacked outside. I hurry out of the office and look around wildly. But I can't see any boxes. No crates. Nothing. I'm too late. I'm too fucking late. I feel like punching something with frustration.

"Excuse me?"

I freeze. Shit. *Shit.*

"Yes?" I turn round, pulling my hair over my face and gazing firmly downward.

"What on earth are you doing here?"

It's a trainee. Bill . . . what's his name? He used to do occasional bits of work for me.

It's all right. He hasn't recognized me.

"I was delivering a bottle of champagne, sir," I mumble in my best drag-queen voice, nodding to the bottle where I left it on the floor. "Surprise for the gentleman. I was just wondering where to put it."

"I'd just leave it on the desk," says Bill curtly. "And you shouldn't be in here."

"I was just going back. Sir." I dump the bottle on the desk, bow my head, and scuttle out. Bloody hell. That was close.

I head to the stairwell and hurry up the stairs, flustered. It's time to exit this building, before anyone else sees me.

The party's still in full swing as I creep out of the stairwell door and hurry toward the room where I left my clothes. I won't bother to change. I can always mail the waitress gear back—

"Trish?" Jan's voice hits the back of my head. "Is that you?"

Fuck. Reluctantly I turn round to face her. She looks hopping mad. "Where the hell have you *been*?"

"Um . . . serving?"

"No, you haven't. I haven't seen you in there once!" she snaps. "You're not working for me again, I can tell you. Now, take these and pull your weight." She thrusts a plate of tiny little éclairs into my arms and pushes me roughly toward the doors of the party.

No. I can't go in there. No way.

"Absolutely! I just have to . . . get some cocktail napkins. . . ." I try to back away, but she grabs me.

"No, you don't! You wanted this job! Now work!"

She shoves me hard, and I stagger into the crowded room. I feel like a gladiator being pushed into the arena. Jan's standing at the door, her arms folded. There's no way out. I'm going to have to do this. I grip the tray more tightly, lower my head—and advance slowly into the crowded room.

I can't walk naturally. My legs feel like boards. The hairs on the nape of my neck are standing on end; I can feel the blood pulsating through my ears. I edge past expensive suits, not daring to look up, not daring to pause in case I attract attention. I can't believe this is happening. I'm dressed up in a green-and-white uniform, serving mini-éclairs to my former colleagues.

But one thing I've learned from doing parties with Eamonn is, the waiting staff are invisible. And sure enough, no one seems to have noticed.

Several hands have plucked éclairs from the tray, without even glancing at me. Everyone's too busy laughing and chatting. The din is tremendous.

I can't see Arnold anywhere. But he has to be here somewhere. I'm compelled to look for him, to raise my head and search him out. But I can't risk it. Instead, I keep on moving steadily around the room. Familiar faces are everywhere. Snatches of conversation are making my ears prick up.

"Where's Ketterman?" someone is asking as I pass by.

"In Dublin for the day," replies Oliver Swan. "But he'll be at the partners' farewell dinner tomorrow night." I breathe out in relief. If Ketterman were here I'm sure his laser eyes would pick me up at once.

"Éclairs. Fab!"

About eight hands dive into my tray at once and I come to a standstill. It's a group of trainees. Hoovering food, as trainees always do at parties.

I'm starting to feel edgy. The longer I stand here without moving, the more exposed I feel. But I can't get away. Their hands keep plunging in for more.

"Are there any more of the strawberry tarts, do you know?" a guy with rimless glasses asks me.

"Um . . . I don't know," I mutter, staring down.

Shit. Now he's peering at me more closely. He's bending down to get a good look. And I can't pull my hair over my face because both hands are holding the tray.

"Is that . . . Samantha Sweeting?" He looks agog. "Is that *you*?"

"Samantha Sweeting?" One of the girls drops her éclair. Another gasps and claps her hand over her mouth.

"Um . . . yes," I whisper at last, my face boiling. "It's me. But please, don't tell anyone. I want to keep a low profile."

"So . . . this is what you do now?" The rimless-glasses guy looks aghast. "You're a *waitress*?"

The trainees are all staring at me as though I'm the Ghost of Failed Lawyers Future.

"It's not so bad." I attempt an upbeat smile. "You get free canapés!"

"So you make one mistake—and that's it?" gulps the girl who dropped her éclair. "Your legal career is ruined forever?"

"Er . . . pretty much." I nod. "Can I offer you another?"

But no one seems hungry anymore. In fact, they all look rather green about the gills.

"I might just . . . pop back to my desk," stammers the guy with rimless glasses. "Just check I haven't got anything outstanding . . ."

"Me too," says the girl, thrusting down her glass.

"Samantha Sweeting is here!" I suddenly hear another of the trainees hissing to a group of junior associates. "Look! She's a waitress!"

"No!" I gasp. "Don't tell anyone else—"

It's too late. I can see all the people in the group turning to look at me with identical expressions of embarrassed horror.

For an instant I'm so mortified I want to curl up on the spot. These are people I used to work with. These are people who respected me. And now I'm dressed up in stripes, serving them.

But then, slowly, I begin to feel defiant.

Fuck you, I find myself thinking. Why shouldn't I work as a waitress?

"Hi," I say, shaking back my hair. "Care for a dessert?"

More and more people are turning to gasp at me. I can hear the whispering round the room. The other waitstaff are all clustered together, goggling at me. Heads are swiveling everywhere now, like iron filings in a magnetic field. There isn't one friendly face among them.

"Jesus Christ!" I hear someone murmur. "*Look* at her."

"Should she *be* here?" exclaims someone else.

"No," I say, trying to sound composed. "You're right. I shouldn't."

I make to leave, but the melee is all around me now. I can't find a way out. And then my stomach plunges. Through a gap in the throng, I spot a familiar shock of woolly hair. Familiar ruddy cheeks. A familiar jovial smile.

Arnold Saville.

Our eyes meet across the room, and although he keeps smiling, there's a hardness to his gaze that I've never seen before. A special anger, just for me.

I feel sick. Almost scared. Not of his anger—but of his duplicity. He's fooled everyone. To everyone else in this room, Arnold Saville is on a par with Father Christmas. A way has parted in the crowd, and he's coming toward me, a glass of champagne in his hand.

"Samantha," he says, in pleasant tones. "Is this appropriate?"

"You had me banned from the building," I hear myself bite back. "I didn't have much choice."

Oh, God. Wrong answer. Too chippy.

I have to get control of myself, or I'm going to lose this confrontation. I'm already at enough of a disadvantage, standing here in waitress gear, being peered at by the entire room as if I'm something the dog dragged in. I need to be calm and steely and inspired. But seeing Arnold in the flesh after all this time has thrown me off balance. As hard as I try to stay calm, I can't. My face is burning, my chest feels tight. All the traumas of the last few weeks are suddenly erupting inside me in a whoosh of hatred.

"You had me fired." The words burst out before I can stop them. "You *lied*."

"Samantha, I know this must have been a very difficult time for you." Arnold has the air of a headmaster dealing with a wayward pupil. "But really . . ." He turns to a man I don't recognize and rolls his eyes. "Former employee," he says in an undertone. "Mentally unstable."

What? *What?*

"I'm not mentally unstable!" I cry. "I just want to know the answer to one simple question. When exactly did you put that memo on my desk?"

Arnold laughs, seemingly incredulous.

"Samantha, I'm retiring. Is this really the time? Could someone get rid of her?" he adds as an aside.

"That's why you didn't want me to come back to the office, isn't it?" My voice is trembling with indignation. "Because I might start asking tricky questions. Because I might work it out."

A little frisson travels around the room. But not in a good way. I can hear people murmuring, "For God's sake," and "How did she get in here?" If I want to retain any credibility or dignity at all I have to stop talking right now. But I can't stop.

"I didn't make that mistake, did I?" I walk toward him. "You *used* me. You wrecked my career, you watched my whole life go into free fall—"

"Really," snaps Arnold, turning away. "This is getting beyond a joke."

"Just answer the question!" I yell at his back. "When did you put that memo on my desk, Arnold? Because I don't believe it was ever there before the deadline."

"Of course it was there." Arnold turns briefly, bored and dismissive. "I came into your office on May twenty-eighth."

May 28th?

Where did May 28th come from? Why does that feel wrong?

"I don't believe you," I say with a helpless anger. "I just don't believe you. I think you set me up. I think—"

"Samantha?" Someone pokes me on the shoulder and I wheel round to see Ernest the security guard. His familiar, gnarled face is awkward. "I'm going to have to ask you to leave the premises."

They're seriously throwing me out of the offices? After practically *living* here for seven years of my life? I can feel my last shreds of composure disappearing. Hot tears of rage and humiliation are pressing against my eyes.

"Just leave, Samantha," says Oliver Swan pityingly. "Don't embarrass yourself any further."

I stare at him for a few seconds, then transfer my gaze to each of the senior partners in turn, searching for a shred of empathy. But there's none.

"I was a good lawyer," I say, my voice shaking. "I did a good job. You all know it. But you just wiped me out, like I never existed." I swallow down the lump in my throat. "Well, your loss."

The room is totally silent as I put the tray of éclairs down on a nearby table and stalk out of the room. The moment I'm out the door I can hear an animated conversation breaking out behind me. I'm even more of a joke than I was before.

I travel down in the lift with Ernest in total silence. If I opened my mouth, I might burst into tears.

When I get out of the building I check my mobile. There's a text from Nat on my phone, asking how things went. I read it several times, but I can't bring myself to reply. Nor can I bring myself to go back to the Geigers' house. Even though I could probably still catch a train, I can't face them tonight.

On automatic pilot, I head down to the Underground and onto a tube. I can see my face in the window opposite, pale and expressionless. And all the way, my mind is buzzing. *May 28th. May 28th.*

I don't hit on the answer until I'm arriving at my building. May 28th. Chelsea Flower Show. Of course. We were at Chelsea all day on May 28th. Arnold, Ketterman, Guy, and I, doing some corporate entertaining. Arnold arrived straight from Paris and afterward he was driven home. He wasn't even in the office.

He lied. Of course he did. I feel a wave of weary anger rising inside me. But there's nothing I can do now. No one will ever believe me. I'll live the rest of my life with everyone convinced it was my mistake.

I get out at my floor, already fumbling for the key, hoping against hope that Mrs. Farley won't hear me, already planning a long, hot bath. And then, as I'm almost at my door, I stop dead, thinking hard.

Slowly I turn and head back to the lift. There's one more chance. I have nothing to lose.

I rise up two floors and come out of the lift. It's almost identical to my floor—same carpet, same wallpaper, same lamps. Just different numbers on the apartment doors. 31 and 32. I can't remember which one I want, so in the end I plump for 31. It has a softer doormat. I sink down on the floor, put my bag down, lean against the door, and wait.

By the time Ketterman appears out of the lift doors I'm drained. I've been sitting here for three solid hours without anything to eat or drink. I feel wan and exhausted. But at the sight of him I scramble to my feet, clutching the wall as I feel a wash of fatigue.

For a moment Ketterman looks shocked. Then he resumes his usual stony expression.

"Samantha. What are you doing here?"

As I stand there I wonder if he's heard about me going to the offices. He must have. He'll have heard the whole gory tale. Not that he's giving anything away.

"What are you doing here?" he repeats. He's holding an enormous metal briefcase in one hand and his face is shadowed under the artificial lights. I take a step forward.

"I know I'm the last person you want to see." I rub my aching neck. "Believe me, I don't want to be here either. Out of all the people in the world I could turn to for help . . . you would be the last. You *are* the last."

I break off for a moment. Ketterman hasn't even flickered.

"So the fact that I'm here, coming to you . . . should prove it to you." I look at him desperately. "I'm serious. I have something to tell you, and you have to listen. You have to."

I can hear a car braking in the street outside and someone laughing raucously. Ketterman's face is still rigid. I can't tell what he's thinking. Then, at last, he reaches in his pocket for a key. He walks past me, unlocks the door to flat 32—and finally turns.

"Come in."

Twenty-two

I wake up to the view of a cracked, grubby ceiling. My eye runs along to a huge cobweb in the corner of the room, then down the wall to a rickety bookshelf stuffed with books, tapes, letters, old Christmas decorations, and the odd bit of discarded underwear.

How did I live in this mess for seven years?

How did I not *notice* it?

I push back the bedcover, get out of bed, and look around blearily. The carpet feels gritty under my feet and I wince. It needs a good Hoover. I guess the cleaner stopped coming after the money stopped appearing.

There are clothes lying all over the floor, and I search around until I find a dressing gown. I wrap it around myself and head out to the kitchen. I'd forgotten how bare and cold and spartan it was in here. There's nothing in the fridge, of course. But I find a chamomile tea bag and fill the kettle, and perch on a bar stool, looking out at the brick wall opposite.

It's already nine-fifteen. Ketterman will be at the office. He'll be taking whatever action he's going to take. In spite of everything, I feel weirdly calm. Matters are out of my hands now; there's nothing further I can do.

He listened to me. He actually listened, and asked questions, and even made me a cup of tea. I was there for over an hour. He didn't tell me what he thought or what he was going to do. He didn't even say whether he believed me or not. But the fact that he took me seriously made all the difference.

The kettle's coming to the boil when the doorbell rings. I pull my dressing gown around me and pad out to the hall. Through the spy-hole I can see Mrs. Farley peering back at me, her arms laden with packages.

Of course. Who else?

I open the door. "Hello, Mrs. Farley."

"Samantha, I *thought* it was you!" she exclaims. "After all this time! I had no idea...I didn't know what to think..."

"I've been away." I muster a neighborly smile. "I'm sorry I didn't let you know I was going away. But I didn't really have any warning myself."

"I see." Mrs. Farley's eyes are darting all around, at my blond hair, at my face, and past me into the flat, as though searching for clues.

"Thanks for taking in my parcels." I hold out my hands. "Shall I . . ."

"Oh! Of course." She hands over a couple of Jiffy bags and a cardboard box, still obviously avid with curiosity. "I suppose these high-powered jobs *do* send you girls abroad with no notice—"

"I haven't been abroad." I put the boxes down. "Thanks again."

"Oh, it's no trouble! I know what it's like when you've had a . . . a difficult family time?" she hazards.

"I haven't had a difficult family time," I say politely.

"Of course not!" She clears her throat. "Well, anyway. You're back now. From . . . whatever you've been doing."

"Mrs. Farley." I try to keep a straight face. "Would you like to know where I've been?"

Mrs. Farley recoils.

"Dear me! No! It's absolutely none of my business! Really, I wouldn't *dream* of . . . I must be getting on. . . ." She starts backing away.

"Thanks again!" I call as she disappears back into her flat.

I'm just closing the door as the phone rings. I pick up the receiver, suddenly wondering how many people must have rung this number over the last few weeks. The machine is crammed with messages, but after listening to the first three, all from Mum and each more furious than the last, I gave up.

"Hello?"

"Samantha," comes a businesslike voice. "John Ketterman here."

"Oh." Suddenly my calmness is replaced by a serious case of nerves. "Hi."

"I'd like to ask that you keep yourself available today. It may be necessary for you to speak to some people."

"People?"

There's a slight pause, then Ketterman says, "Investigators."

Oh, my God. Oh, my *God*. I feel like punching the air or bursting into tears. But somehow I keep my composure.

"So have you found something out?"

"I can't say anything at the moment." Ketterman sounds as distant and formal as ever. "I just need to know that you'll be available."

"Of course. Where will I have to go?"

"We'd like you to come here, to the Carter Spink offices," he says, without any trace of irony.

I look at the phone, almost wanting to laugh. *Would that be the same Carter Spink offices I was thrown out of yesterday?* I feel like saying. *The same Carter Spink offices I've been banned from?*

"I'll call you," adds Ketterman. "Keep your mobile with you. It could be a few hours."

"OK. I will." I take a deep breath. "And please, just tell me. You don't have to go into specifics, but . . . was my theory right?"

There's a crackling silence down the phone. I can't breathe.

"Not in every detail," says Ketterman at last, and I feel a painful thrill of triumph. That means I was right with some details, at least.

The phone goes dead. I put the receiver down and look at my reflection in the hall mirror, my eyes bright.

I was right. And they know it.

They'll offer me my job back, it suddenly hits me. They'll offer me partnership. At the thought I'm seized with excitement—and at the same time, a kind of fear.

I'll cross that bridge when I come to it.

I walk into the kitchen, keyed up, unable to stand still. What the hell am I going to do for the next few hours? I pour hot water onto my chamomile tea bag and stir it round with a spoon. And then I have an idea.

It takes only twenty minutes to pop out and get what I need. Butter, eggs, flour, vanilla, icing sugar. Baking tins. Mixers. A set of scales. Everything, in fact. I cannot *believe* how badly equipped my kitchen is. How did I ever do any cooking in here?

Well. I didn't.

I don't have an apron so I improvise with an old shirt. I don't have a mixing bowl and I forgot to buy one—so I use the plastic basin given to me as part of an aromatherapy kit. Two hours of whisking and baking later, I've produced a cake. Three tiers of vanilla sponge, sandwiched with buttercream, iced with lemon glacé, and decorated with sugar flowers.

I take it in with a glow of satisfaction. This is my fifth cake ever, and the first time I've done more than two tiers. I take off my old shirt, check that my mobile is in my pocket, pick up the cake, and head out of the flat.

As Mrs. Farley answers the doorbell, she looks startled to see me.

"Hi!" I say. "I've brought you something. To say thank you for looking after my post."

"Oh!" She looks at the cake in astonishment. "Samantha! That must have been expensive!"

"I didn't buy it," I say proudly. "I made it."

Mrs. Farley looks staggered.

"You . . . *made* it?"

"Uh-huh." I beam. "Shall I bring it in and make you some coffee?"

Mrs. Farley looks too thunderstruck to answer, so I head past her into the flat. To my shame I realize I haven't been in here before. In three years of knowing her, I never once set foot over the threshold. The place is immaculately kept, full of little side tables and antiques and a bowl of rose petals on the coffee table.

"You sit down," I say. "I'll find what I need in the kitchen." Still looking dazed, Mrs. Farley sinks into an upholstered wing chair.

"Please," she says faintly. "Don't break anything."

"I'm not going to *break* anything! Would you like frothy milk? And do you have any nutmeg?"

Ten minutes later I emerge from the kitchen, bearing two coffees and the cake.

"Here." I cut Mrs. Farley a slice. "See what you think."

Mrs. Farley takes the plate.

"You made this," she says at last.

"Yes!"

Mrs. Farley takes the slice to her mouth. Then she pauses, an anxious expression on her face.

"It's *safe*!" I say, and take a bite of my own slice. "See? I know how to cook! Honestly!"

Mrs. Farley takes a tiny bite. As she's chewing, her eyes meet mine in astonishment.

"It's . . . delicious! So *light*! You really made this?"

"I whisked the egg whites separately," I explain. "It keeps cakes really light. I can give you the recipe if you like. Have some coffee." I hand her a cup. "I used your electric beater for the milk, if that's OK. It works fine, if you get it to just the right temperature."

Mrs. Farley is gazing at me as though I'm talking gobbledygook.

"Samantha," she says at last. "Where have you been these last weeks?"

"I've been . . . away somewhere." My eye falls on a duster and can of Pledge, sitting on a side table. She must have been in the middle of cleaning when I rang. "I wouldn't use those dusters if I were you," I add politely. "I can recommend some better ones."

Mrs. Farley puts down her cup and leans forward in her chair. Her brow is wrinkled in concern.

"Samantha, you haven't joined some sort of religion?"

"No!" I can't help laughing at her face. "I've just been . . . doing something different. More coffee?"

I head into the kitchen and froth up some more milk. When I return to the sitting room, Mrs. Farley is on her second slice of cake.

"This is very good," she says between bites. "Thank you."

"Well . . . you know." I shrug, a little awkward. "Thanks for looking out for me all that time."

Mrs. Farley finishes her cake, puts her plate down, and regards me for a few moments, her head cocked to one side like a bird.

"Dear," she says finally. "I don't know where you've been. Or what you're doing. But whatever it is, you're transformed."

"I know my hair's different—" I begin, but Mrs. Farley shakes her head.

"I used to see you, rushing in and out, arriving home late at night, always looking so *weary*. So troubled. And I used to think you looked like . . . like the empty shell of a person. Like a dried-up leaf. A husk."

A dried-up leaf? I think in indignation. *A husk?*

"But now you've blossomed! You look fitter, you look healthier . . . you look happy." She puts her cup down and leans forward. "Whatever you've been doing, dear, you look wonderful."

"Oh. Well . . . thanks," I say bashfully. "I suppose I do feel different. I suppose I'm more relaxed these days." I take a sip of coffee and lean back in my chair, mulling it over. "I enjoy life a bit more than I used to. I *notice* more than I used to—"

"You haven't noticed your phone's ringing," Mrs. Farley interrupts mildly, nodding at my pocket.

"Oh!" I say in surprise, and grab my phone. "I should get this. Excuse me."

I flip it open and immediately hear Ketterman's voice in my ear.

"Samantha."

I spend three hours at the Carter Spink offices, talking in turn to a man from the Law Society, two of the senior partners, and a guy from Third Union Bank. By the time we finish I feel drained from repeating the same things over and over to the same carefully blank faces. The office lights are making my head ache. I'd forgotten how airless and dry the atmosphere is here.

I still haven't worked out exactly what's going on. Lawyers are so bloody discreet. I know someone's been to see Arnold at his home and that's about it. But even if no one's going to admit it, I know I was right. I've been vindicated.

After the last interview, a plate of sandwiches is brought to the small conference room I'm in, together with a bottle of mineral water and a muffin. I get to my feet, stretch out my arms, and wander over to the window. I feel like a prisoner in here. There's a tapping at the door and Ketterman comes into the room.

"Have we finished yet?" I say.

"We may need to speak to you again." He gestures to the sandwiches. "Have something to eat."

I cannot stay in this room a moment longer. I have to stretch my legs, at least.

"I'll just go and freshen up first," I say, and hurry out of the room before he can object.

As I enter the Ladies, all the women in there stop talking immediately. I disappear into a cubicle and hear the sound of excited whisperings and murmurings outside. As I come out again, not one person has left the room. I can feel all the eyes on me, like sunlamps.

"So are you back now, Samantha?" says an associate called Lucy.

"Is it true you were a waitress?" chimes in a secretary from Litigation.

"Not exactly." I turn away to the sink, feeling self-conscious.

"You look so *different*," says another girl.

"Your arms!" says Lucy as I wash my hands. "They're so brown. And *toned*. Have you been to a spa?"

"Er . . . no." I pull down some paper towel. "But thanks. So, how's life been here?"

"Good." Lucy nods a few times. "Really busy. Clocked up sixty-six billable hours last week. Two all-nighters."

"I had three," puts in another girl. I can see the pride in her face. And the dark gray shadows under her eyes. Is that what I used to look like? All pale and strained and tense?

"Great!" I say politely, drying my hands. "Well, I'd better get back now. See you."

I exit the Ladies and am walking back to the conference room, lost in my own thoughts, when I hear a voice.

"Oh, my God, *Samantha*?"

"*Guy*?" I look up in shock to see him hurrying down the corridor toward me, his smile even more dazzling than ever.

I wasn't expecting to see Guy here. In fact, I feel a bit thrown by the sight of him.

"Wow." He grips my shoulders tightly and scans my face. "You look fantastic."

"I thought you were in Hong Kong."

"Got back this morning. I've just been briefed on the situation. Bloody hell, Samantha, it's incredible." He lowers his voice. "Only you could work all that out. *Arnold,* of all people. I was *shell-shocked*. Everyone is. Those who know," he adds, lowering his voice still further. "Obviously it's not out yet."

"I don't even know what the 'situation' is," I reply, with a touch of resentment. "No one's telling me anything."

"Well, they will." Guy reaches into his pocket, gets out his BlackBerry, and squints at it. "You are flavor of the month right now. I knew it all along." He looks up. "I knew you could never make a mistake."

What? How can he say that?

"No, you didn't," I reply at last, finding my words. "No, you didn't. If you remember, you said I'd made errors. You said I was 'unreliable.' "

I can feel all the old hurt and humiliation starting to rise again and look away.

"I said *other* people had said you made errors." Guy pauses in tapping at his BlackBerry and looks up, frowning. "Shit, Samantha. I did stand up for you. I was on your side. Ask anyone!"

That's why you wouldn't have me to stay.

But I don't say anything out loud. I really don't want to get into it. It's history.

"Fine," I say at last. "Whatever."

We start walking along the corridor together, Guy still engrossed in the BlackBerry. God, he's addicted to that thing, I think with slight irritation.

"So where the hell did you disappear to?" At last he stops tapping. "What have you been doing all this time? You're not really a *waitress*?"

"No." I can't help smiling at his expression. "I'm not. I've got a job."

"I knew you'd get snapped up." He nods with satisfaction. "Who's employed you?"

"Oh . . . no one you'd know."

"You're in the same area, though?" He puts his BlackBerry away. "Doing the same kind of work?"

I have a sudden vision of me in my blue nylon overall, mopping Trish's bathroom floor.

"Er . . . as it happens, not really." Somehow I keep a straight face. Guy seems surprised.

"But you're still in banking law, right? Don't tell me you've made a complete change?" He suddenly looks galvanized. "You haven't gone into commercial law, have you?"

"Um, no . . . not commercial law. I'd better go." I cut him off and open the door to the interview room. "See you later."

I eat my sandwiches, I drink my mineral water. For half an hour no one disturbs me. I feel a bit like I'm in quarantine for some deadly illness. They could have given me some magazines, at least. I've developed quite a habit for gossip, after being surrounded by Trish's endless supply of *Heat* and *Hello!*

At last I hear a knock at the door and Ketterman comes in.

"Samantha. We would like to see you in the boardroom."

The *boardroom*?

I follow Ketterman down the corridors, aware of the nudges and whisperings from everyone we pass. He opens the huge double doors to the boardroom and I walk in to see about half the partners standing there, waiting for me. There's silence as Ketterman closes the doors. I glance at Guy, who grins back encouragingly but says nothing.

Am I supposed to speak? Did I miss the instructions? Ketterman has joined the group of partners. Now he turns to face me.

"Samantha. As you know, an investigation of . . . recent events is under way. The results have not yet been fully determined." He breaks off, looking tense, and I can see some of the others exchanging sober looks. "However, we have come to one conclusion. You were . . . wronged."

I'm stupefied. He's *admitting* it? Getting a lawyer to admit they've made a mistake is like getting a movie star to admit they had liposuction.

"I'm sorry?" I say, just to force him to repeat it.

"You were wronged." Ketterman frowns, clearly not enjoying this part of the conversation at all. I almost want to laugh.

"I was . . . wrong?" I hazard, looking puzzled.

"Wronged!" he snaps. "Wronged!"

"Oh, *wronged.* Well, thank you." I smile politely. "I appreciate that."

They'll probably offer me some kind of bonus, it crosses my mind. A luxury gift basket. Or even a holiday.

"And therefore—" Ketterman pauses. "We would like to offer you full equity partnership in the firm. Effective immediately."

I'm so shocked I nearly sit down on the floor. *Full equity partnership?*

I open my mouth—but I can't speak. I feel winded. I look around helplessly, like a fish on the end of a line. Full equity partnership is the highest pinnacle, way above the first rung of partnership. It's the most prestigious job in law. I never, ever, *ever* expected that.

"Welcome back, Samantha," says Greg Parker.

"Welcome back," chime in a few others. David

Elldridge gives me a warm smile. Guy gives me the thumbs-up.

"We have some champagne." Ketterman nods to Guy, who opens the double doors. The next moment two waitresses from the partners' dining room are coming in with trays of champagne glasses. Someone puts one in my hand.

This is all going too fast.

"Er . . . excuse me?" I call out. "I haven't actually said if I'll accept it."

The whole room seems to freeze, like a videotape on pause.

"I'm sorry?" Ketterman turns to me.

Oh, God. I'm not sure they're going to take this very well.

"The thing is . . ." I break off and take a sip of champagne for Dutch courage, trying to work out how to put this tactfully.

I've been thinking about it all day, over and over. Being a partner at Carter Spink is the dream I've had all my adult life. The glittering prize. It's everything I ever wanted . . .

Except all the things I never knew I wanted. Things I had no idea about until a few weeks ago. Like fresh air. Like evenings off. Unburdened weekends. Making plans with friends. Sitting in the pub after my work is done, drinking cider, with nothing to do, nothing hanging over me.

Even if they're offering me full equity partnership, it doesn't change the way I feel. It doesn't change me. Mrs. Farley was right: I've blossomed. I'm not a husk anymore.

Why would I go back to being a husk?

I clear my throat.

"It's a tremendous honor to be offered such an amazing opportunity," I say earnestly. "And I'm very grateful. Truly. However . . . the reason I came back wasn't to get my job back. It was to clear my name. To prove that I didn't make a mistake." I can't help shooting a look at Guy. "The truth is, since leaving Carter Spink I've . . . well . . . moved on. I have a job. Which I very much enjoy. So I won't be taking up your offer."

There's a stunned silence.

"Thank you," I add again, politely. "And . . . er . . . thanks for the champagne."

"Is she *serious*?" says someone at the back. Ketterman and Elldridge are exchanging frowns.

"Samantha," says Ketterman, coming forward. "You may have found opportunities elsewhere. But you are a Carter Spink lawyer. This is where you trained, this is where you belong."

"If it's a question of salary," adds Elldridge, "I'm sure we can match whatever you're currently—" He glances at Guy. "Which law firm has she gone to?"

"Wherever you are, I'll speak to the senior partner," says Ketterman in a businesslike way. "The personnel director . . . whoever would be appropriate. We'll sort this out. If you give me a number." He's taking out his BlackBerry.

My mouth twists. I desperately want to laugh.

"There isn't a personnel director," I explain. "Or a senior partner."

"There isn't a senior partner?" Ketterman looks impatient. "How can there not be a senior partner?"

"I never said I was working as a lawyer."

It's as if I've said I think the world is flat. I have never seen so many flummoxed faces in my life.

"You're . . . not working as a lawyer?" says Elldridge at last. "What are you working as, then?"

I was hoping it wouldn't come to this. But on the other hand, why shouldn't they know?

"I'm working as a housekeeper." I smile.

" 'Housekeeper?' " Elldridge peers at me. "Is that the new jargon for 'troubleshooter'? I can't keep up with these ridiculous job titles."

"You're on the compliance side?" says Ketterman. "Is that what you mean?"

"No, it's not what I mean," I say patiently. "I'm a housekeeper. I make beds. I cook meals. I'm a domestic."

God, I wish I had a camera. Their *faces*.

"You're literally . . . a *housekeeper*?" stutters Elldridge at last.

"Uh-huh." I look at my watch. "And I'm fulfilled and I'm relaxed and I'm happy. In fact, I should be getting back. Thank you," I add to Ketterman. "For listening to me. You're the only one who did."

"You're turning down our offer?" says Oliver Swan incredulously.

"I'm turning down your offer." I give an apologetic shrug. "Sorry. Bye, everyone."

As I head out of the room I feel slightly wobbly about the legs. And slightly manic inside. I turned it down. I turned down full equity partnership of Carter Spink.

What the hell is my mother going to say?

The thought makes me want to burst into hysterical laughter.

I feel too keyed up to wait for the lift, so I head down the stairwell, clattering down the cold stone steps.

"Samantha!" Guy's voice suddenly echoes above me. Oh, honestly. What does he want?

"I'm going!" I yell back. "Leave me alone!"

"You can't go!"

I can hear him accelerating down the steps, so I pick up speed myself. I've said my piece—what more is there to talk about? My shoes are clacking on the steps as I tear down, gripping on the handrail for balance. But even so, Guy's gaining on me.

"Samantha, this is crazy!"

"No, it's not!"

"I can't let you ruin your career out of . . . out of . . . pique!" he calls, and I wheel round indignantly, nearly falling down the stairs.

"I'm not doing this out of pique!"

"I know you're angry with us all!" Guy joins me on the staircase, breathing hard. "I'm sure it makes you feel really good to turn us down, to say you're working as a housekeeper—"

"I *am* working as a housekeeper!" I retort. "And I'm not turning you down because I'm angry. I'm turning you down because I don't want the job."

"Samantha, you wanted partnership more than anything else in the world!" Guy grabs my arm. "I know you did! You've worked for it for all these years. You can't throw it away! It's too valuable."

"What if I don't value it anymore?"

"It's been less than two months! Everything can't have changed!"

"It has. *I* have."

Guy shakes his head in disbelief. "You're really serious about the housekeeper thing."

"I'm really serious," I snap. "What's wrong with being a housekeeper?"

"Oh, for God's—" He stops himself. "Look, Samantha, come upstairs. We'll talk about it. The human-resources department has come on board. You lost your job . . .

you were badly treated . . . it's no wonder you can't think straight. They're suggesting counseling."

"I don't need counseling!" I turn on my heel and start down the stairs again. "Just because I don't want to be a lawyer, what, I'm *crazy?*"

I reach the bottom of the stairwell and burst into the foyer with Guy in hot pursuit. Hilary Grant, head of PR, is sitting on a leather sofa with some red-suited woman I don't recognize, and they both look up in surprise.

"Samantha you cannot do this!" Guy is shouting after me as he emerges into the foyer. "You are one of the most talented lawyers I know. I cannot let you turn down partnership to be a fucking . . . *housekeeper.*"

"Why not, if it's what I want to do?" I come to a halt on the marble and spin round to face him. "Guy . . . I've found out what it's like to have a life! I've found out what it's like *not* working every weekend. *Not* feeling pressure all the time. And . . . I like it!"

Guy isn't listening to a word I say. He doesn't even want to understand.

"You're going to stand there and tell me you prefer cleaning loos to being a partner at Carter Spink?" His face is flushed with outrage.

"Yes!" I say defiantly. "Yes, I do!"

"Who's that?" says the woman in the red suit with interest.

"Samantha, you're making the biggest mistake of your entire existence!" Guy's voice follows me as I reach the glass doors. "If you walk out now—"

I don't wait to hear any more. I'm out the door. Down the steps. Gone.

You're making the biggest mistake of your entire existence. As I sit on the train back to Gloucestershire, Guy's words keep ringing in my ears.

Once upon a time, just that thought would have sent me into a tailspin. But not anymore. He has no idea.

If I've learned one lesson from all that's happened to me, it's that there *is* no such thing as the biggest mistake of your existence. There's no such thing as ruining your life. Life's a pretty resilient thing, it turns out.

When I arrive at Lower Ebury I head straight to the pub. Nathaniel is behind the bar, wearing a chambray shirt I've never seen before, talking to Eamonn. For a few moments I just watch him from the doorway. His strong hands; the slant of his neck; the way his brow furrows as he nods. I can tell at once he disagrees with whatever Eamonn is saying. But he's waiting, wanting to be tactful about making his point. He knows how people work.

As if he can sense me watching him, he looks up and his face jolts. He smiles in welcome—but I can see the tension underneath. This last couple of days can't have been easy for him. Maybe he thought I'd get suckered in to my old relationship, that I wasn't coming back.

A roar goes up from the dartboard. Bill, a local farmer I've gotten to know, turns and spots me walking toward the bar.

"Samantha!" he shouts. "At last! We need you on our team!"

"In a sec!" I call over my shoulder. "Hi," I say as I reach Nathaniel. "Nice shirt."

"Hi," he says casually. "Good trip?"

"Not bad." I nod. Nathaniel lifts up the bar for me to

come through, his eyes searching my face as though for clues.

"So . . . is it over?"

"Yes." I put my arms around him and hug him tight. "It's over."

And at that moment, I truly believe it is.

Twenty-three

Nothing happens until lunchtime the next day.

I make the breakfast for Trish and Eddie as usual. I hoover and dust as usual. Then I put on Iris's apron, get out the chopping board, and start squeezing oranges. I'm going to make bitter chocolate and orange mousse for the charity lunch tomorrow. We're going to serve it on a bed of crystallized orange slices, and each plate is going to be garnished with a real silver-leaf angel from a Christmas-decoration catalog.

This was Trish's idea. As are the angels hanging from the ceiling.

"How are we doing?" Trish comes tapping into the kitchen, looking flustered. "Have you made the mousses yet?"

"Not yet," I say, briskly squeezing an orange. "Mrs. Geiger, don't worry. It's all under control."

"Do you know what I've *been* through, the last few days?" She clutches her head. "More and more people keep accepting. I've had to change the seating plan..."

"It'll be fine," I say soothingly. "Try to relax."

"Yes." She sighs, holding her head between two lacquered fingernails. "You're right. I'll just go and check the goody bags . . ."

I cannot believe how much Trish is spending on this lunch. Every time I question whether we really need to canopy the dining room in white silk or give every guest an orchid buttonhole, she shrills, "It's all in a good cause!"

Which reminds me of something I've been meaning to ask her for quite a while now.

"Er . . . Mrs. Geiger," I say casually. "Are you charging your guests for entrance to the lunch?"

"Oh, no!" she says. "I think that's rather *tacky*, don't you?"

"Are you holding a raffle?"

"I don't think so." She wrinkles her nose. "People *loathe* raffles."

I hardly dare ask this next question.

"So . . . um . . . how exactly are you planning on making money for Save The Children?"

There's silence in the kitchen. Trish has frozen, her eyes wide.

"Bugger," she says at last.

I knew it. She hadn't given it a thought. Somehow I manage to keep my respectful housekeeper's expression.

"Perhaps we could ask for voluntary donations?" I suggest. "We could hand round a little bag with the coffee and mints?"

"Yes. Yes." Trish peers at me as though I'm a genius. *"That's* the answer." She exhales sharply. "This is really very stressful, Samantha. I don't know how you stay so calm."

"Oh . . . I don't know." I feel a sudden wave of fondness

for her. When I arrived back at the house last night it was like coming home. Even though Trish had left a mountain of dirty crockery on the counter for my return, and a note saying, *Samantha, please polish all silver for luncheon.*

Trish heads out of the kitchen and I start whisking up egg whites for the mousse. Then I notice a man sidling down the drive. He's wearing jeans and an old polo shirt and has a camera slung round his neck. He disappears from view and I frown in puzzlement. Maybe he's a deliveryman. I measure out the caster sugar, with half an ear out for the doorbell, and start folding it into the egg whites, just the way Iris taught me. Then suddenly the man is standing at the kitchen door, peering in through the window.

I'm not ruining my mixture for some door-to-door salesman. He can wait a few moments. I finish folding in the sugar—then head to the door and open it.

"Can I help?" I say politely.

"Are you Samantha Sweeting?" he says, glancing down at a folded-up tabloid newspaper in his hand.

I look back at him warily. "Why?"

"I'm from the *Cheltenham Gazette*." He flashes an ID card at me. "I'm after an exclusive interview with you. 'Why I Chose the Cotswolds as My Secret Hideaway.' That kind of thing."

I look at him blankly for a few seconds.

"Er . . . what are you talking about?"

"You haven't seen it?" He looks surprised. "Haven't your friends been on the phone?"

"No. At least, I don't know," I say, confused. My mobile phone's upstairs in my bedroom. If it has been ringing, I haven't heard it.

"I take it this is you?" He turns the newspaper round and my stomach seizes up.

It's a picture of me. In the *Daily World*. A national tabloid.

It's my official Carter Spink portrait. I'm wearing a black suit and my hair is screwed up. Above it, in bold black letters, is the headline: "I'D RATHER CLEAN LOOS THAN BE A PARTNER AT CARTER SPINK."

What the hell is going on?

With trembling hands I grab the paper from the guy and scan the text.

They are the Masters of the Universe, the envy of their peers. Top law firm Carter Spink is the most prestigious in the country. But yesterday one young woman turned down a high-ranking post as partner in order to work as a humble housekeeper.

GET A LIFE

Partners were left with egg on their faces as star £500-an-hour lawyer Samantha Sweeting rejected their offer, which carried a substantial six-figure salary. Having previously been fired, the high-flyer apparently uncovered a financial scandal at the firm. However, when offered full equity partnership, Sweeting cited the pressure and lack of free time as reason for her decision.

"I've got used to having a life," she said, as partners begged her to stay.

A former Carter Spink employee who declined to be named confirmed the brutal working conditions of the legal firm. "They expect you to sell your soul," he said. "I had to resign from stress. No wonder she prefers manual labor."

A spokeswoman for Carter Spink defended

the firm's practices. "We are a flexible, modern firm with a sympathetic working ethos. We would like to talk to Samantha about her views and would certainly not expect employees to 'sell their soul.' "

VANISHED

She confirmed that Ms. Sweeting's job offer is still open and Carter Spink partners are anxious to talk to her. However, in a further extraordinary twist, this modern-day Cinderella has not been seen since running away from the offices.

WHERE IS SHE?

See comment, page 34.

I peer at it in a daze. See comment? There's *more*? With fumbling hands I turn to page 34.

THE PRICE OF SUCCESS—TOO HIGH?

A high-flying lawyer with everything ahead of her gives up a six-figure salary and turns to domestic drudgery instead. What does this story say about today's high-pressure society? Are our career women being pushed too hard? Are they burning out? Does this extraordinary story herald the start of a new trend?

One thing is for certain. Only Samantha Sweeting can answer.

I stare at the page, numb. How did—what did— *How?*

A flash interrupts me and I lift my head to see the guy pointing his camera at me.

"Stop!" I say, putting my hands up in front of my face.

"Can I have a picture of you holding a toilet brush, love?" he says, zooming his lens in. "It was a waitress in Cheltenham pointed me in the right direction. Reckoned she'd worked with you. Quite a scoop!" The camera flashes again and I flinch.

"No! You . . . you've made a mistake!" I shove the paper back at him in a mess of pages. "My name's Sarah. I'm not a lawyer. Whatever that waitress said . . . she was wrong."

The journalist looks at me suspiciously, and down at the photo again. I can see a flicker of doubt cross his face. I do look fairly different now from the way I did then, with my blond hair and everything.

"Please leave," I say. "My employers won't like it." I wait until he steps off the doorstep, then slam the door shut and turn the key. Then I pull the curtain across the window and lean back against the door, my heart thudding. Fuck. Fuck. What am I going to do?

OK. The important thing is not to panic. The important thing is to stay rational.

On the one hand, my entire past has been exposed in a national tabloid. On the other hand, Trish and Eddie don't read that particular tabloid. Or the *Cheltenham Gazette*. It's one silly story in one silly paper and it will die away by tomorrow. There's no reason to tell them anything. There's no need to rock the boat. I'll just carry on making my chocolate-orange mousses as though nothing has happened. Yes. Total denial is the way forward.

Feeling slightly better, I reach for the chocolate and start breaking chunks into a glass bowl.

"Samantha! Who was that?" Trish pokes her head round the door.

"No one." I look up with a fixed smile. "Nothing. Why don't I make you a cup of coffee and bring it out to the garden?"

Keep calm. Denial. It'll all be fine.

OK. Denial's not going to work, because there are three more journalists in the drive.

It's twenty minutes later. I've abandoned my chocolate mousses and am peering out the hall window in rising dismay. Two blokes and a girl have appeared out of nowhere. They all have cameras and are chatting to the guy in the polo shirt, who's gesticulating toward the kitchen. Occasionally one of them breaks off and takes a shot of the house. Any minute one of them is going to ring the doorbell.

I cannot let this develop. I need a new plan. I need . . .

Diversion. Yes. At least it might buy me some time.

I head to the front door, grabbing one of Trish's floppy straw hats on the way. Then I cautiously step outside and make my way down the gravel drive to the entrance, where the four journalists crowd around me.

"Are you Samantha Sweeting?" says one, thrusting a tape recorder in my face.

"Do you regret turning down partnership?" demands another.

"My name's Sarah," I say, keeping my head down. "You've got the wrong girl. Kindly leave the premises at once."

I wait for the stampede, but no one moves.

"You've all made a mistake!" I try again. "If you don't leave . . . I'll call the police."

One of the journalists peers under the brim of Trish's

hat. "It's her," he says scornfully. "Ned, it's her! Come over here!"

"She's there! She's come out!"

"It's her!"

I hear voices from across the street—and, aghast, I see another load of journalists suddenly appear, hurrying down the road toward the gates, bearing cameras and Dictaphones.

Fuck. Where did they come from?

"Ms. Sweeting, Angus Watts. *Daily Express.*" Blackglasses guy lifts up his microphone. "Do you have a message for young women of today?"

"Do you really enjoy cleaning toilets?" chimes in someone else, snapping a camera in my face. "What brand of toilet cleaner do you use?"

"Stop it!" I say, flustered. "Leave me alone!" I haul at the iron gates until they're closed, then turn and run up the drive, into the house and into the kitchen.

What am I going to do? What?

I catch a glimpse of myself in the mirrored fridge. My face is flushed and my expression wild. I'm also still wearing Trish's floppy straw hat.

I grab it off my head and dump it on the table, just as Trish comes into the kitchen. She's holding a book called *Your Elegant Luncheon Party* and an empty coffee cup.

"Do you know what's going on, Samantha?" she says. "There seems a bit of a *commotion* outside in the road."

"Is there?" I say. "I . . . I hadn't noticed."

"It looks like a protest." She wrinkles her brow. "I do hope they're not still there tomorrow. Protesters are so *selfish* . . ." Her eye falls on the counter. "Haven't you finished the mousses yet? Samantha, really! What have you been *doing*?"

"Um...nothing!" I reach for the bowl and start doling out chocolate mixture into molds. "I'm just getting on with them, Mrs. Geiger."

I feel like I'm in some kind of parallel reality. Everything's going to come out. It's a matter of time. What do I do?

"Have *you* seen this protest?" Trish demands as Eddie saunters into the kitchen. "Outside our gates! I think we should tell them to move on."

"It's not a protest," he says, opening the fridge and peering inside. "It's journalists."

"*Journalists?*" Trish peers at him. "What on earth would journalists be doing here?"

"Maybe we have a new celebrity neighbor?" suggests Eddie, pouring his beer into a glass. At once Trish claps her hand over her mouth.

"Joanna Lumley! I *heard* a rumor she was buying in the village! Samantha, have you heard anything about this?"

"I...er...no," I mumble, my face burning.

I have to say something. But what? Where do I start?

"Samantha, I need this shirt ironed by tonight." Melissa comes wandering into the kitchen, holding a sleeveless print shirt. "And be really careful with the collar, OK? What's going on outside?"

"Nobody knows," says Trish, looking beside herself. "But we think it's Joanna Lumley!"

Suddenly the doorbell rings. For a moment I consider bolting out the back door.

"I wonder if that's them!" exclaims Trish. "Eddie, go and answer it. Samantha, put on some coffee." She looks at me in impatience. "Come on!"

I need to explain but I'm totally paralyzed.

"Samantha?" She peers at me. "Are you all right?"

With an almighty effort I look up.

"Um . . . Mrs. Geiger . . ." My voice comes out a nervous husk. "There's . . . there's something . . . I ought to—"

"Melissa!" Eddie's voice interrupts me. He's hurrying into the kitchen, a huge smile spread across his face. "Melissa, love! They want you!"

"*Me?*" Melissa looks up in surprise. "What do you mean, Uncle Eddie?"

"It's the *Daily Mail*. They want to interview you!" Eddie turns to Trish, glowing with pride. "Did you know that our Melissa has one of the finest legal brains in the country?"

Oh, no. Oh, no.

"What?" Trish nearly drops her copy of *Your Elegant Luncheon Party*.

"That's what they said!" Eddie nods. "They said it might come as quite a surprise to me to learn we had such a high-flying lawyer in the house. I said, nonsense!" He puts an arm around Melissa. "We've always known you were a star!"

"Mrs. Geiger . . ." I say urgently. No one takes any notice of me.

"It must be that prize I won at law school! They must have heard about it somehow!" Melissa is gasping. "Oh, my God! The *Daily Mail*!"

"They want to take photos too!" puts in Eddie. "They want an exclusive!"

"I need to put on some makeup!" Melissa looks totally flustered. "How do I look?"

"Here we are!" Trish wrenches open her handbag. "Here's some mascara . . . and lipstick. . . ."

I have to stop this. I have to break it to them.

"Mr. Geiger . . ." I clear my throat. "Are you sure . . . I mean, did they ask for Melissa by . . . by name?"

"They didn't need to!" He twinkles at me. "Only one lawyer in this house!"

"Make some coffee, Samantha," instructs Trish sharply. "And use the pink cups. Quickly! Wash them up."

"The thing is . . . I have . . . I have something to tell you."

"Not *now*, Samantha! Wash up those cups!" Trish thrusts the rubber gloves at me. "I don't know *what's* wrong with you today—"

"But I don't think they've come to see Melissa," I say desperately. "There's something I . . . I should have told you."

No one pays any attention. They're all focused on Melissa.

"How do I look?" Melissa smooths her hair back self-consciously.

"Lovely, darling!" Trish leans forward. "Just a touch more lipstick. Make you look really glamorous . . ."

"Is she ready for the interview?" An unfamiliar woman's voice comes from the kitchen door and everyone freezes in excitement.

"In here!" Eddie pulls open the door to reveal a dark-haired, middle-aged woman in a trouser suit, whose eyes immediately run appraisingly over the kitchen.

"Here's our legal star!" Eddie gestures to Melissa with a beam of pride.

"Hello." Melissa tosses back her hair, then steps forward with an outstretched hand. "I'm Melissa Hurst."

The woman looks at Melissa blankly for a few moments. "Not her," she says. "*Her.*" And she points at me.

In puzzled silence, everyone turns to stare at me. Melissa's eyes have narrowed to deepest suspicion. I can see the Geigers exchanging glances.

"That's Samantha," says Trish, looking perplexed. "The housekeeper."

"You're Samantha Sweeting, I take it?" The woman

brings out her reporter's pad. "Can I ask you a few questions?"

"You want to interview the *housekeeper*?" says Melissa, with a sarcastic laugh. The journalist ignores her.

"You *are* Samantha Sweeting, aren't you?" she persists.

"I . . . yes," I admit at last. "But I don't want to do an interview. I don't have any comment."

"*Comment?*" Trish's eyes dart around uncertainly. "Comment on what?"

"What's going on, Samantha, love?" Eddie looks anxious. "Are you in some kind of trouble?"

"You haven't *told* them?" The *Daily Mail* journalist looks up from her notepad. "They have no idea?"

"Told us what?" says Trish, agitated. "What?"

"She's an illegal immigrant!" says Melissa in tones of triumph. "I knew it! I knew there was something—"

"Your 'housekeeper' is a top City lawyer." The woman throws down a copy of the *Daily World* onto the kitchen table. "And she's just turned down a six-figure partnership to work for you."

It's as though someone's thrown a grenade into the kitchen. Eddie visibly reels. Trish totters on her high-heeled clogs and grabs a chair for balance. Melissa's face looks like a popped balloon.

"I meant to tell you." I bite my lip awkwardly as I look round the faces. "I was . . . getting round to it . . ."

Trish's eyes are bulging as she reads the *Daily World* headline. Her mouth is opening and closing, but no sound is coming out.

"You're a . . . a *lawyer*?" she stutters at last.

"Not just any old lawyer," chimes in the journalist, consulting her notes. "Highest law degree of her year . . . youngest ever partner of Carter Spink—"

"You're a partner at Carter Spink?" stutters Melissa.

"No!" I say. "I mean . . . well . . . kind of . . . Can I make anyone a cup of tea?" I add desperately.

No one is interested in tea.

"Did you have any idea your housekeeper has an IQ of 158?" The journalist is clearly loving this. "She's a genius."

"We knew she was bright!" says Eddie, defensive. "We spotted that! We were helping her with her—" He breaks off, looking foolish. "With her English GCSE."

"And I'm really grateful!" I put in hurriedly. "Really."

Eddie mops his brow with a tea towel. Trish is still clutching the chair as though she might keel over any minute.

"I don't understand." Eddie suddenly puts the tea towel down and turns to me. "How did you combine being a lawyer with the housekeeping?"

"Yes!" exclaims Trish, coming to life. "Exactly. How on earth could you be a City lawyer . . . and *still* have time to train with Michel de la Roux de la Blanc?"

Oh, God. They still don't get it.

"I'm not really a housekeeper," I say desperately. "I'm not really a Cordon Bleu cook. Michel de la Roux de la Blanc doesn't exist. I have no idea what this thing is really called." I pick up the truffle beater, which is lying on the side. "I'm a . . . a fake."

I can't look at either of them. Suddenly I feel terrible. "I'll understand if you want me to leave," I mumble. "I took the job under false pretenses."

"Leave?" Trish looks horrified. "We don't want you to leave! Do we, Eddie?"

"Absolutely not!" he says, rallying himself. "You've done a fine job, Samantha. You can't help it if you're a lawyer."

" 'I'm a fake,' " says the journalist, writing it carefully

down on her notepad. "Do you feel guilty about that, Ms. Sweeting?"

"Stop it!" I say. "I'm not doing an interview!"

"Ms. Sweeting says she'd rather clean loos than be a partner at Carter Spink," says the journalist, turning to Trish. "Could I see the loos in question?"

"*Our* loos?" Spots of pink appear on Trish's cheeks and she gives me an uncertain glance. "Well! We did have the bathrooms refitted recently; they're all Royal Doulton."

"How many are there?" The journalist looks up from her notepad.

"Stop this!" I clutch my hair. "Look, I'll . . . I'll make a statement to the press. And then I want you all to leave me and my employers alone."

I hurry out of the kitchen, the *Daily Mail* woman following behind, and fling open the front door. The crowd of journalists is still there, behind the gate. Is it my imagination or are there more than before?

"It's Sarah," says the guy in black glasses sardonically as I approach them.

"Ladies and gentlemen of the press," I begin. "I would be grateful if you would leave me alone. There isn't any story here."

"Are you going to stay as a housekeeper?" calls a fat guy in jeans.

"Yes, I am." I lift my chin. "I've made a personal choice, for personal reasons, and I'm very happy here."

"What about feminism?" demands a young girl. "Women have fought for years to gain an equal foothold. Now you're telling them they should go back to the kitchen?"

"I'm not telling women anything!" I say, taken aback. "I'm just leading my own life."

"But you think there's nothing wrong with women

being chained to the kitchen sink?" A gray-haired woman glares at me.

"I'm not chained! I get paid for what I do, and I *choose* to—" My answer is drowned out by a barrage of questions and flashing cameras.

"Was Carter Spink a sexist hellhole?"

"Is this a bargaining ploy?"

"Do you think women should have careers?"

"We'd like to offer you a regular column on household hints!" says a chirpy blond girl in a blue mac. "We want to call it 'Samantha Says.'"

"*What?*" I gape at her. "I don't have any household hints!"

"A recipe, then?" She beams. "Your favorite dish?"

"Could you pose for us in your pinny?" calls out the fat guy, with a lascivious wink.

"No!" I say in horror. "I have nothing else to say! No comment! Go away!"

Ignoring the cries and shouts of "Samantha!" I turn and run with trembling legs back up the drive to the house.

The world is mad.

I burst into the kitchen, to find Trish, Eddie, and Melissa transfixed in front of the *Daily World*.

"Oh, no," I say, my heart plunging. "Don't read it. Honestly. It's just . . . stupid . . . tabloid . . ."

All three of them raise their heads and regard me as though I'm some kind of alien.

"You charge . . . five hundred pounds an hour?" Trish doesn't seem quite in control of her voice.

"They offered you full equity partnership?" Melissa looks green. "And you said *no*? Are you *crazy*?"

"Don't read this stuff!" I try to grab the paper. "Mrs. Geiger, I just want to carry on as usual. I'm still your housekeeper—"

"You're one of the country's top legal talents!" Trish jabs the paper hysterically. "It says so, here!"

"Samantha?" There's a rapping at the door and Nathaniel comes into the kitchen, holding an armful of newly picked potatoes. "Will this be enough for the lunch?"

I stare at him dumbly, feeling a clutch at my heart. He has no idea. He knows nothing. Oh, God.

I should have told him. Why didn't I tell him? *Why didn't I tell him?*

"What are *you*?" says Trish, turning to him wildly. "A top rocket scientist? A secret government agent?"

"I'm sorry?" Nathaniel shoots me a quizzical look.

"Nathaniel . . ."

I trail off, unable to continue. Nathaniel looks from face to face, a crease of uncertainty deepening in his brow.

"What's going on?" he says at last. "Is something up?"

I have never made such a hash of anything as I make of telling Nathaniel. I stammer, I stutter, I repeat myself and go round in circles.

Nathaniel listens in silence. He's leaning against an old stone pillar in front of the secluded bench where I'm sitting. His face is in profile, shadowed in the afternoon sun, and I can't tell what he's thinking.

At last I come to a finish and he slowly lifts his head. If I was hoping for a smile, I don't get it. I've never seen him look so shell-shocked.

"You're a lawyer," he says at last. All the light seems to have gone out of his eyes.

"Yes."

"I can't believe you're a lawyer." There's a hostility to his tone that I've never heard before.

"Nathaniel." I swallow hard. "I know you had a bad experience with lawyers. I'm really sorry about your dad. But . . . I'm not like that. You *know* I'm not—"

"How do I?" he retorts with sudden aggression. "How do I know who you are anymore? You lied to me."

"I didn't lie! I just . . . didn't tell you everything."

"I thought you were in an abusive relationship." He bows his head, clenching his hands behind his neck. "I thought that's why you didn't want to talk about your past. And you let me believe it. When you went up to London, I was *worried* about you. Jesus."

"I'm sorry." I wince with guilt. "I'm so sorry. I just . . . didn't want you to know the truth."

"Why not? What, you didn't trust me?"

"No!" I say in dismay. "Of course I trust you! If it had been anything else . . . Nathaniel, you have to understand. When we first met, how could I tell you? Everyone knows you hate lawyers. You even have a sign in your pub!"

"That sign's a *joke*." He makes an impatient gesture.

"It's not. Not completely! Come on, Nathaniel. If I'd told you I was a City lawyer when we first met, would you have treated me in the same way?"

Nathaniel doesn't reply. He's taken a few steps away and turned to face the house, as if he can't even bear to look at me anymore.

It's all ruined between us. Just as I feared. I can feel the tears rising but somehow keep my chin steady.

"Nathaniel, I didn't tell you the truth about myself because it was incredibly painful," I say quietly. "And because everything was so wonderful between us, I didn't want to ruin it. And because . . . I thought you might look at me differently."

Nathaniel slowly turns to face me, his face still closed and unforgiving.

"Like you're looking at me now." A tear runs down my cheek and I brush it away. "This is what I was afraid of."

The silence seems to last forever. Then Nathaniel exhales heavily, as though coming to a conclusion.

"Come here." He holds out his arms. "Come here."

He wraps them around me and I lean against his chest, almost overcome with relief.

"I'm the same person, you know," I mumble. "Even if I used to be a lawyer—I'm still me. Samantha."

"Samantha Sweeting, corporate lawyer." He surveys me for a few moments. "Nope. I can't see it."

"Me either! That part of my life is over. Nathaniel . . . I'm so sorry. I never meant any of this to happen." A bay leaf falls into his hair from the tree behind and I pick it out, automatically rubbing it to release the sweet scent.

"So what happens now?" says Nathaniel.

"Nothing. The media interest will die down. They'll get bored." I rest my head on his shoulder. "I'm happy in my job. I'm happy in this village. I'm happy with you. I just want everything to stay the same."

Twenty-four

I'm wrong. The media interest doesn't die down. I wake up the next morning to find twice as many reporters as yesterday camped outside, plus two TV vans. My mobile is so jammed with messages from journalists who have got hold of the number, I've given up listening to them. As I enter the kitchen, Melissa and Eddie are sitting at the table, which is covered in newspapers.

"You're in every single paper," Melissa informs me. "Uncle Eddie went down to the shop for them. Look." She shows me a double-page spread in the *Sun*. There's a picture of me superimposed on the background of a loo, and someone's drawn a toilet brush in one of my hands. "I'D RATHER CLEAN LOOS!" is in huge letters next to my face.

"Oh, my God." I sink into a chair and stare at the picture. *"Why?"*

"It's August," says Eddie, flicking through the *Telegraph*. "Nothing else in the news. Says here you're a casualty of today's work-obsessed society." He turns the paper around to show me a small item topped with the headline CARTER SPINK HIGH-FLYER CHOOSES DRUDGERY AFTER RUMORS OF SCANDAL.

"It says here you're a Judas to career women everywhere." Melissa is reading the *Herald*. "This columnist Mindy Morrell is really angry with you."

"Angry?" I echo, bewildered. "Why would anyone be angry with me?"

"But in the *Daily World* you're a savior of traditional values." Melissa reaches for the paper and opens it. *"Samantha Sweeting believes women should return to the hearthside for the sake of their own health and that of society."*

"What? I never said that!" I grab the paper and scan the text in disbelief. "Why are they all so *obsessed*?"

"Silly season," says Eddie, reaching for the *Express*. "Is it true you single-handedly uncovered Mafia connections at your law firm?"

"No!" I look up. "Who said that?"

"Can't remember where I saw it now," he says, riffling through the pages. "There's a picture of your mother in this one. Nice-looking lady."

"My *mother*?" I stare in dismay.

"High-flying daughter of a high-flying mother," Eddie reads aloud. *"Was the pressure to succeed too much?"*

Oh, God. Mum is going to *kill* me.

"This one has a poll, look." Eddie has opened another paper. *"Samantha Sweeting: Heroine or Fool? Phone or text your vote.* Then they give a number to call." He reaches for the phone and frowns. "Which shall I vote for?"

"Fool," says Melissa, grabbing the phone. "I'll do it."

"Samantha! You're up!"

I raise my head to see Trish coming into the kitchen, holding a bundle of newspapers under her arm. As she looks at me she has the same shell-shocked expression of awe that she had yesterday, as though I'm a priceless work of art that has suddenly pitched up in her kitchen. "I've just been reading about you!"

"Good morning, Mrs. Geiger." I put down the *Daily World* and hastily get to my feet. "Um, what can I get you for breakfast? Some coffee to begin with?"

"Don't you make the coffee, Samantha!" she replies, looking flustered. "Eddie, *you* can make the coffee!"

"I'm not making the coffee!" objects Eddie.

"Then . . . Melissa!" says Trish. "Make us all some nice coffee. Samantha, you sit down for once! You're our guest!" She gives an unnatural laugh.

"I'm not your guest!" I protest. "I'm your house-keeper!"

I can see Eddie and Trish exchanging doubtful looks. What do they think? That I'm going to leave?

"Nothing's different!" I insist. "I'm still your house-keeper! I just want to carry on my job as usual."

"Are you crazy?" demands Melissa. "Have you *seen* how much Carter Spink wants to pay you?"

"You wouldn't understand," I retort. "Mr. and Mrs. Geiger . . . *you'll* understand. I've learned a lot living here. I've changed as a person. And I've found a fulfilling way of life. Yes, I could make a lot more money being a lawyer in London. Yes, I could have some high-powered, pressurized career. But it's not what I want." I spread my arms around the kitchen. "This is what I want to do. This is where I want to be."

I'm half expecting Trish and Eddie to look moved by my little speech. Instead, they both peer at me in total incomprehension, then glance at each other again.

"I think you should consider the offer," says Eddie. "It says in the paper they're desperate to woo you back."

"We won't be at *all* offended if you leave," adds Trish, nodding emphatically. "We'll *completely* understand."

Is that all they can say? Aren't they *glad* I want to stay? Don't they *want* me as their housekeeper?

"I don't want to leave!" I say, almost crossly. "I want to stay here and enjoy a fulfilling life at a different pace."

"Right," says Eddie after a pause, then surreptitiously pulls a "What?" face at Trish.

The telephone rings and Trish picks it up.

"Hello?" She listens for a moment. "Yes, of *course,* Mavis. *And* Trudy. See you later!" She puts the receiver down. "Two more guests for the charity lunch!"

"Right." I glance at my watch. "I'd better get going on the starters."

As I'm getting out my pastry the phone rings again and Trish sighs. "If this is more late guests . . . Hello?" As she listens, her expression changes and she puts her hand over the receiver.

"Samantha," she hisses. "It's an ad company. Are you willing to appear in a TV commercial for Toilet Duck? You'd wear a barrister's wig and gown, and you'd have to say—"

"No!" I say, recoiling. "Of course not!"

"You should never turn down television," says Eddie reprovingly. "Could be a big opportunity."

"No, it couldn't! I don't want to be in any commercials!" I can see Eddie opening his mouth to argue. "I don't want to do any interviews," I add quickly. "I don't want to be a role model. I just want everything to go back to normal."

But by lunchtime everything is even more surreal than before.

I've had three more requests to appear on TV and

one to do a "tasteful" photo shoot for the *Sun* in a French maid's uniform. Trish has given an exclusive interview to the *Mail*. Callers to a radio phone-in that Melissa insisted on listening to have described me as "an antifeminist moron," a "Martha Stewart wannabe," and "a parasite on the taxpayers who paid for my education." I was so furious I almost phoned up myself.

But instead I switched the radio off and took three deep breaths. I'm not going to let myself get hassled. I have other things to think about. Fourteen guests have arrived for the charity lunch and are milling around on the lawn. I have wild-mushroom tartlets to bake, asparagus sauce to finish, and salmon fillets to roast.

I desperately wish Nathaniel were here to keep me calm. But he's gone off to Buckingham to pick up some koi carp for the pond, which Trish has suddenly decided she must have. Apparently they cost hundreds of pounds and all the celebrities have them. It's ridiculous. No one ever even *looks* in the pond.

The doorbell rings just as I'm opening the oven, and I sigh. Not another guest. We've had four late acceptances this morning, which has totally thrown my schedule. Let alone the journalist from the *Mirror* who dressed up in a pink floral suit and tried to tell Eddie she was new to the village.

I put the tray of tarts in the oven, gather up the remaining scraps of pastry, and start to wipe down my rolling pin.

"Samantha?" Trish taps at the door. "We have another guest!"

"*Another* one?" I turn round, wiping flour off my cheek. "But I've just put the starters in the oven—"

"It's a friend of yours. He says he needs to speak to you urgently. About business?" Trish raises her eyebrow at me significantly—then steps aside.

It's Guy. Standing in Trish's kitchen. In his immaculate Jermyn Street suit and starched cuffs.

I'm utterly flabbergasted. Judging by his expression, he's pretty gobsmacked too.

"Oh, my God," he says slowly, his eyes running over my uniform, my rolling pin, my floury hands. "You really are a housekeeper."

"Yes." I lift my chin. "I really am."

"Samantha..." says Trish from the door. "*Not* that I want to interrupt, but...starters in ten minutes?"

"Of course, Mrs. Geiger." I automatically bob a curtsy as Trish leaves, and Guy's eyes nearly fall out of his head.

"You *curtsy*?"

"The curtsying was a bit of a mistake," I admit, catching his appalled expression. "Guy, what are you *doing* here?"

"I'm here to persuade you to come back."

Of course he is. I should have guessed.

"I'm not coming back. Excuse me." I reach for the broom and dustpan and start sweeping the flour and pastry scraps off the floor. "Mind your feet!"

"Oh. Right." Guy awkwardly moves out of the way.

I dump the pastry bits in the bin, then get my asparagus sauce out of the fridge, pour it into a pan, and set it on a gentle heat. Guy is watching me in bemusement.

"Samantha," he says as I turn round. "We need to talk."

"I'm busy." The kitchen timer goes off with a shrill ring and I open the bottom oven to take out my rosemary-garlic rolls. I feel a surge of pride as I see them, all golden brown and wafting a delicious, herby scent. I can't resist taking a nibble out of one, then offering it to Guy.

"You *made* these?" He looks astounded. "I didn't know you could cook."

"I couldn't. I learned." I reach into the fridge again for some unsalted butter and break a knob into the foaming asparagus sauce. Then I glance at Guy, who's standing by the utensil rack. "Could you pass me a whisk?"

Guy looks helplessly at the utensils.

"Er . . . which one is the—"

"Don't worry," I say, clicking my tongue. "I'll get it."

"I have a job offer for you," says Guy as I grab the whisk and start beating in the butter. "I think you should look at it."

"I'm not interested." I don't even raise my head.

"You haven't even seen it yet." He reaches into his inside pocket and produces a white letter. "Here. Take a look."

"I'm not interested!" I repeat in exasperation. "Don't you understand? I don't want to be a lawyer."

"You want to be a housekeeper instead." His tone is so dismissive, I feel stung.

"Yes!" I thrust my whisk down. "I do! I'm happy here. I'm relaxed. You have no idea. It's a different life!"

"Yup, I got that," says Guy, glancing at my broom. "Samantha, you have to see sense!" He takes a phone out of his inside pocket and starts dialing. "There's someone you really should speak to. I've been in contact with your mother over the situation."

"You *what*?" I stare at him in horror. "How *dare* you!"

"Samantha, I only want the best for you. So does she. Hi, Jane," he says into the phone. "I'm with her now. I'll pass you over."

I cannot believe this. For an instant I feel like throwing the phone out the window. But no. I can deal with this.

"Hi, Mum," I say, taking the phone from Guy. "Long time."

"Samantha." Her voice is as icy as it was the last time

we spoke. But somehow this time it doesn't make me feel tense or anxious. She can't tell me what to do. She has no idea about my life anymore. "What exactly do you think you're doing? Working as some kind of *domestic*?"

"That's right. I'm a housekeeper. And I suppose you want me to go back to being a lawyer? Well, I'm happy here and I'm not going to." I taste the asparagus sauce and add some salt.

"You may think it's funny to be flippant," she says curtly. "This is your life, Samantha. Your career. I think you fail to understand—"

"*You* don't understand! None of you do!" I glare at Guy, then turn the hob down to a simmer and lean against the counter. "Mum, I've learned a different way to live. I do my day's work, and I finish—and that's it. I'm *free*. I don't need to take paperwork home. I don't need to have my BlackBerry switched on twenty-four/seven. I can go to the pub, I can make weekend plans, I can go and sit in the garden for half an hour with my feet up—and it *doesn't matter*. I don't have that constant pressure anymore. I'm not stressed out. And it suits me." I reach for a glass, fill it with water, and take a drink. "I'm sorry, but I've changed. I've made friends. I've got to know the community here. It's like . . . The Waltons."

"*The Waltons?*" She sounds startled. "Are there children there?"

"No!" I say in frustration. "You don't understand! They just . . . care. Like, a couple of weeks ago they threw me the most amazing birthday party."

There's silence. I wonder if I've touched a sensitive spot. Maybe she'll feel guilty . . . maybe she'll understand . . .

"How very bizarre," she says crisply. "Your birthday was almost two months ago."

"I know it was." I sigh. "Look, Mum, I've made up my mind." The cooker suddenly pings, and I reach for an oven glove. "I've got to go."

"Samantha, this conversation is not over!" she snaps furiously. "We have not finished."

"We have, OK? We *have*!" I switch off the phone and dump it on the table. "Thanks a lot, Guy," I say shortly. "Any other nice little surprises for me?"

"Samantha..." He spreads his hands apologetically. "I was just trying to get through to you—"

"I don't need 'getting through to.' " I turn away. "And now I have to work. This is my job."

I open the bottom oven, take out my trays of tartlets, and start transferring them onto small warmed plates.

"I'll help," says Guy after a moment.

"You can't *help*." I roll my eyes.

"Of course I can." To my astonishment he takes off his jacket, rolls up his sleeves, and puts on an apron adorned with cherries. "What do I do?"

I can't help but laugh. He looks so incongruous.

"Fine." I hand him a tray. "You can take in the starters with me."

As we enter the white-canopied room, the babble of chatter breaks off and fifteen dyed, lacquered heads turn. Trish's guests are seated around the table, sipping champagne, each wearing a suit of a different pastel color. It's like walking into a Dulux paint chart.

"And this is Samantha!" says Trish, whose cheeks are a bright shade of pink. "You all know Samantha, our housekeeper—and also top lawyer!"

To my embarrassment a spattering of applause breaks out.

"We saw you in the papers!" says a woman in cream.

"I need to talk to you." A woman in blue leans forward

with an intense expression. "About my *divorce settlement.*"

I'll pretend I didn't hear that.

"This is Guy, who's helping me out today," I say, beginning to serve the mushroom tarts.

"He's *also* a partner at Carter Spink," adds Trish proudly.

I can see impressed glances being exchanged across the table. An elderly woman at the end turns to Trish, looking bewildered.

"Are *all* your help lawyers?"

"Not all," says Trish airily, taking a deep gulp of champagne. "But you know, having *had* a Cambridge-educated housekeeper . . . I could never go back."

"Where do you get them from?" a red-haired woman asks avidly. "Is there a special agency?"

"It's called Oxbridge Housekeepers," says Guy, placing a mushroom tart in front of her. "Very choosy. Only those with first-class honors can apply."

"Goodness!" The red-haired woman gazes up, agog.

"I, on the other hand, went to Harvard," he continues. "So I'm with Harvard Help. Our motto is: 'Because that's what an Ivy League education is for.' Isn't that right, Samantha?"

"Shut *up*," I mutter. "Just serve the food."

At last all the ladies are served and we retreat to the empty kitchen.

"Very funny," I say, plonking the tray down with a crash. "You're so witty."

"Well, for God's sake, Samantha. Do you expect me to take all this *seriously*? Jesus." He takes off the apron and throws it down on the table. "Serving food to a bunch of airheads. Letting them patronize you."

"I have a job to do," I say tightly, opening the oven to

check on the salmon. "So if you're not going to help me—"

"This is not the job you should be doing!" he suddenly explodes. "Samantha, this is a fucking *travesty*. You have more brains than anyone in that room, and you're serving them? You're *curtsying* to them? You're cleaning their *bathrooms*?"

He sounds so passionate, I turn round. All traces of teasing have gone from his face.

"Samantha, you're one of the most brilliant people I know." His voice is jerky with anger. "You have the best legal mind any of us has ever seen. I cannot let you throw away your life on this . . . deluded crap."

"It's not deluded crap!" I reply, incensed. "Just because I'm not 'using my degree,' just because I'm not in some office, I'm wasting my life? Guy, I'm *happy*. I'm enjoying life in a way I've never done before. I *like* cooking. I *like* running a house. I *like* picking strawberries from the garden—"

"You're living in fantasyland!" he shouts. "This is all a novelty! It's fun because you've never done it before! But it'll wear off! Can't you *see* that?"

I feel a pricking of uncertainty inside. I'll ignore it.

"No." I give my asparagus sauce a determined stir. "I love this life."

"Will you still love it when you've been cleaning bathrooms for ten years? Get real." He comes over to the cooker and I turn away. "So you needed a holiday. You needed a break. Fine. But now you need to come back to real life."

"This *is* real life for me," I shoot back. "It's more real than my life used to be."

Guy shakes his head. "Charlotte and I went to Tuscany last year and learned watercolor painting. I loved it. The olive oil . . . the sunsets—the whole bit." He meets my eyes intently for a moment, then leans forward. "It doesn't mean I'm going to become a fucking Tuscan watercolor painter."

"It's different!" I wrench my gaze away from his. "Guy, I'm not going back to that workload. I'm not going back to that pressure. I worked seven days a week, for seven bloody years——"

"Exactly. Exactly! And just as you get the reward... you *bail out*?" He clutches his head. "Samantha, I'm not sure you understand the position you're in. You've been offered full equity partnership. You can basically demand any income you like. You're in control!"

"What?" I look at him, puzzled. "What do you mean?"

Guy raises his eyes upward, as though summoning the help of the Lawyer Gods.

"Do you realize," he says carefully, "the storm you've created? Do you realize how bad this all looks for Carter Spink? This is the worst week of press since the Storesons scandal in the eighties."

"I didn't *plan* any of it," I say, defensive. "I didn't ask the media to turn up on the doorstep——"

"I know. But they did. And Carter Spink's reputation has plummeted. The human-resources department are *beside* themselves. After all their touchy-feely well-being programs, all their graduate recruitment workshops... you tell the world you'd rather clean loos." He gives a sudden snort of laughter. "Talk about bad PR."

"Well, it's true," I say, lifting my chin. "I would."

"Don't be so perverse!" Guy bangs the table in exasperation. "You have Carter Spink over a barrel! They want the world to see you walking back into that office. They'll pay you whatever you want! You'd be crazy not to take up their offer!"

"I'm not interested in money," I retort. "I've got enough money——"

"You don't understand! Samantha, if you come back, you can earn enough to retire after ten years. You'll be set up for life! *Then* you can go and pick strawberries or sweep floors or whatever crap it is you want to do."

I open my mouth automatically to respond—but all of a sudden I can't quite track my thoughts. They're jumping about all over the place in confusion.

"You earned your partnership," says Guy, his tone quieter. "You earned it, Samantha. Use it."

Guy doesn't say any more on the subject. He's always known exactly when to close an argument; he should have been a barrister. He helps me serve the salmon, then gives me a hug and tells me to call him as soon as I've had time to think. And then he's gone, and I'm left alone in the kitchen, my thoughts churning.

I was so sure of myself. But now . . .

His arguments keep playing out in my mind. They keep hitting true notes. Maybe I am deluded. Maybe this is all a novelty. Maybe after a few years of a simpler life I won't be content, I'll be frustrated and bitter. I have a sudden vision of myself mopping floors with a nylon scarf round my head, assailing people: "I used to be a corporate lawyer, you know."

I have a brain. I have years ahead of me. And he's right. I worked for my partnership. I earned it.

I bury my head in my hands, resting my elbows on the table, listening to the thump of my own heart, beating like a question. *What am I going to do? What am I going to do?*

I've never felt so uncertain in my life. I've always been so positive about what I wanted, what my goals were, where I was headed. Now I feel like a pendulum, swinging from one side to the other, back and forth until I'm exhausted.

And yet all the time I'm being gradually pushed toward one answer. The rational answer. The answer that makes most sense.

I know what it is. I'm just not ready to face up to it yet.

It takes me until six o'clock. The lunch is over and I've cleared the table. Trish's guests have wandered round the garden and had cups of tea and melted away. As I walk out into the soft, balmy evening, Nathaniel and Trish are standing by the pond, with a plastic tank by Nathaniel's feet.

His face lights up as he turns and sees me—and something seems to wrench my stomach. There's no one else whose face lights up like that when they see me. There's no one else who manages to make me laugh and feel secure and teach me about worlds of which I knew nothing.

"This is a kumonryu," Nathaniel is saying as he scoops something out of the tank in a big green net. "Want to have a look?" As I get nearer I see an enormous patterned fish flapping noisily in the net. He offers it to Trish and she hops back with a little shriek.

"Get it away! Put it in the pond!"

"It cost you two hundred quid," says Nathaniel with a shrug. "I thought you might want to say hello."

"Put them all in." Trish shudders. "I'll come and see them when they're swimming about."

She turns on her heel and heads back toward the house.

"All right?" Nathaniel looks up at me. "How was the great charity lunch?"

"It was . . . fine."

"Did you hear the news?" He scoops another fish into the pond. "Eamonn's just got engaged! He's having a party this weekend at the pub."

"That's . . . that's great."

My mouth is dry. Come on. Just tell him.

"You know, we should have a koi pond at the nursery," says Nathaniel, sloshing the rest of the fish into the pond. "Do you know the profit margin on these—"

"Nathaniel, I'm going back." I close my eyes, trying to ignore the stab of pain inside. "I'm going back to London."

For a moment he doesn't move. Then very slowly he turns round, the net still in his hand, his face expressionless.

"Right," he says.

"I'm going back to my old job as a lawyer." My voice shakes a little. "Guy from my old firm came down today, and he convinced me—He showed me. He made me realize—" I break off and gesture helplessly.

"Realize what?" Nathaniel says.

He hasn't smiled. He hasn't said, "Good idea, that's just what I was going to suggest." Why can't he make this *easy* for me?

"I can't be a housekeeper all my life!" I sound more defensive than I'd like. "I'm a trained lawyer! I have a brain!"

"I know you have a brain." Now *he* sounds defensive. Oh, God. I'm not managing this well.

"I've earned partnership. Full equity partnership at Carter Spink." I gaze up at him, trying to convey the significance of this. "It's the most prestigious . . . lucrative . . . amazing . . . I can make enough money in a few years to retire!"

Nathaniel doesn't seem as impressed as he should. He just looks at me steadily. "At what cost?"

"What do you mean?" I avoid his gaze.

"I mean that when you turned up here, you were a nervous wreck. You were like some freaked-out rabbit. White as a sheet. Stiff as a board. You looked like you hadn't ever seen the sun, you looked like you hadn't ever *enjoyed* yourself—"

"You're exaggerating."

"I'm not. Can't you *see* how much you've changed? You're not edgy anymore. You're not a bundle of nerves." He picks up my arm and lets it fall down. "That arm would have stayed there!"

"OK . . . so I've relaxed a bit!" I throw up my hands. "I know I've changed. I've calmed down and I've learned to cook and iron and pull pints—and I've had a wonderful time. But it's like a holiday. It can't last forever!"

"Why not?" His persistence is unnerving me.

"Because!" I say, rattled. "If I stay as a housekeeper I'll be unfulfilled!"

"Is that what your lawyer friend told you?" There's a hostile edge to his tone. "That you'll be more fulfilled working twenty-four hours a day? That they're only thinking of your own good?"

"No! I mean, it's obvious. I can't clean loos forever!"

Nathaniel shakes his head in despair.

"So after all this you're just going to go back, pick up the reins, and carry on as though nothing happened?"

"It'll be different this time! I'll keep a balance. They really want me to come back, they'll listen to what I want—"

"Who are you kidding?" Nathaniel grips my shoulders. "Samantha, they don't give a shit about you! Can't you *see* that? It'll be the same stress, the same lifestyle—"

I feel a sudden surge of anger toward him for not understanding; for not supporting me.

"Well, at least I *tried* something new!" My words pour out in a torrent. "At least I went out and tried a different life for a bit!"

"What's that supposed to mean?" His grasp loosens in shock.

"It means, what have *you* ever tried, Nathaniel?" I know I sound shrill and aggressive but I can't help myself. "You're so narrow-minded! You live in the same village you grew up in, you run the family business, you're buying a nursery down the road . . . you're practically still in the *womb*. So before you lecture me on the way to live my life, try living one of your own, OK?"

I break off, panting, to see Nathaniel looking as though I've slapped him.

"I . . . didn't mean it," I mumble.

I take a few steps away, feeling near to tears. This isn't the way things were supposed to go. Nathaniel was supposed to support me and give me a hug and tell me I was making the right decision. Instead here we are, standing yards apart, not even looking at each other.

"I thought about spreading my wings." Nathaniel suddenly speaks, his voice stiff. "There's a nursery in Cornwall I'd die to own. Fantastic piece of land, fantastic business—but I didn't look at it. I preferred not to be six hours away from you." He shrugs. "I guess you're right. That was pretty narrow-minded of me."

I don't know how to reply. For a while there's silence, except for the cooing of pigeons down at the end of the garden. It is the most spectacular evening, I suddenly realize. Evening sun is slanting through the willow tree and the grass smells sweet underneath my feet.

"Nathaniel . . . I have to go back." My voice isn't quite steady. "I don't have any choice. But we can still be together. The two of us. We can still make it work. We'll have holidays . . . weekends . . . I'll come back for Eamonn's party . . . You won't know I've gone!"

He's silent for a moment, fiddling with the handle of the bucket. When at last he looks up, his expression makes my heart hurt.

"Yeah," he says in a quiet voice. "I will."

Twenty-five

The news makes the front page of the *Daily Mail*. I am a genuine celebrity. SAMANTHA CHOOSES LAW OVER LOOS. As I come into the kitchen the next morning, Trish is poring over it, with Eddie reading another copy.

"Trish's interview has been printed!" he announces. "Look!"

" '*I always knew Samantha was a cut above the average housekeeper,*' *says Trish Geiger, thirty-seven*" reads out Trish proudly. " '*We often discussed philosophy and ethics together over the Hoover.*' "

She looks up and her face changes. "Samantha, are you all right? You look absolutely washed out."

"I didn't sleep that well," I admit, and flip on the kettle.

I spent the night at Nathaniel's. We cooked mushroom omelets together and watched the end of an old war movie and had slow, tender sex. We didn't talk any more about my going. But at three o'clock, when I looked over at him, he was awake too, staring up at the ceiling.

"You need energy!" says Trish, perturbed. "It's your big day! You need to look your best!"

"I will." I try to smile. "I just need a cup of coffee."

It's going to be a huge day. The Carter Spink PR department swung into action as soon as I made my decision and has turned my return into a full media event. There's going to be a big press conference at lunchtime in front of the Geigers' house, where I'll say how delighted I am to be going back to Carter Spink. Several of the partners are going to shake my hand for the photographers and I'll give a few short interviews. And then we're all going back to London on the train.

"So," says Eddie as I spoon coffee into the pot. "All packed up?"

"Pretty much. And Mrs. Geiger . . . here." I hand Trish the blue uniform, which I've been carrying, folded, under my arm. "It's clean and pressed. Ready for your next housekeeper."

As Trish takes the uniform she looks suddenly stricken. "Of course," she says, her voice jumpy. "Thank you, Samantha." She clasps a napkin to her eyes.

"There, there," says Eddie, patting her on the back. He looks rather moist around the eyes himself. Oh, God, now I feel like crying myself.

"I'm really grateful for everything," I gulp. "And I'm sorry for leaving you in the lurch."

"We know you've made the right decision. It's not *that*." Trish dabs her eyes.

"We're very proud of you," chips in Eddie gruffly as the doorbell rings.

I head into the hall, and open the door. The entire PR

team from Carter Spink is standing on the doorstep, all in identical trouser suits.

"Samantha." Hilary Grant, head of PR, runs her eyes over me. "Ready?"

By twelve o'clock I'm wearing a black suit, black tights, black high heels, and the crispest white shirt I've ever seen. I've been professionally made up and my hair has been scraped back into a bun.

Hilary brought the clothes and the hairdresser and makeup artist. Now we're in the drawing room while she preps me on what to say to the press. For the thousand millionth time.

"What's the most important thing to remember?" she's demanding. "Above anything?"

"Not to mention loos," I say wearily. "I promise, I won't."

"And if they ask about recipes?" She wheels round from where she's been striding up and down.

"I answer, 'I'm a lawyer. My only recipe is the recipe for success.'" Somehow I manage to utter the words straight-faced.

I'd forgotten how seriously the PR department takes all of this. But I suppose it's their job. And I suppose this whole business has been a bit of a nightmare for them. Hilary has been outwardly pleasant ever since she got here—but I get the feeling there's a little wax doll of me on her desk, impaled by drawing pins.

"We just want to make sure you don't say anything else . . . *unfortunate*." She gives me a slightly savage smile.

"I won't! I'll stick to the script."

"And then the *News Today* team will follow you back to London." She consults her BlackBerry. "We've given them access for the rest of the day. You're OK about that?"

"Well . . . yes. I suppose."

I cannot believe how big this whole thing has become. A news discussion program actually wants to do a fly-on-the-wall TV documentary section about my return to Carter Spink. Is there nothing else happening in the world?

"Don't look at the camera." Hilary is still briskly issuing instructions. "You should be good-humored and positive. You can talk about the career opportunities Carter Spink has given you and how much you're looking forward to getting back. *Don't* mention your salary—"

"Any chance of a coffee round here?" Guy's voice interrupts us and he comes in, wearing a pair of expensive shades. He takes them off and grins at me. "Maybe you could rustle up some scones?"

"Ha ha," I say politely.

"Hilary, there's some trouble outside." Guy turns to her. "Some TV guy kicking up a fuss."

"Damn." Hilary looks at me. "Can I leave you for a moment, Samantha?"

"Absolutely!" I try not to sound too eager. "I'll be fine!"

As she leaves I breathe a sigh of relief.

"So." Guy raises his eyebrows. "How are you? Excited?"

"Of course!" I smile.

Actually I feel a little surreal, wearing a black suit again, surrounded by Carter Spink PR people. I haven't seen Trish or Eddie for hours. Hilary Grant has totally commandeered the house.

"You made the right decision, you know," says Guy.

"I know." I brush a fleck of lint off my skirt.

"You look sensational. You're going to blow them

away." He perches on a sofa arm opposite me and sighs. "Jesus, I missed you, Samantha. It hasn't been the same."

Does he have any sense of irony? Or did they fix that at Harvard too?

"So now you're my best friend again." I can't help a slight edge. "Funny, that."

Guy blinks at me. "What's that supposed to mean?"

"Come on, Guy." I almost want to laugh. "You didn't want to know me when I was in trouble. Now suddenly we're chums again?"

"That's unfair," retorts Guy hotly. "I did everything I could for you, Samantha. I fought for you in that meeting. It was Arnold who refused to have you back. At the time we had no idea why—"

"You wouldn't let me in your house, though, would you? Friendship wouldn't quite extend that far."

Guy looks genuinely thrown. He pushes his hair back with both hands.

"I felt terrible about that," he says. "It wasn't me. It was Charlotte. I was furious with her—"

"Of course you were."

"I was!"

"Yeah, right," I say sarcastically. "So I suppose you had a huge row about it and broke up."

"Yes," says Guy.

The wind is totally taken out of my sails.

"*Yes?*"

"We've split up." He shrugs. "Didn't you know?"

"No! I had no idea! I'm . . . sorry. I really didn't—" I break off in confusion. "It wasn't . . . it wasn't really over me?"

Guy doesn't answer. His brown eyes are becoming more intense.

"Samantha," he says, not moving his gaze from mine.

"I've always felt . . ." He thrusts his hands in his pockets. "I've always felt we somehow . . . missed our chance."

No. This can't be happening.

We missed our chance?

Now he says this?

"I've always really admired you. I always felt there was a spark between us." He hesitates. "I wondered whether you felt . . . the same."

This is unreal. How many millions of times have I imagined Guy saying these words to me? But now that he's actually *doing* it . . . it's too late. It's all wrong.

"Samantha?"

Suddenly I realize I'm staring at him like a zombie.

"Oh. Right." I try to pull myself together. "Well . . . yes. Maybe I used to feel like that too." I fiddle with my skirt. "But the thing is . . . I've met someone. Since I've been here."

"The gardener," says Guy without missing a beat.

"Yes!" I look up in surprise. "How did you—"

"Some of the journalists were talking about it outside."

"Oh. Well, it's true. His name's Nathaniel." I feel myself blush.

Guy frowns. "But that's just a holiday romance."

"It's not a holiday romance!" I say, taken aback. "It's a *relationship*. We're serious about each other."

"Is he moving to London?"

"Well . . . no. He hates London."

Guy looks incredulous for a moment, then throws back his head and roars with laughter.

"Samantha, you really are living in fantasyland."

"What's that supposed to mean?" I say, incensed. "We'll make it work somehow. If we both want it enough—"

"I'm not sure you've quite got the situation yet." Guy shakes his head. "Samantha, you're *leaving* this place.

You're coming back to London, back to reality, back to work. Believe me, you're never going to keep up some holiday fling."

"It was *not* a holiday fling!" I yell furiously, as the door opens. Hilary looks from Guy to me with alert, suspicious eyes.

"Everything all right?"

"Fine," I say, turning away from Guy. "I'm fine."

"Good!" She taps her watch. "Because it's nearly time!"

The entire world seems to have descended on the Geigers' house. As I venture out the front door with Hilary and two PR managers, there are what looks like hundreds of people in the drive. A row of TV cameras is trained on me, photographers and journalists are in a crowd behind, and Carter Spink PR assistants are milling around, keeping everyone in line and handing out coffee from a refreshments stand that seems to have sprung up from nowhere. At the gate I can see a group of regulars from the pub peering in curiously, and I shoot them a mortified grin.

"It'll be a few more minutes," says Hilary, listening to her mobile. "We're just waiting for the *Daily Telegraph*."

I can see David Elldridge and Greg Parker standing by the cappuccino machine, both typing on their BlackBerrys. The PR department wanted as many partners as possible, but none of the others could make it. Frankly, they were lucky to get this many. As I'm watching, to my disbelief I see Melissa approaching them, dressed up smartly in a beige suit and holding . . . is that a *CV*?

"Hi!" I hear her begin. "I'm a very good friend of Samantha Sweeting, and she recommended I apply to Carter Spink."

I can't help smiling. The girl has some nerve.

"Samantha." I look up to see Nathaniel coming across the gravel, his blue eyes tense. "How are you doing?"

"I'm . . . fine." I feel his hand clasping mine and intertwine my fingers between his as tightly as I can. "You know. It's all a bit crazy."

Guy's wrong. It's going to work. It's going to last. Of course it is.

I can feel his thumb rubbing mine, just like he did that first evening we had together. Like some private language; like his skin is talking to mine.

"Are you going to introduce me, Samantha?" Guy comes sauntering over.

"This is Guy," I say reluctantly. "I work with him at Carter Spink. Guy—Nathaniel."

"Delighted to meet you!" Guy holds out his hand and Nathaniel is forced to let go of mine to shake it. "Thanks for looking after our Samantha so well."

Does he have to sound so *patronizing*? And what's this "our" Samantha?

"It was my pleasure." Nathaniel glowers back.

"So . . . you look after the garden." Guy looks around the drive. "Very nice. Well done!"

I can see Nathaniel's fist forming at his side.

Please don't punch him, I pray urgently. *Don't* punch him—

To my relief I notice Iris coming through the gate, peering around at all the journalists with interest.

"Look!" I say quickly to Nathaniel. "Your mum."

I greet Iris with a wave. She's wearing cropped cotton trousers and espadrilles, her plaits wound round her head. As she reaches me she just looks for a few moments: at my bun, my black suit, my high-heeled shoes.

"Goodness," she says at last.

"I know." I laugh awkwardly. "A bit different."

"So, Samantha." Her eyes rest softly on mine. "You found your way."

"Yes." I take a deep breath. "Yes, I did. This is the right way for me, Iris. I'm a lawyer. I always was. It's a great opportunity. I'd be . . . I'd be crazy not to take it up."

Iris nods, her expression guarded.

"Nathaniel told me all about it. I'm sure you've made the right decision." She pauses. "Well . . . good-bye, chicken. And good luck. We'll miss you."

As I lean forward to hug her I suddenly feel tears pricking my eyes. "Iris . . . I don't know how to thank you," I whisper. "For everything you did."

"You did it all yourself." She squeezes me tight. "I'm very proud of you."

"And it's not really good-bye." I wipe my eyes with a tissue, praying my makeup hasn't run. "I'll be back before you know it. I'm going to visit as many weekends as I can. . . ."

"Here, let me." She takes my tissue from me and dabs my eyes.

"Thanks." I smile but I'm still shaky. "This makeup has got to last all day."

"Samantha?" Hilary calls me from the refreshment stand, where she's talking to David Elldridge and Greg Parker. "Can you come over here?"

"I'll be right there!" I call back.

"Samantha, before you go . . ." Iris takes hold of both my hands, her face filled with concern. "Sweetie . . . I'm sure you're doing what's best for you. But just remember, you only get your youth once." She looks at my hand, smooth against hers. "You only get these precious years once."

"I'll remember." I bite my lip. "I promise."

"Good." She pats my hand. "Off you go."

As I walk over to the refreshment stand, Nathaniel's hand is tightly in mine. We're going to have to say good-bye in a couple of hours.

No. I can't think about that.

Hilary is looking a little stressed as I approach.

"Got your statement?" she says. "Feeling prepared?"

"All set." I take out the folded sheet of paper. "Hilary, this is Nathaniel."

Hilary's eyes run over him without interest. "Hello," she says. "Now, Samantha, let's just run over the order again. You read your statement, then questions, then photos. We'll start in about three minutes. The team are just distributing press packs—" Suddenly she peers more closely at me. "What happened to your *makeup*?"

"Um . . . I was just saying good-bye to someone," I say apologetically. "It's not too bad, is it?"

"We'll have to redo it." Her voice is jerky with annoyance. "This really is *all* I need." She strides away, calling to one of her assistants.

Three more minutes. Three minutes before my old life begins again.

"So . . . I'll be back for Eamonn's party," I say, still clutching Nathaniel's hand. "It's only a few days away. I'll catch the train down on Friday night, spend the weekend—"

"No, you won't," chips in Guy, shaking chocolate onto a cappuccino. He looks up. "You'll be in Hong Kong."

"What?" I say stupidly.

"Samatron are delighted you're back and they've asked for you on this merger. We're flying to Hong Kong to-morrow. Has no one told you?"

"No," I say, taken aback. "No one's even mentioned it."

Guy shrugs. "I thought you knew. Five days in Hong Kong and then on to Singapore. You and I are going to be wooing some new clients." He takes a sip of coffee. "You need to start pulling in business, Samantha Sweeting, equity partner. Can't rest on your laurels."

I haven't even *started* the job yet. And they're already talking about resting on my laurels?

"So . . . when will we be back?"

Guy shrugs. "Couple of weeks?"

"Samantha!" says Elldridge, coming up. "Has Guy mentioned, we want you on a corporate shooting weekend in September? Up in Scotland; should be fun."

"Right. Um, yes, that sounds great." I rub my nose. "The only thing is, I'm trying to keep some weekends free . . . keep a bit of balance in my life . . ."

Elldridge looks puzzled.

"You've *had* your break, Samantha," he says. "Now it's back to work. And I must talk to you about New York." He pats me on the shoulder and turns to the girl manning the coffee machine. "Another espresso, please."

"Realistically, I'd say you're not going to have a free weekend till Christmas," puts in Guy. "I did warn you." He raises his eyebrows meaningfully and moves away to talk to Hilary.

There's silence. I don't know what to say. Everything's moving too fast. I thought it would be different this time. I thought I'd have more control.

"Christmas," echoes Nathaniel at last, looking thunderstruck.

"No," I say at once. "He's exaggerating. It won't be that bad. I'll rearrange things." I rub my brow. "Look, Nathaniel, I'll be back before Christmas. I promise. Things might be busy—but I'll do it somehow. Whatever it takes."

He flinches at my words. "Don't turn it into a duty."

"*Duty?*" I stare at him. "That's not what I meant. You know that's not what I meant."

"Two minutes!" Hilary comes bustling up with the makeup artist, but I ignore her.

"Nathaniel—"

"Samantha!" snaps Hilary, trying to pull me away. "You *really* don't have time for this!"

"You should go." Nathaniel gestures with his head. "You're busy."

This is awful. It feels like everything is disintegrating between us.

"Nathaniel, just tell me." My voice trembles. "Tell me before I go. That day in the farmhouse—what did you say to me?"

Nathaniel looks at me for a long moment, then something in his eyes seems to close up.

"It was long and boring and badly put." He turns away with a half shrug.

"*Please* do something with those smudges!" Hilary is saying. "Could you please move?" she adds sharply to Nathaniel.

"I'll get out of your way." Nathaniel lets go of my hand and retreats before I can say anything.

"You're not in my way!" I call after him, but I'm not sure he hears.

As the makeup artist begins her work, my mind is spinning so fast I feel faint. Suddenly all my certainty has vanished. Am I doing the right thing?

Oh, God. What is *wrong* with me?

"Close, please." The makeup artist is brushing at my eyelids. "Now open..."

I open my eyes to see Nathaniel and Guy standing together, some way away. Guy's talking and Nathaniel is listening, his face taut. I feel a sudden stab of unease. What's Guy saying?

"Close again," says the makeup artist. Reluctantly I close my eyes and feel her brushing yet more shadow on. For God's sake. Hasn't she finished? Does it *matter* what I look like?

At last she withdraws her brush. "Open."

I open my eyes to see Guy standing in the same spot, a few yards away. But Nathaniel's vanished. Where's he gone?

"Put your lips together..." the makeup artist instructs, producing a lipstick brush.

My eyes are darting in panic around the crowded drive, looking for Nathaniel. I *need* him. I need to talk to him before this press conference goes ahead.

"Ready for your big moment? Got your statement?" Hilary is upon me again, smelling of freshly applied scent. "That looks a lot better! Chin up!" She taps my chin so sharply I wince. "Any last-minute questions?"

"Um...yes," I say desperately. "I was just wondering...could we possibly put it off for a little bit? Just a few minutes."

Hilary's face freezes.

"What?" she says at last. I have a dreadful feeling she's going to explode.

"I feel a bit...confused. I need more time to think...." I trail off at Hilary's expression.

She comes toward me and brings her face very close to mine. She's still smiling, but her eyes are snapping and her nostrils flared and white. I take a step back, quailing, but she grabs my shoulders so hard I can feel her nails digging into my flesh.

"Samantha," she hisses. "You will go out there, you will read your statement, and you will say Carter Spink is the best law firm in the world. And if you don't—I will kill you."

I think she's serious.

"We're all confused, Samantha. We all need more time to think. That's life." She gives me a little shake. "Get over it." She breathes out sharply and smooths down her suit. "Right! I'm going to announce you."

She marches onto the lawn. I just stand there, shaking.

"Ladies and gentlemen of the press!" Hilary's voice is blaring through the microphone. "I'm delighted to welcome you all here this morning."

Suddenly I spot Guy, helping himself to a mineral water. "Guy!" I call urgently. "Guy! Where's Nathaniel?"

"I have no idea," says Guy insouciantly.

"What did you say to him? When you were talking just now?"

"I didn't have to say much," Guy replies. "He could tell the way the wind was blowing."

"What do you mean?" I feel like I've missed something. "The wind wasn't blowing any way."

"Samantha, don't be naive." Guy takes a swig of water. "He's a grown man. He understands."

"...our newest partner at Carter Spink, Samantha Sweeting!" Hilary's voice and the applause breaking out barely touch my consciousness.

"Understands what?" I say in horror. "What did you say?"

"Samantha!" Hilary interrupts with a sweetly savage smile. "We're all waiting! Lots of busy people!" She grabs my hand with an iron grip and drags me with surprising force onto the grass. "Off you go! Enjoy!" She gives me a sharp dig in the back and walks away.

I'm stranded in front of the nation's press.

"Move it!" Hilary's tense undertone makes me jump. I feel like I'm on a conveyor belt. The only way is forward.

With wobbling legs I make my way into the middle of the lawn, where a microphone has been set up on a stand. The sun is glinting off all the camera lenses and I feel half blinded. I search the crowd as best I can for Nathaniel, but I can't spot him anywhere. Trish is standing a few yards away to my right, in a fuchsia pink suit, and waves frantically. Beside her, Eddie is holding a camcorder.

Slowly I unfold my statement and smooth it down.

"Good afternoon," I say into the microphone, my voice stilted. "I am delighted to be able to share my exciting news with you. After being made a wonderful offer by Carter Spink, I will be returning to the firm today as a partner. Needless to say . . . I'm thrilled."

Somehow I can't make my voice sound thrilled. The words feel empty as I say them.

"I have been overwhelmed by the warmth and generosity of the Carter Spink welcome," I continue hesitantly, "and am honored to be joining such a prestigious partnership of . . ."

I'm still seeking out Nathaniel. I can't concentrate on what I'm saying.

"Talent and excellence!" snaps Hilary from the sidelines.

"Um . . . yes." I find my place on the sheet. "Talent. And excellence."

A titter goes through the crowd of journalists. I'm not doing a very good job here.

"Carter Spink's quality of service is . . . um . . . second to none," I continue, trying to sound convincing.

"Better quality than the toilets you used to clean?" calls out a journalist with ruddy cheeks.

"We are not taking questions at this stage!" Hilary comes out crossly onto the lawn. "And we are taking no questions on the subject of toilets, bathrooms, or any other form of sanitary ware. Samantha, carry on."

"Unspeakable, were they?" shouts the ruddy-cheeked guy with a guffaw of laughter.

"Samantha, carry *on*," spits Hilary, looking livid.

"They certainly were not unspeakable!" Trish comes striding onto the lawn, her fuchsia heels sinking into the grass. "I will not have my toilets maligned! They're all Royal Doulton. They're Royal Doulton," she repeats into the microphone. "Highest quality. You're doing very well, Samantha!" She pats me on the shoulder.

All the journalists are laughing by now. Hilary's face is puce.

"Excuse me," she says to Trish with suppressed fury. "We are in the middle of a press conference here. Could you please leave?"

"Mrs. Geiger, have you seen Nathaniel?" I look desperately around the crowd for the millionth time. "He's disappeared."

"Who's Nathaniel?" asks one of the journalists.

"He's the gardener," puts in the ruddy-faced guy. "Lover boy. So is that all over?" he adds to me.

"No!" I say, stung. "We're going to keep the relationship going."

"How you going to do that, then?"

I can sense a fresh interest stirring in the crowd of journalists.

"We just will, OK?" Suddenly, I feel near tears.

"Samantha," says Hilary furiously. "Please get back to the official statement!" She pushes Trish away from the microphone.

"Don't you touch me!" shrills Trish. "I'll sue. Samantha Sweeting is my lawyer, you know."

"Oy, Samantha! What does Nathaniel think about you going back to London?" shouts someone.

"Have you put your career over love?" chimes in a bright-faced girl.

"No!" I say desperately. "I just . . . I need to talk to him. Where is he? Guy!" I suddenly spot Guy at the side of the lawn. "Where did he go? What did you say to him?" I hurry toward him over the grass, almost tripping. "You have to tell me. What did you say?"

"I advised him to keep his dignity." Guy gives an arrogant shrug. "To be honest, I told the guy the truth. You won't be back."

"How *dare* you?" I gasp in fury. "How *dare* you say that? I will be back! And he can come to London—"

"Oh, please." Guy raises his eyes. "He doesn't want to hang around like some sad bastard, getting in your way, embarrassing you—"

"Embarrassing me?" I stare at Guy, aghast. "Is that what you *said* to him? Is that why he left?"

"For God's sake, Samantha, give it a rest," snaps Guy impatiently. "He's a *gardener.*"

My fist acts before I can think. It hits Guy right on the jaw.

I can hear gasps and shouts and cameras snapping all around, but I don't care. That is the best thing I have ever done.

"Ow! Fuck!" He clasps his face. "What the fuck was that for?"

The journalists are all crowding round now, hurling questions at us, but I ignore them.

"It's you who embarrass me," I spit at Guy. "You're worth nothing compared to him. *Nothing.*" To my horror

I can feel tears coming to my eyes. I have to find Nathaniel. Right now.

"Everything's fine! Everything's fine!" Hilary comes thundering across the grass, a blur of pinstripe trouser suit. "Samantha's a little overwrought today!" She grabs my arm in a vise, her teeth bared in a rictus smile. "Just a friendly disagreement between partners! Samantha is greatly looking forward to the challenges of leading a world-renowned legal team. Aren't you, Samantha?" Her grip tightens. "*Aren't* you, Samantha?"

"I . . . don't know," I say in despair. "I just don't know. I'm sorry, Hilary." I wrench my arm out of hers.

Hilary makes a furious swipe for my arm, but I evade her and start running over the grass toward the gates.

"Stop her!" Hilary is yelling to all the PR staff. "Block her way!"

Girls in trouser suits start coming at me from all directions like some kind of SWAT team. Somehow I dodge them. One makes a grab for my jacket and I wriggle out of it. I throw off my high heels too, and pick up my pace, barely wincing at the gravel under my soles. And then I'm out, running down the street, not looking back.

By the time I arrive at the pub my tights have been torn to shreds on the road. My hair has come out of its bun and half fallen down my back, my makeup is swimming in sweat, and my chest is burning with pain.

But I don't care. I have to find Nathaniel. I have to tell him he's the most important thing in my life, more important than any job.

I have to tell him I love him.

I don't know why I didn't realize it before, why I never said it before. It's so obvious. It's so blinding.

"Eamonn!" I call urgently as I approach, and he looks

up in surprise from where he's collecting glasses. "I have to talk to Nathaniel. Is he here?"

"Here?" Eamonn appears lost for words. "Samantha, you've missed him. He's already gone."

"Gone?" I come to a halt, panting. "Gone where?"

"To look at this business he wants to buy. He left in the car a short while ago."

"The one in Bingley?" I gulp in relief, still out of breath. "Could you possibly give me a lift there? It's quite important that I talk to him."

"That's not where . . ." Eamonn rubs his neck, looking awkward. I feel a sudden foreboding. "Samantha—he's gone to Cornwall."

Shock slams me in the chest.

"I thought you knew." Eamonn takes a step forward, shading his eyes against the sun. "He said he might be down there a couple of weeks. I thought he'd have told you."

"No," I say, my voice barely working. "He didn't."

Suddenly my legs feel like jelly. I sink down onto one of the barrels, my head pounding. He's gone to Cornwall just like that. Without even saying good-bye. Without even discussing it with me.

"He left a note in case you dropped by." Eamonn feels in his back pocket and produces an envelope. As he hands it over, his face is crumpled up with distress. "Samantha . . . I'm sorry."

"It's fine." I manage a smile. "Thanks, Eamonn." I take the envelope from him and pull out the paper.

> S
> *I think we both know this is the end of the line. Let's quit while we're ahead.*
> *Just know that this summer was perfect.*
> N

Tears are flooding down my cheeks as I read it, over and over. I can't believe he's gone. How can he have given up on us? Whatever Guy said to him, whatever he thought. How can he have just *left*?

We could have made it work. Didn't he *know* that? Didn't he feel it, deep down?

I hear a sound and look up to see Guy and a crowd of journalists gathered around me. I hadn't even noticed.

"Go away," I say in a muffled voice. "Leave me alone."

"Samantha," says Guy, his voice low and conciliatory. "I know you're hurt. I'm sorry if I upset you."

"I'll hit you again." I wipe my eyes with the back of my hand. "I mean it."

"Things may seem bad at the moment." Guy glances at the note. "But you have a fantastic career to get on with."

I don't answer. My shoulders are hunched over, my nose is running, and my hair is falling around my face in lacquered strands.

"Be reasonable. You're not going back to cleaning loos. There's nothing to keep you here now." Guy takes a step forward and puts my glossy high-heeled shoes on the table beside me. "Come on, partner. Everyone's waiting."

Twenty-six

I feel numb. It really is all over. I'm sitting in a first-class compartment on the express train to London, with the other partners. In a couple of hours we'll be back. I have a new pair of tights on. My makeup has been repaired. I've even given a fresh statement to the press, hastily constructed by Hilary: "Although I will always feel affection for my friends in Lower Ebury, nothing is more exciting and important in my life right now than my career with Carter Spink."

I was pretty convincing. I even found a smile from somewhere as I shook David Elldridge's hand. It's just possible they might print a picture of that, rather than the one of me punching Guy. You never know.

As the train pulls out of the station I feel a painful stab and close my eyes for a moment, trying to stay composed. I'm doing the right thing. Everyone's agreed. I take a sip of cappuccino, then another. If I drink enough coffee maybe it'll jolt me alive. Maybe I'll stop feeling as though I'm in a dream.

Wedged in the corner opposite me is the TV camera-man for the news documentary, together with the producer, Dominic, a guy with trendy glasses and a denim jacket. I can feel the camera lens on me, following every move, zooming in and out, catching every expression. I could *really* do without this.

"And so lawyer Samantha Sweeting leaves the village where she was known only as domestic help," Dominic is saying into his microphone in a low, TV-commentary voice. "The question is—does she have any regrets?" He gives me a questioning glance.

"I thought you were supposed to be fly-on-the-wall," I snap with a baleful look.

"Here you go!" Guy dumps a heavy set of contracts on my lap. "Here's the Samatron deal. Get your teeth into that."

I look at the piles of paper, inches thick. Once upon a time, seeing a brand-new, fresh contract gave me a rush of adrenaline. I always wanted to be first to spot an anomaly, first to raise a query. But now I feel blank.

Everyone else in the carriage is working away. I leaf through the contract, trying to summon up some enthusiasm. Come on. This is my life now. Once I get back into the swing of it I'll start to enjoy it again, surely.

But the words are jumbling in front of my eyes. I can't concentrate. All I can think about is Nathaniel. I've tried calling him but he isn't answering. Or replying to texts. It's like he doesn't want to know anymore.

How can everything be over? How can he have just *left*?

My eyes are starting to blur with tears again and I furiously blink them away. I can't cry. I'm a partner. Partners do not cry. Trying to get a grip, I look out the window instead. We seem to be slowing down, which is a bit weird.

"An announcement for all passengers." A voice suddenly comes crackling out of the loudspeakers. "This train has been rescheduled as a slow train. It will be stopping at Hitherton, Marston Bridge, Bridbury . . ."

"What?" Guy looks up. "A *slow* train?"

"Jesus Christ." David Elldridge scowls. "How much longer will it take?"

" . . . and will arrive at Paddington half an hour after the scheduled time," the voice is saying. "Apologies for any—"

"Half an hour?" David Elldridge whips out his mobile phone, looking livid. "I'm going to have to reschedule my meeting."

"I'll have to put off the Pattinson Lobb people." Guy looks equally pissed off, and is already jabbing at the speed-dial on his phone. "Hi Mary? Guy. Listen, total cock-up on this train. I'm going to be half an hour late—"

"Rearrange Derek Tomlinson—" David's instructing.

"We'll have to push back Pattinson Lobb, cancel that guy from *The Lawyer*—"

"Davina," Greg Parker is saying into his phone. "Fucking train's slow. Tell the rest of the team I'll be half an hour late, I'm sending an e-mail—" He puts down his phone and immediately starts typing into his BlackBerry. A moment later Guy is doing the same.

I'm watching all this frenzied action incredulously. They all look so stressed. So the train's going to be late. It's *half an hour*. It's thirty minutes. How can anyone get so het up over thirty minutes?

Is this what I'm supposed to be like? Because I've forgotten how. Maybe I've forgotten how to be a lawyer altogether.

The train pulls into Hitherton station and slowly comes to a halt. I glance out the window—then gasp aloud. A huge hot-air balloon is hovering just a few feet above the station building. It's bright red and yellow, with people waving from a basket. It looks like something out of a fairy tale.

"Hey, look!" I exclaim. "Look at that!"

No one moves their head. They're all frantically tapping at their keyboards.

"*Look!*" I try again. "It's amazing!" There's still no response. No one is interested in anything except the contents of their BlackBerry. And now the balloon's soared away again. In a moment it'll be out of sight. They all missed it.

I look at them, the cream of the legal world, dressed in their thousand-pound handmade suits, holding state-of-the-art computers. Missing out. Not even *caring* that they're missing out. Living in their own world.

I don't belong here. This is not my world anymore. *I'm not one of them.*

I suddenly know it, with the deepest certainty I've ever felt. I don't fit; I don't relate. Maybe I did once, but not anymore. I can't do this. I can't spend my life in meeting rooms. I can't obsess about every little chunk of time. I can't miss out on any more.

As I sit there, the contracts still piled on my lap, I feel tension rising inside me. I've made a mistake. I've made a huge mistake. I shouldn't be here. This isn't what I want from my life. This isn't what I want to do. This isn't who I want to be.

I have to get out. Now.

Up and down the train, people are stepping in and out, banging doors, hefting bags. As calmly as I can I reach for my suitcase, pick up my bag, and stand up.

"I'm sorry," I say. "I made a mistake. I've only just realized."

"*What?*" Guy looks up.

"I'm sorry I've wasted your time." My voice wavers slightly. "But . . . I can't stay. I can't do this."

"Jesus." He clutches his head. "Not this again, Samantha—"

"Don't try and talk me round," I cut across him. "I've decided. I can't be like the rest of you. It's just not right for me. I'm sorry, I should never have come."

"Is this to do with the gardener?" He sounds exasperated. "Because quite frankly—"

"No! It's to do with *me*! I just . . ." I hesitate, searching for the words. "Guy . . . I don't want to be someone who doesn't look out the window."

Guy's face doesn't register an iota of understanding. I didn't expect it to.

"Good-bye." I open the train door and step out, but Guy grabs me roughly.

"Samantha, for the last time, stop this crap! I *know* you. And you're a *lawyer*."

"You *don't* know me, Guy!" My words burst out in a surge of sudden anger. I pull my arm out of his and slam the door shut, shaking all over. The next moment it opens again and Dominic and the cameraman pile out after me.

"And so!" Dominic is murmuring excitedly into his microphone. "In a shocking turn of events, Samantha Sweeting has rejected her glittering legal career!"

As the train pulls out of the station I can see Guy and the other partners on their feet staring out at me in consternation. I guess I've ruined all my chances of a comeback now.

The other passengers start melting away from the platform, leaving me all alone. All alone on Hitherton station with only a suitcase for company. I don't even know where Hitherton is. The TV camera is still trained on me, and as people pass by they give me curious glances.

What am I going to do now?

"As she gazes down onto the railway tracks, Samantha finds herself at a low ebb." Dominic's voice is low and sympathetic.

"I *don't*," I mutter back.

"This morning she was devastated to lose the man she loved. Now . . . she has no career either." He pauses, then adds in sepulchral tones, "Who knows what dark thoughts are going through her mind?"

What's he trying to imply? That I'm going to throw myself under the next train? He'd love that, wouldn't he? He'd probably win an Emmy.

"I'm fine." I lift my chin and clutch my suitcase more tightly. "I'm going to be fine. I've . . . I've done the right thing."

But as I look around the empty station I feel flurries of panic as I take in my situation properly. I have no idea when the next train will be. I have no idea where I want to go even.

"Do you have a plan, Samantha?" asks Dominic, thrusting his microphone at me. "A goal?"

Into my mind come Iris's words that day we made the bread.

"Sometimes you don't need a goal in life," I reply, lifting my chin. "You don't need to know the big picture. You just need to know what you're going to do next."

"And what are you going to do next?"

"I'm . . . I'm . . . working on it." I turn and march away from the camera, toward the waiting room. As I near it, I see a guard coming out.

"Um, hello," I say. "I'd like to know how to get to . . ." I trail off, uncertainly. Where am I going? "To . . . um . . ."

"To . . ." prompts the guard helpfully.

"To . . . Cornwall," I hear myself saying.

"Cornwall?" He looks taken aback. "Whereabouts in Cornwall?"

"I don't know." I swallow. "Not exactly. But I need to get there as quickly as possible."

There can't be that many nurseries for sale in Cornwall. I'll track down the right one. I'll find him. Somehow.

"Well." The guard's brow creases. "I'll have to consult the book." He disappears into his room, then emerges, holding a piece of paper covered in pencil. "Six changes, I'm afraid, to Penzance. And it'll be one hundred and twenty pounds fare. Train'll be a while," he adds as I hand over a wodge of cash. "Platform two."

"Thanks." I take my ticket, pick up my suitcase, and head over the footbridge.

I know this is a crazy plan. I don't have an address. I don't have any backup. Nathaniel may not even want to see me again.

But . . . I have to try.

It seems like hours before I hear the sound of the train in the distance. But it's the wrong side. It's another train for London. As it pulls in I can hear the slam of doors and people disgorging on the other side.

"London train!" the guard is shouting. "Train for London, platform one."

That's the train I should be on. If I was sane. If I hadn't taken leave of my senses. My eyes move idly over the windows, at people in their seats, talking, asleep, reading, listening to iPods—

And then everything seems to freeze. Am I *dreaming*?

It's Nathaniel. On the London train. He's three yards away, sitting in a window seat, staring ahead rigidly.

What—Why is he—

"Nathaniel!" I try to shout, but my voice has turned

into a croak. "Nathaniel!" I wave my arms frantically, trying to get his attention.

"Jesus, it's him!" exclaims Dominic, who has followed me onto the platform. "Nathaniel!" he yells, his voice like a foghorn. "Over here, mate!"

"Nathaniel!" At last my voice is working. "Na-than-iel!"

At my desperate scream he finally looks up. For a moment his expression is sheer disbelief. Then his whole face seems to expand in a slow explosion of delight.

I can hear train doors slamming. It's about to leave.

"Come on!" I yell, beckoning urgently.

I can see him getting up inside the train, grabbing his rucksack, squeezing past the woman in the next seat. Then he disappears from view, just as the train starts pulling out of the station.

I can't move, or even breathe. All I can do is stare at the departing train, moving past carriage by carriage, speeding up, faster and faster . . . until finally it's gone.

And Nathaniel is standing on the platform. He's there.

Without moving my eyes from his I begin to walk along the platform, speeding up as I reach the footbridge. On the opposite side he does the same. We reach the top of the steps, walk forward a way, and both come to a halt, a few feet apart. I feel shell-shocked and exhilarated and uncertain all at the same time.

"I thought you were going down to Cornwall," I say at last. "To buy your nursery."

"I changed my mind." Nathaniel looks pretty shell-shocked himself. "Thought I might . . . visit a friend in London instead." He glances at my suitcase. "Where were you going?"

I clear my throat. "I was thinking . . . Cornwall."

"Cornwall?" He stares at me.

"Uh-huh." I show him my timetable, suddenly wanting to laugh at the ridiculousness of it all.

Nathaniel leans against the barricade, his thumbs in his pockets, and surveys the wooden slats of the bridge. "So . . . where are your friends?"

"Dunno. Gone. And they're not my friends. I hit Guy," I add proudly.

Nathaniel throws back his head and laughs. "So they fired you."

"I fired them," I correct him.

"You did?" says Nathaniel in amazement. He reaches out for my hand but I don't take it. Underneath my joy I'm still feeling unsettled. The hurt of this morning hasn't gone. I can't pretend everything's OK.

"I got your note." I lift my eyes to his and Nathaniel flinches.

"Samantha . . . I wrote you a different one on the train. In case you wouldn't see me in London."

He fishes awkwardly in his pocket and pulls out a letter several sheets long, both sides of the paper covered in writing. I hold it for a few moments without reading it.

"What—what does it say?" I raise my eyes.

"It's . . . long and boring." His gaze burns into mine. "And badly put."

I turn the pages slowly over in my fingers. Here and there I glimpse words that make my eyes fill instantly.

"So," I manage.

"So." Nathaniel's arms come round my waist; his warm mouth is on mine. As he holds me tight I can feel the tears spilling onto my cheeks. This is where I belong. This is where I fit. I finally draw away and look up at him, wiping my eyes.

"Where now?" He looks down over the bridge and I

follow his gaze. The railway track extends in both directions, far into the distance. "Which way?"

I look along the endless line, squinting in the sunshine. I'm twenty-nine years old. I can go anywhere. Do anything. Be anyone I like.

"There's no rush," I say at last, and reach up to kiss him again.

Acknowledgments

I am incredibly grateful to the many people who have gone out of their way to help me with this book. To Emily Stokely, domestic goddess extraordinaire, for teaching me how to bake bread. To Roger Barron for being so generous with his time and giving me a wonderful insight into the world of corporate law (not to mention his Jo Malone expertise!). And especially to Abigail Townley, for acting as legal plot consultant, allowing me to shadow her, and patiently answering a million dumb questions.

A special thank-you to Susan Kamil for so much support and understanding. Many thanks also to Irwyn Applebaum, Nita Taublib, Barb Burg, Sharon Propson, Susan Corcoran, Carolyn Schwartz, Betsy Hulsebosch, Cathy Paine, and Noah Eaker. To the wonderful Araminta Whitley, whose enthusiasm for this book has known no bounds, to Kim Witherspoon as always, to David Forrer and Lizzie Jones. To Valerie Hoskins, Rebecca Watson, and Brian Siberell. Thanks as ever to the members of the Board and to all my boys, big and small.

These acknowledgments would not be complete, of course, without a mention of Nigella Lawson, whom I've never met—but whose books should be required reading for all undomestic goddesses.

ABOUT THE AUTHOR

SOPHIE KINSELLA is a former financial journalist and the author of the bestselling novels *Confessions of a Shopaholic, Shopaholic Takes Manhattan, Shopaholic Ties the Knot, Shopaholic & Sister,* and *Can You Keep a Secret?* She lives in England, where she is at work on her next book.